"Ian, I can't... I just met you."

"You're attracted to me," Ian insisted.

"That doesn't mean I should act on it," Cassie replied. "You're only here for a short time. We can't just...you know."

"Have sex?"

Oh, mercy. The words were out now. Dear Lord. It wasn't as if she hadn't had sex before—she had a baby for crying out loud—but, "Acting on sexual attraction isn't something I normally do."

Ian stepped forward, and stopped when Cassie held up a hand. "Don't. I can't think when you're touching me."

"I'll take that as a compliment."

Cassie rolled her eyes. "You would."

"See? You know me already."

"You're going to have to keep your hands to yourself."

"You're no fun."

Without a word, Ian closed the gap between them. He brought his mouth close to hers. "A woman who kisses like you, who responds to my touch without hesitation, has pent-up passion that needs to be released."

His lips barely brushed hers. "Come find me when you're ready."

***

Single Man Meets Single Mum

is part of the No.1 bestselling series from

M

Powerf   ers.

D0794724

SINGLE MAN
MEETS SINGLE MUM

BY
JULES BENNETT

Published in Great Britain 2014
by Mills & Boon, an imprint of Harlequin (UK) Limited,
Eton House, 18-24 Paradise Road, Richmond, Surrey, TW9 1SR

© 2014 Jules Bennett

ISBN: 978-0-263-91479-5

51-0914

Harlequin (UK) Limited's policy is to use papers that are natural, renewable and recyclable products and made from wood grown in sustainable forests. The logging and manufacturing processes conform to the legal environmental regulations of the country of origin.

Printed and bound in Spain
by Blackprint CPI, Barcelona

National bestselling author **Jules Bennett**'s love of storytelling started when she would get in trouble as a child and would tell her parents her imaginary friends were to blame. Since then, her vivid imagination has taken her down a path she'd only dreamed of. And after twelve years of owning and working in salons, she hung up her shears to write full-time.

Jules doesn't just write Happily Ever After—she lives it. Married to her high school sweetheart, Jules and her hubby have two little girls who keep them smiling. She loves to hear from readers! Contact her at authorjules@gmail.com, visit her website, www.julesbennett.com, where you can sign up for her newsletter, or send her a letter at PO Box 396, Minford, OH 45653, USA. You can also follow her on Twitter and join her Facebook fan page.

To Jill, Amy and Inez.
I love you three more than the frozen yogurt we devour.
Thanks for the road trip and all the laughs.
May we have many, many more!

One

Oomph!

Out of nowhere, Ian Shaffer had his arms full of woman. Curvy, petite woman. A mass of silky red hair half covered her face, and as she shoved the wayward strands back to look up, Ian was met with the most intriguing set of blue eyes he'd ever seen.

"You okay?" he asked, in no hurry to let her down.

He'd taken one step into the stables at Stony Ridge Acres and this beauty had literally fallen into his arms. Talk about perfect timing.

The delicate hand against his shoulder pushed gently, but he didn't budge. How could he, when all those curves felt perfect against his body and she was still trembling?

He may not know much about the horse industry, but women… Yeah, he knew women really well.

"Thank you for catching me."

Her low, husky voice washed over him, making him

even more thankful he'd come to this movie set to see to his client's needs in person...and to hopefully sign another actress to his growing roster of A-listers.

Most agents didn't visit movie sets as regularly as he did, but he sure as hell wasn't missing the opportunity to keep Max Ford happy and allow prospective client Lily Beaumont to witness just what a kick-ass, hands-on agent he was. Given his young age, the fact that he was known as a shark in the industry happened to be good for business.

Ian glanced to the ladder that stretched up into the loft of the spacious stables. His eyes narrowed in on the rung that hung vertically, the culprit of the lady's fall.

"Looks like your ladder needs repairing," he told her, looking back to those big, expressive blue eyes.

"I've been meaning to fix it," she told him, studying his face, his mouth. "You know, you can let me down now."

Yeah, he was probably freaking her out by keeping her in his clutches. But that didn't stop him from easing her down slowly, allowing her body to glide against his.

Hey, he may be there to concentrate on work, but that didn't mean he couldn't enjoy the samplings of a tempting woman when an opportunity presented itself.

Keeping his hand on her arm, Ian allowed his gaze to sweep down her body. He justified the touch by telling himself he was looking for signs of injury, but in all honesty, he simply wanted to get a better look. If this was what they called taking in the local scenery, then sign him up.

"Are you hurt anywhere?" he asked.

"Just my pride." Stepping back, forcing his hand to fall away, she brushed her fingers down her button-up plaid shirt. "I'm Cassie Barrington. And you are?"

He held out his hand. "Ian Shaffer. I'm Max Ford's agent."

And if all went well, he'd be signing Max's costar Lily,

too. There was no way he'd let her go to his rival agency without one hell of a fight first. And then maybe his very unimpressed father would see that Ian had become a success. He was a top agent in L.A. and not just hanging out at parties with women for a living. He'd become a powerful man in the industry.

Though the parties and women were a nice added bonus, Ian enjoyed stepping away from the glamour to be on set with his clients. And it was that extra touch that made him so successful. Between forging connections with producers and getting to know the writers and actors better, he could place his clients in the roles best suited to them.

The role Max was playing was perfect for him. The top actor was portraying the dynamic Damon Barrington, famous horse owner and former jockey. And for Ian, escaping L.A.'s hustle and bustle to spend time on a prestigious Virginia horse farm was a nice change of pace.

"Oh, Max mentioned you'd be coming. Sorry for falling on you." Her brows drew together as she gave him a quick assessment. "I didn't hurt you, did I?"

Ian shoved his hands into his pockets, offering her a smile. She could assess him anytime she wanted. "Not at all," he assured her. "I rather enjoyed the greeting."

Her chin tilted just enough to show defiance. "I don't make a habit of being clumsy...or throwing myself at men."

"That a fact?" he asked, trying not to laugh. "Such a shame."

"Do you make a habit of hitting on women?" she asked.

Unable to resist the gauntlet she'd thrown before him, Ian took a step forward, pleased when her eyes widened and she had to tip her head up to hold his gaze.

"Actually, no. But I'm making an exception in your case."

"Aren't I lucky?" Her tone told him she felt anything

but. "Max should be in his trailer. His name is on the outside, and I believe another trailer was recently brought in for you."

Apparently she was in a hurry for him to be on his way—which only made him want to stay longer. Finding someone who didn't care about his Hollywood status, someone who wasn't impressed with his power and money, was a refreshing change. The fact that someone was curvy, wore jeans as though they were made to mold those curves and had expressive baby blues was the icing on the proverbial cake.

"So you're the trainer and your sister is the famous jockey?" he asked, crossing his arms over his chest.

The warm late-spring sun beat against his back as it came through the wide doors of the stable. Summer blockbuster season was just around the corner and, hopefully, once the film wrapped and he'd signed Lily, his agency would still be on top. His ex-partner-turned-rival would no longer be an issue.

He'd started working for an agency right out of college, thanks to a referral from a professor he'd impressed, but some lucky breaks and smart business sense had had him quickly moving to open his own. Unfortunately, he'd taken on a partner who had stabbed him in the back and secretly wooed most of their clients in the hopes they'd work exclusively with him in a new venture.

For the sake of his pride, he had to win Lily over and get her under contract. But how could his mind be on business with this voluptuous distraction before him?

"You've done your homework," she commented. "I'm impressed you know about me and my sister and our different roles."

"I do my research. You could say I'm pretty hands-on as an agent."

"Apparently you're hands-on with everything."

Oh, that was such a loaded statement—one he wouldn't mind exploring if he had the time. His eyes held hers as he closed the gap between them. The pulse at the base of her throat quickened and her breath caught as she stared, unblinking, at him.

Damn work responsibilities. But surely a little flirting, hell, even a fling, would make this an even more riveting trip.

"Everything," he whispered. "Let me know if you ever want an experience."

When her gaze dropped to his mouth again, Ian resisted the urge to grab her, to taste her. There would be plenty of time for…anything she was willing to give. Besides, wasn't the chase half the fun?

"I think you know where my trailer is."

And because he'd probably crossed some sort of moral, ethical boundary, Ian turned and walked from the barn, leaving her with her mouth open.

Well, this was already the most exciting movie set he'd ever visited and he hadn't even seen his client yet.

Cassie tightened her grip on MacDuff's lead line. He was still new, still skittish, but she was working with him every single day and he was showing improvement. Every now and then he'd let her father, Damon Barrington, ride him, but he had a touch that every horse seemed to love.

At least MacDuff had quit trying to run from her. Now, if she could just get him to understand her silent commands that he had to mimic her pace and direction when they walked.

Her work with MacDuff and the other horses was just one of the many issues that had ended her marriage. Derek had wanted her to stop spending so much time with the "strays" she brought in. He'd insisted she stop trying to save every animal, especially when she'd become pregnant.

Cassie would never stop trying to save animals…especially since she hadn't been able to save her marriage. Her husband had obviously loved women and liquor more than her and their baby. His loss, but the pain still cut deep.

She focused on the line, holding it tight and trying to keep up with the routine because she was running a tad behind now.

Of course, she'd been thrown off her game already this morning after falling into the arms of that handsome, bedroom-eyed stranger. For a split second she'd wanted to revel in the strength with which he held her, but then reality had slapped her in the face, reminding her that she'd fallen for a smooth talker once. Married him, had his child and hadn't seen him since.

Well, except when he'd shown up for the divorce proceedings, mistress in tow. As if that busty bleach blonde would ever play stepmom to Cassie's precious baby. Hell. No.

Cassie swore she'd never let another man play her for a fool again, and she sure as hell wouldn't get swept away by another pretty smile and sultry touch.

Unfortunately, when she'd fallen into Ian's arms, she'd forgotten all about that speech she'd given herself when her husband had left. How could she have a coherent thought when such strong arms were holding her flush against a taut body? No woman would blame her for the lapse in judgment.

But no more. Cassie had her daughter to consider now.

With sweet Emily just turning one, Cassie knew she'd definitely gotten the best part of her marriage, and if Derek didn't want to see their baby, he was the one missing out.

So, no more sexy men who thought they were God's

magnificent gift to this world. Although Cassie had to admit, even if just to herself, that her insides had tingled at Ian's touch. He'd been so strong, had smelled so…manly and had looked in her eyes as if she truly was a beautiful, desirable woman.

She hadn't felt anything but frumpy and still a bit pudgy since having Emily. The extra weight that refused to go away coupled with her husband leaving her for another woman were damaging blows to her self-esteem. Yet, Ian had held her with ease, which wasn't helping her ignore the potency of the mesmerizing man.

Getting swept away by another handsome man with sultry eyes and a powerful presence wouldn't do her any good. She had to concentrate on helping her sister, Tessa, win her way to the Triple Crown. They'd worked side by side nearly their entire lives, always with the dream of being Triple Crown winners like their father. And here they were, about to make history, and Cassie couldn't be more excited.

When Cassie had been too far along with her pregnancy, her father had stepped up to train Tessa. This racing dynasty truly was a family affair.

One race down, two to go.

The fact that the Barrington estate had been turned into a film set was icing on the cake. A script surrounding her father's legacy, legendary racing and past winning streak had piqued the interest of Hollywood A-listers, and, suddenly, the horse farm was all abuzz with lighting, sound guys, extras and security.

Cassie actually loved seeing her father's life played out by Max Ford, the handsome, newly married actor. And playing the role of her late mother was beautiful Southern belle and it-girl Lily Beaumont. So far the two were doing an amazing job, and Cassie couldn't wait to see the final product.

To cap off the racing season, Cassie was moving full throttle toward opening her own riding school for handicapped children. Since having her own child, Cassie wanted to slow down, and she'd always had a soft spot for kids anyway...something she'd thought she and her ex had in common.

Launching the school would be one more step in the healing process. So now she just needed to keep saving up—she wouldn't dream of asking her father or anyone else for money—to get it off the ground.

"Daydreaming?"

Keeping a firm grip on the lead line, Cassie glanced over her shoulder to see Tessa moving toward her in slow, cautious steps. MacDuff really did get treated with kid gloves by everyone until he learned they were his friends.

"Maybe just a little," Cassie admitted, gently pulling MacDuff into a soft trot. "Give me just a few minutes and we'll get to work."

Tessa shoved her hands into the pockets of her jeans. "I'd rather hear what has my big sister so distracted this morning."

Cassie rolled her eyes at Tessa's smirk and quirked brow. She led MacDuff forward a few steps, stopped and moved back a few steps, pleased when the stallion kept up with her exact number and didn't try to fight her.

He was learning. Finally.

"I'm always amazed at how broken they seem to be," Tessa said softly. "You have this patience and gentleness. It's almost as if they know you're determined to help them."

"That's because I am." Cassie reached up to MacDuff's neck, offering him praise. "He's just misunderstood and nobody wanted to work properly with him."

"He was abused."

Cassie swallowed as she led MacDuff back to the sta-

bles. The thought of someone beating him because he
hadn't had the right training sickened her. She'd known
he'd been abused on some level, simply because of how
he'd arrived all wide-eyed and nervous and then threw
Tessa the first time she'd mounted him. But the second
any horse, rescued or not, stepped onto Stony Ridge Acres,
they were treated like royalty. No matter their heritage.
Yes, they bred prizewinning horses and bought from a
long lineage of winners, but it wasn't always about the
win…. It was about the love and care of the animal. And
since Stony Ridge was a massive farm, they could take in
those strays Cassie had a soft spot for.

She'd always loved watching the trainers her father had
for his horses. Years ago, female trainers had been frowned
upon, but her father had insisted women were more gentle
and less competitive by nature than men, thus producing
better-tempered horses—and winners.

"You didn't happen to see a certain new hunk on the
set this morning, did you?" Tessa asked as she pulled out
the tack box and helped to brush MacDuff.

Cassie eyed her sister over the horse's back. "Aren't
you engaged?"

"I'm not dead, Cass." Tessa brushed in large circular
strokes. "I'll take your lack of answering to mean you did
see him."

Saw him, fell into his arms, got lost in those sexy eyes
that could make a woman forget she'd been burned…and
maybe reveled in that powerful hold a tad too long.

"Even you have to admit he's one attractive man," Tessa
went on.

"I can admit that, yes." Cassie switched from the curry-
comb to the dandy brush. "I may have had an incident this
morning involving that loose rung on the ladder to the loft
and Mr. Shaffer."

Tessa stepped around MacDuff's head, dropped the brush into the tack box and crossed her arms over her chest. "Okay, spill it. You know his name and you said 'incident.' I want all the details."

Cassie laughed. "It's no big deal, Tess. I fell off the ladder. Ian happened to be there, and he caught me."

"Oh, so we've gone from Mr. Shaffer to Ian."

"He's Max's agent and apparently visits his clients' film sets. We exchanged names," Cassie defended herself. "Seemed like the thing to do since he was holding me."

"I love where this story is going." Tessa all but beamed as she clasped her hands together.

Laughing, Cassie tossed her brush aside, as well. "No story. That was pretty much it."

"Honey, you haven't even mentioned a man's name since *you know who* left and—" Tessa held up a hand when Cassie tried to intervene "—your face seemed to brighten up a bit when you said his name."

"It did not," Cassie protested.

Tessa's smile softened. "If you want to argue, that's fine. But he's hot, you finally showed a spark of life about a man and I'm clinging to hope that you haven't given up on finding love. Or, for heaven's sake, at least allowing yourself a fling."

Cassie rolled her eyes and patted MacDuff's side. "Just because this romance business is working for you doesn't mean it will for me. I tried that once—it didn't last. Besides, I have no time for love or even a date between training with you and Emily."

"There's always time. And, romance aside, have a good time. A little romp with a sexy stranger might be just what you need," Tessa said with a naughty smile. "Aren't you the one who forced me to take a few days off last month? You have to make time for yourself."

Cassie had conspired with Tessa's now fiancé, producer Grant Carter, to whisk Tessa away during her training and the filming of the movie. Grant had wanted to get Tessa far from the limelight, the stress and the demands of their busy schedules, and Cassie had been all too happy to help because her sister needed a break.

Tess had found the right man, but Cassie seriously doubted there was a "right man" for her. All she required was someone who loved her and didn't mind her smelling like horses more often than not, someone who would offer stability in her life, make her feel desirable and love her daughter. Was that too tall of an order?

"I'm not looking for a fling," Cassie insisted, even though she'd pretty much already envisioned a steamy affair with Ian.

Tessa raised a brow. "Maybe a fling is looking for you."

"I just met the man. I'm sure he's not going to be around me that much anyway, so there's very little chance of seduction. Sorry to burst your bubble."

"Maybe you should show Ian around the estate," Tessa suggested as she went to grab a blanket and saddle for her racing horse, Don Pedro.

Cassie sighed, closing the gate to MacDuff's stall. "I don't want to show him around. Max is his client—he can do it."

"Max is going to be busy filming the scene with Lily down by the pond. I want to make sure we're there to see that taping."

Cassie smiled and nodded in agreement. She loved watching the two actors get into character, loved watching her father's reaction to reliving his life through the eyes of a director, and there was no way she'd miss such a monumental scene. This was the scene where Max would propose to Lily. The replay of such a special moment in her parents' lives was something she had to witness.

"I'll make sure we're done here about the time shooting starts," Cassie assured her sister. "All the more reason I don't have time to show Ian around."

"Now, that's a shame."

Cassie and Tessa both turned to see the man in question. And just like with their earlier encounter, the mere sight of him caused a flutter to fill her belly. Of course, now she couldn't blame the sensation on the scare from the fall... only the scare from the enticing man.

"I'd like to have a look around the grounds if you have time," he said, looking directly into her eyes, seeming to not even notice Tessa.

Cassie settled her hands on her hips, cursing herself when his gaze followed her movements. Great, now she'd drawn his attention to her hips...not an area a woman wanted a man looking.

"I thought you went to see Max," Cassie said, refusing to acknowledge his request.

"I saw him for a brief moment to let him know I was here. He actually was talking with Grant and Lily."

Cassie cast a glance at her sister, whose face had split into a very wide grin. *Darn her.*

With a gracefulness that would've pleased their late mother, Tessa turned, extended her hand and smiled. "I'm Tessa Barrington, Cassie's sister. We're so glad to have you here at the farm."

Ian shook Tessa's hand as the two exchanged pleasantries. He finally settled his gaze back on Cassie. Did those eyes have some magical power? Seriously, why did she have to feel a jolt every single time he looked at her?

"Go ahead and show Ian around, Cassie. I'm fine here."

If Cassie could've reached out and strangled her sister

with the lead line she so would have, but then Ian would be a witness.

"It will have to be tomorrow or later this evening." No, she wasn't too busy right now, but she wouldn't allow Mr. Hollywood Hotshot to hold any control over her. "I'll come find you when I'm ready."

"Well, I'm going to walk Don Pedro out," Tessa said. "It was a pleasure to meet you, Ian. Cass, I'll see you later."

Great, now they were alone. Cassie would definitely kill her sister for that little stunt.

Ian stepped closer, and Cassie held her ground. This was her property and no matter how charming, how sexy and how...

Damn, he smelled good. She lost all train of thought; Ian's masculine scent was enough to render her mind blank. How long had it been since she'd been with a man, felt his touch?

Too long. So why did this man with an inflated ego turn her on? Could she not attract the right kind of guy just once?

"I can wait till tomorrow," he told her. His eyes searched her face as a hint of a smile played around his lips. "I'm a pretty patient man."

Placing a hand on his chest to stop him may have been a mistake. A jolt of awareness tingled up her arm. The strength, the chiseled pecs beneath her palm... Yeah, she was very aware of the sexiness that encompassed Ian Shaffer.

"I appreciate the fact you're taking the time to use your charm on me, but I'm too busy for games. Besides, I'm pretty sure I'm a lot older than you."

Ian shrugged. "Age hadn't entered my mind."

Cassie laughed. "I'm pretty sure I know what entered your mind."

He stepped forward again, giving her no choice but to

back up until the gate to a stall stopped her. Ian put one hand on either side of her head, blocking her.

"Then I'm sure you're aware I find you attractive." His eyes dropped to her mouth, then traveled back up. "I can't wait for that tour, Cassie."

He pushed off the stall and walked out of the stable. When was the last time a man had caught her attention, inspired her sexual desire so fast? The danger of falling into lust scared her to death.

But she had to be realistic. There was nothing special about her. And if she did allow herself to act on these very new, very powerful emotions, she highly doubted he'd remember her name in a few months.

No way could she succumb to his charms.

Two

Cassie's parents had been married nearly twenty years when her mother was killed suddenly in a car accident. She'd always admired the love her parents had for each other, always wanted a marriage like that for herself.

Unfortunately, a happy, loving marriage wasn't in the cards for her. And hindsight was a harsh slap in the face because Cassie realized she'd probably married Derek too quickly.

She'd craved the love her parents had had and thought for sure Derek—the Barringtons' onetime groom—had the same outlook on marriage.... As in, it was long-term and between only two people.

How could she trust her feelings for a man again? Cassie swiped the tear from her cheek as she headed back toward the stable. The sun was slowly sinking behind the hills surrounding the estate. Spring was gradually turning into summer, giving the evenings just a bit more light.

The day's filming was complete and the scene she'd just witnessed had left her raw and hopeful all at the same time.

Max Ford and Lily Beaumont had beautifully reenacted Cassie's parents' proposal. Cassie had heard stories, had seen pictures of her parents' early love. But to witness that moment in person… Cassie had no words for how precious the experience had been.

She'd stood with Tessa off to the side, and even with the directors and producers stopping and starting and re-arranging in the middle of the scene, the moment had captured her heart.

Added to that, each time she'd glanced at Ian, his gaze had been on hers. He hadn't even bothered trying to hide the heat that lurked in those dark, heavy-lidded eyes. Thankfully, at one point he'd slid on his aviator shades, but his dominating presence still captured her attention…and her hormones.

There went those lustful emotions again. She couldn't afford to get swept away by a sexy body and killer smile. Lust was the evil that had overtaken her once before and look where that had gotten her. Oh, she didn't regret her marriage because she had Emily, but the pain from the rejection and having her love blatantly thrown back in her face was humiliating. Who wanted to be rejected?

Cassie reached the stable, intending to work with MacDuff again, but her eyes moved up to the rung of the ladder that still hung vertically.

She'd meant to mention the problem to Nash, the new groom, but between the emotional shoot and a certain hot agent plaguing her mind, she'd simply forgotten. Besides, he'd been so busy today cleaning out all the stalls, she really hated to add to his list.

Her father took pride in his stables, always making sure everything looked pristine and perfect. Cassie would bite the bullet and fix the ladder herself. At least working on something would keep her mind off Ian...hopefully. Her tendency to fix things and have everything in her life make sense would have to be satisfied with just this piece of wood for now. The Ian issue—and she feared he was fast becoming an issue—would have to wait.

She grabbed the hammer and several long nails from the toolbox in the equipment room. She shoved the nails in her back pocket and held on to the hammer as she climbed the ladder that stretched to the loft of the stable.

The setting sun cast a soft glow into the structure. Horses neighed, stomped hooves and rustled in their stalls. The sounds, the smells—none of it ever got old. Cassie loved her life here and she looked forward to bringing her daughter up in such a beautiful, serene environment.

During her four years of marriage, she'd been away from the estate. Even though she and Derek had lived only ten minutes away, it just wasn't the same as being on the grounds. Cassie loved living in the cottage, being with the horses and knowing her family was all right here helping with her emotional recovery.

With her tears mostly dry, Cassie sniffed. Crying had never been her thing. Anger fit more into her life, especially since she'd been abandoned only two months after giving birth. Tears hadn't brought her cheating husband back, not that she'd wanted him after the fact, and tears certainly weren't helping her raise her daughter or move on like the strong mother she needed to be.

Halfway up the ladder, she eyed the broken rung, then carefully slid it back into place. Widening her stance as far as she could to balance her body while holding the hammer, she reached around into her back pocket for a nail.

"I can help you with that."

Cassie glanced over her shoulder to see Ian at the base

of the ladder, his watchful gaze raking over her body. *Great.* She had red-rimmed eyes and a red-tipped nose, she was sure. She was not a pretty crier. She always got the snot-running, red-splotchy-face and puffy-eyes look.

Cassie slid a nail out and turned back around to place it against the wood. "I've got it, but thanks."

She knew he hadn't left, but Cassie didn't say anything else as she worked quickly and repaired the rung. With a hefty tug on the wood, she made sure it was securely in place before she started her descent. Just as she'd gotten to the last rung, Ian moved his hard body against hers, trapping her between the ladder and a most impressive chest. Her body was perfectly aligned with his, causing ripples of heat to slide through her. They were both fully dressed, but the sensations spiraling through her had never occurred before, even when she'd been completely naked with her ex.

Yeah, she was doomed where this sexy stranger was concerned.

Cassie swallowed, closed her eyes. Ian made her aware of just how feminine she was. When was the last time she'd felt desirable? Was it so wrong to want a man to find her attractive? After being married to someone who kept looking elsewhere for his desires to be fulfilled, Cassie knew she was probably grasping at any attention at this point.

She also knew she didn't care—not when his body was so hard, so perfectly perfect against hers. Not when his soft, warm breath tickled the side of her neck, and not when his masculine aroma enveloped her.

"What are you doing here?" she whispered.

Ian slid his arms up to align with hers, his hands covering hers on the wood. "I saw you walking this way. You looked upset."

No. He didn't care. He couldn't. Not this soon and not about her. Sexual desires were clouding his mind...and

hers, too, apparently, because she was enjoying the heat
of his body a little too much.

What man would follow a woman into a stable just
because she looked upset? No. He'd followed her for one
reason and one reason only. A reason she certainly didn't
think she was ready for.

"I'm fine," she lied.

Ian nuzzled her hair. Oh…when he did that she forgot
all arguments about why being attracted to someone so
full of himself was wrong. Her mind completely voided
out any pep talks she'd given in regard to steering clear of
lustful feelings and attractive charmers.

"You're a very beautiful woman, Cassie." His soft voice
slid over her body, reinforcing those tremors that were
becoming the norm where he was concerned. "I tried to
ignore this pull I have toward you, but it was damn hard
when I saw you during the shoot. How do you do that to
a guy?"

Um…she had no clue. Power over men had certainly
never been something she'd mastered. If it had, she'd still
be married.

"Ian, we just mct and…"

He used one hand and slid the hammer from her grasp,
letting it fall to the concrete floor with a loud thud.

"And I'm older than you," she continued. "I'm thirty-
four. You can't even be thirty."

With an arm around her waist, he hauled her off the
ladder and spun her around until she faced him—their
mouths inches apart.

"I'm twenty-nine, and I assure you I'm old enough to
not only know what I want, but to act on it."

His mouth came down on hers, hard, fast, hungry. Cassie
didn't have time to think or refuse because her body was
already melting into his.

The passion pouring from him stirred her desire even more as she gripped his thick biceps. Giving in to just a few seconds of bliss wouldn't hurt.

And when Ian's mouth traveled from her mouth down the column of her throat, Cassie tipped her head back as her breath caught. What was he doing to her? A full-on body attack. His mouth may be in one spot, but Cassie could feel every inch of her body tingling and wanting more.

Wait…this wasn't right. She couldn't do this.

Pushing him away, Cassie slid her hand up over the exposed skin peeking out of her shirt…the skin his mouth had just explored.

"Ian, I can't… We can't…" Words were useless because her mind was telling her one thing and her body was telling her another. "I just met you."

"You're attracted to me."

She couldn't deny the statement. "That doesn't mean I should act on it. I don't just go around kissing strangers."

"After you learned my name this morning, I was no longer a stranger."

Those dark eyes held her gaze. Even without a word the man exuded power, control. Derek had been so laid-back, so uncaring about everything that this was quite a change.

And Cassie would be lying if she didn't admit the fact that Ian was the polar opposite of her ex turned her on even more.

"You're only here for a short time," she went on, crossing her arms over her chest. "We can't just…you know."

"Have sex?" he asked, quirking a brow.

Oh, mercy. The words were now out, hovering in the air, and from the smirk on his face, she was the only one feeling awkward at this moment.

"Yes, that." *Dear Lord.* It wasn't as if she hadn't had

sex before; she'd had a baby, for crying out loud. But she couldn't discuss something like that with him. Now she felt foolish and juvenile. "Acting on sexual attraction isn't something I normally do."

That was an understatement, considering she'd had sex with one man and that had been her husband. What if she did throw caution to the wind? What if she had some sordid affair?

Seriously? Was she contemplating that? She was a mother—a mother to a little girl. What kind of example was she?

"You're thinking too hard." Ian started to step forward, but he stopped when Cassie held up a hand.

"Don't. I can't think when you're touching me."

"I'll take that as a compliment."

Cassie rolled her eyes. "You would."

"See? You know me already."

One of them had to think rationally. Apparently it would be her. She maneuvered around him toward the opening of the stable.

"You're going to have to keep your hands and your mouth to yourself."

Those tempting lips curved into a smile. "You're no fun."

"I don't have time for fun, Ian."

And more than likely he was the proverbial good time back in L.A. She could easily see him hopping from one party to the next, beautiful women draped over his arm, falling into his bed.

Cassie flicked the main switch to light up the pathways between the stalls. The brightness from the antique horseshoe-style chandeliers put a screeching halt to any romantic ambience that had been lurking in the darkening stable.

When she turned back around, Ian had his hands on his narrow hips, his focus still locked on her. There was a hunger in his eyes she'd never seen from any man before.

Without a word, he closed the gap between them. Cassie's heart had just started to settle, but now it picked back up again. She should've known better than to think the intense moment would pass.

Ian framed her face with his hands and brought his mouth to within a fraction of an inch of hers. "A woman who kisses, who responds to my touch without hesitation, has pent-up passion that needs to be released."

His lips barely brushed hers. "Come find me when you're ready."

Ian walked around her, leaving her still surrounded by that masculine scent, his arousing words and the tingling from his touch still on her lips.

She'd known the man twelve hours. There was no way she could handle him being on the grounds for two more months. She was a woman—a woman with needs.

And a part of her wondered just what would happen if she allowed herself to put those needs first for once.

Three

Two days had passed since she'd been up close and personal with Ian, but Cassie was more than aware of his quiet, yet dominating, presence on the estate. She'd seen him from a distance as he talked with Max. She'd found out she'd just missed him on the set of one scene she'd gone to watch, but she refused to admit she was wondering about his schedule, about when she'd see him again. Feel his body against hers.

She refused to fall for another man who set her hormones into overdrive, so where did that leave her? Considering a fling?

Groaning, she made her way from the stables to the main house. The sun was making its descent behind the mountains and Emily was at her weekly sleepover with Tessa and Grant. After witnessing the shooting of the engagement scene over the past couple of days, Cassie was feeling more and more nostalgic.

She missed her mother with each passing day; seeing Rose's life depicted in the film had Cassie wanting to feel closer to her. And with Emily away for the night, this was the perfect opportunity to reminisce and head up to the attic, where all her mother's things were stored.

Rose's unexpected death had shaken up the family in ways they'd never even imagined. As teen girls, Tessa and Cassie had really taken it hard, but they'd all been there for each other, forming an even stronger bond. But Cassie still ached for her mother's sweet smile, her encouraging words and her patient guidance.

Because right now she truly wanted a mother's advice. Ian had her completely tied in knots. When he'd left her in the stables two days ago, Cassie had never felt so torn, so conflicted in her life. And he hadn't approached her since. What was up with that? Had he changed his mind? Had he decided she wasn't worth the trouble?

Why was she even worried about this anyway? No doubt Ian was used to those flawless women who had been surgically perfected. More than likely Cassie's extra pounds and shapelier curves were not what Ian was looking for in a...fling? What was he doing exactly with his flirting? Where had he expected this to go?

Never mind. He'd thrown out the word *sex* like nothing. Cassie knew exactly where he was headed with his flirting.

Leaving the attic door propped open, Cassie headed up the narrow wooden staircase. At the top she flicked on the small light that was so soft, it really only set off a glow on one wall. But that was the wall where her mother's boxes were stacked.

In the silence of the evening, Cassie was all alone with her thoughts, her memories. She pulled the lid off the first bin and choked back tears.

How could anyone's life, especially that of her beautiful,

loving, vivacious mother, be condensed to a few boxes? All the memories, all the smiles, all the comfort Rose Barrington had offered to the world…all gone. Only tangible items remained stored neatly in plastic bins.

Cassie couldn't help but smile. Her very organized mother wouldn't have had it any other way.

After going through pictures from her parents' simple, elegant wedding day, Cassie knew the wedding dress was around. Tessa actually planned on wearing it for her upcoming vows, and Cassie couldn't wait to see her baby sister in their mother's gown. Just that image was enough to have her tearing up again.

This film was certainly wreaking havoc on her emotions, that was for sure.

Cassie kept searching through storage bins, looking for a box or a folded garment bag. Would the crew need to duplicate that dress for the wedding scene? More than likely they'd already researched pictures to find inspiration for the costumes, just as they had for the settings.

Cassie had been itching for a chance to look through the old photos again herself.

Moving from the bins, Cassie went and looked inside the narrow antique wardrobe, where she discovered a white garment bag. Slowly unzipping, so as not to tear the precious material inside, Cassie peeled back the bag and pulled out the classy gown she'd been hunting for.

The dress had been preserved so that the cream-colored material was still perfect. Tessa would be just as beautiful a bride as their mother had been.

Cassie had thought about wearing it for her own wedding, but her ex had insisted on getting married at the courthouse. She should've known then that he wasn't the one. Not that there was anything wrong with a small civil ceremony, but Derek had known she'd always wanted a wedding in the small church where her parents had married. She'd wanted the lacy gown, the rice in her hair as they ran to their awaiting car...the special wedding night.

None of those young-girl dreams had come true.

Unable to resist, Cassie stripped from her jeans, boots, button-up and bra and pulled on the strapless floor-length dress. A straight cut with lace overlay may be simple to some, but the design was perfect to Cassie.

Smoothing a hand down the snug bodice, Cassie went to the antique mirror in the corner. If she fell in love one day—real love this time—maybe she could wear it. Wouldn't that be a beautiful tradition? Rose, Tessa and Cassie all wearing the same gown. Perhaps if the material held up and the gown was well preserved again, little Emily would one day walk down the aisle wearing the dress her grandmother had.

If it weren't for baby weight, the frock would fit perfectly. Unfortunately, right now her boobs threatened to spill out the top and lace was definitely not a forgiving material, so her curves were very...prominent.

Behind her, the attic door clicked. Cassie turned, her hand to her beating heart as footsteps sounded up the stairs. No time to cover up all her goods, so she kept her hand in place over her generous cleavage.

"Hello?" she called.

Ian rounded the landing and froze. He took in her state of dress—or undress, really—of course zeroing in on where her hand had settled.

So much for her evening of reminiscing. Could fate be any more mocking? Dangling this sexy stranger in her face when she knew full well that nothing could or should happen?

"What are you doing?" she asked, keeping her hand in place and trying to remain calm. Kind of hard when she was on display and just the sight of the man had her heart accelerating.

"I wanted to apologize for the other day," he told her, coming up the last couple of steps. "I never force myself on a woman, and I didn't want you to have that impression of me. But if I'm going to be here any length of time, and I am, we need to clear the air."

Clear the air? Cassie sighed and prayed because she had a sinking feeling they may be there for a while.

"Well, now's the perfect time because if that door latched all the way, we're locked in here."

Ian drew his brows together. "Locked in?"

"The door locks from the outside. That's why I had left it standing open."

Pulling up the hem of the dress with one hand and trying to keep the bodice up with the other, she moved around him down the steps and tugged on the handle. She leaned her forehead against the door and groaned.

"I didn't know," he murmured behind her.

Cassie turned and looked up the steps to see Ian looking menacing and dangerous—in that sexy way only he could—standing at the top. His muscles filled out his long-sleeved T, those wide shoulders stretching the material, and his dark jeans fit his narrow hips beautifully.

She knew firsthand exactly how that body felt against hers. Knew just how well he could kiss a woman into forgetting her morals.

In a house this size, with only her father living here and his bedroom on the first floor, no one would hear them yell until morning, when they could open the small window and catch someone's attention.

Risking another full-body glance at Ian, Cassie knew she was in big, big trouble. Her attraction to him was the strongest she'd ever felt toward a man. But it wasn't so much the level of heat between them that scared her; it was the quick onset of it. It felt as if she had no control over her own reaction. She'd been helplessly drawn to this intriguing man. How could she trust her emotions right now? He was honestly the first man to find her desirable since her ex. Was he just a sexy diversion or were her feelings more in-depth than that?

Earlier tonight she'd flirted with the idea of a fling, but now the reality of being trapped with Ian made her heart flutter and nerves dance in her belly.

Her gaze met his. Crackling tension vibrated between them in the soft glow and the silence.

And Cassie had all night to decide what to do with all her attraction and the hungry look in Ian's eyes...

Ian stared down at Cassie, struck by those creamy exposed shoulders, that poured-on, vintage-style wedding gown molded to her sweet curves. From his vantage point, he could see even more of her very exposed breasts and most impressive cleavage—even though she was trying her hardest to keep gravity from taking over the top of that dress.

Mercy. Being straight in front of her had been torture, but this angle offered a much more interesting, gut-clenching view. Not that he was complaining.

Being stuck in an attic with Cassie would be no hardship because he'd caught a glimpse of the passion she held beneath her vulnerability. And there wasn't a doubt in his mind that her war with herself stemmed from some past hurt.

Cassie attempted to cross her arms over her breasts, which only tortured him further, because she failed to cover the goods and actually ended up offering him an even more enticing view. Was she doing this as punishment?

"Text Max and have him come to the main house and ring the doorbell. Dad won't be in bed yet."

Ian shook his head. "Sorry. I only came over to apologize to you, so I left my phone in my trailer to charge."

Groaning, Cassie tipped her head back against the door and closed her eyes. "This isn't happening to me," she muttered. "This cannot be happening."

Ian had to smile. Of all the scenarios he'd envisioned on his short walk from his trailer to the main house, he hadn't once thought of being stuck for hours with someone so sexy, so unexpected, and wearing a wedding dress to boot.

This couldn't have been scripted any worse...or better, depending on the point of view.

Cassie lifted the dress and stomped back up the steps, her shoulder slamming into him as she stormed by.

"Wipe that smirk off your face, Ian. Nothing about this is comical."

"Can't you call someone with your phone?" he asked, turning to face her.

Cassie propped her hands on her hips. "No. I came up here to be alone, to think."

Damn, she was even sexier when she was angry. But getting too wrapped up with Cassie Barrington was a dangerous move. She wasn't a fling type of girl and he'd pushed too hard in the stables. Had she given in to his blatant advances, he knew she would've regretted it later.

He needed to do the right thing and keep his hands off her. He was here for two main purposes: keep Max happy and sign Lily so she didn't go to his rival. Period.

But his hormones didn't get the memo, because the more he was around Cassie, the more alluring and sexy she became. Of course, now that he'd seen a sample, he had to admit, he wanted to see more. That dress... Yeah, she looked like a 1950s pinup. Sexy as hell, with all the right curves and none of that stick-thin, anorexic nonsense, and she was even hotter with a slight flush from anger.

For the past two days he'd seen her working with her sister, training the horses and driving him unbelievably mad with the way her lush body filled out a pair of jeans. He'd seriously had to get his damn hormones in check and then approach her with a much-needed apology for his Neanderthal tendencies.

But now that he was here, those hormones were front and center once again, overriding all common sense and rational thoughts.

"How did you know I was up here?" she asked. "I figured all the crew was either in their trailers or back at the hotel."

"I ran into Grant on my way to your cottage. He told me you were here. As I was coming in the back door, your cook, Linda, was going out for the night and she said you mentioned coming to the attic."

"You came all this way just to apologize? I'm sure you would've seen me tomorrow."

Ian shrugged, shoving his hands into his pockets. "True, but I knew too many people would be around tomorrow. I assumed you wouldn't want to discuss this in front of an audience. Besides, I think we need to address this spark between us and figure out what to do with it since I'll be here several weeks."

Cassie threw her hands in the air. "Could you at least turn around so I can put my clothes back on?"

His eyes traveled down her body, darting to the pile of clothes behind her, zeroing in on the leopard-print bra lying on top.

"Sure," he said, trying to get the visual of her in that leopard bra out of his mind before he went insane.

Fate may have landed him up here with the sassy, sexy

Ms. Barrington, and fate also provided a window directly in front of him, where he was afforded a glorious view of Cassie's reflection as she changed. Of course, that made him a bit of a jerk, but no man with air in his lungs would look away from that enticing view. This evening just kept getting better and better.

Cassie would probably die before she asked for help with the zipper, so he didn't offer. And she didn't have any trouble. As the dress slid down her body, Ian's knees nearly buckled.

Lush didn't even begin to describe her. Her full breasts, rounded belly and the slight flare of her hips were a lethal combination.

"As I was saying," he went on, cursing his voice when it cracked like that of an adolescent. "I realize that neither of us was prepared for the instant physical attraction—"

"You're delusional," she muttered as she tugged her jeans up over her hips and matching bikini panties.

"But just because I find you sexy as hell doesn't mean I can't control myself."

Her hands froze on her back as she fastened her bra. Apparently his words had struck a chord. She glanced up and caught his gaze in the reflection. Busted.

"Seriously?" she asked with a half laugh. "Why did you even turn around?"

"I didn't know the window was there." That was the truth.

"And you weren't going to say anything?"

Ian spun around—no point in being subtle now. "I'm a guy. What do you think?"

Rolling her eyes, Cassie shrugged into her shirt and buttoned it up with jerky, hurried motions.

Fighting the urge to cross the room and undress her again, Ian slid his hands into his pockets and met her gaze.

"You are stunning," he told her, suddenly feeling the need to drive that point home. "I'm not sure why that statement caught you off guard."

Most women in Hollywood would pause at such a comment, try to deny it in order to hear more pretty words in a vain attempt to boost their own egos, but Ian knew Cassie was different. She truly didn't believe she was beautiful, and he had a feeling all that insecurity circled back to whatever the basis was for her vulnerability.

Damn, he didn't have time to delve into distressed damsels. But there was a desire in him, something primal, almost possessive that made him want to dig deeper, to uncover more of Cassie Barrington. And not just physically.

That revelation alone scared the hell out of him.

"I don't need to be charmed, Ian." She propped her hands on her hips. "We're stuck up here and lying or trying to make me want you isn't going to work."

"I don't lie, Cassie." When she quirked a brow, he merely shrugged. "I find you sexy. Any man would be insane or blind not to."

Cassie shook her head. After zipping the dress into a white garment bag, she headed over to a storage box and popped off the lid. She flopped down on the floor, crossing her legs and offering him the view of her back.

He waited for her to say something, but she seemed to have dismissed him or was so wrapped up in the memories of the photos she was pulling out, she just didn't care that he was there.

"You ever look at a picture and remember that moment so well, you can actually feel it?" she asked, her soft voice carrying across the room.

Ian took that as his invitation to join her. He closed the distance between them, taking a seat directly beside her. Cassie held a picture. A young girl, he presumed it was her, sat atop a horse, and a dark-haired beauty, who he assumed was her mother, held the lead line.

"That was my first horse," she told him, her eyes still on the picture. "I'd always ridden with Dad and helped him around the stables, but this one was all mine. I'd picked him out at auction and Mom and Dad told me I had to care for him all by myself."

Ian looked at the image of a young Cassie. "How old were you?"

"Eight. But I knew as soon as I saw him that I'd want him. He was skittish and shied away from the men, but when I approached him, against my father's advice, he came right to me and actually nuzzled my neck."

Ian listened to her, refusing to let himself fall into her sea of emotions. He'd noticed her and Tessa holding hands at the shoot, tears swimming in both of their eyes.

"I've never ridden a horse," he admitted.

Cassie dropped the picture back into the bin and turned to stare at him. "Seriously? We'll have to rectify that while you're here."

Ian laughed. "I wasn't asking for an invitation. Just stating a fact."

She turned a bit more to face him, her thigh rubbing against his. Did she have a clue that she was playing with fire? She may be older than him, but something told him she wasn't necessarily more experienced.

Arrogance had him believing they weren't on a level playing field. He had plenty he wanted to show her.

"I love teaching people how to ride," she went on, oblivious to his thoughts. "It's such an exhilarating experience."

Cassie's wide smile lit up her entire face. The room had a soft glow from the single-bulb sconce on the wall and Ian could resist those full lips for only so long…especially now that he knew exactly how they tasted.

Without warning, he slid his hands through her hair and captured her lips. She opened freely, just like when they'd been in the stables.

Ian tipped her head, taking the kiss deeper. He wanted more, so much more. He wanted to feel her hands on him as he explored her mouth, relishing her taste, but she didn't touch him. Maybe she did know how to play this age-old game of catch and release.

Easing back, Ian took in her swollen lips, her heavy lids and flushed cheeks and smiled. "Actually, *that's* an exhilarating experience."

And God help them both because between the interlude in the stables and that kiss, he had the whole night to think about how this sexual chemistry would play out.

The real question was: Could he make it all night without finding out?

Four

Cassie jumped to her feet, instantly feeling the chill without Ian's powerful touch. The man was beyond potent and he damn well knew it.

"You seriously think because we're locked in here and we kissed a few times that I'll just have sex with you?" Cassie ran a shaky hand through her hair, cursing her nerves for overtaking her as fast as those heated kisses had. "I don't know what lifestyle you lead in L.A., but that's not how I work."

Ian stared up at her, desire still lurking in those dark-as-sin eyes. "Are you denying you were just as involved in those kisses as I was?"

"You had your hands all over me," she threw back. "Just because I like kissing doesn't mean I always use it as a stepping-stone for sex. I technically just met you, for crying out loud. I don't know anything about you."

Moving as slowly as a panther hunting its prey, Ian came

to his feet and crossed to her. "You know how quick you respond to my touch, you know how your heartbeat quickens when you wonder what my next move will be and you know you're fighting this pull between us."

Cassie raised a brow, trying for her best bored look. "That has nothing to do with Ian Shaffer. That's all chemistry."

"So you don't deny you want me?" he asked with a smirk.

Crossing her arms and taking a step back, Cassie narrowed her eyes. "Drop the ego down a notch. You just proved how very little we know about each other. You may sleep with virtual strangers, but I don't."

Ian laughed, throwing his arms in the air. "Okay. What do you want to know?"

"Are you married?"

Shock slid over his face. "Hell no. Never plan to be."

Commitment issues? Lovely. Hadn't she just gotten out of a relationship with a man of the same nature?

On the other hand, Ian wasn't cheating on a wife back in California. That was at least one mark in his favor. Okay, the toe-curling kisses were major positive points in his favor, but she'd never confess that out loud. And she wasn't actually looking to jump back into another relationship anyway.

"No girlfriend?" she asked.

"Would I be all over you if I did?"

Cassie shrugged. "Some guys wouldn't care."

That heated gaze glided over her and was just as effective as a lover's touch. Her body trembled.

"I'm not like a lot of other guys."

He was powerful, sexy and wanted in her pants. Yeah, he was just like some guys.

With a sigh, Cassie laughed. "I can't believe this," she

muttered more to herself than to Ian. "I'm actually playing twenty questions because I want to have sex."

"Sweetheart, I don't care a bit to answer a hundred questions if you're considering sex."

Lord have mercy, it was hot up there. Not just because of the ridiculous way her body responded to this charmer, but literally. The heat in the attic was stifling.

Cassie unbuttoned the top two buttons of her shirt, exposing her cleavage area, but she needed air. She rolled her sleeves up and caught Ian's eyes taking in her actions.

"Don't get excited there, hotshot. I'm just trying to cool off."

Sweat trickled between her shoulder blades and she so wished she'd at least pulled her hair up earlier. There had to be something up here. As she started to look around in boxes for a rubber band of any type, she tried not to think of Ian and if he had sweat on the taut muscles beneath his shirt.

Okay, that mental blocker was broken because all she could see was glistening bronzed skin. And while she hadn't seen him without a shirt, she had a very good imagination.

"Can I help you find something?" he asked.

Throwing a glance over her shoulder, she caught his smirk as he crossed his arms over his chest. "I just need something to pull my hair up. I'm sweating."

There, that should douse his oversexed status a little. What man found a sweaty woman attractive? And she was pretty sure her wavy red hair was starting to look like Bozo the Clown's after a motorcycle ride...sans helmet. She lifted the flap off a box in the far corner and shuffled things around in her hunt.

"So, why is an agent needed on a film set?" she asked,

truly wondering but also wanting to keep his mind on work—which was what he should be doing anyway.

"Max is one of my top clients." Ian unbuttoned his shirt halfway. "I often visit my clients on set to make sure they're taken care of. And with this being a very impressive script and plot, I knew I had to be here. I've actually blocked off a good bit of time to spend at Stony Ridge."

And wasn't that just the news she needed to hear? Mr. Tall, Dark and Tempting would be spending "a good bit of time" here. Just what her very inactive sexual life needed... temptation.

"Yes," she shouted as she grabbed a rubber band off a stack of school papers from her primary days.

"Max is a great guy, from what I've seen." After pulling her hair into a knot on top of her head, she turned to Ian. "He and Lily are doing an amazing job, too. Lily seems like a sweetheart."

Nodding his agreement, Ian rested a hip against an old dresser. "She's rare in the industry. L.A. hasn't jaded her or sucked the goodness out of her. She had a rough patch with a scandal at the start of her career, but she's overcome it. She's a rare gem."

"And I'm sure you've tried to get her into bed."

Rich laughter filled the space. The fact he was mocking her only ticked Cassie off more. But, if she were honest, she was ticked at herself for wanting him.

"I've never slept with Lily," he told her, a grin still spread across his handsome face. "I've never even tried to. I'm actually hoping to sign her to my agency. I respect my clients and they respect me. This business is too risky and too exposed for anything like that to remain a secret. There are no secrets in Hollywood."

"Is that all that's stopped you? The fact that people could find out?"

Ian straightened to his full height and took a step toward her. *Great.* She'd awoken the sex beast again.

"What stopped me," he said as he took slow steps toward her, "was the fact that, yes, she's beautiful, but I'm not attracted to her. Added to that, I want a professional relationship with her, not a sexual one. If I want a woman in my bed, she won't be on my client list. Plain and simple."

He'd come close enough that Cassie had to tip her head back. Thankfully, he hadn't touched her. Too much more touching—or, heaven forbid, kissing—and she feared her self-control would be totally shot.

Cassie swiped a hand over her damp neck. "Is everything a business strategy with you?"

"Not at all. Right now, I'm not thinking anything about business."

The way his eyes held hers, as if she was the only person that mattered right now, made her wonder…

She may be naive and she was certainly still recovering from Derek walking out on her, but what would a fling hurt? Tessa had even verbally expressed Cassie's thoughts on the matter. She'd married for "love," or so she'd thought. Hell, she'd even saved herself for marriage and look how that had turned out.

"I promise I won't ravage you if you'd like to take something off," he told her with a naughty grin. "I'm sure your shirt will be long enough to cover things if you need to get out of those jeans. If not, I've seen naked women before."

Yeah? Well, not *this* naked woman, and with that last bit of baby weight still hanging on for dear life, she most definitely wasn't comfortable enough with her body to flaunt it. Even if she did indulge in a fling with the sexy agent—and she couldn't believe she was seriously considering such a thing—she wasn't going to make the catch so easy for him. What fun would that be?

Deciding to teach him a lesson, Cassie reached up and patted the side of his face. "You're so sweet to sacrifice yourself that way."

Cassie knew her mother had a box of old clothes up here. Perhaps something could be used to cool her off and make Ian squirm just a bit more.

As she went toward the area with the clothing boxes, she opted to keep Ian talking.

"So, tell me more about Lily." Cassie pulled the lid off an oblong box and nearly wept with relief at the colorful summer dresses inside. "She's very striking and has a strong resemblance to my mother."

"When this film came across my desk, I knew I wanted Max to try for it and I was sincerely hoping they paired him with Lily. This role was made for her. She's already got that Southern-belle charm your mother had, according to everyone on set. Lily has the sweet little twang in her voice like all of you Barringtons do."

Cassie turned, clutching a simple strapless cotton dress to her chest. "I do not have a twang."

Ian quirked a brow. "It's actually even more prominent when you get ticked. Very cute and sexy."

Rolling her eyes, Cassie turned back to the box and placed the lid back on. "I'm going to change. Could you try not to stare at me through the reflection again?"

Ian shrugged one broad shoulder. "I promise."

Cassie waited for him to turn around or move, but he just sat there smiling. Damn that man. Now that she'd reminded him he'd seen her pretty much naked, Cassie had no doubt she'd just thrown gasoline on the fire.

"Aren't you going to turn around?" she finally asked.

"Oh, when you just said not to look at you through the reflection, I assumed you wanted to let me in on the full viewing."

"I didn't want to let you into this room…let alone treat you to a viewing."

Cassie resisted the urge to kiss that smirk off his face. He knew he was getting to her, and she wondered just how much longer she'd deny it to herself.

"I'll move, then," she told him, stomping to the other end of the attic behind a tall stack of boxes. "And don't you follow me."

"Wouldn't dream of it." He chuckled. "But you're just putting off the inevitable, you know."

She quickly wrestled out of her clothes and yanked the strapless dress up over her heated body. Her bare arms and legs cooled instantly.

"I'm not putting anything off," she informed him as she came back around the boxes. "I know your type, Ian. Sex shouldn't just be a way to pass the time. It should mean something, and the couple should have feelings for each other."

"Oh, I feel something for you. And I plan on making you feel something, too."

Why did her body have to respond to him? And why did she always have to be so goody-goody all the time?

She didn't even have the ability to make him squirm. No wonder her husband had left her for another woman.

"I'm not sure what put that look on your face, but I hope it wasn't me."

Cassie drew her attention back to Ian, who had now moved in closer and was very much in her personal space. His dark eyes stared at her mouth and Cassie really tried to remember why she was putting up such a fight.

Had her husband ever looked at her like this? As though he was so turned on that all that mattered was the two of them? Had he ever made her tingle like this or feel so feminine and sexy?

No to all the above.

Cassie swallowed. If she was really going to do this, she needed to be in control. She'd been dominated enough in her marriage and right now she wanted something totally different. She wanted sex and she wanted Ian.

Mustering up all her courage, Cassie looked up at him with a wide smile and said, "Strip."

Five

It wasn't often Ian was shocked—he did live in Hollywood, after all. But that one word that had just slid from Cassie's lips truly took his breath and left him utterly speechless.

"Excuse me?"

Raising a brow, she crossed her arms as if she dared him to refuse. "I said strip. You want this, fine. But on my terms."

"I don't do sex with rules."

Cassie shrugged. "I don't do flings, but here we both are, stepping outside of our comfort zones."

Damn, she was hot. He never would've guessed the shy, quiet sister had this vixen streak. Of course, she admitted she was stepping outside her comfort zone, so perhaps this was all new territory. He had to hand it to her—she was doing a spectacular job. But he couldn't let her have all the control.

Reaching behind his neck, Ian fisted his shirt and tugged it off, flinging it to the side. Hands on his hips, he offered a grin.

"Now you."

Cassie laughed. "You're not done yet."

"No, but I'm ahead of you." He met her gaze, the silent challenge thrown down between them. "I'm waiting."

Even though her eyes never left his, he didn't miss the way her hands shook as she reached beneath the dress and pulled her panties down her bare legs.

Just that simple piece of silk lying discarded at her feet had his pulse racing, his body responding.

She quirked a brow again, as if waiting for him to proceed.

Without hesitation he toed off his shoes and ripped off his socks. "Looks like you're down to only one garment now," he told her, taking in the strapless dress she'd donned.

And it was about to get a whole hell of a lot hotter in here.

She eyed the lamp across the room and started for it.

"No," he told her. "Leave it on."

Glancing over her shoulder, she met his stare. "Trust me when I say you'll want that off."

"And why is that?"

Turning fully to face him, she pointed to her body. "In case you haven't noticed, I'm not one of those Hollywood types who starve themselves for the sake of being ultra-thin."

Crossing the narrow space between them, Ian ran both his hands up her bare arms and tucked his fingers in the elastic of the top of the dress, causing her arms to fall to her side.

"Oh, I've noticed." He yanked the dress down until it

puddled at her feet, leaving her bare to him. "And that's precisely why I want that light on."

Her body trembled beneath his. No way did he want her questioning her gorgeous curves or the fact that he wanted the hell out of her.

Without a word he shucked off his pants and boxer briefs and tossed them aside.

Her eyes drank him in, causing the same effect as if she'd touched his entire body with her bare hands. Dying to touch her, to run his fingers along her curves, Ian snaked his arms around her waist and tugged her against him.

"As much as I want to explore that sexy body of yours, I'm hanging on by a thread here," he admitted as his mouth slammed down onto hers.

Cassie wrapped her arms around his neck. Their damp bodies molded together from torso to thigh, and she felt so perfect against him.

Perfect? No, she couldn't be perfect for him. Perfect for right now, which was all either of them was after.

They were simply taking advantage of the moment...of the sexual attraction that had enveloped them since she'd literally fallen into his arms only a few days ago.

Ian gripped her waist and lifted her.

"Ian, don't—"

"Shh," he whispered against her mouth. "I've got you."

Her lips curved into a smile. "What about a condom? Do you have that, too?"

Condom, yes. They needed a condom. His mind had been on the subtle moans escaping from her lips and getting those curves beneath his hands.

He eased her down his body and went to his jeans, where he pulled a condom from his wallet and in record time had it on.

When he turned back to her, he fully expected her to

have her arms wrapped around her waist, maybe even be biting her lip out of nerves. But what he saw was a secure woman, hands on her hips, head tilted and a naughty grin on her face.

"Your confidence is sexy," he told her as he came back to her.

"You make me feel sexy."

Yeah, she wasn't a Hollywood size zero. Cassie Barrington was more old-school Hollywood starlet. She was a natural, stunning, vibrant woman, and now that she'd agreed to leave the light on, he could fully appreciate the beauty she was.

And when she reached for him and nearly wrapped herself around him as she claimed his mouth, her sexy status soared even higher.

Damn, he wasn't going to make it through this night.

Ian backed her against the wall and lifted her once again. This time her legs went around his waist and he had no control. None. The second he'd shucked that dress off her he'd been holding on by that proverbial thin thread.

Ian took her, causing her body to bow back, and her head tilted, eyes closed as she groaned once again.

As their hips moved together, Ian took the opportunity to kiss his way across her shoulders and the column of her throat before taking her face between his palms and claiming her mouth.

Sweat slick between them, the air around them grew even hotter as Cassie gripped his bare shoulders. Her nails bit into his skin; her heels dug into his back.

He wouldn't have it any other way.

She tore her mouth from his. "Ian, I—"

Yeah, he knew. He was right there with her as her body stilled, trembled. Following her over the edge, watching her face as she succumbed to the passion was one of the most erotic moments of his life.

Her body slid down his and he was pretty sure she would've collapsed to the floor had he not been leaning against her. He needed to lean into her or he'd be a puddle, too.

And the night had just begun.

Cassie slid back into her dress, ignoring the panties. Why bother with modesty at this point?

She may not live in Hollywood, but she'd put on one hell of an acting display. Ian thought her confident? She'd played along simply because she secretly wanted to be that wanton, take-charge woman, that woman who claimed what she wanted. And if he thought she was so comfortable with her body in this situation, then who was she to tell him different?

She'd been meek in her marriage, not a sex goddess in any way. But the way Ian had looked at her, touched her, was nothing like she'd ever experienced.

How could a man she'd known only a handful of days provide so much self-assurance? He'd awakened something within her she hadn't even known existed.

Cassie was certainly not used to one-night stands or flings, but she couldn't regret what had just happened. A virtual stranger had just given her one of the greatest gifts…self-esteem. Not too long ago she'd thought she'd never have that back, but right now, with her body still tingling from his talented hands and lips, Cassie knew without a doubt that she was better than the husband who had left her for another woman.

She'd just scooped up her discarded panties from the floor when Ian placed his hands around her waist and tugged her back against his bare chest.

"How's that age thing now?" he asked, nipping her ear. "Any complaints about how young I am?"

Laughing, Cassie shook her head. "You certainly know what you're doing."

His lips trailed over her neck. "I'm not done, either."

Oh, mercy. Her entire body shivered as she let her head fall back against his shoulder, enjoying the kisses he sprinkled across her heated skin.

"I'm not sure why you put this dress back on," he told her between kisses. "It's so hot in here and all."

Yes, yes, it is.

Cassie turned in his arms, noticing he was still completely naked. Those ripped muscles beneath taut, tanned skin begged for her touch.

"I didn't get to appreciate all of this a moment ago, before you attacked me," she told him, trailing her fingertips along his biceps and across his pecs.

"Appreciate me all you want," he told her with a crooked grin. "But let it be known, I didn't attack. You ordered me to strip, so I believe you started this."

Cassie playfully smacked his chest. "Who started what? You were the one who propositioned me in the stables."

"How's a man supposed to react when a sexy woman falls into his arms?"

"Yes, naturally that's what most people would do," she said, rolling her eyes.

Ian reached down, cupped her backside and widened his sexy smile. "I'm glad this little incident happened with the lock."

Cassie had to admit she was, too. There was no way she would've been able to focus on work with all her emotions fluttering around inside her. Now hopefully she wouldn't have to worry about this overwhelming physical attraction to Ian. They'd had sex, gotten it out of their systems and could move on.

His body stirred against hers. Okay, maybe they hadn't gotten it out of their systems.

"We still have hours before anyone will find us." He started backing her up again. "I have so many ideas to fill the time."

The backs of Cassie's thighs hit the edge of an old table. Ian wasted no time hoisting her up onto the smooth wooden surface.

"Do you have more condoms?" she asked.

His heavy-lidded gaze combined with that Cheshire-cat smile had her quivering before he even spoke.

"I may be out of condoms, but not out of ways to pleasure you."

And when he proceeded to show her, Cassie was suddenly in no hurry for daylight to come.

Six

Unable to sleep for appreciating the feel of this sexy woman tangled all around him on the old chaise, Ian smoothed a hand down Cassie's bare back. Trailing down the dip in her waist, up over the curve of her hip had his body stirring again.

What on earth was he doing? Sex was one thing, but to lie awake most of the night rehashing it over and over in his head like some lovesick fool was, well…for fools. Not that he was any expert on relationships.

His mother was gearing up to divorce husband number four, no doubt with number five waiting in the wings, and his father… Ian sighed. His father probably wasn't even capable of love. Ian hadn't spoken to his father in years and rarely talked with his mother. He had nothing to say to either and it was obvious both of his parents were battling their own issues that didn't include him.

It shouldn't come as a surprise that Ian didn't do relationships.

He was great at his job, however, and what he wanted was to take his client roster to the next level. Lily Beaumont was the key.

Yet here he was, getting involved with Cassie Barrington. And, yes, they'd just had sex, but during the moments in between their intimacy, he'd gotten a brief glimpse of a playful, confident woman and he couldn't deny he liked what he saw.

The sound of a car door jarred him from his thoughts. He eased out from beneath Cassie's warm, lush body and moved over to the small window that faced the side of the house.

Tessa and Grant had arrived. He didn't know if he wanted to call for their attention or crawl back over to Cassie and give her a proper good-morning wake-up.

But their night was over, and he had responsibilities. He honestly had no clue how she'd react once she woke up. Would she regret what they'd done? Would she want more and expect some sort of relationship?

Ian gave the window a tug and it rose slowly with a groan.

"Hey," he yelled down. "Up here."

Tessa and Grant both looked around and Ian eased his arm out to wave. "We're locked in the attic," he called.

"Ian?" Grant shouted. "What on earth? We'll be right up."

Of course, now it dawned on him that both he and Cassie were as naked as the day they were born, and he turned around to see her already getting up. Shame that he hadn't ignored the rescue party and gone with his original idea of waking her, especially now that she was covering that made-for-sex body.

"Was that Tessa and Grant?" she asked, tugging on her jeans from the previous day.

"Uh-huh." He pulled on his own clothes, trying to keep his eyes off her as she wrestled into her bra.

Several moments later, the door below creaked open and Ian rushed over to the top of the stairs to see Tessa.

"We'll be right down," he told her, hoping to save Cassie some time to finish dressing.

He didn't know if she wanted it public knowledge that they'd slept together. This was all her call. He was much more comfortable with a fling than he figured she was. Plus this was her home, her family, and the last thing he wanted to do was put her in an awkward position.

"Who's up there with you?" Tessa asked, her brows drawn together.

"Your sister."

Tessa smiled. "Really? Well, we'll meet you all down in the kitchen. Take your time."

Once she walked away, Ian glanced up to Cassie, who was wearing a lovely shade of red over her neck and face.

"I tried," he defended, holding out his hands. "But I'd say your sister knows."

Cassie nodded. "That's okay. Tessa won't say anything."

Okay, maybe he hadn't wanted a relationship, but her statement hit a nerve. Seconds ago he'd thought he was fine with a fling and she wasn't, but perhaps he'd had that scenario backward.

"Is that what we're going to do? Keep this quiet?"

Smoothing her tousled hair away from her face, Cassie eyed him from across the room and sighed. "I don't know. This is all new to me. Can we just go downstairs and talk later?"

The voice of reason had him nodding. He didn't want to

analyze what had happened too much. They both needed to concentrate on their jobs. After all, he had a mission and she was in the middle of the biggest racing season of her life.

Cassie started to ease by him when he stepped in front of her, blocking her exit. Her eyes went wide, then dropped to his mouth. Why was he doing this?

Quit stalling and let her go.

But he needed one more taste before their night officially came to an end.

He shoved his hands into her hair, tilting her head as he closed the distance between them. "Before you go," he whispered as his mouth slid across hers.

She melted into him as she returned the kiss. Her hands gripped his wrists as he held on to her. As much as Ian wanted her naked once again, he knew that was not an option.

Easing back, he smiled when her eyes took a moment to open. He released her, and, without a word, she walked by him and down the stairs.

And like some nostalgic sap, he glanced around the attic and smiled. This was definitely his favorite place on the estate.

Ian met up with Cassie in the kitchen. As soon as he entered the open room, he took in several things at once.

Tessa and Grant were seated at the bar, where Linda was serving cinnamon rolls. Both Tessa and Grant were eyeing Ian with knowing grins on their faces.

But it was Cassie, yet again, who captured his attention.

The woman he'd spent the night with was currently squatting down in front of a little girl with soft blond curls. The little girl looked nothing like Cassie, but the interaction didn't lie. The way she clung to Cassie, Cassie's sweet smile and laughter as she kissed her—it all had a sickening feeling settling deep in his gut.

"And who's this?" he asked, hoping it was Linda's grandchild or something because he knew Tessa and Grant had no children.

Coming to her feet with the little girl wrapped in her arms, Cassie still wore that vibrant smile as she turned to face him. "This is my daughter, Emily."

All eyes were on Ian. Granted, they were watching him because of the unspoken fact that he and Cassie had spent the night together, but they couldn't know the turmoil that flooded him. Cassie had a child and hadn't told him.

Not that they'd played the getting-to-know-you game before they'd shed their clothes, but wasn't that something that would come up?

Cassie's smile faded as Ian remained silent. Her protective hands held Emily close to her chest.

"Why don't you have some breakfast?" Linda asked, breaking the silence.

His eyes darted to her, then back to Cassie, who still watched him with a questioning look. Tessa and Grant had yet to move as they also took in the unfolding scene.

"I have things to do," he said as he walked by Cassie, ignoring the hurt in her eyes, and out the back door.

He couldn't stay in there another second. Rage filled him at the idea that Cassie had kept such a vital part of her life a secret. Was she the mother who pawned her kid off on other people so she could go have a good time? She'd been so confident, so eager to please him last night. Perhaps he was just the latest in a long line of men she threaded into her web.

No, he hadn't wanted anything beyond sex. And he sure as hell didn't want to discover that the woman he'd spent the night with was manipulative and selfish, looking for attention…just like his mother.

Humiliation flooded her.

The look of utter shock layered with anger had consumed Ian when she'd announced Emily was her daughter.

"Cass?"

Swallowing the hurt, Cassie turned to see her sister watching her. Because this awkward moment didn't need any more fuel added to the fire, Cassie smiled.

"Thanks for watching her last night," Cassie said as she held Emily with one arm and grabbed the overnight bag off the counter. "I need to go change and then I'll meet you at the stables."

"Cassie." Tessa slid from the stool and crossed to her. "Don't do this."

"Do what?"

Blue eyes stared back at her and Cassie wanted nothing more than to sit and cry, but feeling sorry for herself wouldn't accomplish anything. She'd tried that when Derek had left her.

"I just want to go feed Emily and change." Cassie blinked back the burn of tears. "I'll meet you in an hour."

"Leave Emily here," Linda said. "I'm keeping her today anyway. Do what you need to do. I'll make sure she's fed."

As much as Cassie wanted to keep Emily with her, she knew it was silly. She'd just have to put her in her crib with toys while she grabbed a shower.

"All right," she conceded, dropping the bag back onto the counter and easing Emily into the wooden high chair next to the wide granite island. "Thanks, guys."

Barely keeping it together, she started for the door. When Tessa called her name again, Cassie raised a hand

and waved her off. She just wanted to be alone for a minute, to compose herself.

How could she be so naive? Of course some big-city bachelor would be turned off by kids, but to act so repulsed by the fact made her flat-out angry.

She'd sworn when Derek had left she wouldn't allow herself to get hurt again. So, what did she do? Sleep with the first man who showed her any kind of affection.

Seriously, she thought she had more self-respect than that.

More angry at herself now, Cassie marched across the Barrington estate to her cottage next to the stables. Swatting at her damp cheeks, she squinted against the bright early-morning sun.

And because of the light in her eyes she didn't see Ian until she was in the shadow of her house. There he stood, resting against one of the porch posts as if he belonged there.

"Don't you have a client who needs your attention?" she asked, not stopping as she brushed past him and slid her key from her pocket to let herself in.

When she tried to close the door behind her, Ian's muscular arm shot out and his hand gripped the edge.

Those dark eyes leveled hers as she reined in her tears. No way would she let him see just how upset she truly was.

Tension crackled between them as Ian stood on the threshold, making no move to come in or leave.

"What do you want?" she asked.

"I want to know why you didn't tell me you had a daughter."

"Do you have kids?" she retorted.

He blinked. "No."

"Why didn't you tell me you didn't?"

"It never came up."

She threw her arms out. "Exactly. We didn't discuss too much personal stuff before…"

Shaking her head, Cassie looked up to the ceiling and sighed. "Just go. I made a mistake—it's over."

When her front door slammed, she jumped.

"I don't like being played." Ian fisted his hands on his narrow hips.

"This is my life, Ian." She gestured toward the Pack 'n Play in the corner and the toys in a basket next to the sofa. "I'm a mom. I'm not apologizing for it, and you won't make me feel bad."

When he continued to stare, muscle ticking in his jaw, Cassie tried her hardest not to wilt under his powerful presence. His gray T-shirt stretched over taut muscles, and she instantly recalled him taking her against the wall.

"Look, you're going to be here for a while," she said, reality sinking in. "I'm going to be here for the most part except during races. We're going to see each other."

His eyes roamed over her as if he were recalling last night, too. A shiver crept through her, but she remained still, waiting on his response.

"I wish you were different," he told her, his voice low.

Stunned, Cassie crossed her arms. "What?"

Cursing, Ian turned for the door. "Nothing. You're right," he said, gripping the handle and glancing over his shoulder. "We have to see each other, so why make this harder than necessary? Last night was a mistake, so let's just forget it happened."

He walked out the door and Cassie resisted the urge to throw something. For a second, when he'd said he wished she were different, she'd seen a sliver of vulnerability in his eyes. But he'd quickly masked it with his cruel, hurtful words. *Fine.* She didn't need anybody, especially someone who acted as if her child was a burden. Emily came first in her life. Period.

And no man, not her ex-husband and certainly not this sexy stranger, would make her feel ashamed.

Cassie turned toward her bedroom and cursed her body. She hated Ian Shaffer for his words, his actions, but her body still tingled from everything he'd done to her last night. How could someone so passionate and gentle turn into someone so hurtful?

Something about Emily had triggered such a dramatic turnaround. Unfortunately, Cassie didn't have the time or the energy to care. Whatever issues Ian had didn't concern her.

Now she just had to figure out how to see him on a daily basis and block out the fact he'd made her so alive, so confident for a brief time. Because now she didn't feel confident at all. She wished she could have a do-over of last night.

This time she'd keep her clothes on.

done a complete one-eighty since they'd spent the night together. That night had been full of passion and surrender. Now Cassie had erected walls, thanks to him, and the only thing he saw in her eyes was exhaustion.

"I'll let you get in to dinner," he told her, not answering her question. "See you tomorrow."

When he turned away, Cassie called his name. He glanced over his shoulder and found two sets of beautiful blue eyes staring at him.

"We're not having much, but you're welcome to join us."

The olive branch had been extended and he wondered if this was her manners and upbringing talking or if she truly wanted him to stay.

"I'd be a fool to turn down dinner with two pretty ladies," he told her, turning back to face her. "Are you sure?"

With a shaky nod, Cassie smiled. "I'm sure."

Well, hell. Looked as if he was getting in deeper after all. But he followed her through the back door like the lost man that he was.

They could be friends, he thought. Friends ate dinner together; friends apologized when they were wrong. That was where they were at now because Cassie and her little girl deserved a commitment, a family life—things he couldn't offer.

As Cassie slid Emily into her high chair, Ian watched her delicate skin as her shoulder peeked from her shirt once again. Anything he was feeling right now went way beyond friendship and ventured down the path at warp speed toward carnal desire.

Nine

Cassie had no clue what had prompted her to invite Ian inside. She wasn't weak. She didn't need a man and had been just fine on her own for the better part of a year now. But something about Ian kept pulling her toward him, as if some invisible force tugged on her heart.

And when Emily had reached for him, Cassie had waited to see his reaction. Thankfully, he'd played right along. She'd barely noticed his hesitation and hard swallow, but he hadn't disappointed Emily. Maybe kids weren't the issue with him; perhaps he was just upset because she hadn't said anything. But really, when would that conversation have occurred? When she had fallen into his arms that first day or when she'd told him to strip in the attic?

The image of him doing just that flooded her mind. Cassie was thankful her back was to him as she turned on the oven.

"Hope you like grilled cheese and French fries." Cassie

reached into the narrow cabinet beside the oven and pulled out a cookie sheet.

"Considering I was going to probably have microwave popcorn back in my trailer, grilled cheese and fries sounds gourmet."

Her phone vibrated on the counter next to the stove. She saw Derek's name flash across the screen. No and no. If he was so determined to talk to her, he knew where she was.

Right where he'd left her months ago. Pompous jerk.

As she busied herself getting the meager dinner ready for the other man who was driving her out of her mind in a totally different way, she mentally cursed. Ian was probably used to fine dining, glamorous parties and beautiful women wearing slinky dresses and dripping in diamonds. Unfortunately, tonight he was getting a single mother throwing together cheese sandwiches while wearing an old, oversize T-shirt to hide her extra weight.

More than likely he'd said yes because he felt sorry for her. Regardless, he was in her house now. Surprisingly he'd pulled up a kitchen chair next to the high chair and was feeding puff snacks to Emily.

The sight had Cassie blinking back tears. Emily's father should be doing that. He should be here having dinner with them, as a family. He should've stuck it out and kept his pants zipped.

But he'd decided a wife and a baby were too much of a commitment and put a damper on his lifestyle.

In the back of her mind, Cassie knew she was better off without him. Any man that didn't put his family first was a coward. Not suitable material for a husband or father to her child.

But the reality of being rejected still hurt. Cassie could honestly say she'd gotten over her love, but the betrayal... That was something she would probably never recover from. Because he'd not just left her; he'd left a precious, innocent baby behind without even attempting to fight for what he'd created.

Being rejected by Ian was just another blow to her already battered self-esteem.

"You okay?"

Cassie jerked back to the moment and realized two things. One, Ian was staring at her, his brows drawn together, and two, she'd worn a hole in the bread from being too aggressive applying the butter.

Laughing, Cassie tossed the torn bread onto the counter and grabbed another piece from the bag. "Yeah. My mind was elsewhere for a minute."

"Were you angry with that slice of bread?" he asked with a teasing grin.

"I may have had a little aggression I needed to take out." Cassie couldn't help but laugh again. "You're pretty good with her. Do you have nieces or nephews?"

Ian shook his head. "I'm an only child. But there was a set I visited not too long ago that had a baby about Emily's age. He was the cutest little guy and instantly wanted me over anyone else. I guess kids just like me."

Great. Now he had a soft spot for kids. Wasn't that the exact opposite of the image he'd portrayed the other morning when seeing Emily for the first time?

Ian Shaffer had many facets and she hated that she wanted to figure out who the real Ian was deep down inside.

Dinner was ready in no time, and thankfully, the silence wasn't too awkward. Eating and caring for a baby helped fill the void of conversation. When they were done, Ian went to clear the table and Cassie stopped him.

"I'll get it," she told him, picking up her own plate. "It's not that much."

"You cooked. The least I could do is help clean." He picked up his plate and took it to the sink. "Besides, if you cook more often, I'll gladly clean up after."

Cassie froze in the midst of lifting Emily from her high chair. "You want to come back for dinner?" she asked.

"I wouldn't say no if you asked."

Cassie settled Emily on her hip and turned to Ian, who was putting the pitcher of tea into the refrigerator. Okay, now she knew this wasn't pity. He obviously wanted to spend time with her. But why? Did he think she'd be that easy to get into bed again? Of course he did. She'd barely known his name when she'd shed her clothes for him. What man wouldn't get the impression she was easy?

Cassie turned and went into the living room, placed Emily in her Pack 'n Play and handed her her favorite stuffed horse. Footsteps shuffled over the carpet behind her and Cassie swallowed, knowing she'd have to be up front with Ian.

"Listen," she said as she straightened and faced the man who stood only a few feet away. "I have a feeling you think I'm somebody that I'm not."

Crossing his arms over his wide chest, Ian tilted his head and leveled those dark eyes right on her. "And what do you believe I think of you?"

Well, now she felt stupid. Why did he make this sound like a challenge? And why was she getting all heated over the fact he was standing in her living room? No man had been there other than her father and her soon-to-be brother-in-law. She'd moved into the guest cottage on the estate after Derek had left her so she could be closer to the family for support with Emily.

So seeing such a big, powerful man in her house was a little...arousing. Which just negated the whole point she was trying to make. Yeah, she was a juxtaposition of nerves and emotions.

"I think because we slept together you think I'm eager to do it again." She rested her hands on her hips, willing them to stop shaking. She had to be strong, no matter her physical attraction to Ian. "I'm really not the aggressive, confident woman who was locked in that attic."

Ian's gaze roamed down her body, traveled back up and landed on her mouth as he stepped forward. "You look like the same woman to me," he said, closing the gap between them. "What makes you think you're so different from the woman I spent the night with?"

She couldn't think with him this close, the way his eyes studied her, the woodsy scent of his cologne, the way she felt his body when he wasn't even touching her.

"Well, I..." She smoothed her hair back behind her ears and tipped her head to look him in the eye. "I'm afraid you think that I look for a good time and that I'm easy."

A ghost of a smile flirted around those full lips of his. "I rushed to judgment. I don't think you're easy, Cassie. Sexy, intriguing and confident, but not easy."

Sighing, she shook her head. "I'm anything but confident."

Now his hands came up, framed her face and sent an insane amount of electrical charges coursing through her. As much as she wanted his touch, she couldn't allow herself to crave such things. Hadn't she learned her lesson? Physical attraction and sexual chemistry did not make for a solid base for family, and, right now, all she could focus on was her family. Between Emily and the race with her sister, Cassie had no time for anything else.

But, oh, how she loved the feel of those strong, warm palms covering her face, fingertips slipping into her hair.

"You were amazing and strong in the attic," he told her.

He placed a finger over her lips when she tried to speak. "You may not be like that all the time, but you were then. And that tells me that the real you came out that night. You had no reason to put on a front with me and you were comfortable being yourself. Your passion and ability to control the situation was the biggest turn-on I've ever experienced."

Cassie wanted to tell him he was wrong, that she wasn't the powerful, confident woman he thought she was.

But she couldn't say a word when he leaned in just a bit more, tickling his lips across hers so slowly that Cassie feared she'd have to clutch on to his thick biceps to stay upright.

She didn't reach up, though. Didn't encourage Ian in tormenting her any further.

But when his mouth opened over hers so gently, coaxing hers open, as well, Cassie didn't stop him. Still not reaching for him, she allowed him to claim her. His hands still gripped her face, his body pressed perfectly against hers and she flashed back instantly to when they'd had nothing between them. He'd felt so strong, so powerful.

More than anything to do with his looks or his charming words, he made her feel more alive than she'd ever felt.

Ian's lips nipped at hers once, twice, before he lifted his head and looked her straight in the eyes.

The muscle ticked in his jaw as he slowly lowered his hands from her face and stepped back. "No, Cassie. Nothing about you or this situation is easy."

Without another word, he turned and walked through her house and out the back door. Cassie gripped the edge of the sofa and let out a sigh. She had no clue what had just happened, but something beyond desire lurked in Ian's dark eyes. The way he'd looked at her, as if he was wrestling his own personal demon...

Cassie shook her head. This was not her problem. Sleeping with the man had brought up so many complications—the main reason she never did flings.

Was that why she kept feeling this pull? Because sex just wasn't sex to her? For her to sleep with someone meant she had some sort of deeper bond than just lust. How could she not feel attached to the man who made her feel this alive?

Glancing down to sweet Emily, who was chewing on her stuffed horse, Cassie rested her hip against the couch. This baby was her world and no way would she be that mother who needed to cling to men or have a revolving door of them.

Better to get her head on straight and forget just how much Mr. Hollywood Agent affected her mind.

Trouble was, she was seriously afraid he'd already affected her heart.

Ten

"My girls ready for next week?"

Cassie slid the saddle off Don Pedro and threw a glance over her shoulder to her father. Damon Barrington stalked through the stables that he not only owned, but at one time had spent nearly every waking hour in.

Even though the Barringtons' planned to retire from the scene after this racing season, Damon still wasn't ready to sell the prizewinning horses. He'd had generous offers, including one from his biggest rival in the industry, Jake Mason, but so far no deal had been made. Cassie highly doubted her father would ever sell to Jake. The two had been competitors for years and had never gotten along on the track…or off it.

"We're as ready as we'll ever be," Tessa said as she started brushing down the Thoroughbred. "My time is even better than before. I'm pretty confident about the Preakness."

Damon smiled, slipping his hands into the pockets of his worn jeans. The man may be a millionaire and near royalty in the horse industry because of his Triple Crown win nearly two decades ago, but he still was down-to-earth and very much involved in his daughters' careers.

"I know you'll do the Barrington name proud, Tess." He reached up and stroked the horse's mane as Cassie slid in beside her father.

"What are you doing down here?" Cassie asked. "Thought you'd be keeping your eye on the film crew."

Damon patted the horse and reached over to wrap an arm around Cassie's shoulders. A wide grin spread across his tanned, aged face. His bright blue eyes landed on hers.

"The lighting guys are reworking the living room right now," he explained. "The scene they shot the other day wasn't quite what they wanted. They're shooting a small portion again this afternoon."

This whole new world of filming was so foreign to her, but the process was rather fascinating. "I plan on heading into town and picking up some feed later," she told him. "I guess I'll miss watching that."

And more than likely miss seeing Ian again—which was probably for the best. She needed space after that simple dinner and arousing kiss last night. He hadn't been by the stables and she hadn't seen him around the grounds, so he was probably working…which was what she needed to concentrate on.

"I thought I'd take Emily with me and maybe run her by that new toy store in town," Cassie went on. "She's learning to walk now and maybe I can find her something she can hold on to and push around to strengthen her little legs."

Damon laughed. "Once she starts walking, she'll be all over this place."

Cassie smiled. "I can't wait to see how she looks in a saddle."

Tessa came around Don Pedro and started brushing his other side. "Why don't you take her for a ride now? I'm sure she'd love it and it's such a nice day out. We're done for a while anyway."

The idea was tempting. "I still need to get feed, though."

"I'll send Nash to get it," Damon spoke up. "He won't mind."

Cassie leaned her head against her father's strong shoulder. "Thanks, Dad."

Patting her arm, Damon placed a kiss on top of her head. "Anytime. Now go get my granddaughter and start training her right."

Excited for Emily's first ride, Cassie nearly sprinted to the main house and through the back door to the kitchen, where Linda was washing dishes.

"Hey, Linda." Cassie glanced over the island to see Emily in her Pack 'n Play clapping her hands and gibbering to her animals. "I'm going to take Emily off your hands for a bit."

"Oh, she's no trouble at all." Linda rinsed a pan and set it in the drainer before drying her hands and turning. "I actually just sat her in there. We've been watching the action in the living room. She likes all the lights."

Cassie scooped up her girl and kissed her cheek. "I'm sure she does. She'd probably like to crawl all over and knock them down."

Laughing, Linda crossed to the double ovens in the wall and peeked inside the top one. "I'm sure she would, but I held on tight. The cranberry muffins are almost done if you'd like one."

Yeah, she'd love about six warm, gooey muffins dripping with butter, but she'd resist for the sake of her backside.

"Maybe later. I'm taking Emily for her first ride."

A wide smile blossomed across Linda's face. "Oh, how fun. She's going to love it."

"I hope so," Cassie said. "I'll be back in a bit."

When Cassie stepped back into the barn, Tessa had already saddled up Oliver, the oldest, most gentle horse in the stables. Cassie absolutely couldn't wait to see Emily's excitement as she took her first horseback ride.

"He's all ready for you," Tessa exclaimed, reaching for Emily.

Cassie mounted the horse and lifted Emily from Tessa's arms. Settling her daughter in front of her and wrapping an arm around her waist, Cassie reached for the rein and smiled down to Tessa.

"Get a few pics of us when we're in the field, would you?"

Tessa slid her hand into her pocket and held up her phone. "I'm set. You guys look so cute up there," she said, still grinning. "My niece already looks like a pro."

Cassie tugged on the line and steered Oliver out of the barn and into the field. The warm late-spring sunshine beat down on them and Cassie couldn't help but smile when Emily clapped her hands and squealed as the horse started a light trot.

"This is fun, isn't it, sweetie?" Cassie asked. "When you get big, Mommy will buy you your own horse and he will be your best friend."

Cassie didn't know how long they were riding, and she didn't really care. Memories were being made, and even though Emily wouldn't recall this day at all, Cassie would cherish it forever. She thought of her own mother and held Emily a little tighter. Her mom lived in her heart and there was an attic full of pictures and mementos to remember her by.

Turning Oliver to head back toward the front fields, Cassie swallowed as new memories overtook her. That attic wasn't just a room to store boxes and old furniture. Now the attic was a place where she'd given herself to a man…a dangerous man. He made her feel too much, want too much.

And what was with him wanting to eat dinner with her and Emily? Not that she minded, but having him in her house just once was enough to have her envisioning so much more than just a friendly encounter.

She had to admit, at least to herself, that Ian intrigued her. And if she was going that far, she also had to admit that every part of her wished he weren't just passing through. She missed the company of a man…and not just sex. She missed the conversation, the spark of excitement in harmless flirting… Okay, fine, she missed the sex, too.

But it really was so much more than that. There was a special connection, a certain bond that strengthened after being intimate. At least there was for her. Perhaps that was why she couldn't dismiss what had happened between her and Ian so easily.

As she neared the stables, she caught sight of Ian walking toward the main house with the beautiful Lily Beaumont at his side. The gorgeous actress was laughing and Cassie had to ignore the sliver of jealousy that shot through her. Ian wasn't hers by any means, no matter what she may wish for.

And Lily was a very sweet woman, from what Cassie had experienced on the set. As Cassie watched the two head toward the front door, she couldn't help but get a swift kick back into reality. Ian and Lily were from the same world. They were near the same age, for crying out loud.

In comparison, Cassie was just a worn-out single mom. Squeezing Emily tight and placing a kiss on her little mop of curls, Cassie knew she wouldn't wish to be anything else. Being the solid foundation for Emily was the most important job of her life, and for now, all her daughter's needs had to come first. One day, Cassie vowed, she'd take time for herself and perhaps find love.

"I'm actually considering your offer and one other," Lily stated.

Ian rested his hand on the knob of the front door. "You don't have to tell me the other agency. I already know."

And damn if he'd lose this starlet to his rival. They'd ruin her and not give a damn about reputation, only the bottom line, which was money to them.

"It's not a decision I'm going to make overnight." Lily lifted her hand to shield her eyes from the afternoon sun. "I am glad you're on set, though, because that will give us more of a chance to discuss terms and what I'm looking for in an agency."

Good. That sounded as though she was interested in him. "I'm ready to talk anytime you are."

A bright smile spread across her face. "Well, right now I'm needed for a scene, but perhaps we could have lunch or dinner one day while we're both here?"

Returning her smile, Ian nodded and opened the door for her, gesturing her in. "Let me know when you're not filming and we'll make that happen."

Nodding her thanks, Lily headed into the house. Ian wasn't sticking around for the short scene retake. He had other pressing matters to attend to. Like the beauty he'd seen out in the field moments ago. With red hair blazing past her shoulders and a heart-clenching smile on her face, Cassie had captured his attention instantly. So what else was new? The woman managed to turn him inside out without even being near. More times than not she consumed his thoughts, but when he'd seen her taking her daughter on a horseback ride, Ian had to admit that the sight had damn near stopped him in his tracks.

Emily's sweet squeals of delight, the loving expression on Cassie's face... The combination had shifted something in Ian's heart, something he wasn't quite ready to identify.

But he did know one thing. He'd been wrong. He was wrong about Cassie in thinking she was just like his mother. His mother never would've taken the time to have precious moments with him like the ones he'd seen with Cassie and Emily. His mother had been too busy on her quest for love and Mr. Right.

Ian ran a hand over his hair and sighed. He'd turned out just fine, no thanks to Mom and Dad, but getting involved with a woman and an innocent child was a hazardous mistake that would leave all parties vulnerable and in a risky position. What did he know about children or how to care for them?

And why was he even thinking this way? He was leaving in a few weeks. No matter his attraction and growing interest in Cassie Barrington, he couldn't afford to get personally involved.

Hours later, after he'd drafted a contract he hoped would entice Lily Beaumont into signing with his agency, Ian found himself leaving his trailer and heading toward Cassie's cottage.

Night had settled over the grounds and all was quiet. No bustling crew or noisy conversation. Max's wife and baby had shown up earlier in the evening, so they were probably holed up in his trailer for family time. And the producer's and director's families had arrived the day before. Bronson Dane and Anthony Price were at the top 1 percent of the film industry and still made time for their growing families.

Everyone had a family, a connection and the promise of love.

Ignoring the pang of envy he didn't want to feel, Ian stepped up onto Cassie's porch, which was illuminated with a lantern-style light on either side of the door. As soon as he knocked, he glanced down to his watch. Damn, maybe it was too late to be making a social call.

The door swung open and Ian took in the sight of Cassie wearing a long T-shirt and her hair down, curling around her shoulders. Long legs left uncovered tempted him to linger, but he brought his eyes back up to her surprised face.

"I'm sorry," he said, shoving his hands into his pockets. "I just realized how late it was."

"Oh, um…it's fine." She rested her hand on the edge of the oak door and tilted her head. "Is everything okay?"

Nodding, Ian suddenly felt like an idiot. "Yeah, I was working and lost track of time. Then I started walking and ended up here."

A sweet smile lit up her features. "Come on in," she told him, opening the door and stepping aside. "I just put Emily to bed, so this is fine."

He stepped inside and inhaled a scent of something sweet. "Is that cookies I smell?"

Cassie shut the door and turned to face him. "I thought I'd make some goodies for the wives who arrived. This way they can stock their trailers with snacks. I already made a batch of caramel corn."

His heart flipped in his chest. He hated the fact he kept going back to his mother, but he honestly couldn't recall a time when his mother had baked anything or even reached out to others by doing a kind act.

A shrink would have a field day in his head with all his Mommy and Daddy issues. *Jeez*. And here he'd thought once he'd left for L.A. he'd left all of those years behind.

"They will really appreciate that," he told her.

Shrugging, Cassie maneuvered around him and grabbed a small blanket from the couch and started folding it. "I'm no Linda, but I do enjoy baking when I have the time."

She laid the folded blanket across the back of the couch and looked back at him. He couldn't stop his eyes from traveling over her again. How could he help the fact he found her sexier than any woman he'd ever met? She probably wouldn't believe him if he told her that her curves were enticing, her low maintenance a refreshing change.

Cassie tugged on the hem of her shirt. "I should probably go change."

"No." He held up his hand to stop her. "This is your house—you should be comfortable. Besides, I've seen it all."

Her eyes flared with remembrance and passion as Ian closed the space between them and looked down at her mouth. "I've tasted it all, too, if you recall."

With a shaky nod, she said, "I remember."

The pulse at the base of her throat increased and Ian ran a hand over his face as he took a step back. "I swear, I didn't come here for this."

Cassie's bright blue eyes darted away. "I understand."

"No, you don't." Great, now she thought he was rejecting her. "It's not that I don't want you, Cassie. That's the furthest from the truth."

Shoving her hair back from her shoulders, Cassie shook her head. "Ian, it's okay. You don't have to make excuses. I'm a big girl. I can handle the truth. Besides, we're past this awkward stage, right?"

"Yeah," he agreed because right now he was feeling anything but awkward. Excited and aroused, but not awkward. "I don't know what possessed me to show up at your door this late, but…"

Cassie produced that punch-to-the-gut smile. "You can stop by anytime."

How did she do that? Instantly make him feel welcome, wanted…needed. There was so much more to Cassie Barrington than he'd first perceived. There were sides to the confident vixen, the single mother and the overworked trainer he had yet to discover.

Cassie was giving, loving and patient. He'd known instantly that she was special, but maybe he just hadn't realized how special. This woman embodied everything he hadn't known he'd been looking for.

"Why are you looking at me like that?" she asked, brows drawn together, smile all but gone.

Ian took a step toward her. He'd been mentally dancing around her for days and now he was physically doing it as he made up his mind on how to approach her.

"Because I just realized that all of your layers are starting to reveal themselves, one at a time." He slid his fingertips up her arms and back down, relishing the goose bumps he produced with such a simple touch. "I didn't want to see all of that before. I wanted you to be unattainable. I wanted you to be all wrong and someone I could easily forget."

Those vibrant eyes remained locked on his as her breath caught.

"But there's no way I could ever forget you, Cassie. Or us."

He didn't give her time to object. He claimed her lips and instantly she responded—opening her mouth to him, wrapping her arms around his neck and plunging her fingers into his hair.

Ian knew he wasn't leaving anytime soon. He also knew her T-shirt had to go.

Eleven

Cassie had no idea what she was doing. Okay, she knew what she was doing and who she was doing it with, but hadn't she just had a mental talk with herself about the hazards of getting wrapped up in Ian's seductive ways? Hadn't she told herself she'd already been burned once and was still recovering?

But the way his mouth captured hers, the way he held her as if she were the rarest of gems, Cassie couldn't help but take pleasure in the fact that Ian pulled out a passion in her that she'd never known existed.

When Ian's hands gripped the hem of her T-shirt and tugged up, she eased back and in an instant the unwanted garment was up and over her head, flung to the side without a care.

Dark-as-sin eyes raked over her body, which was now bare of everything except a pair of red lacy panties. The old Cassie wanted to shield herself with her hands, but the way Ian visually sampled her gave her the confidence of a goddess.

"I could look at you forever," he said, his voice husky.

Forever. The word hovered in the air, but Cassie knew he was speaking only from lust, not in the happily-ever-after term.

Ian pulled his own shirt off and Cassie reached out, quickly unfastening his pants. In no time he was reaching for her, wearing only a smile.

"Tell me you know this is more than sex," he muttered against her lips. "I want you to know that to me, this is so much more."

Tears pricked the backs of her eyes as she nodded. The lump in her throat left her speechless. She really didn't know what label he wanted to put on this relationship, but right now, she couldn't think beyond the fact that Ian's hands were sliding into her panties and gliding them down her shaky legs.

Cassie wrapped her arms around his broad shoulders and kicked aside the flimsy material. Ian's hands cupped her bottom as he guided her backward.

"Tell me where your room is," he muttered against her lips.

"Last door on the right."

He kissed her on the throat, across the swells of her breasts, all the while keeping his hands firmly gripped on her backside as he maneuvered her down the hallway and into her room.

A small bedside lamp gave the room a soft glow. Ian gently shut the door behind him and looked her right in the eyes. There was an underlying vulnerability looking back at her, and Cassie knew what he was thinking.

"I've never had a man in this room," she told him. "And there's no other man I want here."

As if the dam had broken, Ian reached for her, capturing her lips once again and lifting her by the waist.

When she locked her legs around his hips and they tumbled onto the bed, Ian broke free of her lips and kissed a path down to her breasts. Leaning back, Cassie gripped his hair as he tasted her.

"Ian," she panted. "I don't have any protection."

His dark gaze lifted to hers. "I didn't bring any. I hadn't planned on ending up here."

Biting her lip, Cassie said, "I'm on birth control and I'm clean. I've only been with my ex-husband and you."

Ian's hands slid up to cup her face as he kissed her lips. "I've never been without protection and I know I'm clean, too."

She smiled. "Then why are we still talking?"

Cassie moved her hands to his waist. Before she could say another word, Ian slid into her. Closing her eyes, Cassie let out a soft groan as he began to move above her.

"Look at me," he demanded in that low tone. "I want you to see me and only me."

As if any other man could take his place? But as she stared into his eyes, she saw so much more than lust, than sex and passion. This man was falling for her. He may not even recognize the emotion himself, but it was there, plain as day, looking back at her.

When his pace increased, Cassie gripped his shoulders and arched her back. "Ian…I…"

Eyes still locked on to her, he clenched the muscle in his jaw. "Go ahead, baby."

Her body trembled with her release, but she refused to close her eyes. She wanted him to see just how affected she was by his touch…his love.

When his arms stiffened and his body quivered against

hers, Cassie held on, swallowing back the tears that clogged her throat.

One thing was very certain. The night in the attic may have been all about lust, but this moment right here in her bed, Cassie had gone and fallen in love with Ian Shaffer.

"I have to be on set early," Ian whispered into her ear.

Pulling himself away from the warm bed they'd spent the night in, Ian quickly gathered his clothes and dressed. Cassie eased up onto one elbow, and the sheet slipped down to stop just at the slope of her breasts. All that creamy exposed skin had him clenching his jaw and reliving what had just transpired hours before between those sheets.

"How early?" she asked, her voice thick with sleep.

"I'd like to see Max before he starts."

Okay, so the lie rolled easily off his tongue, but he couldn't stay. He couldn't remain in her bed, smelling her sweet scent, playing house in her little cottage, with her innocent baby sleeping in the next room.

What did he know about family or children…or whatever emotion was stirring within him? His career had always taken precedence over any social life or any feelings. With his parents' example of the epitome of failed marriages and love, he knew he wanted something completely different for his own life, so perfecting his career was the path he'd chosen.

How could he put his career, his agency and the impending addition of Lily to his client roster in jeopardy simply because he'd become entangled with Cassie Barrington? She was the poster child for commitment, and an instant family was something he couldn't get wrapped up in.

Cassie was a beautiful, intriguing complication. His eyes darted to the bed, where she studied him with a hint of desire layered with curiosity.

"Everything okay?" she asked.

Nodding, he shoved his feet into his shoes. "Of course. I'll lock the door behind me."

Unable to avoid temptation completely, Ian crossed the room, leaned down and kissed her lips. Just as her hand came up to his stubbled jaw, he pulled away and left her alone.

He stepped onto the front porch, closed the door behind him and leaned against it to catch his breath. The easy way Cassie welcomed him into her bed—and into her life with Emily—terrified him. Last night she'd accepted him without question and she'd given him everything she had... including love. He'd seen it in her eyes, but even more worrisome was what she may have seen reflected in his.

Because in those moments, when they were one and her bright blue eyes sought his, Ian had found himself completely and utterly lost. He wanted so much, but fear of everything he'd ever known regarding love and family made him question his emotions and his intentions.

Damn it. His intentions? What the hell was this? He wasn't the kind of man who had dreams of driving a minivan or heading up a household. He was a top Hollywood agent and if he didn't get his head on straight, he could lose one of the most important clients he'd ever had the chance of snagging.

Shaking his head, Ian pushed off the door and forced himself to walk toward his trailer. Twenty-nine years old and doing the walk of shame? *Classy, Shaffer. Real classy.*

Darkness and early-morning fog settled low over the estate. He shoved his hands into his pockets and decided he needed to shower and change before seeing Max...especially considering he was wearing the same clothes as yesterday.

He hadn't totally lied when he'd left Cassie's bed. He would talk to Max, but it wasn't dire and they could always talk later. Yet he worried if he stayed, he'd give Cassie false hope.

Okay, he worried he'd give himself false hope, too, because being with her was like nothing he'd ever experienced before and he wanted to hold on to those moments.

But the reality was, he was passing through.

Ian took his time getting ready for the day, answered a few emails and jotted down notes for calls he needed to make later in the week. He hated to admit he was shaken up by this newfound flood of emotions, but he had to come to grips with the fact that whatever he was feeling for Cassie Barrington was most definitely not going away.... It was only getting stronger.

By the time he exited his trailer, he had a plan of action, and today would be all about work and focusing on the big picture and his agency.

Crew members were gathered around the entrance of the stables, and off to the side were Max and Lily, holding their scripts and chatting. Ian headed in their direction, eager to get the day started.

"Morning," he greeted them as he approached.

Max nodded. "Came by your trailer last night to discuss something. Have a late night?"

The smile on Max's face was devilish—and all-knowing.

"What did you need?" Ian asked, dodging the question.

With a shrug, Max shook his head. "It can wait. I'm going to talk to Bronson before we start filming. Excuse me."

Ian figured Max left so Ian could chat with Lily. *Good boy*.

"I glanced over today's filming schedule." Ian stepped in front of Lily to shade her face from the sun. "Looks like after three today you guys are free."

Lily smiled. "We are indeed. Are you available to talk then?"

He'd be available anytime she wanted if it meant persuading her to sign with him. "I am. Would you like to stay here or go out to grab something for dinner?"

"I say go out," she replied. "Hopefully we can talk privately without everyone around."

Before he could respond, Lily's gaze darted from his to a spot over his left shoulder. A smile like he'd never seen before lit up her face and Ian couldn't help but glance around to see who she was connecting with.

Nash.

More confirmation that this Hollywood starlet and the groom on the Barrington estate had something going on.

Ian only hoped whatever was happening with the two of them was kept quiet and didn't interfere with filming or hinder her judgment in signing with him.

"Going out is fine," he told her.

Blinking, she focused back on him. "I'm sorry. What?"

Yeah, definitely something going on there.

"I said we could go out for a bite to eat. I can come by your trailer about five. Does that work?"

"Of course," she replied with a nod. "I'll see you then."

As she walked away, Ian turned and caught Nash still staring as Lily entered the stable. Nash had the look of a man totally and utterly smitten and Ian couldn't help but feel a twinge of remorse for the guy. Nash and Lily were worlds apart.

Exactly like Ian and Cassie.

What a mess. A complicated, passion-induced mess.

Ian stood to the side as lighting and people were set in place to prepare for filming. Bronson was talking with Max, and Lily's hair was being smoothed one last time.

Grant and Anthony were adjusting the bales of hay at the end of the aisle.

Ian wasn't sure what Cassie's plans were for the day, but he intended to keep his distance for now. He needed to figure out exactly how to handle this situation because the last thing she needed was more heartache. And he, who knew nothing about real intimacy, would most certainly break her heart if he wasn't careful.

Damon Barrington settled in beside him and whispered, "Their chemistry on set is amazing."

Ian watched Max and Lily embrace in the middle of the aisle, horses' heads popping out over their stalls. The set was utterly quiet except for Lily's staged tears as she clung to Max. The couple was the perfect image of a younger Damon and Rose Barrington, according to the pictures Ian had seen.

As soon as Anthony yelled, "Cut!" the couple broke apart and Lily dabbed at her damp cheeks.

Damon glanced around. "I can't believe my girls aren't down here. You haven't seen Cassie or Tessa, have you?"

Ian shook his head. "I haven't."

No need to tell Cassie's father that just a few hours ago Ian had slipped from her bed. Best not bring that up.

"I'm sure they'll be along shortly." Damon looked over at Ian and grinned. "My girls haven't let too many scenes slip by. They've enjoyed this process."

"And you?" Ian asked. "Have you enjoyed the Hollywood invasion?"

Nodding, Damon crossed his arms over his chest. "It's not what I thought it would be. The scenes vary in length and everything is shot out of order. But I'm very interested in seeing how they piece this all together."

Ian liked Damon, appreciated the way the man had taken charge of his life, made something of it and encouraged his children to do the same. And when his wife had passed, the man had taken over the roles of both parents and loved his children to the point where both women were now two of the most amazing people he'd met.

Ian had never received encouragement from his father and couldn't help but wonder what his life would've been like had his father been more hands-on.

Shrugging off years that couldn't be changed, Ian excused himself from Damon. If Cassie was going to come watch the filming, he needed to be elsewhere.

Because he had no doubt that if he hung around and had to look Cassie in the eye in front of all these people, there would be no hiding the fact that he'd developed some serious feelings for her.

Twelve

Who was he kidding? There was no way he could stay away from Cassie. All during the business dinner with Lily, his mind had been on Cassie and what she was doing.

By the end of the night he'd nearly driven himself crazy with curiosity about what Cassie and Emily had done all day. Added to that, Lily hadn't signed with him. Not yet. She'd looked over his proposed contract and agreed with most of it, but she'd also said she needed to look over one other contract before deciding.

He was still in the running, but he'd rather have this deal signed and completed so he could move on to other deals waiting in the wings…not so he could focus on the woman who had his head spinning and his gut tied in knots.

After walking Lily to her trailer, Ian crossed the estate toward the two cottages. Only one of Cassie's outdoor lights was on and she was on her porch switching out the bulb in the other.

"Hey," he greeted her as he stepped onto the top step. "Need help?"

"I can manage just fine."

As she stood on her tiptoes and reached, her red tank top slid up over her torso, exposing a tantalizing band of flesh.

"I can get that so you don't have to stretch so far," he told her.

She quickly changed out the bulb and turned to face him, tapping the dead bulb against her palm. "I've been doing things on my own for a while now. Besides, I won't be anybody's second choice. I figured you were smart enough to know that."

"I'm sorry?"

Somehow he was not on the same page as her and she was mad at someone. From the daggers she was throwing him, he'd done something to upset her. Considering he hadn't sneaked out of her bed that morning without saying goodbye, he really had no clue what was going on.

"Forget it." She shook her head and opened her front door, then turned before he could enter. "I'm pretty tired, but thanks for stopping by."

Oh, hell no. He wasn't going to just let her be mad and not tell him what was going on. More than that, did she really believe he'd just leave her when she was this upset?

His hand smacked against the door as she tried to close it. "I'm coming in."

Cassie stepped back and let him pass. Emily sat in her Pack 'n Play and chattered with a stuffed horse, oblivious to the world around her.

"I need to get Emily ready for bed." Cassie maneuvered around him and picked up Emily. "I may be a while."

Code for "I'm going to take my time and let you worry." That was fine; he had no intention of going anywhere.

If Cassie was gearing up for a fight, he was ready. Seeing her pain, masked by anger, had a vise gripping his heart, and he cared too much about her to just brush her feelings aside.

Ian glanced around the somewhat tidy living area and started picking up toys before he thought better of it. He tossed them into the Pack 'n Play; then he folded the throw and laid it on the back of the sofa, neatened the pillows and took a plate and cup into the kitchen and placed them in the dishwasher.

By the time he'd taken a seat on the couch, he found himself smiling. Where had this little domestic streak come from? He hadn't even thought twice about helping Cassie, and not just because she was angry. He found himself wanting to do things to make her life easier.

Ian had no clue what had happened with her life before he'd come along, but he knew she was divorced and assumed the ex had done a number on her.

Well, Ian intended to stick this out, at least for as long as he was here. He would make her smile again, because she deserved nothing less.

Cassie wasn't jealous. Just because she'd heard Ian and Lily had had dinner didn't mean a thing. Really.

But that green-eyed monster reared its ugly head and reminded Cassie that she'd fallen for a cheating man once before.

On the other hand, what hold did she have over Ian? He wasn't staying and he'd never confessed his undying love to her. But she'd seen his eyes last night, she'd seen how he looked at her, and she'd experienced lovemaking like she never had before. How could he deny that they'd formed an unspoken bond?

Cassie quickly dried off Emily and got her dressed in

her footed bunny pajamas. After giving her a bottle and rocking her gently, Cassie began to sing.

This was the time of night she enjoyed most. Just her and her precious baby girl. Cassie might sing off-key, she might even get an occasional word wrong, but Emily didn't care. She just reached her little hands up and patted Cassie's hand or touched her lips.

They had a nightly ritual and just because Ian was out in her living room didn't mean she would change her routine. Before Emily fell asleep in her arms, Cassie laid her in her crib, giving her a soft kiss on her forehead, then left the room.

Cassie took a moment to straighten her tank and smooth her hair over her shoulders before she started down the hallway. As she entered the living room, she noticed that Ian was reclined on her sofa, head tilted back, eyes closed, with his hands laced across his abdomen. He'd picked up the toys and neatly piled them in the Pack 'n Play in the corner.

No. She didn't want that unwelcome tumble of her heart where this man was concerned. She couldn't risk everything again on the chance that he could love her the way she loved him.

Tears pricked her eyes as she fully confessed just how much she did love this man. But he could never know.

Her feet shuffled over the hardwood floors, and Ian lifted his lids, his gaze seeking hers.

"Thank you for picking up," she told him, still standing because she intended to show him out the door.

Shifting to fully sit up, Ian patted the cushion beside him. "Come here, Cassie."

She didn't like being told what to do, but she wasn't going to act like a teenager who pouted over a boy, either.

She was a big girl, but that didn't exempt her from a broken heart.

Taking a seat on the opposite end of the couch, she gripped her hands in her lap. "What do you want, Ian? I don't have time for games."

His eyes locked on to hers. "I don't play games, Cassie, and I have no idea what you're so upset about."

Of course he didn't. Neither had her ex when he'd cheated.

She eased back against the arm of the sofa and returned his stare. "Do you know why I'm divorced?"

Ian shook his head and slid his arm along the back of the couch as if to reach for her.

"My husband got tired of me," she told him, tamping down the sliver of hurt and betrayal that threatened to make her vulnerable. Never again. "The whole marriage-baby thing was cramping his style. Apparently he'd been cheating on me for most of our marriage and I was too naive and dumb to realize it. You see, I assumed that when we took our vows they meant something to him."

"Cassie—"

"No," she said, holding up her hand. "I'm not finished. After Emily was born, Derek left. She was barely two months old. He left me a note and was just…gone. It seems the sexy wife he once knew was no longer there for him, so, in turn, his cheating and the divorce were my fault. I know now that he was a coward and I'm glad he's gone because I never want Emily to see me settle for someone who treats me like I'm not worth everything.

"I want my daughter to see a worthy example of how love should be," she went on, cursing her eyes for misting up. "I want her to see that love does exist. My parents had it, and I will find it. But I won't be played for a fool while I wait for love to come into my life."

Ian swallowed, his eyes never leaving hers as he scooted

closer. He wasn't stupid; he could put the pieces together and know she'd assumed the worst about his dinner meeting with Lily.

"I didn't play you for a fool, Cassie." His tone was light as he settled his hand over both of hers, which were still clasped together in her lap. "I have never lied to a woman and I've never pretended to be something I wasn't."

With a deep sigh, Cassie shook her head. "Forget I said anything. I mean, it's not like we're committed to each other," she said as she got to her feet.

But Ian jumped right up with her and gripped her shoulders before she could turn from him.

"Do you seriously think for one second that I believe you're so laid-back about the idea of me seeing you and another woman?" he demanded. "I had a business meeting with Lily. I told you I've wanted to sign her to my agency for months. She's the main reason I came to the set and why I'm staying so long."

Cassie's eyes widened, but he didn't give her a chance to speak. He needed her to know she didn't come in second… and she should never have to.

"I spent the entire evening trying to win her over, outlining every detail of the contract and all the perks of having me as her agent." Ian loosened his grip as he stepped closer to Cassie and slid his hands up to frame her face. "But the entire evening, I was thinking of you. Wondering what you were doing, how long it would be until I could see you again."

Her shoulders relaxed and her face softened as she kept those stunning baby blues locked on his. The hope he saw in her eyes nearly melted him on the spot. He knew she wanted to trust. He knew she'd been burned once and he completely understood that need, the yearning for that solid foundation.

"I'm sorry," she whispered. Cassie's lids lowered as she shook her head before she raised her gaze to his once more. "I don't want to be that woman. I seriously have no hold on you, Ian. You've promised me nothing and I don't expect you to check in."

Ian kissed her gently, then rested his forehead against hers. A soft shudder rippled through her and Ian wanted nothing more than to reassure her everything would be all right.

But how could he, when he knew he wasn't staying? How could they move forward with emotions overtaking them both?

"I hate what he did to me," she whispered, reaching up to clasp his wrists as he continued to cup her face. "I hate that I've turned bitter. That's not who I want to be."

Ian eased back and tipped her face up to his. "That's not who you are. You're not bitter. You're cautious and nobody blames you. You not only have yourself to think of—you have Emily, too."

Cassie's sweet smile never failed to squeeze his heart, and Ian had no clue how a man could leave behind a wife and child. Ian wouldn't mind getting ahold of Cassie's ex. He obviously was no man, but a coward. Selfishly, Ian was glad Derek was out of the picture. If the man could throw away his family so easily, he wasn't worthy.

"What's that look for?" she asked. "You're very intense all of a sudden."

He had to be honest because she was worth everything he had inside him.

"Where is this going?" he asked. "I care about you, Cassie. More than I thought I would, and I think we need to discuss what's happening between us."

A soft laugh escaped her. "You sound like a woman."

Ian smiled with a shrug. "I assure you I've never said this to anyone else, but I don't want you getting hurt."

Cassie nodded and a shield came over her eyes as if she was already steeling herself. "Honestly, I don't know. I care for you, too. I question myself because I'm still so scarred from the divorce and I told myself I wouldn't get involved again. Yet, here we are and I can't stop myself."

Her inner battle shouldn't make him happy, but he couldn't help but admit he liked the fact she had no control over her feelings for him.... At least he wasn't in this boat of emotions alone.

"I don't want you to be the rebound guy," she murmured. "But I'm so afraid of how you make me feel."

Stroking her silky skin, wanting to kiss her trembling lips, Ian asked, "How do I make you feel?"

He shouldn't have asked. Cassie pursed her lips together as if contemplating her response, and Ian worried he'd put her on the spot. But he had to know. This mattered too much. *She* mattered too much.

"Like I'm special."

She couldn't have zeroed in on a better word that would hit him straight in the heart. *Special*. She was special to him on so many levels. She was special because he'd never felt more alive than he did with her. He'd never let his career come second to anything before her, and he sure as hell had never thought, with his family issues, that he'd be falling for a woman with a child.

Cassie inspired him to be a better person, to want to care for others and put his needs last.

But most of all he understood that need to feel special. He'd craved it his entire life, and until this very moment, he hadn't realized that was what he'd been missing.

"You make me feel special, too." Before now he never would've felt comfortable opening up, showing how vulnerable he was on the inside. "I don't want to be the rebound guy, either."

Her eyes widened as she tried to blink back the moisture. "So what does that mean?"

Hell if he knew. Suddenly he wanted it all—his career, the Hollywood lifestyle, Cassie and Emily. Cassie had him rethinking what family could be.

There was that other part of him that was absolutely terrified and wanted to hightail it back to Hollywood. But for now, he would relish their time together until he could come to grips with this mess of emotions.

"It means for now, you're mine." He kissed the corners of her mouth. "It means you are more to me than any other woman has ever been." He kissed her directly on the mouth, coaxing her lips apart before murmuring, "It means I'm taking you to bed to show you just how much you mean to me."

Only wanting to keep her smiling, keep her happy for as long as he was here, Ian slid his arms around her waist and pulled her body flush against his own.

When Cassie's fingers slid up around his neck and threaded into his hair, Ian claimed her mouth and lifted her off the ground. She wrapped her legs around his waist and he carried her toward the bedroom, where he fully intended to make good on his promise.

Thirteen

The day couldn't be more perfect. God had painted a beautiful setting with the sun high in the sky and the temperature an ideal sixty degrees. The stage was set for Tessa to win the Preakness and take the second step toward the Triple Crown.

But no matter the weather, the thrill that always slid through Cassie at each race had to do with the stomp of the hooves in the stalls as the horses eagerly awaited their shining moment, the thick aroma of straw, the colorful silks adorning each horse, the tangible excitement of the jockeys as they shared last-minute talks with their trainers.

Which was exactly what Cassie and Tessa had just finished doing. Cassie had the utmost confidence that this race would go in their favor, but strange things always happened and they both knew better than to get cocky—especially at this point.

The first third of the Triple Crown was theirs, but this

was a new day, a new race and a whole other level of adrenaline rushes.

Cassie followed behind as Tessa rode Don Pedro from the stables through the paddock and entered the track. No matter the outcome, Cassie was proud of her sister, of what they'd accomplished in their years together.

Soon their racing season would come to an end and Cassie would move on with her goal of opening a riding camp for handicapped children. Training a Triple Crown winner would put her in high demand in the horse-breeding world, but she hoped to use that reputation as a launching point for her school.

And beyond the school worries, her father was getting offers from his most heated rival, Jake Mason, to buy the prizewinning horses. Their season wasn't even over yet, for heaven's sake.

But those thoughts would have to wait until after the competition.

As would her thoughts of a certain Hollywood agent who had stayed behind on the estate to get some work done without distractions. The majority of the film crew had accompanied the Barringtons to Baltimore, Maryland, but today they were spectators, enjoying the race. They'd gotten many great shots from Louisville a couple of weeks ago, so now they were able to relax…somewhat. Cassie knew they were still taking still shots for the ad campaign, but not as many as at the derby.

As Tessa rode onto the track, Cassie couldn't help but smile. There was so much to be thankful for right now in her life. One chapter of her career was coming to an end. Another was going to begin in a few months. Her daughter was happy and healthy and nearing her first birthday.

And, delicious icing on the cake, Ian Shaffer had entered her life. For how long she didn't know. But she did know that, for now, they were together and he had admitted his feelings were strong. But did that mean he'd want to try something long distance? Or would he stay around a little longer after the film was finished?

So many questions and none of them would be answered today. She needed to concentrate and be there for Tessa. All else could wait until this race was over.

In no time the horses were in their places and Cassie felt her father's presence beside her. His arm snaked around her waist, the silent support a welcome comfort. Each race had nerves balling up in her stomach, but nothing could be done now. The training for the Preakness was complete and now they waited for the fastest, most exciting moment in sports.

Cassie glanced toward the grandstands, and the colorful array of hats and suits had her smile widening. Excitement settled heavily over the track as everyone's gaze was drawn to the starting gate.

"You're trembling," her father whispered into her ear.

Cassie let out a shaky laugh. "I think that's you."

His arm tightened around her waist as a robust chuckle escaped. "I believe you're right, my dear."

The gun sounded and Cassie had no time for nerves. She couldn't keep her eyes off the places switching, the colored numbers on the board swapping out as horses passed each other and inched toward the lead.

Don Pedro was in forth. Cassie fisted her hands so tight, her short nails bit into her palms.

"Come on. Come on," she muttered.

Tessa eased past third and into second on the last turn.

The announcer's tone raised in excitement as Tessa inched even farther toward the head of the race. Cassie wanted to close her eyes to pray, but she couldn't take her gaze off the board.

Just as the first two horses headed to the finish line, Cassie started jumping up and down. Excitement, fear, nerves... They all had her unable to stand still.

And when the announcer blared that the winner was Don Pedro by a nose, Cassie jumped even higher, wrapped her arms around her father's neck and squealed like a little girl.

"We did it," he yelled, embracing her. "My girls did it!"

Damon jerked back, gripped her hand and tugged her toward the winner's circle, where Tessa met them. Her radiant smile, the mass of people surrounding her and the flash of cameras all announced there was a new winner.

Grant was right there in the throng of people, his grin so wide there was no way to hide the pride beaming off him.

Cassie's heart lurched. She loved that Tessa had found the man of her dreams, couldn't be happier for the couple. But, for the first time, Cassie was not the first one Tessa turned to after a race.

And that was not jealousy talking.... Cassie loved seeing Tessa and Grant so happy, and sharing Tessa's affection was fine. It was the fact that Cassie still felt empty when monumental things happened. Whom did she turn to to celebrate or for a shoulder to cry on?

Tessa turned her head, caught Cassie's eye and winked down at her. Returning the wink, Cassie smiled to hide her sad thoughts.

Soon reporters were thrusting microphones in her face, as well. Very few ever won the Triple Crown, and a team of females was practically unheard of. History was definitely in the making.

The Barrington sisters had done it again, and with only one more race to go to round out the season and secure the coveted Triple Crown, Cassie knew she needed to focus now more than ever on training for the Belmont.

Which meant keeping her heart shielded from Ian, because if he penetrated too much more, she feared she'd
never be able to recover if it all fell apart.

They were gone for days, weeks.

Okay, maybe it wasn't weeks, but Ian felt as if he hadn't
seen Cassie forever. Which told him he was going to be
in trouble when it came time for him to head back to L.A.

She'd arrived home late last night and he'd known she'd
be tired, so he had stayed away to let her rest and spend
time with Emily. But knowing she was so close was hard.

As he headed toward the stables just as the sun peeked
overtop the hilltops, Ian wanted to spend some time with
her. He'd actually ached for her while she'd been away.
Like most of the nation, he'd watched with eyes glued to
the television during the Preakness and he'd jumped out
of his seat and cheered when Don Pedro crossed the finish line for the win.

The familiar smell of hay greeted him before he even
hit the entrance. As soon as he crossed the threshold, Ian
spotted Nash cleaning out a stall.

"Morning," Ian greeted him.

Nash nodded a good-morning and continued raking old
hay. "Cassie isn't here yet," he said without looking up.

Ian grinned. Apparently he and Cassie weren't very
discreet...not that they'd tried to be, but they also hadn't
been blatant about their relationship, either.

"Hey, Ian."

He turned to see Tessa striding into the stables, all
smiles with her hair pulled back.

"Congrats on the win." Ian couldn't help but offer a
quick hug with a pat on her back. "That was one intense
race."

Tessa laughed. "You should've seen it from my point of view."

Her eyes darted to Nash, then back to Ian. "What brings you out this early?"

Ian shrugged, sliding his hands into his pockets. "Just looking for Cassie."

Tessa's grin went into that all-knowing mode as she quirked a brow. "She actually was up most of the night with Emily. Poor baby is teething and nobody is getting any sleep."

"But Cassie has to be exhausted. You just got back late last night," he argued, realizing he was stating nothing new to Tessa.

Shrugging, Tessa sighed. "I know. I offered to take Emily for the night, but Cassie wouldn't hear of it."

Probably because the last time Cassie had been without her child, she had been locked in the attic with him.

"She's spreading herself too thin," Ian muttered.

Nash walked around them and pulled a bale of hay from the stack against the wall, then moved back into the stall. Ian shifted closer to the doorway to get out of the quiet groom's way.

"Follow me," Tessa said with a nod.

Intrigued, Ian fell into step behind the famous jockey. She stopped just outside the stables, but away from where Nash could overhear.

"This isn't where you tell me if I hurt your sister you'll kill me, is it?" he asked with a smile.

Tessa laughed and shook her head, eyes sparkling with amusement. "You're smart enough to know that goes without saying. I wanted to discuss something else, actually."

"And what's that?"

"Did Cassie ever tell you about the little getaway she and Grant came up with for me? Grant felt I was pushing myself too hard, never taking time for myself to regroup and recharge."

Ian grinned. "Must run in the family."

"Yeah, we Barringtons are all made of the same stubborn stuff."

Ian had no doubt the almighty Damon Barrington had instilled all his work ethic into his girls and that hard work and determination were paying off in spades.

"I'd like to return the favor," Tessa went on. "Are you up for taking a few days away from here?"

Was he? Did he want to leave Lily when they were still negotiating a contract? He didn't mind leaving Max. The actor could handle anything and Ian was very confident with their working relationship.

It was Lily that worried him. But he couldn't be in her face all the time. He'd spoken with her a few times since their dinner meeting. She'd promised a decision once she realized which agency would offer her the most and which one she'd feel most at home with.

He had to believe she'd see that his company was hands down the front-runner.

And a few days away with Cassie? He had deals and meetings to get back to, but after days without her, how could he not want to jump at that chance?

"Should I take that smile to mean you're going to take me up on this offer?"

Ian nodded. "I think I will. What did you have in mind?"

Fourteen

How long could a baby be angry and how many teeth would be popping through?

Cassie had just collapsed onto the couch for the first time all day when someone knocked on her door. She threw a glance to Emily, who was playing on the floor and crawling from toy to toy...content for now.

Stepping over plush toys and blankets, Cassie opened the door and froze. Ian stood on her porch looking as handsome as ever, sporting aviator sunglasses and a navy T-shirt pulled taut across his wide shoulders and tucked into dark jeans.

She didn't need to look down at her own outfit to know she was just a step above homeless chic with her mismatched lounge pants with margarita glasses on them and her oversize T-shirt with a giant smiley face in the middle.

And her hair? She'd pulled it up into a ponytail for bed and hadn't touched it since. Half was falling around her face; the other half was in a nest on the side of her head.

Yeah, she exuded sex appeal.

"Um…are you going to invite me in?"

Cassie shoved a clump of hair behind her ear. "Are you sure you want to come in? Emily is teething. She's cranky more often than not since last night, and I'm…well…"

Ian closed the gap between them, laying a gentle kiss on her lips. "Beautiful."

Okay, there was no way she couldn't melt at that sweet declaration even if he was just trying to score points. He'd succeeded.

When he stepped into the house, Cassie stepped back and closed the door behind him. Emily grabbed hold of the couch cushion and pulled herself to her feet, throwing an innocent smile over her shoulder to Ian.

Cassie laughed. "Seriously? She smiles for you and I've had screaming for over twelve hours?"

"What can I say? I'm irresistible."

No denying that. Cassie still wasn't used to his powerful presence in her home, but she was growing to love it more and more each time he came for a visit.

"Hey, sweetheart," he said, squatting down beside Emily. "Did you have your mommy up last night?"

Emily let go of the couch to clap her hands and immediately fell down onto her diaper-covered butt. She giggled and looked up at Ian to see his reaction.

Cassie waited, too. She couldn't help but want to know how Ian would be around Emily. He hadn't spent too much time with her, considering he stopped by at night and he'd gone straight to Cassie's bed.

Reaching forward, Ian slid his big hands beneath Emily's delicate arms and lifted her as he came to his full height.

Cassie couldn't deny the lurch of her heart at the sight of this powerful man holding her precious baby. Was there a sexier sight than this? Not in Cassie's opinion.

"I know we talked on the phone, but congratulations." A smile lit up his already handsome face. "I'm so happy for you and Tessa."

Cassie still couldn't believe it herself. Of course they'd trained to win, but what trainer and jockey didn't? The fact they were that much closer to winning that coveted Triple Crown still seemed surreal.

"I'm still recovering from all the celebrating we did in Baltimore," she told him. "I've never been so happy in all my life. Well, except for when Emily was born."

"I have a surprise for you," Ian told her as Emily reached up and grabbed his nose.

Cassie went to reach for Emily, but Ian stepped back. "She's fine," he told her. "I love having my nose held so my voice can sound a little more like a chipmunk when I ask a sexy woman to go away with me for a few days."

Shocked at his invitation, Cassie shook her head, trying to make sense of it. "Go away with you?"

Ian nodded as Emily reached up on his head and tugged his glasses off. Immediately they went to her mouth.

"She's still fine," Ian told Cassie as he dodged her again. "They're sunglasses. She can chew on them all she wants."

"They'll have drool on them."

Ian's eyes darted to the lenses, but he just sighed. "Oh, well. So, what do you say? You up for getting away for a few days?"

Oh, how Cassie would love to get away. To not worry or train or do anything but be with Ian because their time together was coming to an end and she was certainly not ready to let go.

"Ian, going away with you sounds amazing, but I can't."

Ian glanced at Emily. "She's going to use you as an excuse, isn't she?"

Cassie laughed. "Actually, yes. But she's not an excuse.

I mean, I can't ask anyone to keep her for days, especially with her teething and upset."

Bringing his gaze back to Cassie, Ian crossed the space between them until he stood so close she could see the flecks of amber in his dark eyes.

"I'm not asking you to hand her off to anybody. I want to take you both away."

Cassie stared back at him, sure she'd heard him wrong. He wanted to take her and a baby? A cranky baby?

"But…but…are you sure?"

Ian dipped his head and gently kissed her before easing back and giving her that heart-melting grin. "I wouldn't have asked if I wasn't sure."

A million things ran through her mind. Could she actually take off and be with Ian for a few days? Did he honestly know what he was asking? Because she really didn't think he knew how difficult playing house could be.

"Stop thinking so hard." He shifted Emily to his other side and reached out to cup the side of Cassie's face. "Do you want to go?"

Cassie nodded. "Of course I do. It's just—"

"Yes, you want to go. That's what I need to hear. Everything else is taken care of."

Intrigued, Cassie raised her brows. "Oh, is it?"

A corner of Ian's mouth quirked into a devilish half smile. "Absolutely. How about I come back and get you in an hour. Just pack simple clothing and whatever Emily can't live without. I'll be back to help you finish up and then we'll go."

"Where are we going?" she asked.

Handing Emily back to Cassie, Ian shrugged. "I guess you'll find out when we get there."

She tried to get the sunglasses away from Emily and

noticed slobber bubbles along the lenses. Ian waved a hand and laughed.

"No, really, keep them," he said as he headed toward the door. "She apparently gets more use out of them than I did."

Cassie was still laughing after he'd closed the door behind him. A getaway with Ian and Emily? How could she not want to jump at this chance?

And how could she not read more into it? Was Ian silently telling her he wanted more? Or was he getting in all the time he could before he said his final goodbye?

Ian didn't know if he was making a mistake or if he was finally taking a leap of faith by bringing Cassie and Emily to his beachfront home. They'd flown from the East Coast to the West and he'd questioned himself the entire way.

Tessa had suggested he take Cassie to Grant's mountain home for a getaway, but Ian wanted Cassie on his turf. Deep down inside he wanted her to see how he lived, see part of his world.

And he wanted to find out how well she fit into his home. Would she feel out of place or would she enjoy the breathtaking views from his bedroom, which overlooked the Pacific Ocean?

Surprisingly, Emily was wonderful on the plane ride, thanks to the pain reliever aiding in her teething process. As Ian maneuvered his car—it had been waiting for him at the airport—into his drive, he risked a glance over to Cassie. He wanted to see her initial reaction.

And he wasn't disappointed. Her eyes widened at the two-story white beach house with the porch stretching across the first floor and the balcony wrapping around the house on the second. He'd had that same reaction when his Realtor had shown him the property a few years ago. Love at first sight.

"Ian, this is gorgeous," she exclaimed. "I can't believe you managed to get a beach house on such short notice."

He hadn't told her he was bringing her to his home. He'd wanted to surprise her, and he was afraid if he told her, then she'd back out.

As he pulled into the garage and killed the engine, Ian turned to face her. "Actually, this is my house."

Cassie gasped, jerking her head toward him. "Your house? Why didn't you tell me we were coming to your house?"

He honestly didn't have an excuse unless he wanted to delve way down and dig up the commitment issues he still faced. His fear of having her reject his plan, his fear of how fast they'd progressed and his fear of where the hell all of this would lead had kept him silent.

"I can't believe you live on the beach," she said, still smiling. "You must love it here."

Yeah, he did, but for the first time in his life, he suddenly found himself loving another location, as well. Who knew he'd fall in love with a horse farm on the other side of the country?

While Cassie got Emily out of the car, Ian took all the luggage into the house. He put his and Cassie's in the master bedroom and took Emily's bag into the room across the hall.

Thankfully, he'd called ahead and had his housekeeper pick up a few items and set them up in the makeshift nursery. Since she was a new grandmother, she knew exactly what a baby would need. And judging from the looks of the room, she'd gone all out.

Ian chuckled. The woman was a saint and deserved a raise...as always.

"Ian, this house is—"

He turned around to see Cassie in the doorway, Emily on her hip, eyes wide, mouth open.

"I had a little help getting the place ready," he informed her, moving aside so she could enter. "I hope you don't mind that I had my housekeeper get Emily some things to make her comfortable while you guys are here."

Cassie's gaze roamed around the room, pausing on the crib in the corner. "I don't know what to say," she whispered as her eyes sought his. "This is... Thank you."

Warmth spread through him. Cassie was absolutely speechless over a package of diapers, a bed and some toys. Cost hadn't even factored into his plan; Emily's comfort and easing Cassie's mind even a little had been his top priorities.

Before he could respond, Emily started fussing. Cassie kissed her forehead and patted her back. "It's okay, baby. You're all right."

The low cries turned into a full-fledged wail and a sense of helplessness overtook him. Yes, he could buy anything for her, but what did he know about consoling a child or what to do when they were hurting or sick?

With a soft smile, Cassie looked back to him. "Sorry. I'm sure this isn't the getaway you'd hoped for."

Ian returned her smile and reached out to slide his hand over Emily's back. "The only expectation I had was spending time with both of you. She can't help that she's teething."

Her eyes studied him for a moment before she said, "I don't know what I did to deserve you, Ian."

"You deserve everything you've ever wanted."

He wanted to say more, he wanted to do more and give more to her, but they were both in uncharted territory, and taking things slow was the best approach. God knew they hadn't started out slow. Working backward might not have been the most conventional approach, but it was all they had to work with.

"Can you get in the side of her diaper bag and get out the Tylenol?" she asked.

While Cassie got Emily settled with pain medication and started to sing to her, Ian watched from the doorway. Had his father ever felt this way about him? Had the man wanted to be hands-on? Because Ian desperately found himself wanting to be more in not just Cassie's life, but Emily's, as well. He didn't have the first clue about caring for children, but he wanted to learn.

How could he ever be what they needed?

But how could he ever let either of them go?

Fifteen

Thankfully, after a round of medicine and a short nap, Emily was back to her happy self. Cassie put on her bathing suit, wrapping a sheer sarong around her waist, then put Emily into her suit, as well.

Why waste time indoors when there was a beach and rolling waves just steps away?

"You ready to play in the ocean?" Cassie asked Emily as she carried her toward the back door. "You're going to love it, baby girl."

The open-concept living room and kitchen spread across the entire back of the house, and two sets of French doors led out onto the patio. Cassie stepped out into the warm sunshine and stopped.

At the edge of the water, Ian stood with his back to her wearing black trunks and flaunting his excellent muscle tone. The fabric clinging to the back of his well-toned thighs, his slicked-back hair and the water droplets glistening on his tanned shoulders and back indicated he'd already tested the waters.

The man was sinful. He tempted her in ways she never thought possible, made her want things that could never be. They couldn't be more opposite, yet they'd somehow found each other. And they'd grown so close since their encounter in the attic.

The night of the lock-in had been filled with nothing but lust and desire. Now, though, Cassie was wrestling with so many more emotions. At the top of her list was one she'd futilely guarded her heart against…love.

She completely loved this man who had brought her to his home, shown her his piece of the world. But the clincher was when he'd assumed Emily would accompany them. He knew Cassie and Emily were a package deal, and he'd embraced the fact and still welcomed them.

How could she not fall hard for this intriguing man? He was nothing like her ex, nothing like any man she'd ever known, really. And that was what made him so special.

Emily started clapping and pointing toward Ian. Cassie laughed. "Yeah, we're going, baby."

Sand shifted beneath her toes as she made her way toward the man who'd taught her heart to trust again. Just the sight of him had her anticipating their night alone after Emily went to bed.

It wasn't as if she hadn't seen or touched him all over, but still, his sexiness never got old.

Emily squealed and Ian turned to face her. His gaze traveled over her modest suit and Cassie tamped down that inner demon that tried to tell her that her extra baby weight was hideous. Ian never, ever made her feel less than beautiful, so that inner voice could just shut the hell up.

"You look good in a suit, Cass."

His low voice, combined with that heavy-lidded gaze, had her insides doing an amazing little dance number.

"I was thinking the same thing about you," she told him with a grin.

"Mom, Mom, Mom," Emily squealed again, clapping her little hands and staring out at the water.

"Can I?" Ian asked, reaching for Emily.

Handing Emily over, Cassie watched as Ian stepped into the water. Slowly, he waded in deeper, all the while taking his hand and cupping water to splash up onto her little pudgy legs. Emily's laughter, her arms around Ian's neck and seeing Ian bounce around in the water like a complete goofball had Cassie laughing herself.

This getaway was exactly what she needed. Coming off the win at the Preakness and rolling right into a special weekend had Cassie realizing that her life was pretty near perfect right now. For this moment, she would relish the fact that Ian had to care for her on some deep level… possibly even love her. If he only had feelings of lust, he wouldn't have brought her to his home, wouldn't have invited a teething, sometimes cranky kid, and he certainly wouldn't be playing in the water with Emily like a proud daddy.

Cassie hated to place all her hope, all her heart, on one man…but how could she not, when he'd captured her heart the instant they'd been intimate in that attic?

Not wanting to miss out on a single moment, Cassie jumped into the ocean, reached beneath the water and pinched Ian on the butt.

The grin he threw over his shoulder at her told her she was in for a fun night.

Rocking a now peaceful baby had Ian truly wishing for so much. He'd convinced Cassie that he could put Emily to bed. He figured the little one was so tired from the day of playing in the ocean and taking a stroller ride around his neighborhood that she'd fall fast asleep.

She'd been fussy at first and Cassie had shown Ian how to rub some numbing ointment onto Emily's gums. He'd given Emily a bottle, even burped her, and rocked her until her sweet breath evened out.

He glanced down to the puckered lips, the pink cheeks from the sun—even though they'd slathered her with sunscreen—and smiled. Was it any wonder Cassie worked herself to death? How could a parent not want to sacrifice herself to make such an innocent child happy?

Cassie worked so hard with her sister, worked harder in the stables caring for horses, and she busted her butt to make a secure life and happy home for Emily...all without a husband.

Oh, she'd be ticked if she knew he worried about her not having someone in her life to help her. Granted, she had her father, Tessa and Linda, but whom did she have at night? Who helped her at home?

God help him, but Ian wanted to be that man. The weight of a sleeping baby in his arms, the sweet smell of her skin after her bath and the thought that this innocent child had complete and total trust in him were truly humbling.

Once he knew she was asleep, Ian eased from the rocking chair and laid Emily into the new crib, complete with pink-and-white-striped sheets. When he stood up, she stirred a little, but she settled right in.

A sigh of relief escaped Ian. He'd mastered numerous multimillion-dollar movie deals, he rubbed elbows with A-list actors and he'd managed to start his own agency at the age of twenty-four. But putting a child to sleep all by himself felt like quite an accomplishment.

He glanced at the monitor beside the crib and made sure it was on before he stepped out into the hall and quietly shut the door behind him.

He barely managed not to jump when he noticed Cassie across the hall, leaning against the doorway to his bedroom.

"You did it," she said with a wide smile. "I'm impressed."

All thoughts fled his mind as he took in the muted glow that surrounded her from the small lamp in his room. Her long red curls slid around her shoulders, lying against the stark white silk robe she wore—and what she wasn't wearing beneath. The V in the front plunged so deep, the swells of her breasts begged for his touch.

"I like your pajamas," he told her, crossing the hallway and immediately going to the belt on her robe. "Reminds me of something..."

Cassie lifted her arms to wrap around his neck. "What's that?"

"The fact I haven't seen you naked in several days."

She shifted, allowing the material to slide from her shoulders and puddle at her feet. Ian's hands roamed over the soft, lush curves he'd come to love and crave.

"You feel so good," he groaned as he trailed his lips from her jawline down the smooth column of her neck. "So perfect."

When she trembled beneath his touch, Ian cupped her behind and pulled her flush against his body. Nothing had ever felt so right. Every time Cassie was in his arms, contentment settled deeper and deeper into his heart.

She undressed him rapidly, matching his own frenzy. Ian had brought other women to his home. Not many, but a few. Yet he knew the second he laid Cassie beneath him and looked down into her blue eyes...he never wanted another woman in this bed.

* * *

He knew she wasn't asleep. The full moon shone through the wide expanse of windows across the room from the king-size bed and directly across their tangled bodies.

Cassie's breathing wasn't even and he'd felt the soft flutter of her lashes against his arm. Whatever thoughts consumed her mind, they were keeping her awake.

More than likely they were the same things that had him awake hours after they'd made love...twice.

Ian trailed his fingertips over her hip, down into the dip of her waist and back again. Goose bumps prickled beneath his touch.

"Talk to me," she whispered in the darkened room.

Words that had frightened him on more than one occasion after sex. But this was so different from any other time. First, Cassie was like no other woman. Second, what had just happened between them was so far beyond sex. And third, he actually didn't cringe as the words hovered in the air between them.

Moreover, he *wanted* to talk to her. He wanted her to know about his past, his life and what had brought him to this point...and why the thought of commitment scared the hell out of him.

Part of him truly wanted to try for her. Never before had he even considered permanent anything in his life, let alone a woman and a child. Cassie changed everything for him, because she was starting to *be* everything for him.

Of course, there was that devil on his shoulder that kept telling him he couldn't just try out playing house with this woman. She was genuine, with real feelings and a heart of gold that she had to protect. If he attempted to try for a long-term spot in her life and things didn't work out, he would never be able to forgive himself.

"My childhood wasn't quite as rosy and enjoyable as

yours." The words tumbled out before he thought better of opening up about the past he hated to even think about. "My father was a military man. Things had to be perfect, and not just perfect, but done five minutes ago. When he was home on leave, if I had a chore, I had better get to it the second he told me or I would face punishment."

Cassie gasped next to him. "He hit you?"

Ian stared up at the darkened ceiling as he continued to trail his fingertips over her lush, naked curves. "On occasion. But it wasn't a beating. He was old-school and a hand to my backside wasn't unheard of. But then he came home less and less because he and my mother divorced. That's when she started bringing her male friends into the house."

Ian recalled how weird it felt having a strange man at the breakfast table when he woke up, but eventually he didn't question his mother...and he didn't ask the names of the men. Would it matter? They'd be gone when she finished with them anyway.

"My mom is currently in the middle of her fourth divorce and I've no doubt number five is waiting in the wings absolutely convinced he's the one."

Cassie's arm tightened around his abdomen. "I'm sorry. I can't imagine."

Her warm breath tickled his chest, but Ian wouldn't have it any other way. He loved the feel of her tucked perfectly against him, her hair falling over his shoulder, the flutter of her lashes against his side.

"Don't be sorry," he told her. "There are kids way worse off than I was. But I always wished I had parents who loved each other, who loved me. A family was everything to me when I was younger, but I wanted the impossible."

A drop of moisture slid down his side. Ian shifted his body, folding Cassie closer as he half loomed over her.

"Don't cry for me." In the pale moonlight, her eyes glistened. Had anyone ever cried for him before? "I'm fine, Cassie. I guess I just wanted you to know what I came from."

Soft fingertips came up to trail down his cheek. Her thumb caressed his bottom lip, and his body responded instantly.

"I'm crying for the little boy who needed love and attention," she whispered. "And I'm crying for the man who fits so perfectly into my family, I'm terrified of how we'll get along without him."

Her declaration was a punch to his gut. The fact that they'd never mentioned his leaving after the film wrapped hung heavy in the air between them. And knowing she not only worried about his absence, but she'd cried over it had him hating himself on so many levels.

"I don't want to hurt you," he murmured as he slid his lips across hers. "That's the last thing I'd ever want."

Adjusting her body so she could frame his face with her hands, Cassie looked up at him with those damn misty eyes and smiled. "I know. I went into this with my eyes wide-open. For right now, though, you're mine and I don't want to think about tomorrow, Ian. I don't want to worry about that void that will inevitably come when you're gone."

Her hips tilted against his. "I just want you. Here. Now."

As he kissed her lips he had a hard time reining in his own emotions, because Cassie was dead-on about one thing.... There would most definitely be a void—the one he would feel without her by his side.

Sixteen

Cassie reached across the bed, only to encounter cool sheets. Quickly she sat up, clutching the material to her chest and glancing to the nightstand clock.

How on earth had she slept until nine? Between having a career set around a working horse farm and being a single mother, sleeping in was a foreign concept and a luxury she simply couldn't afford.

Another reality hit her hard as she jerked to look at the baby monitor on the dresser across the room. The red light wasn't on, which meant at some point the device had been turned off. Throwing the covers aside, Cassie grabbed the first available article of clothing—which happened to be Ian's T-shirt—and pulled the soft cotton over her head. She inhaled the embedded masculine scent of Ian as she darted across the hall.

The nursery was empty. Giggling erupted from downstairs, so Cassie turned and headed toward the sweet sound. At the base of the steps, Cassie froze as she stared into the living room. Ian stood behind Emily, her little hands held high, clutching on to his as he helped her walk across the open space. He'd pushed the coffee table against one wall, leaving the dark hardwood floor completely open.

Emily squealed as she waddled through the area, and Cassie, who still stood unnoticed, had to bite her lip to control the trembling and wash of emotions that instantly consumed her.

Ian Shaffer had officially stolen her heart, and there was no way she could go back to her life before she'd ever met him. The man had opened his home to her and her daughter. He wasn't just interested in having her in his bed. Granted, that was how they'd started out, but over a brief period of time they'd grown together and meshed in such a way that had Cassie hopeful and wishing. Dare she set her sights so high and dream for things that once seemed unattainable?

"Mamamama," Emily cried when she saw Cassie in the doorway.

Cassie stepped toward her daughter and squatted down. "Hey, sweet pea. Are you making Ian work this morning?"

Emily's precious two-toothed grin melted her heart. When she glanced up to meet Ian's gaze, her breath literally caught. He still clung to Emily's fingers and he'd been hunched over so he could accommodate her height, but he just looked so at peace and happy.

"What time did she get up?"

Ian shrugged. "Maybe around seven."

Cassie straightened. "Why didn't you get me up?"

Scooping Emily into his arms, Ian smiled. "Because you needed to sleep, so I turned the monitor off and got her out of the crib. She's been changed and fed—probably not how you'd do it, but it's done nonetheless."

Cassie was utterly speechless. The man had taken such care of her daughter all so Cassie could sleep in. He'd been watching and loving over Emily…over another man's baby, and all without a care or second thought. And now he stood holding her as if the act were the most natural thing in the world.

"Don't look at me like that," he told her. Emily turned her head into Ian's shoulder and his wide, tanned hand patted her tiny back. "I wanted to help and I knew you'd refuse if you even thought she was awake. Besides, I kind of wanted to see how Emily and I would get along. I'm pretty sure she loves me."

Cassie couldn't help but laugh. "I'm sure she does love you. She knows a good thing when she sees it."

Ian's eyes widened, and the muscle in his jaw moved as if he were hiding his words deep within. Had she said too much? At this point, with time against them, Cassie truly believed she couldn't hold back. She needed to be up front and honest.

"I'm not saying that to make you uncomfortable," she informed him, crossing her arms over her chest. "But you have to know this is so much more than physical for me, Ian."

Those dark eyes studied her a second before he nodded. "I'd be lying if I said this was all sexual for me. You and Emily…"

He shook his head as his words died on his lips. Cassie wanted him to go on, but she knew the internal battle he waged with himself and she didn't want to push him. He'd opened up to her last night, bared his soul, and she knew what he'd shared hadn't come easy for him.

Placing a hand on his arm, Cassie smiled. "We don't need to define anything right now," she assured him. "I just wanted you to know this thing between us—it matters so much to me."

With Emily lying against one shoulder, Ian pulled Cassie to his other side and wrapped an arm around her. "Everything in my arms right now matters more to me than I ever thought possible," he told her with a kiss to the top of her head.

Before she could completely melt into a puddle at his feet over his raw, heartfelt words, Ian's hand slid down her side and cupped her bottom beneath his T-shirt.

"This shirt never looked this sexy on me," he growled into her ear. "So unless you want to end up back in bed, you better go get some clothes on."

Shivers of arousal swept through her. Would she ever get enough of him? More so, would he get enough of her?

Tipping her head back, she stared up into his eyes. Desire and, dare she say, love stared back at her. No, she didn't think they'd get enough of each other, which meant whatever they were building wouldn't come crumbling down when he left Virginia after the film was done shooting. But how they would manage was a whole other hurdle to jump.

Extracting herself from his side, Cassie pulled Emily from his arms. "How about we spend the day on the beach?" she suggested.

Emily's little hand went into Cassie's hair, and she started winding the strands around her baby fingers.

"You in a suit?" Ian's gaze raked over her once more. "I'd never say no to that."

With this being their last day of complete relaxation, Cassie wanted to live for the moment, this day, and not worry about what obstacles they faced tomorrow or even next week. She was completely in love with Ian. He wasn't a rebound; he wasn't a filler or a stepping-stone until the next chapter of her life.

Ian Shaffer *was* the next chapter of her life.

Seventeen

"I just need someone who's good with advertising," Cassie muttered as she stared down at the new plans for her riding school for handicapped children.

"How about that hunky agent you're shacking up with?"

Cassie threw a glare across the room at her sister. Tessa silently volleyed back a wicked grin.

"We're not shacking up." Not technically, anyway. "And that's not his job."

"Maybe not," Tessa replied, coming to her feet. "But he'd know more about it than we would, and I guarantee he'd do anything to help you."

More than likely, but Cassie wasn't going to ask. Venturing into personal favors would imply something…something they'd yet to identify in their relationship.

Yes, they'd admitted they had strong feelings for each other, but after the giant leap into intimacy, they'd pulled back the emotional roller coaster and examined where they were going.

And they still didn't know.

Cassie spoon-fed another bite of squash and rice to Emily. Right now she needed to focus on the final race of the season, getting her school properly advertised and caring for her daughter. Ian, unfortunately, would have to fall in line behind all of that and she highly doubted he would want to. What man would? He deserved more than waiting on her leftover time.

"You're scowling." Tessa came to stand beside the high chair and leaned against the wall. "What's really bothering you?"

Sisters. They always knew when to dig deeper and pull the truth from the depths of hell just to make you say the words aloud.

"Ian is out to dinner with Lily."

A quirk of a smile danced around Tessa's mouth. "You're jealous? Honey, the man is absolutely crazy about you. All you'd have to do is see how he looks at you when you aren't paying attention."

The idea that he studied her enough to show emotion on his face for others to see made her way more thrilled than she should be. She wanted to tell him she'd fallen for him—she wanted to tell everybody. But there was that annoying little voice that kept telling her this was too good to be true and that she needed to come back to reality before she ended up hurt.

"He's not like Derek," Tessa informed her as if she were reading her mind. "Ian may be younger, but he's all man and he's only got eyes for you."

Cassie smiled with a nod and scooped up the last bite, shoving it into Emily's waiting mouth. "I know. There's just that thread of doubt that gets to me, and I know it's not Ian's fault. He can't help the mess that is my life."

Laying a hand over Cassie's arm, Tessa squeezed. "Your

life is beautiful. You have a precious baby, an awesome career and the best sister anyone could ever ask for. What more could a girl want?"

To be loved. The words remained in her head, in her heart.

"So where's your guy tonight?" Cassie asked, wiping off the orange, messy mouth, hoping to unearth her daughter. "You two aren't normally separated for more than an hour at a time."

With a smile that could only be equated to love, Tessa positively beamed. "He's going over some things with Bronson and Anthony. I'm pretty sure Dad weaseled his way into that meeting, as well."

Cassie scooped Emily from the high chair and settled her on her hip. "I've no doubt Dad is weighing in with his opinion. I need to give her a bath. You sticking around?"

Shaking her head, Tessa sighed and started across the living room. "I think I'll head home and make some dinner. It's not often I get to cook for Grant, and he's worked so hard lately. He needs to relax."

Cassie squeezed her eyes shut. "I don't want to hear about you two relaxing. Just a simple no would've answered my question."

With a naughty laugh, Tessa grabbed her keys from the entry table and waved. "See you tomorrow."

Once Cassie was alone, she couldn't help that her thoughts drifted to Ian, to the days they'd spent at his home in L.A. and to the fact he'd taken such good care of her sweet Emily.

Yes, the man may be five years her junior, but so what? Her ex-husband had been two years older and look how well that had turned out. Cassie couldn't hang a single argument on age, not when Ian went above and beyond to show her just what type of man he was.

After Emily was bathed and dressed in her lightweight

sleeper, Cassie set some toys on a blanket and let her daughter have some playtime before bed. Settling on the couch, curling her legs to the side, Cassie rested her elbow on the arm of the sofa and watched Emily smack soft yellow and red cubes together, making them jingle.

Exhaustion consumed her, but how could she not be tired? Her plate was not only full—it was overflowing. Physically, mentally, she was drained. Her head was actually pounding so fiercely her eyes ached. Maybe she could just lay her head on the arm of the couch while Emily played for a bit longer.

Adjusting her arm beneath her head, Cassie closed her eyes, hoping to chase away the dull throb.

After the flash of panic in seeing Cassie slumped over the arm of the couch and Emily holding herself up against the edge of the couch by her mama, Ian realized Cassie had merely fallen asleep.

"Hey, sweetie," he said softly when Emily smiled up at him, flashing her two little baby teeth. "Your mama is pretty tired. Why don't we let her sleep?"

Ian scooped Emily up, set her in her Pack 'n Play across the room and made sure she had her favorite stuffed horse. He had to ignore her slight protesting as he crossed back and gently lifted Cassie into his arms. Murmuring something, she tilted her head against his chest and let out a deep sigh. She was exhausted and apparently couldn't even keep her eyes open. It was so unlike her to fall asleep with Emily still up and not confined to one area.

A small bedside lamp sent a soft glow through her bedroom. After gently laying her down, he pulled the folded blanket from the foot of the bed and draped it over her curled form. Smoothing her hair from her face, Ian frowned and leaned in closer to rest his palm across her forehead.

She wasn't burning up, but she wasn't far from it. Careful not to wake her, he peeled the throw back off her to hopefully get her fever down. Her cheeks were pink and the dark circles beneath her eyes were telltale signs of an illness settling in. He had a feeling Cassie would only be angry to know she was getting sick.

He went into her adjoining bath, got a cool cloth and brought it back out, carefully laying it across her forehead. She stirred and her lids fluttered open as she tried to focus.

"Ian?"

"Shh." He curled a hand over her shoulder to get her to remain down. "It's all right. You need to rest."

"Emily..." Cassie's eyes closed for a moment before she looked back up at him. "I don't feel very well."

"I know, baby. I'm not going anywhere and Emily is fine. Just rest."

He had no clue if she heard him; her eyes were closed and her soft, even breathing had resumed.

The woman worked herself too hard. Not that he could judge. After all, he hadn't grown to be one of Hollywood's most sought-out agents at such a young age by playing assistant and errand boy. No, he'd done grunt work, made his career his since he'd left home determined to prove to his free-spirited mother and domineering father that he could manage on his own and succeed way above anything they'd ever dreamed.

And he'd done just that.

But now that he looked down at Cassie resting peacefully, he couldn't help but wonder if there wasn't more in store for him. Work was satisfying on so many levels, but it didn't keep his bed warm, didn't look to him for support and compassion and sure as hell didn't make his heart swell to the point of bursting.

Cassie and Emily, on the other hand...

After clicking off the bedside lamp, he went straight to the hall bath to wash his hands. If Cassie was contagious, he didn't want to get her daughter sick. Granted, the child had been with her mother all evening, but still. Weren't people supposed to wash their hands before dealing with kids?

Yeah, he had a lot to learn. As he lathered up and rinsed, he glanced across the open floor plan to Emily, who had long since forgotten she was angry with being confined. Ian dried his hands on a plaid towel and smiled. Definitely had a lot to learn about little people.

And suddenly it hit him that he actually wanted to do just that. Who knew that when he came out here to sway Lily into signing with his agency that he'd completely get sidetracked by a beauty who literally fell into his arms?

After getting a bottle ready—thank God he'd had those alone days with Cassie and Emily in California so he knew a bit more about Emily's care—Ian set it on the end table and went to retrieve one happy baby.

"Are you always in a good mood?" he asked as he lifted her from the baby prison. "Your mama isn't feeling good, so it's just you and me."

Emily patted his face and smiled. "Dadadada."

Ian froze. *Oh, no. No, no, no.* As if a vise was being tightened around his chest, Ian's breath left him.

"No, baby. Ian."

Emily patted his cheek again. "Dadada."

Okay, he had to put his own issues aside at the thought of someone calling him Daddy because this poor girl honestly didn't know her daddy. She didn't remember the man who was supposed to be here for her and her mother.

Ian held her closer, silently wanting to reassure her that she was not alone. But was he also silently telling himself that he'd be here beyond the rough night right now? Would he be here after the film wrapped up?

Since he was alone with his thoughts he might as well admit to himself that being with Cassie and Emily for the long term was something he wanted and, dare he say... ached for?

As he settled into the corner of the couch with Emily, he slid the bottle between her little puckered lips and smiled as those expressive blue eyes looked back up at him. Eyes like her mother's. Both ladies had him wrapped around their fingers.

Emily drifted off to sleep about the time the bottle was empty. He set it back on the table and shifted her gently up onto his shoulder. If she spit up on his dress shirt, so be it. He hadn't taken the time to change after his dinner meeting with Lily. She was pretty confident she'd be signing with his agency.

And the fact this was the first time he'd thought of that monumental career development since he'd come in and discovered Cassie ill should tell him exactly how quickly his priorities had changed where the Barrington females were concerned.

Once Emily had fallen asleep, he figured it was okay for him to rest on the couch with her. He carefully got up and turned off the lights in the living room, leaving on only the small light over the stove in the kitchen. Pulling the throw off the back of the sofa with one hand and holding Emily firmly with the other, Ian toed off his shoes and laid the little girl against the back of the sofa before he eased down onto his side beside her. Not the most comfortable of positions, but he was so tired he could've slept standing up, and there was no way he'd leave Cassie alone with the baby tonight.

Resting with the baby on a couch was probably some

sort of Parenting 101 no-no, but since he'd taken no crash courses in this gig, he was totally winging it.

The next thing he knew someone was ringing the door-bell. Ian jerked up, taking in the sunlight streaming in through the windows. It was Sunday and the crew was taking the day off. Was someone looking for him? The doorbell chimed again and Emily's eyes popped open, too.

Ian picked her up and raked a hand over his hair as he padded to the door. The last thing he needed was for some-one to ring that bell again and wake Cassie. Apparently they'd all slept uneventfully through the night.

As he flicked the lock, Ian glanced out the sidelight, frowning when he didn't recognize the stranger on the porch.

Easing the door open slightly, Ian met the other man's gaze. "Can I help you?"

The stranger's eyes went from Emily back to Ian be-fore the muscle in his jaw jumped. "Who the hell are you, and where is Cassie?"

Shocked at the immediate anger, Ian instantly felt de-fensive. "I should be asking you who you are, considering you're on the outside."

Narrowed eyes pierced Ian. "I'm Cassie's husband. I'll ask again. Who the hell are you?"

Husband. Ian didn't miss the fact the prick left out the "ex" part.

"I'm her lover," Ian said, mentally high-fiving himself for wiping that smug look off the man's face.

Eighteen

Cassie held on to the side of her head, which was still pounding, but now she had a new problem.

Frozen at the end of her hallway, she had full view of Ian holding Emily and the front door wide-open with Derek standing on the other side looking beyond pissed. This was the dead-last thing she wanted to deal with in her life, particularly at this moment.

"Derek, what are you doing here?" she asked, slowly crossing the room, praying she didn't collapse.

"Go back to bed, honey." Ian turned to her, his face softening as he took in what she knew was impressive bed head. "Emily is fine and he can come back later."

"Don't tell my wife what to do," Derek practically shouted as he shouldered his way past Ian and into the living room.

"She's not your wife." Ian's eyes narrowed. When Emily started to fidget, Ian patted her back and murmured something to her. "I need to feed her and change her diaper."

Derek's gaze darted from Ian to Cassie and back to Ian.

"What the hell is this? You move in your lover to shack up? Never took you for a whore."

Cassie didn't think she could feel worse. She was wrong. But before she could defend herself, Ian had turned back, clenching the muscle in his jaw.

"Apologize," Ian said in a low, threatening tone.

Cassie had no doubt if Ian hadn't been holding the baby, he would've been across the room in an instant.

"This has nothing to do with you," Derek shot back. "Why don't you give me my daughter and get out."

No matter how awful Cassie felt, she raised her hand to silence Ian and moved closer to Derek. Too bad whatever bug she'd picked up couldn't be fast-acting or she'd so exhale all over him.

"You relinquished any right you had when you walked out on us." Cassie laid a hand on the back of the couch for support. She'd be a little more intimidating if she wasn't freezing and ready to fall onto her face. "You can't just barge into my house and try to take control. I don't know why you're here, but I don't really care."

Cassie felt Ian's hard body behind her, his strong hand settled around her waist. The man offered support both physically and emotionally with one simple, selfless touch. And the sea of differences between the two men in this room was evident without so much as a spoken word.

Ian had watched her with care, concern and, yes, even love. Derek stood glaring, judging and hating. When he'd first walked out she would've done anything to get her family back, but now that he was here, she loathed the sight of him.

"I'm here to see my wife and daughter," Derek told her.

"I'm not your wife," Cassie fired back. "And if you want to see Emily, you can contact your attorney and he can call mine. You can't just charge in here after being gone for nearly a year and expect me to just let you see her. Did you think she'd be comfortable with you?"

"She seems fine with him." Derek nodded his chin in Ian's direction.

"That's because she knows who I am," Ian stated from behind her. "Now, Cassie has asked you to leave. She's not feeling good and my patience has just about run out. Leave now or I'll escort you out personally, then notify the crew's security to take you off the estate property."

Derek looked as if he wanted to say more, but Ian stepped around Cassie, keeping his arm wrapped around her waist. He said nothing and kept his gaze on Derek until Derek stepped back toward the front door.

"I plan on seeing my daughter," Derek threatened. "And my wife. I'll go through my lawyer, but I will be getting my family back."

He slammed the door, leaving the echoing sound to fill the silence. Cassie hadn't seen Derek in so long, she had no idea how to feel, how to react. She didn't feel like battling him.

And had he threatened to take Emily? Was that what he'd implied?

Cassie sank onto the back of the couch and wrapped her arms around her waist. Maybe she should have listened to those voice mails.

"Go back to bed, Cass. Don't think about him—just go rest for now."

Cassie looked up at Ian, still holding Emily. The image just seemed so...right. The three of them *felt* right. They'd all been random puzzle pieces and when they'd come together they'd instantly clicked into place without question.

Shoving her wayward hair behind her ears, Cassie shook her head. "I can't rest, Ian. He just made a veiled threat to take Emily. He can't do that, right? I mean, what judge would let him have my baby after he walked out on us?"

Tears pricked her eyes. She couldn't fathom sharing custody of her baby. Emily belonged here.

"She doesn't even know him," Cassie murmured, thinking aloud. "There's no way he could take her. Emily would be terrified."

Ian rested a hand on her shoulder and held on to Emily with his other strong arm. "You're jumping the gun here. He didn't say he was going to ask for custody. I honestly think those were just hollow words. He wants to scare you because he's angry I was here. I guarantee had you been alone, his attitude would've been completely different. One look at me, especially holding his daughter, and he was instantly on the defensive."

Emily started to reach for Cassie, but Ian shifted his arm away. "Go on back to rest. I'll feed her breakfast and then I'll check on you to see if you feel like eating. You're exhausted and working too hard."

Cassie raised a brow. "Working too hard? Are you the pot or the kettle?"

Laughing, Ian shrugged. "Does it matter?"

Cassie pushed away from the couch and sighed. "Thanks, Ian. Really. I don't know what I would've done without you here last night."

After a light kiss across her forehead, Ian looked into her eyes. "There's nowhere else I would've rather been."

As Cassie got back into bed, she knew Ian wasn't just saying pretty words to try to win her over. The man was full of surprises, and she found herself falling harder with each passing revelation.

And now here she was, 100 percent in love with a man who lived on the other side of the country, who would be leaving in a couple of weeks to go back to his life. And, of all the rotten timing, her ex had decided to show up now.

Cassie curled into her pillow and fisted her hands beside her face as the tears threatened to fall. Somehow this would all work out. She had faith, she had hope and, for the first time in her life, she had love. All of that had to count for something...didn't it?

Once Cassie had gotten a little food in her, she seemed even more tired, so Ian insisted on taking Emily for a few hours and then checking back. There was no way he could leave her alone with a baby, but he still had work to do.

Single parents worked while caring for their babies all the time, right? Shouldn't be too hard to send some emails and make a few phone calls.

After fighting with the straps on the stroller and narrowly missing pinching Emily's soft skin in the buckle, he finally had her secured and ready to go. Diaper bag over his shoulder, Ian set out across the estate, pushing Emily toward his trailer.

Bright purple flats covered her feet as she kicked her little legs the entire way. Ian knew he was smiling like an idiot, but how could he not? Emily was an absolute doll and she was such a sweet kid. He was actually looking forward to spending time with her.

Max Ford and his wife, Raine, were just stepping out of their trailer as he passed by. Max held their little girl, Abby, who was almost two now.

"Look at this," Max said with a wide grin. "You seeing how the family life fits you?"

Ian didn't mind the question. Actually, he kind of warmed at the idea of it. "Cassie isn't feeling too great, so I told her I'd take Emily for the day."

Max's daughter pointed down to Emily. "Baby."

Laughing, Raine took the little girl and squatted down to the stroller to see Emily. "Her name is Emily," Raine explained.

"You're pretty serious about Cassie," Max said in a softer tone. "Happened pretty quick."

Ian shook his head and raked a hand over his hair, which was probably still sporting a messy look after sleeping on the sofa all night. "Yeah, it did. But I can't help it, man. I didn't see this coming."

"You plan on staying after the film is done?" Max asked.

Ian watched the interaction between the two little girls and Raine and his heart swelled. "I honestly don't know," Ian said, looking back to Max. "How hard was it for you with the transition?"

Max's gaze drifted to his family, and a genuine smile, not what he used for the cameras or his on-screen love interests, but the one that Ian had seen directed only at Raine, transformed his face. "When you want something so bad you'd die without it, there's no transition. It's the easiest and best decision I've ever made."

Yeah, that was kind of where Ian's mind was going. Having Cassie and Emily in his life made him feel things on a level he hadn't even known existed inside him.

Ian said his goodbyes to Max and his family and stepped inside his trailer. After settling Emily on a pink fuzzy blanket from her house, Ian placed her favorite toys all around her. Standing back to admire his feat of babysitting, he went to boot up his laptop, grabbed his phone and sat at the small kitchenette. Thankfully, the trailer was all open and small, so Emily couldn't leave his sight.

After answering a few emails, Ian glanced at the little girl, who was chewing on one toy and pounding the other one against the side of her rainbow-striped leggings. So far so good.

As he dialed one of his clients, rising star Brandon Crowe, who was on his way to Texas for filming, Ian scrolled back through his emails, deleting the junk so he could wade through and find things that actually needed his attention.

"Hello."

"Brandon, glad I caught you." Ian closed out his email and opened the document with his client's name on it to make notes. "You arrive in Houston yet?"

"About an hour ago. I'm ready for a beer, my hotel room and about five days of sleep. In that order."

Ian chuckled. His client had been filming all over with a tight schedule; the crew had literally been running from one location to another.

"What's up?" Brandon asked.

"I know your mind is on overload right now, but I need to discuss the next script. I have a film that will be set in Alaska and the producer has specifically asked for you. I'd like to send this script to you and see what you think."

Brandon sighed. "Sure. Did you look it over?"

"Yeah. I think this character would be a perfect fit for you. I can see why they want you for the role."

"Who's the producer?" Brandon asked.

Ian told him more specifics and turned to see Emily... only she wasn't there. Panic rushed through him as he jerked to his feet, sending his chair toppling to the floor behind him.

"Emily," he called, glancing around the very tiny area.

"Excuse me?"

Ian glanced at the phone. For a second he'd forgotten about the call. "I need to call you back. The baby is gone."

"Baby?"

Ian disconnected the call and tossed his phone on the

table. Stepping over the toys and blanket, Ian crossed to the other end of the trailer. He peeked into the tiny bathroom: no Emily.

"Emily," he called. "Sweetheart?"

In the small bedroom, Ian saw bright rainbow material sticking out from the side of the bed. He rounded the bed. Emily sat on her bottom, still chewing her favorite stuffed horse. Of course, when she saw him she looked up and gave that heart-melting smile.

"You're rotten," he told her. "Your mom is not going to let you come play with me anymore if you give me a heart attack."

He scooped her up and was rewarded with a wet, sloppy horse to the side of the face. *Nice.*

The next hour went about as stellar as the first, and by the end of hour two, Ian knew he was an amateur and needed reinforcements. There was just no way he could do this on his own.

How the hell did Cassie manage? Not only manage, but still put up the front of keeping it together and succeeding at each job: mother, sister, daughter, trainer. She did it all.

Of course, now she was home, in bed, flat-out exhausted and literally making herself sick.

As Ian gathered up all Emily's things, she started crying. The crying turned into a wail in about 2.5 seconds, so Ian figured she was hungry. Wrong. He changed her diaper. Still not happy.

He picked up the bag and Emily, stepped outside and strapped her into the stroller. Perhaps a walk around the estate would help.

Keeping toward the back of the main house, Ian quickly realized this also wasn't making her very happy. That was it. Reinforcements were past due.

He made his way to the back door, unfastened the very

angry Emily and carried her into the house, where—*thank you, God*—Linda greeted him with a smile and some heavenly aroma that could only be her cinnamon rolls.

"I've done something wrong," Ian yelled over Emily's tantrum. "We were fine." A slight lie. "But then she started screaming. She's not hungry. She has a clean diaper. We took a walk. I don't know what to do."

Linda wiped her hand on a plaid towel and tossed it onto the granite counter before circling the island and holding her hands out for Emily. The baby eagerly went to the middle-aged woman and Ian nearly wept with gratitude that someone else surely knew what they were doing.

"She probably needs a nap," Linda told him as she jostled and tried to calm Emily.

Ian laughed and pushed a hand through his hair. "After all of that, I need one, too."

Smiling, Linda patted Emily's back. "You say you fed her?"

Ian nodded. "She took a bottle. I have some jar food, but Cassie said to save that for a bit later."

"If she's had her bottle, then her little belly is full and she's ready to rest. I'll just take her into the master bedroom. Damon has a crib set up in there for when Cassie is over here."

Ian sank to the bar stool, rested his elbow on the island and held his head in his hands. Good grief, being in charge of one tiny little being was the hardest job he'd ever had... and he'd had the job only a few hours.

Hands down, parenting was not for wimps.

A slither of guilt crept through him. Had he been too hard on his parents all those years? His free-spirited mother who was always seeking attention and his by-the-book father who could never be pleased...were they just struggling at this whole parenting thing, too?

Ian didn't have the answers and he couldn't go back in time and analyze each and every moment. The most pressing matter right now was the fact that he was in love with Cassie and her sweet baby, and the ex had just stepped back into the picture.

Great freakin' timing.

But Ian needed to wait, to let Cassie deal with this matter in her own way. He wasn't stepping aside, not by any means. He'd offer support any way she wanted it, but this was her past to handle, and with a baby involved, Ian had a bad feeling things were about to get worse before they could get better.

Nineteen

Cassie jerked when the loud knock on her door pulled her out of her sleep. Glancing to the clock on the bedside table, she realized she'd slept most of the day. Damn, she'd never slept that much.

Throwing off the covers and coming to her feet, Cassie was thrilled when she didn't sway and within moments knew she was feeling better. Perhaps her body was just telling her she needed to slow it down every now and then. The pounding on her door continued and Cassie rolled her eyes. There wasn't a doubt in her mind who stood on the other side of the door. Ian wouldn't pound on her door. He'd knock or just come on in, and so would her father and Tessa.

And that left only one rude, unwanted guest.

Shuffling down the hall, probably looking even more stellar than earlier today when Derek had stopped by, Cassie actually laughed. Was he really here to plead for his family back when she looked like death and after he'd left her for some young, hot bimbo? Oh, the irony was not lost on her.

Cassie took her time flipping the lock on the knob and opening the door. Sure enough, Derek stood there, clutching a newspaper. Disapproval settled in his eyes.

"Funny," she told him, leaning against the edge of the door. "That's the same look you wore when you left me. What do you want now?"

He slapped the paper to her chest and pushed past her to enter.

"Come on in," she muttered, holding on to the paper and closing the door. "I thought I told you to have your lawyer contact mine."

Derek scanned the living area, then stretched his neck to see down the hall. "Where's Emily?"

"With Ian." Crossing her arms, crinkling the paper, Cassie sighed. "What do you want, Derek?"

"First of all, I don't want my daughter with a stranger."

Hysterical laughter bubbled out before she could even try to control it. "Seriously? If anyone is a stranger to her, it's you. We've already established what you think of Ian, so state your reason for this unwanted visit or that threat of calling security will become a fast reality."

He pointed toward the paper. "Apparently you haven't seen today's local paper. Maybe your pretty boy is a stranger to you, as well."

Cassie unfolded the paper. She'd play his game if it meant he'd leave sooner.

Her eyes settled on the picture of Lily and Ian. Cassie had known they were having a business meeting the evening before, she'd known they were discussing a major career move for both of them, but she hadn't known the media would spin the story into something…romantic.

Her eyes landed on the headline: Hollywood Starlet on Location Still Finds Time for Romance.

The way their two heads were angled together in the grainy picture did imply something more than a business meeting. The intimate table for two complete with bouquet and candles also added to the ambience of love.

Cassie glanced back up to Derek. "What about it?"

She would not give her ex the satisfaction of letting it get to her, of coming between something she and Ian had built and worked hard at.

"Looks like your boy toy has someone else on the side." Derek smirked. "Is this really what you've moved on to?"

"Why are you here?" she demanded. "What do you want from me?"

"If you'd answered my calls or texts you'd know I want my family back. I had no idea you opted to replace me with such a younger man."

Cassie smacked the paper down on the table beside the door. "Don't you dare judge me. You left me, remember? And if we're casting stones, I'll remind you that when you left, you moved on with a much younger woman with boobs as her only major asset."

Fired up and more than geared for a fight, Cassie advanced on him. "You're just upset because Ian is a real man. He cares about me, about Emily. My looks don't matter, my size doesn't matter and he's taken to Emily like she is his own, which is a hell of a lot more than you ever did for either of us."

Derek clenched his jaw as he loomed over her and held her gaze. "I just want you to know that this man, this kid, really, will get bored with the family life. He'll move on, and then where will you be? I'm man enough to admit I was wrong and that I'm willing to try again."

She hated that she felt a small tug, hated that for months

she'd prayed for this moment. But she loved Ian. How could she deny herself the man she felt she'd been waiting for her whole life?

But on the other hand, how could she deny her daughter the bond of her parents raising her in the same house?

Cassie shook her head, refusing to listen to the conflicting voices in her head. She needed to think, needed to be alone.

"I waited for months for you to come back," she told him, hoping her words would make him squirm, make him feel the heavy dose of guilt he was due. "I cried myself to sleep when I thought of Emily not knowing her father. But you know what? After the tears were spent, I realized that Emily was better off. Both of us were, actually. Neither of us needed a man in our life who didn't put us first. We needed a man who would love us, put our needs above his own selfish ones and be there for us no matter what."

When he opened his mouth, Cassie raised a hand to silence him. "I would've given you the same in return. I married you thinking we were both in love, but I was wrong. You didn't love me, because if you did, you wouldn't have found it so easy to leave me."

"I'm back, though." He reached out, touched her face. "I want my family back, my wife back. I know I made a mistake, but you can't tell me you're ready to throw everything away."

When the door opened behind her, Cassie didn't have to turn to know Ian stood just at the threshold. She closed her eyes and sighed.

"Actually," she whispered. "You already threw it all away."

Derek's eyes darted from hers to just over her shoulder before he dropped his hands. "You can keep the paper. Maybe it will give you something to think about."

She didn't move as he skirted around her. When the door shut once again, Cassie turned slowly to see Ian, hands on his hips. Even with the space between them, Cassie saw so many emotions dancing in his eyes: confusion, hurt, love.

"Where's Emily?" she asked, hoping to keep the conversation on safer ground.

"I actually just left her with Linda. She's taking a nap."

Cassie nodded, worry lacing through her. "What you just saw was—"

"I know what I saw," he murmured. "I know he wants you back. He'd be a fool not to. It's just—"

Ian glanced down, smoothing a hand over the back of his neck, then froze when his gaze landed on the paper. Slowly he picked it up, skimming the front page.

Cassie waited, wondering how he would react.

When he muttered a curse and slammed the paper down, Cassie jumped.

"Tell me this wasn't Derek's defense," Ian begged. "He surely wasn't using me as his battle to win you back."

Shrugging, Cassie crossed her arms around her waist. "It's a pretty damning photograph."

Closing the spacious gap between them, Ian stood within a breath of her and tipped her chin up so she looked him in the eyes. "The media is known for spinning stories to create the best reaction from viewers. It's how they stay in business."

Cassie nodded. "I'm aware of that."

Ian studied her for a moment before he plunged his fingers through her disheveled hair and claimed her lips. The passion, desire and fury all poured from him, and Cassie had to grip his biceps to hold on for the ride.

He attacked her mouth, a man on a mission of proving something, of taking what was his and damning the consequences.

When he pulled away, Ian rested his forehead against hers. "Tell me you believe that I could kiss you like that and have feelings for another woman. Tell me that you don't trust me and all we have here is built on lies. Because if that's the case, I'll leave right now and never come back."

Cassie's throat tightened as she continued to clutch his arms. "I don't believe that, Ian. I know you wouldn't lie to me. You've shown me what a real man is, how a real man treats a lady."

Taking a deep breath, she finally stepped back, away from his hold. "But I also know that this is something I'm going to have to deal with if we're together. The media spinning stories, always being in the limelight."

"I'm an agent, Cassie. Nobody cares about me. If I had been out alone, nobody would've known who I was."

Cassie smiled. "But you were out with the breathtaking Lily Beaumont. All of your clients are famous, Ian. There will be other times, other photos."

Shaking her head, she walked around and finally sank onto the sofa. Ian joined her but didn't touch her. She hated this wedge that had settled between them…a wedge that had formed only once Derek had entered the picture.

"I want to be with you, Cassie," he told her. "As in beyond the movie, beyond next month or even next year. I want to see where this can go, but if the idea of my work will hold you back, maybe we both need to reevaluate what we're doing."

Tears pricked her eyes as she turned to face him fully. "You want to be with me?"

Reaching out to swipe the pad of his thumb across her cheek to clear the rogue tear, Ian smiled. "Yes. I know it's crazy and we've only known each other a short time, but I do want to be with you."

"Is this because my ex is back? Are you feeling threatened?"

Shaking his head, Ian took her shoulders and squeezed. "This has nothing to do with Derek. His appearance is just bad timing, that's all. I can't deny myself the fact that being with you has made me a better person. Finding myself wrapped around yours and Emily's lives makes me want more for myself. I never thought about a family before, but I want to see where this will lead and how we can make it work."

Hope filled Cassie as she threw her arms around Ian's neck and sniffed. "I know I'm a hot mess right now," she told him. "I have no idea how I was lucky enough to get you, but I want to see where we go, too. I'm just sorry you'll have to deal with Derek." Cassie eased back and wiped her cheeks. "He's Emily's father, and even though he abandoned us, I can't deny him if he wants to see her."

"What if he wants custody? Did he mention that again?"

"No. I hope he was just trying to scare me, like you said."

Smoothing her hair behind her ear, Ian smiled and settled his palm against her cheek. "No matter what, I'm here for you. Okay?"

For the first time in a long time, Cassie knew there was something to be hopeful about, something more than her career and Emily to fight for. And that was the love of a good man.

Ian was right. Damn if Derek's visit hadn't come at the worst possible time. Not only was the estate covered in film crew and actors, but Ian had settled so perfectly into her life and now the Belmont Stakes was upon them.

The final of the three most prestigious races in the horse world. There was no way Cassie could possibly think of

Derek and his threats right now...and yet he had left her with a doozy last night.

He'd called her and issued an ultimatum—either she take him back and give their marriage another go or he would go to his lawyer with a plea to get full custody. Of course, she doubted he could, but the threat was there, and even if he didn't get full, there was always a chance he could get shared. And then where would she be?

Cassie sank down onto the bed in her hotel room and rested her head in her hands. Crying would be of no use, but she so wished she could cut loose and absolutely throw a fit. Being an adult flat-out sucked sometimes.

The adjoining door to the bedroom next to hers creaked open and Cassie glanced up to see Tessa standing in the doorway wearing a gray tank top and black yoga pants.

"I know you're not in a good spot, and as much as I think you could use a drink, that won't help us any in tomorrow's race." Tessa held up a shiny gold bag. "But I do have chocolates and I'm willing to share."

Cassie attempted a smile. "Are they at least rum balls?"

Laughing, Tessa crossed the room and sank onto the bed, bumping Cassie's hip. "Sorry. Just decadent white-chocolate truffles. You ready to talk about Derek being back and wreaking havoc? Because it's been all I could do not to say something to you, but I figured you'd tell me on your own."

Cassie took the bag and dug out a chocolate. No, the sweetness wouldn't cure all, but it would certainly take the edge off her rage.

"I was hoping if I ignored the fact he was in town he'd just go away," Cassie said as she bit into the chocolate.

"How's that working?"

"Not well. How did you find out anyway? He's only been in town two days."

Tessa reached into the bag and pulled out a piece for herself. "Ian and Max were discussing the problem, and I may have eavesdropped on their conversation."

Swallowing the bite and reaching for another truffle, Cassie shifted on the bed to face her sister, settling the bag between them. "I planned on telling you. I was just trying to focus on Ian, make sure Emily was all settled with Linda before we left and praying Derek didn't try to get back onto Stony Ridge while we were gone. I've got security keeping an eye out for him."

"Can you legally do that?" Tessa asked.

Shrugging, Cassie smoothed her hair back and tugged the rubber band from her wrist to secure the knotty mess. "I have no clue. But if he's trespassing on the property, that's all the guards need to know to have him escorted off. If he wants to play the poor-father card, I doubt he'll have a leg to stand on."

"After the race tomorrow, go on home." Tessa reached in the bag and offered Cassie another chocolate, but Cassie wasn't in the mood anymore. "Nash and I will make sure everything is handled and taken care of. Take the truck Nash brought, and he and I can take the trailer and other truck."

Cassie bit her lip when tears threatened. "I don't want him to ruin this, Tessa. We've worked too hard, come too far, and we're both retiring after this season. I can't let him destroy our dreams of going out on top."

Reaching between them to take Cassie's hand, Tessa smiled. "Derek won't destroy anything. You won't give him that power. He's a jerk and he'll probably be gone when we get back because you weren't falling all over yourself to take him back when he appeared on your doorstep."

"He's threatening to file for custody," Cassie whispered.

Tessa let out a string of words that would've made their mother's face turn red. "He's an ass, Cassie. No judge will let him take Emily."

"What about joint custody?"

With a shrug, Tessa shook her head. "Honestly, I don't know, but the man has been gone almost a year, so I would certainly hope no judge would allow someone so restless to help raise a child."

Cassie had the same thoughts, but life and the legal system weren't always fair.

Flinging herself onto the bed, Cassie crossed her arms over her head. "I just never thought I'd be in this situation, you know? I mean, I married Derek thinking we'd be together forever. Then when we had Emily I really thought my family was complete and we were happy. Derek leaving was a bomb I hadn't expected, but now that he's back, I don't want him. I feel nothing but anger and resentment."

Tessa lay on her back next to Cassie and sighed. "You know, between me, Dad, Grant, Linda and Ian, Derek doesn't stand a chance. There's no way we'd let him just take Emily without a fight. If the man wants to play daddy, he'll have to actually stick around and prove he can man up."

"I agree," Cassie told her, lacing her fingers behind her head and staring up at the ceiling. "I won't deny my daughter the chance of knowing her father if I truly believe he won't desert her in a year just when she's getting used to him. I will do everything in my power to protect her heart from him."

And wasn't that just the saddest statement? Protecting a little girl's heart from her own father. But Derek had given her little choice.

"So, you want to tell me what you and Ian are doing?"

Tessa asked. "Because I'm pretty sure the two of you are much more than a fling."

Cassie laughed. "Yeah, we're definitely much more than a fling."

"Who knew when you got locked in that attic the man of your dreams would come to your rescue?"

"Technically he didn't rescue me," Cassie clarified.

Tessa glanced over, patted Cassie's leg and smiled. "Oh, honey. He's rescued you—you just might not see it yet."

She was right. Ian had come along at a time in her life when the last thing she'd wanted was a man. But he'd shown her love, shown her daughter love. He'd shown her what true intimacy was all about. When she'd been sick he hadn't thought twice about taking Emily, even though he knew next to nothing about babies.

He made Cassie's life better.

There was no way that she could not fight for what they had. Maybe she should look into a riding school in California. With her income and her knowledge, she technically could start it anywhere.

She had to deal with Derek first; then she would figure out how being far away from her family would work.

Tessa's brows lifted. "I know that look," she said. "You're plotting something. Share or I'll take my chocolates back to my room."

"Just thinking of the future," Cassie replied with a smile. "Thinking of my school. I've already started putting the wheels in motion for Stony Ridge, but who's to say that's where it has to be?"

Tessa hugged her. "I was so afraid this is what you'd do. Damn, I'm going to miss you if you move."

"Don't go tearing up on me," Cassie ordered. "Ian hasn't asked me, but if he did, I can't say that I would tell him no. On the other hand, Grant has a home out in L.A., too, so I'm sure you'd spend time out there."

"It wouldn't be the same." Tessa sniffed, blinked back tears. "But I want you happy and this is truly the happiest I've seen you in your entire life. I'll support any decision you make."

Cassie reached out, grabbed Tessa's hand and settled in with the fact she'd move heaven and earth to be with Ian. And now she couldn't wait to get home to tell him just that.

Twenty

Ian had a wonderful surprise planned for Cassie. He couldn't wait for her to get home.

Not only had Tessa and Cassie taken the Belmont Stakes and the coveted Triple Crown, but Cassie was on her way back and Ian had to get the stage set. They had so much to celebrate.

Very few had ever taken home the Triple Crown title, and Tessa was the first female jockey to own the honor. The Barrington sisters had officially made history and Ian was so proud he'd been able to witness a small portion of their success. He hated he wasn't there in person, though.

Ian had opted to stay behind for two reasons. So they could both concentrate on their own work without distractions and to see if he could handle being without her.

He couldn't.

After a perfect morning in which Lily officially signed with his agency, he was now in town hitting up the quaint little florist, about to buy an exorbitant amount of flowers in a variety of colors and styles. He wanted her cottage to be drowning in bouquets for the evening he had planned. Not only because he had high hopes about their future, but because she deserved to be placed on a pedestal after such a milestone win.

He may have also had Linda's help in the matter of planning.

The days they'd been apart had been a smack of reality to the face. He didn't want to be without her, without Emily. He was ready to make a family with them.

He also realized that love and marriage—and fatherhood—weren't scary at all once you found the person who totally completed you.

This family had instantly been so welcoming, so loving, and Ian couldn't be happier. From Linda to sweet Emily, he was so overwhelmed by how easily they accepted him. And now Cassie was about to get the surprise of her life.

As Ian rounded the building that housed the flower shop, he smacked into someone…Derek. *Great.*

"You're still in town?" Ian asked, eyeing the man clutching a massive bouquet of roses.

Derek shielded his eyes from the warm afternoon sun. "I'm not leaving until I get what I want."

Becoming more irritated by the moment, and a tad amused, Ian crossed his arms over his chest. "That will be a while, considering what you want is mine."

"Yours? My family is not your property," Derek clarified.

"They're also not your family. Not anymore. Cassie made her choice."

"Did she? Because the Cassie I know loves family." Derek adjusted the flowers to his other hand and shifted beneath the awning of the flower shop to shield himself from the sun. "It means more to her than anything. Do you think she'd honestly choose some young guy who she just met over the father of her child? Because I can assure you, she'll put Emily's needs ahead of her own."

There was a ring of truth to Derek's words, but there was also no way Ian would show any emotion or allow this guy to step into the life he was trying to build.

"Don't blame me or Cassie because you realized too late that you made a mistake," Ian said, propping his hands on his hips and resisting the urge to take those flowers, throw them on the ground and crush them. "Cassie and I have something, and there's no way you're going to come charging in like you belong. You missed your chance."

Derek smiled. "I didn't miss anything. You see, no matter how much you hate me, I am Emily's father. She will want to know me and I will make damn sure my lawyer does everything he can to get my baby girl in my life. Now, if Cassie wants to come, too, that's her decision, but I'll fight dirty to get what I want. Considering the fact that you are a Hollywood playboy, combined with the perfectly timed image in the paper, I don't see how I can't use that against Cassie. Obviously she's eager to get any man's attention—"

All control snapped as Ian fisted Derek's shirt and slammed him against the old brick building. Petals flew everywhere as the bouquet also smacked against the wall.

"Listen here, you little prick." It was all Ian could do not to pummel the jerk. "I will not be bullied into giving up what I want, and Cassie will not be blackmailed, either. If you want to see your daughter, then go through your attorney the proper way, but don't you dare use your own child as a pawn. Only a sick ass would do that."

Stepping back, Ian jerked the bouquet from Derek's hand and threw it down on the sidewalk. He'd held back long enough and Ian knew full well whom that arrangement was meant for.

Ian issued one final warning through gritted teeth. "Stay away from me and mine."

As he walked away, he didn't go into the flower store as originally intended. He had some thinking to do.

No, he wouldn't be intimidated by some jerk who thought he could blackmail his way back into Cassie's life, but if Ian's presence was going to cause issues with custody of Emily, Ian knew he had a difficult decision to make.

As he headed back to his sporty rental car, the small box in his pocket felt heavier than ever.

Cassie had never been so eager to return from a race, especially one as important as this one.

They'd done it. The Barrington women had conquered the racing world and brought home the Triple Crown. Cassie was pretty sure she'd be smiling in her sleep for years to come. She and Tessa had worked so hard, prayed even harder, and all their endless hours and years of training had paid off.

But beyond the joy of the racing season coming to an amazing end, Cassie couldn't wait to celebrate with Emily and Ian and wanted to get Derek taken care of so he would leave her alone once and for all.

Because she'd gotten home later than intended, Linda had stayed in the cottage and put Emily to bed. Now Cassie was alone, her baby sleeping down the hall and unpacked bags still just inside the door where she'd dropped them.

She had to see Ian now. Too many days had passed since she'd seen him, touched him. Each day she was away from him she realized just how much she truly loved him.

A gentle tap on her front door had her jerking around. The glow of the porch light illuminated Ian's frame through the frosted glass. She'd know that build anywhere and a shiver of excitement crept over her at the thought of seeing him again. She hadn't realized she could miss someone so much.

But the second she flung the door open, ready to launch into his strong hold, she froze. Something was wrong. He wasn't smiling, wasn't even reaching for her. Actually, his hands were shoved in his pockets.

"What's wrong?" she asked, clutching the door frame.

Ian said nothing as his gaze moved over her. Something flashed through his eyes as he settled back on her face...regret?

"Ian?"

He stepped over the threshold, paused within a breath of her and then scooted around her. After closing the door behind her, she leaned against it, unsure of what to say or how to act.

Her eyes locked on to Ian's as silence quickly became the third party present. Moments ago she'd had nothing but hope filling her heart. Now fear had laid a heavy blanket over that hope.

"This is so much harder than I thought it would be," he whispered, his eyes glistening. "I had tonight planned so different."

"You're scaring me, Ian."

Wrapping her arms around her waist, Cassie rubbed her hands up and down her bare arms to ward off the chill.

"I love you, Cassie. I've never said that to another human being, not even my own parents." Ian stepped closer but didn't touch her. "Tonight I thought I would tell you I loved you, show you that I can't live without you and Emily, but I've thought about it all evening and came to the hardest decision of my life."

Cassie wasn't a fool. She knew exactly what he was

going to say. "How dare you," she whispered through tears clogging her throat. "You tell me you love me a breath before you're about to break things off? Because that's what this is, right?"

Ian ran a hand over his face. "Damn it, Cassie. I'm letting you go to make things easier. I can't keep you in my life, knowing I could be the one thing that stands between you and keeping custody of your daughter."

Realization quickly dawned on Cassie. "You bastard. You let Derek get to you, didn't you? I never took you for a coward, Ian."

"I'm not a coward, and if Emily weren't in the picture I would stay and fight for you…and I'd win. But Emily deserves a chance to know her father, and I can't stand the thought of you sharing custody or possibly losing because Derek is going to fight dirty. He said it himself. This way, with me gone, maybe you two can come to some sort of peaceful middle ground."

Torn between hurt, love and anger, Cassie tried to rein in her emotions. "You're leaving me because you're afraid. I understand that you didn't have a great childhood, which makes me respect you all the more for stepping up and loving Emily the way you have. But don't you dare leave now when things get tough. I thought you were more of a man than that."

He jerked as if she'd slapped him. "Trust me, Cass. In the long run, this is the best for Emily."

"What about me?" she cried. "I love my daughter and her needs will always come first, but you say you love me. So what about that? What about us?"

The glistening in his eyes intensified a second before a tear slid down his cheek. He didn't make a move to swipe it away and Cassie couldn't stop staring at the wet track.

Her heart literally ached for the man who was trying

to be strong and, in his own way, do the right thing. But damn it, she wanted more and she thought she'd found it with him.

As she stepped forward, Ian took a step back. And that lone action severed any thread of hope she had been holding on to.

"I'm barely hanging on here," he whispered. "You can't touch me. I have to be strong for both of us. Just think about what I said. You'll know that I'm right. There's no other way if you want to keep Emily. Derek won't play fair, and if I'm in your life, he'll use that against you."

He took in a deep, shuddering breath. "I want to be part of your life, Cass. I want to be part of Emily's. But it's because I want so much to be a part of your family that I must protect you both, and unfortunately, that means I need to step aside."

Cassie hated the emotions whirling about inside her. So much love for this man and so much hatred toward another. Damn Ian for being noble.

"If you're not staying to fight for me and with me, then leave." Blinking back tears and clenching her fists at her side to keep from wrapping her arms around him, Cassie held his gaze. "You've done what you came to do, so go."

Ian slid a hand from his pocket, clutched something and reached out to place it on the end table by the sofa. "What I came to do was quite the opposite," he told her as he took a step toward her. "But I want you to have that and remember that I do love you, Cassie. No matter what you think right now. I'll always love you."

Without touching her, without even a kiss goodbye, Ian stepped around her and quietly walked out of her life. Drawing in a shaky breath, she took a step toward the end table and saw a blue box. Her heart in her throat, Cassie reached for the box. Her hands shook because she knew exactly what would be beneath that velvety lid.

Lifting the lid with a slow creak, Cassie gasped. Three square-cut stones nestled perfectly in a pewter band had tears spilling down both cheeks. Cassie's hand came to her mouth to hold back the sob that threatened to escape.

Ian had put all of their birthstones in the ring...a ring he'd planned on giving her when he told her he loved her.

Unable to help herself, she pulled the band from the box and slid it on. A perfect fit—just like the man who had walked out the door moments ago.

As she studied the ring on her finger, Cassie knew there was no way she would go down without a fight. No way at all. Emily would come first, as always, but who said she couldn't have the man of her dreams *and* her family?

If Derek wanted to fight dirty, well, bring it on, because Cassie had just gotten a whole new level of motivation to fuel her fire. And there was no way in hell Derek would take her child or the dreams Cassie had for a future with Ian.

The depth of Ian's love was so far beyond what she'd dared to imagine. His strength as a man and father was exactly what she needed, wanted...deserved. She wouldn't let his sacrifice go to waste.

Twenty-One

Ian wasn't sure why he didn't book a trip somewhere exotic to just get away. He'd come back to L.A. after breaking things off with Cassie. Max had more than understood his need to leave, but his friend had also had some choice words for him regarding the stupidity of his decision.

Ian wished there'd been another way. He'd had many sleepless nights looking for another way to protect Cassie and Emily, but it was because he loved them so much—because they *were* his family—he knew he needed to remove himself from their lives.

The pain after he'd left was unlike anything he'd ever known. Sharp, piercing pain had settled into the void in his heart that Cassie and Emily had left. But he also knew, in the long run, this was the best for the ladies he'd quickly grown to love.

Now, back in his beachfront home, he saw Cassie and that precious baby. How had two females he'd known only a short time infiltrated every single corner of his life? There wasn't a spot in his house, his mind or his heart that they hadn't left their imprint on.

He'd been home almost a month, and in the phone calls and texts between Max and Lily, he knew the filming was nearing the end. He hadn't asked about Cassie.... He just couldn't. The thought of her possibly playing house with Derek to keep the peace for Emily nearly crippled him.

Ian sank down onto the sand and pulled his knees up to his chest. The orange glow from the sunset made for a beautiful backdrop and not for the first time was he elated to have all of this for his backyard.

But he'd give it up in a heartbeat for a chance at happiness with Cassie. Letting her go was hands down the hardest thing he'd ever done in his entire life.

He hadn't been lying when he'd said this decision was better for Emily in the long run. When he'd been younger he would've given anything for his parents to have stayed together. Perhaps his father would've been a little more relaxed and his mother not so much of a free spirit always seeking attention from men.

Ian couldn't alter Emily's future by coming between her parents. His broken heart was minor in comparison to their safety. All that mattered was that sweet Emily wasn't a pawn, that he gave her the best chance to know her father. A chance he'd never had.

Damn it, he loved that little girl. He missed those little fingers wrapped around his thumb as he gave her a nighttime bottle. He missed that little two-toothed grin she'd offer for no apparent reason.

He missed everything...even the diaper changes.

"Beautiful place you have here."

Ian jerked his head over his shoulder, his heart nearly

stopping at the sight of Cassie in a little green sundress, her hair whipping about her shoulders and Emily on her hip.

"I was just in the neighborhood and was curious if you had room for two more," she went on, not coming any closer.

In an instant, Ian was on his feet. "Room for two? Were you wanting to stay here?"

Cassie shrugged, her face tipped up to hold his gaze as he moved in closer. "Your house, your heart. Wherever you have room."

Ian's knees weakened. She'd come for him. When he'd thought they were finished, when he'd thought he'd done the right thing by setting her free, she'd come to him.

"I'll always have room in my heart for you and Emily." Ian reached out, slid a crimson curl behind her ear. "But my house? That depends on what's going on with you and Derek."

Cassie grabbed his hand before he could pull away from her. "Derek is being taken care of by my team of attorneys. I hired three to make sure he didn't blackmail me, you or use Emily as a bargaining chip. He's agreed to supervised visitation because Emily is young and would view him as a stranger. He's not allowed to take her from the state for any reason and I have approval over any and all visits."

Shocked, Ian merely stared. When Emily reached for him, his heart tumbled. Pulling her into his arms, he held her tight, breathing in her sweet scent.

"I've missed you," he whispered into her ear. Her little arms came around his neck and Ian had to physically fight back tears.

"We've missed *you*," Cassie told him. "But I had to make sure Derek was being handled before I could come to you."

Ian lifted his head, slid his arm around Cassie's waist

and pulled her against his side. This right here was worth everything. The heartache he'd felt, the worry, the sleepless nights.

"If you ever try to be noble again, I'll go to the press with horrid lies." Cassie smiled up at him. "I know why you left—I even admire your decision on some level—but being without you for weeks was a nightmare. I never want to be without you again."

Ian slid his lips over hers. "What about your family? What about the school?"

Reaching up to pat his cheek, Cassie smiled. "Emily and I are staying here for a while. As for the school, I'd really like to open it on the estate, but I'll move it to California if you're needed here."

Ian couldn't believe what he was hearing. She was willing to part with her life, live across the country from her family, her rock, all because of him.

"I'd never ask you to leave your family," he told her. "I actually want to be near them. What do you say we keep this home for our getaways and vacations? We can live on the estate or build nearby. The choice is totally up to you, but I want you to have the school at Stony Ridge."

Cassie's smile widened, those sparkling blue eyes glistening. "Sounds like a plan. Of course, we're missing something, you know."

Curious, Ian drew back slightly. "What's that?"

"Well, I've worn my ring since you left." She held up her left ring finger and the sight had his heart jumping. "I assumed that this ring had a question that went along with it. I mean, I'm assuming the man I've fallen in love with plans on carrying out his intentions."

Ian looked to Emily. "What do you think, sweetheart? Should I ask your mommy to marry me?"

Emily clapped her hands and grinned. "Mom-mom-mom."

Laughing, Ian glanced back to Cassie. So many emotions swam in her eyes. So much hope and love, and it was all for him.

"How did I get to be so lucky?" he murmured.

Shrugging, Cassie said, "I'd say fate has been pushing us together since the moment I fell into your arms."

Pulling her tighter against him, he held the two most precious ladies. "This right here, in my arms, is my world. Nothing will come between us again. Not an ex, not my tendency to be noble, nothing. You're mine, Cassie."

Easing back to look down into her eyes, Ian saw his entire future looking back at him. "Tell me you'll marry me. Tell me you'll let me be Em's dad. That you'll even teach me all about horses. I want to be part of everything in your life."

"I wouldn't have it any other way," she told him, wiping a lone tear that had slid down her cheek. "Besides, I still owe you that horseback ride you've never been on."

Ian laughed. "How about we lay Emily down for a nap and we'll discuss other plans for our family?"

The gleam in her eye told him she hadn't missed his hidden meaning. "*Our family.* Those are two of the most beautiful words I've ever heard."

He kissed her once again. "Then let's get started on building it."

* * * * *

Chadwick was sitting behind his desk.

Serena knew she shouldn't think of him as Chadwick—it was too familiar. Too personal. Mr Beaumont was her boss. She worked hard for him, pulling long hours whenever necessary.

It wasn't a secret that Serena would go to the ends of the earth for this man. It *was* a secret that she'd always done just a little more than admire his commitment to the company.

Chadwick Beaumont was an incredibly handsome man—a solid six-two, his sandy-blond hair neatly trimmed at all times. He would be one of those men who aged like a fine wine, only getting better with each passing year. Some days, Serena would catch herself staring as if she were trying to savor him.

But that secret admiration was buried deep.

She had an excellent job with benefits and she would never risk it by doing something as unprofessional as falling in love with her boss. They worked together. Their relationship was nothing but business-professional.

She had no idea how being pregnant was going to change things.

***

Not the Boss's Baby
is part of The Beaumont Heirs series:
One Colorado family, limitless scandal!

NOT THE
BOSS'S BABY

BY
SARAH M. ANDERSON

Published in Great Britain 2014
by Mills & Boon, an imprint of Harlequin (UK) Limited,
Eton House, 18-24 Paradise Road, Richmond, Surrey, TW9 1SR

© 2014 Sarah M. Anderson

ISBN: 978-0-263-91479-5

51-0914

Harlequin (UK) Limited's policy is to use papers that are natural, renewable and recyclable products and made from wood grown in sustainable forests. The logging and manufacturing processes conform to the legal environmental regulations of the country of origin.

Printed and bound in Spain
by Blackprint CPI, Barcelona

Award-winning author **Sarah M. Anderson** may live east of the Mississippi River, but her heart lies out west on the Great Plains. With a lifelong love of horses and two history teachers for parents, she had plenty of encouragement to learn everything she could about the tribes of the Great Plains.

When she started writing, it wasn't long before her characters found themselves out in South Dakota among the Lakota Sioux. She loves to put people from two different worlds into new situations and to see how their backgrounds and cultures take them someplace they never thought they'd go.

Sarah's book *A Man of Privilege* won the 2012 RT Reviewers' Choice Award for Best Mills & Boon® Desire™.

When not helping out at her son's school or walking her rescue dogs, Sarah spends her days having conversations with imaginary cowboys and American Indians, all of which is surprisingly well-tolerated by her wonderful husband. Readers can find out more about Sarah's love of cowboys and Indians at www.sarahmanderson.com.

To Leah Hanlin. We've been friends for over twenty years now, and I'm so glad I've been able to share this journey—and my covers!—with you.
Let's celebrate by getting more sleep!

One

"Ms. Chase, if you could join me in my office."

Serena startled at the sound of Mr. Beaumont's voice coming from the old-fashioned intercom on her desk. Blinking, she became aware of her surroundings.

How on earth had she gotten to work? She looked down—she was wearing a suit, though she had no memory of getting dressed. She touched her hair. All appeared to be normal. Everything was fine.

Except she was pregnant. Nothing fine or normal about *that*.

She was relatively sure it was Monday. She looked at the clock on her computer. Yes, nine in the morning—the normal time for her morning meeting with Chadwick Beaumont, President and CEO of the Beaumont Brewery. She'd been Mr. Beaumont's executive assistant for seven years now, after a yearlong internship and a year working in Human Resources. She could count the number

of times they'd missed their 9:00 a.m. Monday meeting on two hands.

No need to let something like a little accidental pregnancy interrupt that.

Okay, so everything had turned upside down this past weekend. She wasn't just a little tired or a tad stressed out. She wasn't fighting off a bug, even. She was, in all likelihood, two months and two or three weeks pregnant. She knew that with certainty because those were the last times she'd slept with Neil.

Neil. She had to tell him she was expecting. He had a right to know. God, she didn't want to see him again—to be rejected again. But this went way beyond what she wanted. What a huge mess.

"Ms. Chase? Is there a problem?" Mr. Beaumont's voice was strict but not harsh.

She clicked the intercom on. "No, Mr. Beaumont. Just a slight delay. I'll be right in."

She was at work. She had a job to do—a job she needed now more than ever.

Serena sent a short note to Neil informing him that she needed to talk to him, and then she gathered up her tablet and opened the door to Chadwick Beaumont's office. Chadwick was the fourth Beaumont to run the brewery, and it showed in his office. The room looked much as it might have back in the early 1940s, soon after Prohibition had ended, when Chadwick's grandfather John had built it. The walls were mahogany panels that had been oiled until they gleamed. A built-in bar with a huge mirror took up the whole interior wall. The exterior wall was lined with windows hung with heavy gray velvet drapes and crowned with elaborately hand-carved woodwork that told the story of the Beaumont Brewery.

The conference table had been custom-made to fit the

room—Serena had read that it was so large and so heavy that John Beaumont had to have the whole thing built in the office because there was no getting it through a doorway. Tucked in the far corner by a large coffee table was a grouping of two leather club chairs and a matching leather loveseat set. The coffee table was supposedly made of one of the original wagon wheels that Phillipe Beaumont had used when he'd crossed the Great Plains with a team of Percheron draft horses back in the 1880s on his way to settle in Denver and make beer.

Serena loved this room—the opulence, the history. Things she didn't have in her own life. The only changes that reflected the twenty-first century were a large flat-screen television that hung over the sitting area and the electronics on the desk, which had been made to match the conference table. A door on the other side of the desk, nearly hidden between the bar and a bookcase, led to a private bathroom. Serena knew that Chadwick had added a treadmill and a few other exercise machines, as well as a shower, to the bathroom, but only because she'd processed the orders. She'd never gone into Chadwick's personal space. Not once in seven years.

This room had always been a source of comfort to her—a counterpoint to the stark poverty that had marked her childhood. It represented everything she wanted—security, stability, *safety*. A goal to strive for. Through hard work, dedication and loyalty, she could have nice things, too. Maybe not this nice, but better than the shelters and rusted-out trailers in which she'd grown up.

Chadwick was sitting behind his desk, his eyes focused on his computer. Serena knew she shouldn't think of him as Chadwick—it was far too familiar. Too personal. Mr. Beaumont was her boss. He'd never made a move on her, never suggested that she "stay late" to work

on a project that didn't exist—never booked them on a weekend conference that didn't exist. She worked hard for him, pulling long hours whenever necessary. She did good work for him and he rewarded her. For a girl who'd lived on free school lunches, getting a ten-thousand-dollar bonus *and* an eight-percent-a-year raise, like she had at her last performance review, was a gift from heaven.

It wasn't a secret that Serena would go to the ends of the earth for this man. It *was* a secret that she'd always done just a little more than admire his commitment to the company. Chadwick Beaumont was an incredibly handsome man—a solid six-two, with sandy blond hair that was neatly trimmed at all times. He was probably going gray, but it didn't show with his coloring. He would be one of those men who aged like a fine wine, only getting better with each passing year. Some days, Serena would catch herself staring at him as if she were trying to savor him.

But that secret admiration was buried deep. She had an excellent job with benefits and she would never risk it by doing something as unprofessional as falling in love with her boss. She'd been with Neil for almost ten years. Chadwick had been married as well. They worked together. Their relationship was nothing but business-professional.

She had no idea how being pregnant was going to change things. If she'd needed this job—and health benefits—before, she needed them so much more now.

Serena took her normal seat in one of the two chairs set before Chadwick's desk and powered up her tablet. "Good morning, Mr. Beaumont." Oh, heavens—she'd forgotten to see if she'd put on make-up this morning in her panic-induced haze. At this point, she could only pray she didn't have raccoon eyes.

"Ms. Chase," Chadwick said by way of greeting, his

gaze flicking over her face. He looked back at his monitor, then paused. Serena barely had time to hold her breath before she had Chadwick Beaumont's undivided attention. "Are you okay?"

No. She'd never been less okay in her adult life. The only thing that was keeping her together was the realization that she'd been less okay as a kid and survived. She'd survive this.

She hoped.

So she squared her shoulders and tried to pull off her most pleasant smile. "I'm fine. Monday mornings, you know."

Chadwick's brow creased as he weighed this statement. "Are you sure?"

She didn't like to lie to him. She didn't like to lie to anyone. She had recently had her fill of lying, thanks to Neil. "It'll be fine."

She had to believe that. She'd pulled herself out of sheer poverty by dint of hard work. A bump in the road— a baby bump—wouldn't ruin everything. She hoped.

His hazel eyes refused to let her go for a long moment. But then he silently agreed to let it pass. "Very well, then. What's on tap this week, beyond the regular meetings?"

As always, she smiled at his joke. What was on tap was beer—literally and figuratively. As far as she knew, it was the only joke he ever told.

Chadwick had set appointments with his vice presidents, usually lunch meetings and the like. He was deeply involved in his company—a truly hands-on boss. Serena's job was making sure his irregular appointments didn't mess up his standing ones. "You have an appointment at ten with your lawyers on Tuesday to try and reach a settlement. I've moved your meeting with Matthew to later in the afternoon."

She carefully left out the facts that the lawyers were divorce attorneys and that the settlement was with his soon-to-be-ex-wife, Helen. The divorce had been dragging on for months now—over thirteen, by her count. She did not know the details. Who was to say what went on behind closed doors in any family? All she knew was that the whole process was wearing Chadwick down like waves eroding a beach—slowly but surely.

Chadwick's shoulders slumped a little and he exhaled with more force. "As if this meeting will go any differently than the last five did." But then he added, "What else?" in a forcefully bright tone.

Serena cleared her throat. That was, in a nutshell, the extent of the personal information they shared. "Wednesday at one is the meeting with the Board of Directors at the Hotel Monaco downtown." She cleared her throat. "To discuss the offer from AllBev. Your afternoon meeting with the production managers was cancelled. They're all going to send status reports instead."

Then she realized—she wasn't so much terrified about having a baby. It was the fact that because she was suddenly going to have a baby, there was a very good chance she could lose her job.

AllBev was an international conglomerate that specialized in beer manufacturers. They'd bought companies in England, South Africa and Australia, and now they had their sights set on Beaumont. They were well-known for dismantling the leadership, installing their own skeleton crew of managers, and wringing every last cent of profit out of the remaining workers.

Chadwick groaned and slumped back in his chair. "That's this week?"

"Yes, sir." He shot her a wounded look at the *sir*, so she corrected herself. "Yes, Mr. Beaumont. It got moved

up to accommodate Mr. Harper's schedule." In addition to owning one of the largest banks in Colorado, Leon Harper was also one of the board members pushing to accept AllBev's offer.

What if Chadwick agreed or the board overrode his wishes? What if Beaumont Brewery was sold? She'd be out of a job. There was no way AllBev's management would want to keep the former CEO's personal assistant. She'd be shown the door with nothing more than a salvaged copier-paper box of her belongings to symbolize her nine years there.

Maybe that wouldn't be the end of the world—she'd lived as frugally as she could, tucking almost half of each paycheck away in ultra-safe savings accounts and CDs. She couldn't go back on welfare. She *wouldn't*.

If she weren't pregnant, getting another job would be relatively easy. Chadwick would write her a glowing letter of recommendation. She was highly skilled. Even a temp job would be a job until she found another place like Beaumont Brewery.

Except...except for the benefits. She was pregnant. She *needed* affordable health insurance, and the brewery had some of the most generous health insurance around. She hadn't paid more than ten dollars to see a doctor in eight years.

But it was more than just keeping her costs low. She couldn't go back to the way things had been before she'd started working at the Beaumont Brewery. Feeling like her life was out of control again? Having people treat her like she was a lazy, ignorant leech on society again?

Raising a child the way she'd been raised, living on food pantry handouts and whatever Mom could scavenge from her shift at the diner? Of having social workers threaten to take her away from her parents unless they

could do better—*be* better? Of knowing she was always somehow less than the other kids at school but not knowing why—until the day when Missy Gurgin walked up to her in fourth grade and announced to the whole class that Serena was wearing the exact shirt, complete with stain, she'd thrown away because it was ruined?

Serena's lungs tried to clamp shut. *No,* she thought, forcing herself to breathe. It wasn't going to happen like that. She had enough to live on for a couple of years— longer if she moved into a smaller apartment and traded down to a cheaper car. Chadwick wouldn't allow the family business to be sold. He would protect the company. He would protect her.

"Harper. That old goat," Chadwick muttered, snapping Serena back to the present. "He's still grinding that ax about my father. The man never heard of letting bygones be bygones, I swear."

This was the first that Serena had heard about this. "Mr. Harper's out to get you?"

Chadwick waved his hand, dismissing the thought. "He's still trying to get even with Hardwick for sleeping with his wife, as the story goes, two days after Harper and his bride got back from their honeymoon." He looked at her again. "Are you sure you're all right? You look pale."

Pale was probably the best she could hope for today. "I...." She grasped at straws and came up with one. "I hadn't heard that story."

"Hardwick Beaumont was a cheating, lying, philandering, sexist bigot on his best day." Chadwick repeated all of this by rote, as if he'd had it beaten into his skull with a dull spoon. "I have no doubt that he did exactly that—or something very close to it. But it was forty years ago. Hardwick's been dead for almost ten years.

Harper…." He sighed, looking out the windows. In the distance, the Rocky Mountains gleamed in the spring sunlight. Snow capped off the mountains, but it hadn't made it down as far as Denver. "I just wish Harper would realize that I'm not Hardwick."

"I know you're not like that."

His eyes met hers. There was something different in them, something she didn't recognize. "Do you? Do you, really?"

This…this felt like dangerous territory.

She didn't know, actually. She had no idea if he was getting a divorce because he'd slept around on his wife. All she knew was that he'd never hit on her, not once. He treated her as an equal. He respected her.

"Yes," she replied, feeling certain. "I do."

The barest hint of a smile curved up one side of his lips. "Ah, that's what I've always admired about you, Serena. You see the very best in people. You make everyone around you better, just by being yourself."

Oh. *Oh.* Her cheeks warmed, although she wasn't sure if it was from the compliment or the way he said her name. He usually stuck to Ms. Chase.

Dangerous territory, indeed.

She needed to change the subject. *Now.* "Saturday night at nine you have the charity ball at the Denver Art Museum."

That didn't erase the half-cocked smile from his face, but it did earn her a raised eyebrow. Suddenly, Chadwick Beaumont looked anything but tired or worn-down. Suddenly, he looked hot. Well, he was always hot—but right now? It wasn't buried beneath layers of responsibility or worry.

Heat flushed Serena's face, but she wasn't entirely sure why one sincere compliment would have been enough to

set her all aflutter. Oh, that's right—she was pregnant. Maybe she was just having a hormonal moment.

"What's that for, again? A food bank?"

"Yes, the Rocky Mountain Food Bank. They were this year's chosen charity."

Every year, the Beaumont Brewery made a big splash by investing heavily in a local charity. One of Serena's job responsibilities was personally handling the small mountain of applications that came in every year. A Beaumont Brewery sponsorship was worth about $35 million in related funds and donations—that's why they chose a new charity every year. Most of the non-profits could operate for five to ten years with that kind of money.

Serena went on. "Your brother Matthew planned this event. It's the centerpiece of our fundraising efforts for the food bank. Your attendance will be greatly appreciated." She usually phrased it as a request, but Chadwick had never missed a gala. He understood that this was as much about promoting the Beaumont Brewery name as it was about promoting a charity.

Chadwick still had her in his sights. "You chose this one, didn't you?"

She swallowed. It was almost as if he had realized that the food bank had been an important part of her family's survival—that they would have starved if they hadn't gotten groceries and hot meals on a weekly basis. "Technically, I choose all the charities. It's my job."

"You do it well." But before the second compliment could register, he continued, "Will Neil be accompanying you?"

"Um...." She usually attended these events with Neil. He mostly went to hobnob with movers and shakers, but Serena loved getting all dressed up and drinking cham-

pagne. Things she'd never thought possible back when she was a girl.

Things were different now. So, *so* different. Suddenly, Serena's throat closed up on her. God, what a mess.

"No. He..." *Try not to cry, try not to cry.* "We mutually decided to end our relationship several months ago."

Chadwick's eyebrows jumped up so high they almost cleared his forehead. "Several *months* ago? Why didn't you tell me?"

Breathe in, breathe out. Don't forget to repeat.

"Mr. Beaumont, we usually do not discuss our personal lives at the office." It came out pretty well—fairly strong, her voice only cracking slightly over the word *personal*. "I didn't want you to think I couldn't handle myself."

She was his competent, reliable, loyal employee. If she'd told him that Neil had walked out after she'd confronted him about the text messages on his phone and demanded that he recommit to the relationship—by having a baby and finally getting married—well, she'd have been anything but competent. She might be able to manage Chadwick's office, but not her love life.

Chadwick gave her a look that she'd seen before— the one he broke out when he was rejecting a supplier's offer. A look that blended disbelief and disdain into a potent mix. It was a powerful look, one that usually made people throw out another offer—one with better terms for the Brewery.

He'd never looked at her like that before. It bordered on terrifying. He wouldn't fire her for keeping her private life private, would he? But then everything about him softened as he leaned forward in his chair, his elbows on the table. "If this happened several months ago, what happened this weekend?"

"I'm sorry?"

"This weekend. You're obviously upset. I can tell, although you're doing a good job of hiding it. Did he…" Chadwick cleared his throat, his eyes growing hard. "Did he do something to you this weekend?"

"No, not that." Neil might have been a jerk—okay, he *was* a cheating, commitment-phobic jerk—but she couldn't have Chadwick thinking Neil had beaten her. Still, she was afraid to elaborate. Swallowing was suddenly difficult and she was blinking at an unusually fast rate. If she sat there much longer, she was either going to burst into tears or black out. Why couldn't she get her lungs to work?

So she did the only thing she could. She stood and, as calmly and professionally as possible, walked out of the office. Or tried to, anyway. Her hand was on the doorknob when Chadwick said, "Serena, stop."

She couldn't bring herself to turn around and face him—to risk that disdainful look again, or something worse. So she closed her eyes. Which meant that she didn't see him get up or come around his desk, didn't see him walk up behind her. But she heard it—the creaking of his chair as he stood, the footsteps muffled by the thick Oriental rug. The warmth of his body as he stood close to her—much closer than he normally stood.

He placed his hand on her shoulder and turned her. She had no choice but to pivot, but he didn't let go of her. Not entirely. Oh, he released her shoulder, but when she didn't look up at him, he slid a single finger under her chin and raised her face. "Serena, look at me."

She didn't want to. Her face flushed hot from his touch—because that's what he was doing. *Touching* her. His finger slid up and down her chin—if she didn't know

better, she'd say he was caressing her. It was the most intimate touch she'd felt in months. Maybe longer.

She opened her eyes. His face was still a respectable foot away from hers—but this was the closest they'd ever been. He could kiss her if he wanted and she wouldn't be able to stop him. She *wouldn't* stop him.

He didn't. This close up, his eyes were such a fine blend of green and brown and flecks of gold. She felt some of her panic fade as she gazed up into his eyes. She was not in love with her boss. Nope. Never had been. Wasn't about to start falling for him now, no matter how he complimented her or touched her. It wasn't going to happen.

He licked his lips as he stared at her. Maybe he was as nervous as she was. This was several steps over a line neither of them had ever crossed.

But maybe…maybe he was hungry. Hungry for her.

"Serena," he said in a low voice that she wasn't sure she'd ever heard him use before. It sent a tingle down her back that turned into a shudder—a shudder he felt. The corner of his mouth curved again. "Whatever the problem is, you can come to me. If he's bothering you, I'll have it taken care of. If you need help or…" She saw his Adam's apple bob as he swallowed. His finger stroked the same square inch of her skin again and she did a whole lot more than shudder. "Whatever you need, it's yours."

She needed to say something here, something professional and competent. But all she could do was look at his lips. What would they taste like? Would he hesitate, waiting for her to take the lead, or would he kiss her as if he'd been dying to do for seven years?

"What do you mean?" She didn't know what she wanted him to say. It *should* sound like an employer expressing concern for the well-being of a trusted em-

ployee—but it didn't. Was he hitting on her after all this time? Just because Neil was a jerk? Because she was obviously having a vulnerable moment? Or was there something else going on there?

The air seemed to thin between them, as if he'd leaned forward without realizing it. Or perhaps she'd done the leaning. *He's going to kiss me,* she realized. *He's going to kiss me and I want him to. I've always wanted him to.*

He didn't. He just ran his finger over her chin again, as if he were memorizing her every feature. She wanted to reach up and thread her fingers through his sandy hair, pull his mouth down to hers. Taste those lips. Feel more than just his finger.

"Serena, you're my most trusted employee. You always have been. I want you to know that, whatever happens at the board meeting, I will take care of you. I won't let them walk you out of this building without anything. Your loyalty *will* be rewarded. I won't fail you."

All the oxygen she'd been holding in rushed out of her with a soft "*oh.*"

It was what she needed to hear. God, how she needed to hear it. She might not have Neil, but all of her hard work was worth something. She wouldn't have to think about going back on welfare or declaring bankruptcy or standing in line at the food pantry.

Then some of her good sense came back to her. This would be the time to have a business-professional response. "Thank you, Mr. Beaumont."

Something in his grin changed, making him look almost wicked—the very best kind of wicked. "Better than *sir*, but still. Call me Chadwick. Mr. Beaumont sounds too much like my father." When he said this, a hint of his former weariness crept into his eyes. Suddenly, he dropped his finger away from her chin and took a step

back. "So, lawyers on Tuesday, Board of Directors on Wednesday, charity ball on Saturday?"

Somehow, Serena managed to nod. They were back on familiar footing now. "Yes." She took another deep breath, feeling calmer.

"I'll pick you up."

So much for that feeling of calm. "Excuse me?"

A little of the wickedness crept back into his smile. "I'm going to the charity gala. You're going to the charity gala. It makes sense that we would go to the charity gala together. I'll pick you up at seven."

"But...the gala starts at nine."

"Obviously we'll go to dinner." She must have looked worried because he took another step back. "Call it...an early celebration for the success of your charity selection this year."

In other words, don't call it a date. Even if that's what it sounded like. "Yes, Mr. Beau—" He shot her a hot look that had her snapping her mouth shut. "Yes, Chadwick."

He grinned an honest-to-God grin that took fifteen years off his face. "There. That wasn't so hard, was it?" Then he turned away from her and headed back to his desk. Whatever moment they'd just had, it was over. "Bob Larsen should be in at ten. Let me know when he gets here."

"Of course." She couldn't bring herself to say his name again. Her head was too busy swimming with everything that had just happened.

She was halfway through the door, already pulling it shut behind her, when he called out, "And Serena? Whatever you need. I mean it."

"Yes, Chadwick."

Then she closed his door.

Two

This was the point in his morning where Chadwick normally reviewed the marketing numbers. Bob Larsen was his handpicked Vice President of Marketing. He'd helped move the company's brand recognition way, way up. Although Bob was closing in on fifty, he had an intrinsic understanding of the internet and social media, and had used it to drag the brewery into the twenty-first century. He'd put Beaumont Brewery on Facebook, then Twitter—never chasing the trend, but leading it. Chadwick wasn't sure exactly what SnappShot did, beyond make pictures look scratched and grainy, but Bob was convinced that it was the platform through which to launch their new line of Percheron Seasonal Ales. "Targeting all those foodies who snap shots of their dinners!" he'd said the week before, in the excited voice of a kid getting a new bike for Christmas.

Yes, that's what Chadwick *should* have been thinking

about. He took his meetings with his department heads seriously. He took the whole company seriously. He rewarded hard work and loyalty and never, ever allowed distractions. He ran a damn tight ship.

So why was he sitting there, thinking about his assistant?

Because he was. Man, was he.

Several months.

Her words kept rattling around in his brain, along with the way she'd looked that morning—drawn, tired. Like a woman who'd cried her eyes out most of the weekend. She hadn't answered his question. If that prick had walked out several months before—and no matter what she said about what 'we decided,' Chadwick had heard the 'he' first—what had happened that weekend?

The thought of Neil Moore—mediocre golf pro always trying to suck up to the next big thing every time Chadwick had met him—doing anything to hurt Serena made him furious. He'd never liked Neil. Too much of a leech, not good enough for the likes of Serena Chase. Chadwick had always been of the opinion that she deserved someone better, someone who wouldn't abandon her at a party to schmooze a local TV personality like he'd witnessed Neil do on at least three separate occasions.

Serena deserved so much better than that ass. Of course, Chadwick had known that for years. Why was it bothering him so much this morning?

She'd looked so...different. Upset, yes, but there was something else going on. Serena had always been unflappable, totally focused on the job. Of course Chadwick had never done anything inappropriate involving her, but he'd caught a few other men assuming she was up for grabs just because she was a woman in Hardwick Beaumont's old office. Chadwick had never done busi-

ness with those men again—which, a few times, meant going with the higher-priced vendor. It went against the principles his father, Hardwick, had raised him by—the bottom line was the most important thing.

Hardwick might have been a lying, cheating bastard, but that wasn't Chadwick. And Serena knew it. She'd said so herself.

That had to be why Chadwick had lost his mind and done something he'd managed not to do for eight years— touch Serena. Oh, he'd touched her before. She had a hell of a handshake, one that betrayed no weakness or fear, something that occasionally undermined other women in a position of power. But putting his hand on her shoulder? Running a finger along the sensitive skin under her chin? Hell.

For a moment, he'd done something he'd wanted to do for years—engage Serena Chase on a level that went far beyond his scheduling conflicts. And for that moment, it'd felt wonderful to see her dark brown eyes look up at him, her pupils dilating with need—reflecting his desire back at him. To feel her body respond to his touch.

Some days, it felt like he never got to do what he wanted. Chadwick was the responsible one. The one who ran the family company and cleaned up the family messes and paid the family bills while everyone else in the family ran amuck, having affairs and one-night stands and spending money like it was going out of style.

Just that weekend his brother Phillip had bought some horse for a million dollars. And what did his little brother do to pay for it? He went to company-sponsored parties and drank Beaumont Beer. That was the extent of Phillip's involvement in the company. Phillip always did exactly what he wanted without a single thought for how

it might affect other people—for how it might affect the brewery.

Not Chadwick. He'd been born to run this company. It wasn't a joke—Hardwick Beaumont had called a press conference in the hospital and held the newborn Chadwick up, red-faced and screaming, to proclaim him the future of Beaumont Brewery. Chadwick had the newspaper articles to prove it.

He'd done a good job—so good, in fact, that the Brewery had become the target for takeovers and mergers by conglomerates who didn't give a damn for beer or for the Beaumont name. They just wanted to boost their companies' bottom lines with Beaumont's profits.

Just once, he'd done something he wanted. Not what his father expected or the investors demanded or Wall Street projected—what *he* wanted. Serena had been upset. He'd wanted to comfort her. At heart, it wasn't a bad thing.

But then he'd remembered his father. And that Chadwick seducing his assistant was no better than Hardwick Beaumont seducing his secretary. So he'd stopped. Chadwick Beaumont was responsible, focused, driven, and in no way controlled by his baser animal instincts. He was better than that. He was better than his father.

Chadwick had been faithful while married. Serena had been with—well, he'd never been sure if Neil was her husband, live-in lover, boyfriend, significant other, life partner—whatever people called it these days. Plus, she'd worked for Chadwick. That had always held him back because he was not the apple that had fallen from Hardwick's tree, by God.

All of these correct thoughts did not explain why Chadwick's finger was hovering over the intercom button, ready to call Serena back into the office and ask her

again what had happened this weekend. Selfishly, he almost wanted her to break down and cry on his shoulder, just so he could hold her.

Chadwick forced himself to turn back to his monitor and call up the latest figures. Bob had emailed him the analytics Sunday night. Chadwick hated wasting time having something he could easily read explained to him. He was no idiot. Just because he didn't understand *why* anyone would take pictures of their dinner and post them online didn't mean he couldn't see the user habits shifting, just as Bob said they would.

This was better, he thought, as he looked over the numbers. Work. Work was good. It kept him focused. Like telling Serena he was taking her to the gala—a work function. They'd been at galas and banquets like that before. What difference did it make if they arrived in the same car or not? It didn't. It was business related. Nothing personal.

Except it was personal and he knew it. Picking her up in his car, taking her out to dinner? Not business. Even if they discussed business things, it still wouldn't be the same as dinner with, say, Bob Larsen. Serena usually wore a black silk gown with a bit of a fishtail hem and a sweetheart neckline to these things. Chadwick didn't care that it was always the same gown. She looked fabulous in it, a pashmina shawl draped over her otherwise bare shoulders, a small string of pearls resting against her collarbone, her thick brown hair swept up into an artful twist.

No, dinner would not be business-related. Not even close.

He wouldn't push her, he decided. It was the only compromise he could make with himself. He wasn't like his father, who'd had no qualms about making his secretar-

ies' jobs contingent upon sex. He wasn't about to trap Serena into doing anything either of them would regret. He would take her to dinner and then the gala, and would do nothing more than enjoy her company. That was that. He could restrain himself just fine. He'd had years of practice, after all.

Thankfully, the intercom buzzed and Serena's normal, level voice announced that Bob was there. "Send him in," Chadwick replied, thankful to have a distraction from his own thoughts.

He had to fight to keep his company. He had no illusions that the board meeting on Wednesday would go well. He was in danger of becoming the Beaumont who lost the brewery—of failing at the one thing he'd been raised to do.

He did not have time to be distracted by Serena Chase. And that was final.

The rest of Monday passed without a reply from Neil. Serena was positive about this because she refreshed her email approximately every other minute. Tuesday started much the same. She had her morning meeting with Chadwick where, apart from when he asked her if everything was all right, nothing out of the ordinary happened. No lingering glances, no hot touches and absolutely no near-miss kisses. Chadwick was his regular self, so Serena made sure to be as normal as she could be.

Not to say it wasn't a challenge. Maybe she'd imagined the whole thing. She could blame a lot on hormones now, right? So Chadwick had stepped out of his prescribed role for a moment. She was the one who'd been upset. She must have misunderstood his intent, that's all.

Which left her more depressed than she expected. It's not like she *wanted* Chadwick to make a pass at her. An

intra-office relationship was against company policy—
she knew because she'd helped Chadwick rewrite the
policy when he first hired her. Flings between bosses and
employees set the company up for sexual harassment law-
suits when everything went south—which it usually did.

But that didn't explain why, as she watched him walk
out of the office on his way to meet with the divorce lawyers with his ready-for-battle look firmly in place, she
wished his divorce would be final. Just because the process was draining him, that's all.

Sigh. She didn't believe herself. How could she con-
vince anyone else?

She turned her attention to the last-minute plans for
the gala. After Chadwick returned to the office, he'd
meet with his brother Matthew, who was technically in
charge of planning the event. But a gala for five hundred
of the richest people in Denver? It was all hands on deck.

The checklist was huge, and it required her full attention. She called suppliers, tracked shipments and checked
the guest list.

She ate lunch at her desk as she followed up on her
contacts in the local media. The press was a huge part of
why charities competed for the Beaumont sponsorship.
Few of these organizations had an advertising budget.
Beaumont Brewery put their name front and center for
a year, getting television coverage, interviews and even
fashion bloggers.

She had finished her yogurt and wiped down her desk
by the time Chadwick came back. He looked *terrible*—
head down, hands jammed into his pockets, shoulders
slumped. Oh, no. She didn't even have to ask to know
that the meeting had not gone according to plan.

He paused in front of her desk. The effort to raise his
head and meet her eyes seemed to take a lot out of him.

Serena gasped in surprise at how *lost* he looked. His eyes were rimmed in red, like he hadn't slept in days.

She wanted to go to him—put her arms around him and tell him it'd all work out. That's what her mom had always done when things didn't pan out, when Dad lost his job or they had to move again because they couldn't make the rent.

The only problem was, she'd never believed it when she was a kid. And now, as an adult with a failed long-term relationship under her belt and a baby on the way?

No, she wouldn't believe it either.

God, the raw pain in his eyes was like a slap in the face. She didn't know what to do, what to say. Maybe she should just do nothing. To try and comfort him might be to cross the line they'd crossed on Monday.

Chadwick gave a little nod with his head, as if he were agreeing they shouldn't cross that line again. Then he dropped his head, muttered, "Hold my calls," and trudged into his office.

Defeated. That's what he was. *Beaten.* Seeing him like that was unnerving—and that was being generous. Chadwick Beaumont did not lose in the business world. He didn't always get every single thing he wanted, but he never walked away from a negotiation, a press conference—anything—looking like he'd lost the battle *and* the war.

She sat at her desk for a moment, too stunned to do much of anything. What had happened? What on earth would leave him that crushed?

Maybe it was the hormones. Maybe it was employee loyalty. Maybe it was something else. Whatever it was, she found herself on her feet and walking into his office without even knocking.

Chadwick was sitting at his desk. He had his head

in his hands as if they were the only things supporting his entire weight. He'd shed his suit coat, and he looked smaller for having done it.

When she shut the door behind her, he started talking but he didn't lift his head. "She won't sign off on it. She wants more money. Everything is finalized except how much alimony she gets."

"How much does she want?" Serena had no business asking, but she did anyway.

"Two hundred and fifty." The way he said it was like Serena was pulling an arrow out of his back.

She blinked at him. "Two hundred and fifty dollars?" She knew that wasn't the right answer. Chadwick could afford that. But the only other option was…

"Thousand. Two hundred and fifty thousand dollars."

"A year?"

"A month. She wants three million a year. For the rest of her life. Or she won't sign."

"But that's—that's insane! No one needs that much to live!" The words burst out of her a bit louder than she meant them to, but seriously? Three million dollars a year forever? Serena wouldn't earn that much in her entire lifetime!

Chadwick looked up, a mean smile on his face. "It's not about the money. She just wants to ruin me. If I could pay that much until the end of time, she'd double her request. Triple it, if she thought it would hurt me."

"But why?"

"I don't know. I never cheated on her, never did anything to hurt her. I tried…" His words trailed off as he buried his face in his hands.

"Can't you just buy her out? Make her an up-front offer she can't refuse?" Serena had seen him do that before, with a micro-brew whose beers were undercutting

Beaumont's Percheron Drafts line of beers. Chadwick had let negotiations drag on for almost a week, wearing down the competitors. Then he walked in with a lump sum that no sane person would walk away from, no matter how much they cared about the "integrity" of their beer. Everyone had a price, after all.

"I don't have a hundred million lying around. It's tied up in investments, property…the horses." He said this last bit with an edge, as if the company mascots, the Percherons, were just a thorn in his side.

"But—you have a pre-nup, right?"

"Of *course* I have a pre-nup," he snapped. She flinched, but he immediately sagged in defeat again. "I watched my father get married and divorced four times before he died. There's no way I wouldn't have a pre-nup."

"Then how can she do that?"

"Because." He grabbed at his short hair and pulled. "Because I was stupid and thought I was in love. I thought I had to prove to her that I trusted her. That I wasn't my father. She gets half of what I earned during our marriage. That's about twenty-eight million. She can't touch the family fortune or any of the property—none of that. But…"

Serena felt the blood drain from her face. "Twenty-eight *million*?" That was the kind of money people in her world only got when they won the lottery. "But?"

"My lawyers had put in a clause limiting how much alimony would be paid, for how long. The length of the marriage, fifty thousand a month. And I told them to take it out. Because I wouldn't need it. Like an idiot." That last bit came out so harshly—he really did believe that this was his fault.

She did some quick math. Chadwick had gotten mar-

ried near the end of her first year at Beaumont Brewery—
her internship year. The wedding had been a big thing,
obviously, and the brewery had even come out with a
limited-edition beer to mark the occasion.

That was slightly more than eight years ago. Fifty
thousand—still an absolutely insane number—times
twelve months times eight years was...*only* $4.8 mil-
lion. And somehow, that and another $28 million wasn't
enough. "Isn't there...anything you can do?"

"I offered her one fifty a month for twenty years. She
laughed. *Laughed*." Serena knew the raw desperation
in his voice.

Oh, sure, she'd never been in the position of losing a
fortune, but there'd been plenty of desperate times back
when she was growing up.

Back then, she'd just wanted to know it was going
to be okay. They'd have a safe place to sleep and a big
meal to eat. To know she'd have both of those things the
next day, too.

She never got those assurances. Her mother would
hum "One Day At a Time" over and over when they had
to stuff their meager things into grocery bags and move
again. Then they finally got the little trailer and didn't
have to move any more—but didn't have enough to pay
for both electricity and water.

One day at a time was a damn fine sentiment, but it
didn't put food on the table and clothes on her back.

There had to be a way to appease Chadwick's ex, but
Serena had no idea what it was. Such battles were beyond
her. She might have worked for Chadwick Beaumont for
over seven years, might have spent her days in this office,
might have attended balls and galas, but this was not her
world. She didn't know what to say about someone who
wasn't happy with *just* $32.8 million.

But she could sympathize with staring at a bill that could never be paid—a bill that, no matter how hard your mom worked as a waitress at the diner or how many overtime shifts as a janitor your dad pulled, would never, ever end. Not even when her parents had filed for bankruptcy had it truly ended, because whatever little credit they'd been able to use as a cushion disappeared. She loved her parents—and they loved each other—but the sinking hopelessness that went with never having enough...

That's not how she was going to live. She didn't wish it on anyone, but especially not on Chadwick.

She moved before she was aware of it, her steps muffled by the carpeting. She knew it would be a lie, but all she had to offer were platitudes that tomorrow was a new day.

She didn't hesitate when she got to the desk. In all of the time she'd spent in this office, she'd never once crossed the plane of the desk. She'd sat in front of the massive piece of furniture, but she'd never gone around it.

Today she did. Maybe it was the hormones again, maybe it was the way Chadwick had spoken to her yesterday in that low voice—promising to take care of her.

She saw the tension ripple through his back as she stepped closer. The day before, she'd been upset and he'd touched her. Today, the roles were reversed.

She put her hand on his shoulder. Through the shirt, she felt the warmth of his body. That's all. She didn't even try to turn him as he'd turned her. She just let him know she was there.

He shifted and, pulling his opposite hand away from his face, reached back to grab hers. Yesterday, he'd had all the control. But today? Today she felt they were on equal footing.

She laced their fingers together, but that was as far as

it went. She couldn't make the same kinds of promises he had—she couldn't take care of him when she wasn't even sure how she was going to take care of her baby. But she could let him know she was there, if he needed her.

She chose not to think about exactly what *that* might mean.

"Serena," Chadwick said, his voice raw as his fingers tightened around hers.

She swallowed. But before she could come up with a response, there was a knock on the door and in walked Matthew Beaumont, Vice President of Public Relations for the Beaumont Brewery. He looked a little like Chadwick—commanding build, the Beaumont nose— but where Chadwick and Phillip were lighter, sandier blondes, Matthew had more auburn coloring.

Serena tried to pull her hand free, but Chadwick wouldn't let her go. It was almost as if he wanted Matthew to see them touching. Holding hands.

It was one thing to stick a toe over the business-professional line when it was just her and Chadwick in the office—no witnesses meant it hadn't really happened, right? But Matthew was no idiot.

"Am I interrupting?" Matthew asked, his eyes darting between Serena's face, Chadwick's face, and their interlaced hands.

Of course, Serena would rather take her chances with Matthew than with Phillip Beaumont. Phillip was a professional playboy who flaunted his wealth and went to a lot of parties. As far as Serena could tell, Phillip might be the kind of guy who wouldn't have stopped at a simple touch the day before. Of course, with his gorgeous looks, he probably had plenty of invitations to keep going.

Matthew was radically different from either of his brothers. Serena guessed that was because his mother

was Hardwick's second wife, but Matthew was always working hard, as if he were trying to prove he belonged at the brewery. But he did so without the intimidation that Chadwick could wear like a second skin.

With a quick squeeze, Chadwick released her hand and she took a small step back. "No," Chadwick said. "We're done here."

For some inexplicable reason, the words hurt. She didn't know why. She had no good reason for him to defend their touch to his half brother. She had absolutely no reason why she would want Chadwick to defend their relationship—because they didn't have one outside of boss and trusted employee.

She gave a small nod of her head that she wasn't sure either of them saw, and walked out of his office.

Minutes passed. Chadwick knew that Matthew was sitting on the other side of the desk, no doubt waiting for something, but he wasn't up for that just yet.

Helen was out to ruin him. If he knew why, he'd try to make it up to her. But hadn't that pretty much described their marriage? She got her nose bent out of shape, Chadwick had no idea why, but he did his damnedest to make it up to her? He bought her diamonds. She liked diamonds. Then he added rubies to the mix. He'd thought it made things better.

It hadn't. And he was more the fool for thinking it had.

He replayed the conversation with Serena. He hadn't talked much about his divorce to anyone, beyond informing his brothers that it was a problem that would be taking up some measure of his time. He didn't know why he'd told Serena it was his fault that negotiations had gotten to this point.

All he knew was that he'd had to tell someone. The

burden of knowing that this whole thing was a problem he'd created all by himself was more than he could bear.

And she'd touched him. Not like he'd touched her, no, but not like she'd ever touched him before. More than a handshake, that was for damn sure.

When was the last time a woman had touched him aside from the business handshakes that went with the job? Helen had moved out of the master bedroom almost two years before. Not since before then, if he was being honest with himself.

Matthew cleared his throat, which made Chadwick look up. "Yes?"

"If I thought you were anything like our father," Matthew began, his voice walking the fine line between sympathetic and snarky, "I'd assume you were working on wife number two."

Chadwick glared at the man. Matthew was only six months younger than Chadwick's younger brother, Phillip. It had taken several more years before Hardwick's and Eliza's marriage had crumbled, and Hardwick had married Matthew's mother, Jeannie, but once Chadwick's mother knew about Jeannie, the end was just a matter of time.

Matthew was living proof that Hardwick Beaumont had been working on wife number two long before he'd left wife number one.

"I haven't gotten rid of wife number one yet." Even as he said it, though, Chadwick flinched. That was something his father would have said. He detested sounding like his father. He detested *being* like his father.

"Which only goes to illustrate how you are *not* like our father," Matthew replied with an easy-going grin, the same grin that all the Beaumont men had. A lingering

gift from their father. "Hardwick wouldn't have cared. Marriage vows meant nothing to him."

Chadwick nodded. Matthew spoke the truth and Chadwick should have taken comfort in that. Funny how he didn't.

"I take it Helen is not going quietly into the night?"

Chadwick hated his half brother right then. True, Phillip—Chadwick's full brother, the only person who knew what it was like to have both Hardwick and Eliza Beaumont as parents—wouldn't have understood either. But Chadwick hated sitting across from the living symbol of his father's betrayal of both his wife and his family.

It was a damn shame that Matthew had such a good head for public relations. Any other half relative would have found himself on the street long ago, and then Chadwick wouldn't have had to face his father's failings as a man and a husband on a daily basis.

He wouldn't have had to face his own failings on a daily basis.

"Buy her out," Matthew said simply.

"She doesn't want money. She wants to hurt me." There had to be something wrong with him, he decided. Since when did he air his dirty laundry to anyone—including his executive assistant, including his half brother?

He didn't. His personal affairs were just that, personal.

Matthew's face darkened. "Everyone has a price, Chadwick." Then, in an even quieter voice, he added, "Even you."

He knew what that was about. The whole company was on pins and needles about AllBev's buyout offer. "I'm *not* going to sell our company tomorrow."

Matthew met his stare head-on. Matthew didn't flinch. Didn't even blink. "You're not the only one with a price, you know. Everyone on that board has a price, too—and

probably a far sight less than yours." Matthew paused, looking down at his tablet. "Anyone else would have already made the deal. Why you've stuck by the family name for this long has always escaped me."

"Because, unlike *some* people, it's the only name I've ever had."

Everything about Matthew's face shut down, which made Chadwick feel like an even bigger ass. He remembered his parents' divorce, remembered Hardwick marrying Jeannie Billings—remembered the day Matthew, practically the same age as Phillip, had come to live with them. He'd been Matthew Billings until he was five. Then, suddenly, he was Matthew Beaumont.

Chadwick had tortured him mercilessly. It was Matthew's fault that Eliza and Hardwick had fallen apart. It was Matthew's fault that Chadwick's mom had left. Matthew's fault that Hardwick had kept custody of both Chadwick and Phillip. And it was most certainly Matthew's fault that Hardwick suddenly hadn't had any time for Chadwick—except to yell at him for not getting things right.

But that was a child's cop-out and he knew it. Matthew had been just a kid. As had Phillip. As had Chadwick. Hardwick—it had been all *his* fault that Eliza had hated him, had grown to hate her children.

"I'm...that was uncalled for." Nearly a lifetime of blaming Matthew had made it damn hard to apologize to the man. So he changed the subject. "Everything ready for the gala?"

Matthew gave him a look Chadwick couldn't quite make out. It was almost as if Matthew was going to challenge him to an old-fashioned duel over honor, right here in the office.

But the moment passed. "We're ready. As usual, Ms.

Chase has proven to be worth far more than her weight in gold."

As Matthew talked, that phrase echoed in Chadwick's head.

Everyone did have a price, he realized.

Even Helen Beaumont. Even Serena Chase.

He just didn't know what that price was.

Three

"The Beaumont Brewery has been run by a Beaumont for one hundred and thirty-three years," Chadwick thundered, smacking the tabletop with his hand to emphasize his point.

Serena jumped at the sudden noise. Chadwick didn't normally get this worked up at board meetings. Then again, he'd been more agitated—more abnormal—this entire week. Her hormones might be off, but he wasn't behaving in a typical fashion, either.

"The Beaumont name is worth more than $52 dollars a share," Chadwick went on. "It's worth more than $62 a share. We've got one of the last family-owned, family-operated breweries left in America. We have the pleasure of working for a piece of American history. The Percherons? The beer? That's the result of hard American work."

There was an unsettled pause as Serena took notes. Of

course there was a secretary at the meeting, but Chadwick liked to have a separate version against which he could cross-check the minutes.

She glanced up from her seat off to the side of the hotel ballroom. The Beaumont family owned fifty-one percent of the Beaumont Brewery. They'd kept a firm hand on the business for, well, forever—easily fending off hostile takeovers and not-so-hostile mergers. Chadwick was in charge, though. The rest of the Beaumonts just collected checks like any other stockholders.

She could see that some people were really listening to Chadwick—nodding in agreement, whispering to their neighbors. This meeting wasn't a full shareholders' meeting, so only about twenty people were in the room. Some of them were holdovers from Hardwick's era—handpicked back in the day. They didn't have much power beyond their vote, but they were fiercely loyal to the company.

Those were the people nodding now—the ones who had a personal stake in the company's version of American history.

There were some members—younger, more corporate types that had been brought in to provide balance against the old-boys board of Hardwick's era. Chadwick had selected a few of them, but they weren't the loyal employees that worked with him on a day-to-day basis.

Then there were the others—members brought in by other members. Those, like Harper and his two protégées, had absolutely no interest in Beaumont beer, and they did nothing to hide it.

It was Harper who broke the tense silence. "Odd, Mr. Beaumont. In my version of the American dream, hard work is rewarded with money. The buyout will make you a billionaire. Isn't that the American dream?"

Other heads—the younger ones—nodded in agreement.

Serena could see Chadwick struggling to control his emotions. It hurt to watch. He was normally above this, normally so much more intimidating. But after the week he'd had, she couldn't blame him for looking like he wanted to personally wring Harper's neck. Harper owned almost ten percent of this company, though. Strangling him would be frowned upon.

"The Beaumont Brewery has already provided for my needs," he said, his voice tight. "It's my duty to my company, my *employees*...." At this, he glanced up. His gaze met Serena's, sending a heated charge between them.

Her. He was talking about her.

Chadwick went on, "It's my duty to make sure that the people who *choose* to work for Beaumont Brewery also get to realize the American dream. Some in management will get to cash out their stock options. They'll get a couple of thousand, maybe. Not enough to retire on. But the rest? The men and women who actually make this company work? They won't. AllBev will walk in, fire them all, and reduce our proud history to nothing more than a brand name. No matter how you look at it, Mr. Harper, that's not the American dream. I take care of those who work for me. I reward loyalty. I do not dump it by the side of the road the moment it becomes slightly inconvenient. I cannot be bought off at the expense of those who willingly give me their time and energy. I expect nothing less from this board."

Then, abruptly, he sat. Head up, shoulders back, he didn't look like a man who had just lost. If anything, he looked like a man ready to take all comers. Chadwick had never struck her as a physical force to be reckoned with—but right now? Yeah, he looked like he could fight for his company. To the death.

The room broke out into a cacophony of arguments—the old guard arguing with the new guard, both arguing with Harper's faction. After about fifteen minutes, Harper demanded they call a vote.

For a moment, Serena thought Chadwick had won. Only four people voted to accept AllBev's offer of $52 a share. A clear defeat. Serena breathed a sigh of relief. At least something this week was going right. Her job was safe—which meant her future was safe. She could keep working for Chadwick. Things could continue just as they were. There was comfort in the familiar, and she clung to it.

But then Harper called a second vote. "What should our counteroffer be? I believe Mr. Beaumont said $62 a share wasn't enough. Shall we put $65 to a vote?"

Chadwick jolted in his seat, looking far more than murderous. They voted.

Thirteen people voted for the counteroffer of $65 a share. Chadwick looked as if someone had stabbed him in the gut. It hurt to see him look so hollow—to know this was another fight he was losing, on top of the fight with Helen.

She felt nauseous, and she was pretty sure it had nothing to do with morning sickness. Surely AllBev wouldn't want to spend that much on the brewery, Serena hoped as she wrote everything down. Maybe they'd look for a cheaper, easier target.

Everything Chadwick had spoken of—taking care of his workers, helping them all, not just the privileged few, reach for the American dream—that was why she worked for him. He had given her a chance to earn her way out of abject poverty. Because of him, she had a chance to raise her baby in better circumstances than those in which she'd been raised.

All of that could be taken away from her because Mr. Harper was grinding a forty-year-old ax.

It wasn't fair. She didn't know when she'd started to think that life was fair—it certainly hadn't been during her childhood. But the rules of Beaumont Brewery had been more than fair. Work hard, get promoted, get benefits. Work harder, get a raise, get out of a cube and into an office. Work even harder, get a big bonus. Get to go to galas. Get to dream about retirement plans.

Get to feel secure.

All of that was for sale at $65 a share.

The meeting broke up, everyone going off with their respective cliques. A few of the old-timers came up to Chadwick and appeared to offer their support. Or their condolences. She couldn't tell from her unobtrusive spot off to the side.

Chadwick stood stiffly and, eyes facing forward, stalked out of the room. Serena quickly gathered her things and went after him. He seemed to be in such a fog that she didn't want him to accidentally leave her behind.

She didn't need to worry. Chadwick was standing just outside the ballroom doors, still staring straight ahead.

She needed to get him out of there. If he was going to have another moment like he'd had yesterday—a moment when his self-control slipped, a moment where he would allow himself to be lost—by no means should he have that moment in a hotel lobby.

She touched his arm. "I'll call for the car."

"Yes," he said, in a weirdly blank voice. "Please do." Then his head swung down and his eyes focused on her. Sadness washed over his expression so strongly that it brought tears to her eyes. "I tried, Serena. For you."

What? She'd thought he was trying to save his com-

pany—the family business. The family name. What did he mean, he'd tried for *her*?

"I know," she said, afraid to say anything else. "I'll go get the car. Stay here." The driver stayed with the car. The valet just had to go find him.

It took several minutes. During that time, board members trickled out of the ballroom. Some were heading to dinner at the restaurant up the street, no doubt to celebrate their brilliant move to make themselves richer. A few shook Chadwick's hand. No one else seemed to realize what a state of shock he was in. No one but her.

Finally, after what felt like a small eternity, the company car pulled up. It wasn't really a car in the true sense of the word. Oh, it was a Cadillac, but it was the limo version. It was impressive without being ostentatious. Much like Chadwick.

The doorman opened the door for them. Absent-mindedly, Chadwick fished a bill out of his wallet and shoved it at the man. Then they climbed into the car.

When the door shut behind them, a cold silence seemed to grip the car. It wasn't just her security on the line.

How did one comfort a multi-millionaire on the verge of becoming an unwilling billionaire? Once again, she was out of her league. She kept her mouth shut and her eyes focused on the passing Denver cityscape. The journey to the brewery on the south side of the city would take thirty minutes if traffic was smooth.

When she got back to the office, she'd have to open up her resume—that was all. If Chadwick lost the company, she didn't think she could wait around until she got personally fired by the new management. She *needed* uninterrupted health benefits—prenatal care trumped

any thought of retirement. Chadwick would understand that, wouldn't he?

When Chadwick spoke, it made her jump. "What do you want?"

"Beg pardon?"

"Out of life." He was staring out his own window. "Is this what you thought you'd be doing with your life? Is this what you wanted?"

"Yes." Mostly. She'd thought that she and Neil would be married by now, maybe with a few cute kids. Being single and pregnant wasn't exactly how she'd dreamed she'd start a family.

But the job? That was exactly what she'd wanted.

So she wasn't breaking through the glass ceiling. She didn't care. She was able to provide for herself. Or had been, anyway. That was the most important thing.

"Really?"

"Working for you has been very...stable. That's not something I had growing up."

"Parents got divorced too, huh?"

She swallowed. "No, actually. Still wildly in love. But love doesn't pay the rent or put food on the table. Love doesn't pay the doctor's bills."

His head snapped away from the window so fast she thought she'd heard his neck pop. "I...I had no idea."

"I don't talk about it." Neil knew, of course. He'd met her when she was still living on ramen noodles and working two part-time jobs to pay for college. Moving in with him had been a blessing—he'd covered the rent for the first year while she'd interned at Beaumont. But once she'd been able to contribute, she had. She'd put all her emphasis on making ends meet, then making a nest egg.

Perhaps too much emphasis. Maybe she'd been so fo-cused on making sure that she was an equal contributor

to the relationship—that money would never drive them apart—that she'd forgotten a relationship was more than a bank account. After all, her parents had nothing *but* each other. They were horrid with money, but they loved each other fiercely.

Once, she'd loved Neil like that—passionately. But somewhere along the way that had mellowed into a balanced checkbook. As if love could be measured in dollars and cents.

Chadwick was staring at her as if he'd never seen her before. She didn't like it—even though he no longer seemed focused on the sale of the company, she didn't want to see pity creep into his eyes. She hated pity.

So she redirected. "What about you?"

"Me?" He seemed confused by the question.

"Did you always want to run the brewery?"

Her question worked; it distracted Chadwick from her dirt-poor life. But it failed in that it created another weary wave that washed over his expression. "I was never given a choice."

The way he said it sounded so…cold. Detached, even. "Never?"

"No." He cut the word off, turning his attention back to the window. Ah. Her childhood wasn't the only thing they didn't talk about.

"So, what *would* you want—if you had the choice?" Which he very well might have after the next round of negotiations.

He looked at her then, his eyes blazing with a new, almost feverish, kind of light. She'd only seen him look like that once before—on Monday, when he'd put his finger under her chin. But even then, he hadn't looked quite this…heated. The back of her neck began to sweat under his gaze.

Would he lean forward and put his hand on her again? Would he keep leaning until he was close enough to kiss? Would he do more than just that?

Would she let him?

"I want…" He let the word trail off, the raw need in his voice scratching against her ears like his five-o'clock shadow would scratch against her cheek. "I want to do something for me. Not for the family, not for the company—just for me."

Serena swallowed. The way he said that made it pretty clear what that 'something' might be.

He was her boss, she was his secretary, and he was still married. But none of that seemed to be an issue right now. They were alone in the back of a secure vehicle. The driver couldn't see through the divider. No one would barge in on them. No one would stop them.

I'm pregnant. The words popped onto her tongue and tried frantically to break out of her mouth. That would nip this little infatuation they both seemed to be indulging right in the bud. She was pregnant with another man's baby. She was hormonal and putting on weight in odd locations and wasn't anyone's idea of desirable right now.

But she didn't. He was already feeling the burden of taking care of his employees. How would he react to her pregnancy? Would all those promises to reward her loyalty and take care of her be just another weight he would struggle to carry?

No. She had worked hard to take care of herself. So she was unexpectedly expecting. So her job was possibly standing on its last legs. She would not throw herself at her boss with the hopes that he'd somehow "fix" her life. She knew first-hand that waiting for someone else to fix your problems meant you just had to keep on waiting.

She'd gotten herself into her current situation. She could handle it herself.

That included handling herself around Chadwick.

So she cleared her throat and forced her voice to sound light and non-committal. "Maybe you can find something that doesn't involve beer."

He blinked once, then gave a little nod. He wasn't going to press the issue. He accepted her dodge. It was the right thing to do, after all.

Damn it.

"I like beer," he replied, returning his gaze to the window. "When I was nineteen, I worked alongside the brew masters. They taught me how to *make* beer, not just think of it in terms of units sold. It was fun. Like a chemistry experiment—change one thing, change the whole nature of the brew. To those guys, beer was a living thing—the yeast, the sugars. It was an art *and* a science." His voice drifted a bit, a relaxed smile taking hold of his mouth. "That was a good year. I was sorry to leave those guys behind."

"What do you mean?"

"My father made me spend a year interning in each department, from the age of sixteen on. Outside of my studies, I had to clock in at least twenty hours every week at the brewery."

"That's a lot of work for a teenager." True, she'd had a job when she was sixteen, too, bagging groceries at the local supermarket, but that was a matter of survival. Her family needed her paycheck, plus she got first crack at the merchandise that had been damaged during shipping. She kept the roof over their heads and occasionally put food on the table. The satisfaction she'd gotten from accomplishing those things still lingered.

His smile got less relaxed, more cynical. "I learned

how to run the company. That's what he wanted." She must have given him a look because he added, "Like I said—I wasn't given any choice in the matter."

What his father had wanted—but not what Chadwick had wanted.

The car slowed down and turned. She glanced out the window. They were near the office. She felt like she was running out of time. "If you had a choice, what would you want to do?"

It felt bold and forward to ask him again—to demand he answer her. She didn't make such demands of him. That's not how their business relationship worked.

But something had changed. Their relationship was no longer strictly business. It hadn't crossed a line into pleasure, but the way he'd touched her on Monday? The way she'd touched him yesterday?

Something had changed, all right. Maybe everything.

His gaze bore into her—not the weary look he wore when discussing his schedule, not even the shell-shocked look he'd had yesterday. This was much, much closer to the look he'd had on Monday—the one he'd had on his face when he'd leaned toward her, made the air thin between them. Made her want to feel his lips pressing against hers. Made her want things she had no business wanting.

A corner of his mouth curved up. "What are you wearing on Saturday?"

"What?"

"To the gala. What are you wearing? The black dress?"

Serena blinked at him. Did he seriously *want* to discuss the shortcomings of her wardrobe? "Um, no, actually...." It didn't fit anymore. She'd tried it on on Monday night, more to distract herself from constantly refreshing her email to see if Neil would reply than anything else.

The dress had not zipped. Her body was already changing. How could she not have realized that before she peed on all those sticks? "I'll find something appropriate to wear by Saturday."

They pulled up in front of the office building. The campus of Beaumont Brewery was spread out over fifteen acres, with most of the buildings going back to before the Great Depression.

That sense of permanence had always attracted Serena. Her parents moved so frequently, trying to stay one step ahead of the creditors. The one time Serena had set them up in a nice place with a reasonable rent—and covered the down payment and security deposit, with promises to help every month—her folks had fallen behind. Again. But instead of telling her and giving her a chance to make up the shortfall, they'd done what they always did—picked up in the middle of the night and skipped out. They didn't know how to live any other way.

The Beaumonts had been here for over a century. What would it be like to walk down halls your grandfather had built? To work in buildings your great-grandfather had made? To know that your family not only took care of themselves, but of their children and their children's children?

The driver opened up their door. Serena started to move, but Chadwick motioned for her to sit. "Take the afternoon off. Go to Neiman Marcus. I have a personal shopper there. He'll make sure you're appropriately dressed."

The way he said it bordered on condescending. "I'm sorry—was my black dress inappropriate somehow?"

It had been an amazing find at a consignment shop. Paying seventy dollars for a dress and then another twenty to get it altered had felt like a lot of money, but

she'd worn it more than enough to justify the cost, and it had always made her feel glamorous. Plus, a dress like that had probably cost at least five hundred dollars originally. Ninety bucks was a steal. Too bad she wouldn't be able to wear it again for a long time. Maybe if she lost the baby weight, she'd be able to get back into it.

"On the contrary, it would be difficult to find another dress that looks as appropriate on you. That's why you should use Mario. If anyone could find a better dress, it would be him." Chadwick's voice carried through the space between them, almost as if the driver wasn't standing three feet away, just on the other side of the open car door.

Serena swallowed. He didn't have her backed against a door and he certainly wasn't touching her, but otherwise? She felt exactly as she had Monday morning. Except then, she'd been on the verge of sobbing in his office. This? This was different. She wouldn't let her emotions get the better of her today, hormones be damned.

So she smiled her most disarming smile. "I'm afraid that won't be possible. Despite the generous salary you pay me, Neiman's is a bit out of my price range." Which was not a lie. She shopped clearance racks and consignment stores. When she needed some retail therapy, she hit thrift stores. Not an expensive department store. Never Neiman's.

Chadwick leaned forward, thinning the air between them until she didn't care about the driver. "We are attending a work function. Dressing you appropriately is a work-related expense. You will put the dress on my account." She opened her mouth to protest—that was not going to happen—when he cut her off with a wave of his hand. "Not negotiable."

Then, moving with coiled grace, he exited the ve-

hicle. And made the driver shut the door before Serena could follow him out. "Take her to Neiman's," she heard Chadwick say.

No. No, no, no, *no*. This wasn't right. This was wrong on several levels. Chadwick gave her stock options because she did a good job on a project—he did not buy her something as personal, as *intimate*, as a dress. She bought her own clothing with her own money. She didn't rely on any man to take care of her.

She shoved the door open, catching the driver on the hip, and hopped out. Chadwick was already four steps away. "*Sir,*" she said, putting as much weight on the word as she could. He froze, one foot on a step. Well, she had his attention now. "I must respectfully decline your offer. I'll get my own dress, thank you."

Coiled grace? Had she thought that about him just moments ago? Because, as Chadwick turned to face her and began to walk back down toward where she was standing, he didn't look quite as graceful. Oh, he moved smoothly, but it was less like an athlete and more like a big cat stalking his prey. *Her.*

And he didn't stop once he was on level ground. He walked right up to her—close enough that he could put his finger under her chin again, close enough to kiss her in broad daylight, in front of the driver.

"You asked, Ms. Chase." His voice came out much closer to a growl than his normal efficient business voice. "Did you not?"

"I didn't ask for a dress."

His smile was a wicked thing she'd never seen on his face before. "You asked me what I wanted. Well, this is what I want. I want to take you out to dinner. I want you to accompany me to this event. And I want you to feel as beautiful as possible when I do it."

She sucked in a breath that felt far warmer than the ambient air temperature outside.

His gaze darted down to her lips, then back up to her eyes. "Because that black dress—you feel beautiful in it, don't you?"

"Yes." She didn't understand what was going on. If he was going to buy her a dress, why was he talking about how she felt? If he was going to buy her a dress and look at her with this kind of raw hunger in his eyes—talk to her in this voice—shouldn't he be talking about how beautiful he *thought* she was? If he was going to seduce her—because that's what this was, a kind of seduction—wasn't he going to tell her she was pretty? That he'd always thought she was pretty?

"It is a work-related event. This is a work-related expense. End of discussion."

"But I couldn't possibly impose—"

Something in him seemed to snap. He did touch her then—not in the cautious way he'd touched her on Monday, and not in the shattered way he'd laced his fingers with hers just yesterday.

He took her by the upper arm, his fingers gripping her tightly. He moved her away from the car door, opened it himself, and put her inside.

Before Serena could even grasp what was happening, Chadwick had climbed in next to her. "Take us to Neiman's," he ordered the driver.

Then he shut the door.

Four

What was wrong with this woman?

That was the question Chadwick asked himself over and over as they rode toward the Cherry Creek Shopping Center, where the Neiman Marcus was located. He'd called ahead and made sure Mario would be there.

Women in his world loved presents. It didn't matter what you bought them, as long as it was expensive. He'd bought Helen clothing and jewelry all the time. She'd always loved it, showing off her newest necklace or dress to her friends with obvious pride.

Of course, that was in the past. In the present, she was suing him for everything he had, so maybe there were limits to the power of gifts.

Still, what woman didn't like a gift? Would flatly refuse to even entertain the notion of a present?

Serena Chase, that's who. Further proving that he didn't know another woman like her.

"This is ridiculous," she muttered.

They were sitting side by side in the backseat of the limo, instead of across from each other as they normally did. True, Serena had scooted over to the other side of the vehicle, but he could still reach over and touch her if he wanted to.

Did he want to?

What a stupid question. Yes, he wanted to. Wasn't that why they were here—he was doing something he wanted, consequences be damned?

"What's ridiculous?" he asked, knowing full well she might haul off and smack him at any moment. After all, he'd forced her into this car with him. He could say this was a work-related expense until he was blue in the face, but that didn't make it actually true.

"This. *You*. It's the middle of the afternoon. On a Wednesday, for God's sake. We have *things* to do. I should know—I keep your schedule."

"I hardly think…" He checked his watch. "I hardly think 4:15 on a Wednesday counts as the middle of the afternoon."

She turned the meanest look onto him that he'd ever seen contort her pretty face. "*You* have a meeting with Sue Colman this afternoon—your weekly HR meeting. *I* have to help Matthew with the gala."

Chadwick got his phone and tapped the screen. "Hello, Sue? Chadwick. We're going to have to reschedule our meeting this afternoon."

Serena gave him a look that was probably supposed to strike fear in his heart, but which only made him want to laugh. Canceling standing meetings on a whim—just because he felt like it?

If he didn't know better, he'd think he was having fun.

"Did the board meeting run long?" Sue asked.

"Yes, exactly." A perfect excuse. Except for the fact that someone might have seen them return to the brewery—and then leave immediately.

"It can wait. I'll see you next week."

"Thanks." He ended the call and tapped on the screen a few more times. "Matthew?"

"Everything okay?"

"Yes, but Serena and I got hung up at the board meeting. Can you do without her for the afternoon?"

There was silence on the other end—a silence that made him shift uncomfortably.

"I suppose I could make do without *Ms. Chase*," Matthew replied, his tone heavy with sarcasm. "Can you?"

If I thought you were anything like our father, Matthew had said the day before, *I'd assume you were working on wife number two.*

Well, he wasn't, okay? Chadwick was not Hardwick. If he were, he'd have Serena flat on her back, her prim suit gone as he feasted on her luscious body in the backseat of this car.

Was he doing that? No. Had he ever done that? *No.* He was a complete gentleman at all times. Hardwick would have made a new dress the reward for a quick screw. Not Chadwick. Just seeing her look glamorous was its own reward.

Or so he kept telling himself.

"I'll talk to you tomorrow." He hung up before Matthew could get in another barb. "There," he said, shoving his phone back into his pocket. "Schedule's clear. We have the rest of the afternoon, all forty-five minutes of it."

She glared at him, but didn't say anything.

It only took another fifteen minutes to make it to the shopping center. Mario was waiting by the curb for them. The car had barely come to a complete stop when he had

the back door open. "Mr. Beaumont! What a joy to see you again. I was just telling your brother Phillip that it's been too long since I've had the pleasure of your company."

"Mario," Chadwick said, trying not to roll his eyes at the slight man. Mario had what some might call a *flamboyant* way about him, what with his cutting-edge suit, faux-hawk hair and—yes—eyeliner. But he also had an eagle eye for fashion—something Chadwick didn't have the time or inclination for. Much easier to let Mario put together outfits for him.

And now, for Serena. He turned and held a hand out to her. When she hesitated, he couldn't help himself. He notched an eyebrow in challenge.

That did it. She offered her hand, but she did not wrap her fingers around his.

Fine. Be like that, he thought. "Mario, may I introduce Ms. Serena Chase?"

"Such a delight!" Mario swept into a dramatic bow—but then, he didn't do anything that wasn't dramatic. "An honor to make your acquaintance, Ms. Chase. Please, come inside."

Mario held the doors for them. It was only when they'd passed the threshold that Serena's hand tightened around Chadwick's. He looked at her and was surprised to see something close to horror on her face. "Are you all right?"

"Fine," she answered, too quickly.

"But?"

"I've just…never been in this particular store before. It's…" She stared at the store. "It's different than where I normally shop."

"Ah," he said, mostly because he didn't know what else to say. What if she hadn't been refusing his offer due to stubborn pride? What if there was another reason?

Mario swept around them and clapped his hands in what could only be described as glee. "Please, tell me how I can assist you today." His gaze darted to where Chadwick still had a hold of Serena's hands, but he didn't say anything else. He was far too polite to be snide.

Chadwick turned to Serena. "We have an event on Saturday and Ms. Chase needs a gown."

Mario nodded. "The charity gala at the Art Museum, of course. A statement piece or one of refined elegance? She could easily pull off either with her shape."

Serena's fingers clamped down on Chadwick's, and then she pulled her hand away entirely. Perhaps Mario's extensive knowledge of the social circuit was a surprise to her. Or perhaps it was being referred to in the third person by two men standing right in front of her. Surely it wasn't the compliment.

"Elegant," she said.

"Fitting," Mario agreed. "This way, please."

He led them up the escalator, making small talk about the newest lines and how he had a spotted a suit that would be perfect for Chadwick just the other day. "Not today," Chadwick said. "We just need a gown."

"And accessories, of course," Mario said.

"Of course." When Chadwick agreed, Serena shot him a stunned look. He could almost hear her thinking that he'd said nothing about accessories. He hadn't, but that was part of the deal.

"This way, please." Mario guided them back to a private fitting area, with a dressing room off to the side, a seating area, and a dais surrounded by mirrors. "Champagne?" he offered.

"Yes."

"No." Serena's command was sudden and forceful. At first Chadwick thought she was being obstinate again, but

then he saw the high blush that raced across her cheeks. She dropped her gaze and a hand fluttered over her stomach, as if she were nervous.

"Ah." Mario stepped back and cast his critical eye over her again. "My apologies, Ms. Chase. I did not realize you were expecting. I shall bring you a fruit spritzer—non-alcoholic, of course." He turned to Chadwick. "Congratulations, Mr. Beaumont."

Wait—what? *What?*

Chadwick opened his mouth to say something, but nothing came out.

Had Mario just said...*expecting?*

Chadwick looked at Serena, who suddenly seemed to waver, as if she were on the verge of passing out. She did not tell Mario that his critical eye was wrong, that she was absolutely *not* expecting. She mumbled out a pained "Thank you," and then sat heavily on the loveseat.

"My assistant will bring you drinks while I collect a few things for Ms. Chase to model," Mario said. If he caught the sudden change in the atmosphere of the room, he gave no indication of it. Instead, with a bow, he closed the door behind him.

Leaving Chadwick and Serena alone in the silence.

"Did he just say...."

"Yes." Her voice cracked, and then she dragged in a ragged breath.

"And you're..."

"Yes." She bent forward at the waist, as if she could make herself smaller. As if she wanted to disappear from the room.

Or maybe she was on the verge of vomiting and was merely putting her head between her knees.

"And you—you found out this weekend. That's why you were upset on Monday."

"Yes." That seemed to be the only word she was capable of squeezing out.

"And you didn't tell me?" The words burst out of him. She flinched, but he couldn't stop. "Why didn't you *tell* me?"

"Mr. Beaumont, we usually do not discuss our personal lives at the office." At least that was more than a syllable, but the rote way she said it did nothing to calm him down.

"Oh? Were we going to *not* discuss it when you started showing? Were we going to not discuss it when you needed to take maternity leave?" She didn't reply, which only made him madder. Why was he so mad? "Does Neil know?" He was terrified of what she might say. That Neil might not be the father. That she'd taken up with someone else.

He had no idea why that bothered him. Just that it did.

"I…" She took a breath, but it sounded painful. "I sent Neil an email. He hasn't responded yet. But I don't need him. I can provide for my child by myself. I won't be a burden to you or the company. I don't need help."

"Don't lie to me, Serena. Do you have any idea what's going to happen if I lose the brewery?"

Even though she was looking at her black pumps and not at him, he saw her squeeze her eyes shut tight. Of course she knew. He was being an idiot to assume that someone as smart and capable as Serena wouldn't already have a worst-case plan in place. "I'll be out of a job. But I can get another one. Assuming you'll give me a letter of reference."

"Of course I would. You're missing the point. Do you know how hard it'll be for a woman who's eight months pregnant to get a job—even if I sing your praises from the top of the Rocky Mountains?"

She turned an odd color. Had she been breathing, beyond those few breaths she'd taken a moment before?

Jesus, what an ass he was being. *She* was pregnant—so *he* was yelling at her.

Something his father would have done. Dammit.

"Breathe," he said, forcing himself to speak in a quiet tone. He wasn't sure he was nailing "sympathetic," but at least he wasn't yelling. "Breathe, Serena."

She gave her head a tiny shake, as if she'd forgotten how.

Oh, hell. The absolute last thing any of them needed was for his pregnant assistant to black out in the middle of the workweek in an upscale department store. Mario would call an ambulance, the press would get wind of it, and Helen—the woman he was still technically married to—would make him pay.

He crouched down next to Serena and started rubbing her back. "Breathe, Serena. Please. I'm sorry. I'm not mad at you."

She leaned into him then. Not much, but enough to rest her head against his shoulder. Hadn't he wanted this just a few days before? Something that resembled his holding her?

But not like this. Not because he'd lost his temper. Not because she was...

Pregnant.

Chadwick didn't have the first clue how to be a good father. He had a great idea of how to be a really crappy father, but not a good one. Helen had said she didn't want kids, so they didn't have kids. It had been easier that way.

But Serena? She was soft and gentle where Helen, just like his own mother, had been tough and brittle. Serena worked hard and wasn't afraid to learn new things—wasn't afraid to get her hands dirty down in the trenches.

Serena would be a good mother. A *great* mother.

The thought made him smile. Or it would have, if he hadn't been watching her asphyxiate before his very eyes.

"Breathe," he ordered her. Finally, she gasped and exhaled. "Good. Do it again."

They sat like that for several minutes, her breathing and him reminding her to do it again. The assistant knocked on the door and delivered their beverages, but Serena didn't pull away from him and he didn't pull away from her. He sat on his heels and rubbed her back while she breathed and leaned on him.

When they were alone again, he said, "I meant what I said on Monday, Serena. This doesn't change that."

"It changes *everything*." He'd never heard her sound sadder. "I'm sorry. I didn't want anything to change. But it did. *I* did."

They'd lived their lives in a state of stasis for so long—he'd been not-quite-happily married to Helen, and Serena had been living with Neil, not quite happily, either, it turned out. They could have continued on like that forever, maybe.

But everything had changed.

"I won't fail you," he reminded her. Failure had not been an option when he was growing up. Hardwick Beaumont had demanded perfection from an early age. And it was never smart to disappoint Hardwick. Even as a child, Chadwick had known that.

No, he wouldn't fail Serena.

She leaned back—not away from him, not enough to break their contact, but far enough that she could look at him. The color was slowly coming back into her face, which was good. Her hair was mussed up from where her head had been on his shoulder and her eyes were wide. She looked as if she'd just woken up from a long

nightmare, like she wanted him to kiss her and make it all better.

His hand moved. It brushed a few strands of hair from her cheek. Then his fingers curved under her cheek, almost as if he couldn't pull away from her skin.

"I won't fail you," he repeated.

"I know you won't," she whispered, her voice shaking.

She reached up—she was going to touch him. Like he was touching her. She was going to put her fingers on his face and then pull him down and he would kiss her. God, how he would kiss her.

"Knock, knock!" Mario called out from the other side of the door. "Is everybody decent in there?"

"Damn."

But Serena smiled—a small, tense smile, but a smile all the same. In that moment, he knew he hadn't let her down yet.

Now he just had to keep it that way.

Five

"Breathe in," Mario instructed as he held up the first gown.

Serena did as she was told. Breathing was the only thing she was capable of doing right now, and even that was iffy.

She'd almost kissed Chadwick. She'd almost let herself lean forward in a moment of weakness and *kiss him*. It was bad enough that she'd been completely unprofessional and had a panic attack, worse that she'd let him comfort her. But to almost kiss him?

She didn't understand why that felt worse than letting him kiss her. But it did. Worse and better all at the same time.

"And breathe *all* the way out. All the way, Ms. Chase. There!" The zipper slid up the rest of the way and she felt him hook the latch. "Marvelous!"

Serena looked down at the black velvet that clung to

every single size-ten curve she had and a few new ones. "How did you know what size I'd need?"

"Darling," Mario replied as he made a slow circle around her, smoothing here and tugging up there, "it's Mario's job to know such things."

"Oh." She remembered to breathe again. "I've never done this before. But I guess you figured that out." He'd guessed everything else. Her dress size, her shoe size— even her bra size. The strapless bra fit a lot better than the one she owned.

"Which part—trying on gowns or being whisked out of the office in the middle of the day?"

Yeah, she wasn't fooling anyone. "Both." Mario set a pair of black heels before her and balanced her as she stepped into them. "I feel like an imposter."

"But that's the beauty of fashion," Mario said, stepping back to look her over yet again. "Every morning you can wake up and decide to be someone new!" Then his face changed. "Even Mario." His voice changed, too— it got deeper, with a thicker Hispanic accent. "I'm really Mario from the barrio, you know? But no one else does. That's the beauty of fashion. It doesn't matter what we were. The only thing that matters is who we are today. And today," he went on, his voice rising up again, "you shall be a queen amongst women!"

She looked at him, more than a little surprised at what he'd said. Was it possible that he really was Mario from the barrio—that he might understand how out of place she felt surrounded by this level of wealth? She decided it didn't matter. All that mattered was that he'd made her feel like she could do this. She felt herself breathe again—and this time it wasn't a strain. "You really are fabulous, you know."

"Oh," he said, batting her comment away with a

pleased grin, "I tell my husband that all the time. One of these days, he's going to believe me!" Then he clapped his hands and turned to the cart that had God only knew how many diamonds and gems on it. "Mr. Beaumont is quite the lucky man!"

But he wasn't. He wasn't the father of her baby and he wasn't even her boyfriend. He was her boss. The walls started to close in on her again.

She needed to distract herself and fast. "Does this happen a lot? Mr. Beaumont showing up with a fashion-challenged woman?" The moment she asked the question, she wished she could take it back. She didn't want to know that she was the latest in a string of afternoon makeovers.

"Heavens, no!" Mario managed to look truly shocked at the suggestion as he turned with a stunning diamond solitaire necklace the size of a pea. "His brother, Mr. Phillip Beaumont? Yes. But not Mr. Chadwick Beaumont. I don't believe he ever even joined his wife on such an afternoon. Certainly not here. I would recall *that*."

Serena breathed again. There wasn't a particularly good reason for that to make her so happy. She had no claim on Chadwick, none at all. And just because he hadn't brought a girl shopping didn't mean he hadn't been seeing anyone else.

But she didn't think he had. He worked too much. She knew. She managed his schedule.

"Now," Mario went on, draping the necklace around her neck and fastening it, "you may have woken up this morning a frugal..." He tilted his head to the side and looked at her suit, now neatly hanging by the door. "Account executive?"

"Close," she said. "Executive assistant."

He snapped his fingers in disappointment, but it didn't

last. "By the time Mario gets done with you, you will *be* royalty."

He held his arm out to her, for which she was grateful—those heels were at least two inches higher than her dress shoes. Then he opened the door and they walked out into the sitting room.

Chadwick was reclined in the loveseat, a glass of champagne in one hand. He'd loosened his tie, a small thing that made him look ten times more relaxed than normal.

Then he saw her. His eyes went wide as he sat up straight, nearly spilling his drink. "Serena...wow."

"And this is just the beginning!" Mario crowed as he led her not to Chadwick but over to the small dais in front of all the mirrors. He helped her up and then guided her in a small turn.

She saw herself in the mirrors. Mario had smoothed her hair out after he'd gotten her suit off her. Her face still looked a little ashen, but otherwise, she couldn't quite believe that was her.

Royalty, indeed. Chadwick had been right. This dress, just like her black dress at home, made her feel beautiful. And after the day she'd had, that was a gift in itself.

She got turned back around and saw the look Chadwick was giving her. His mouth had fallen open and he was now standing, like he wanted to walk right up to her and sweep her into his arms.

"Now," Mario said, although it didn't feel like he was talking to either Serena or Chadwick. "This dress would be perfect for Saturday, but half the crowd will be wearing black and we don't want Ms. Chase to blend, do we?"

"No," Chadwick agreed, looking at her like she hadn't announced half an hour ago that she was pregnant. If anything, he was looking at her like he'd never really

seen her before. And he wanted to see a lot more. "No, we don't want that."

"Plus, this dress is not terribly forgiving. I think we want to try on something that has more flow, more grace. More…"

"Elegant," Chadwick said. He seemed to shake back to himself. He backed up to the loveseat and sat again, one leg crossed, appraising her figure again. "Show me what else you've got, Mario."

"With pleasure!"

The next dress was a pale peachy pink number with a huge ball gown skirt and a bow on the back that felt like it was swallowing Serena whole. "A classic style," Mario announced.

"Too much," Chadwick replied, with a shake of his hand. She might have been hurt by this casual dismissal, but then he caught her gaze and gave her a smile. "But still beautiful."

Then came a cornflower blue dress with an Empire waist, tiny pleats that flowed down the length of the gown, and one shoulder strap that was encrusted with jewels. "No necklace," Mario informed her as he handed her dangling earrings that looked like they were encrusted with real sapphires. "You don't want to compete with the dress."

When she came out this time, Chadwick sat up again. "You are…*stunning*." There was that look again—like he was hungry. Hungry for her.

She blushed. She wasn't used to being stunning. She was used to being professional. Her black dress at home was as stunning as she'd ever gotten. She wasn't sure how she was going to pull off stunning while pregnant. But it didn't seem to be bothering Chadwick.

"This one has a much more forgiving waistline. She'll

be able to wear it for several more months and it'll be easier to get back into it." Mario was talking to Chadwick, but Serena got the feeling that he was really addressing her—greater wearability meant better value.

Although she still wasn't looking at the price tags.

"I don't know where else I'd wear it," she said.

Chadwick didn't say anything, but he gave her a look that made her shiver in the best way possible.

They went through several dresses that no one particularly loved—Mario kept putting her in black and then announcing that black was too boring for her. She tried on a sunflower yellow that did horrible things to her skin tone. It was so bad, Mario wouldn't even let her go out to show Chadwick.

She liked the next, a satin dress that was so richly colored it was hard to tell if it was blue or purple. It had an intricate pattern in lace over the bodice that hid everything she didn't like about her body. That was followed by a dark pink strapless number that reminded her of a bridesmaid gown. Then a blue-and-white off-the-shoulder dress where the colors bled into each other in a way that she thought would be tacky but was actually quite pretty.

"Blue is your color," Mario told her. She could see he was right.

She didn't think it was possible, but she was having fun. Playing dress-up, such as it was. High-end dress-up, but still—this was something she'd had precious little of during her childhood. Chadwick was right—she *did* feel beautiful. She twirled on the dais for him, enjoying the compliments he heaped upon her.

It was almost like…a fairy tale, a rags-to-riches dream come true. How many times had she read some year-old fashion magazine that she'd scavenged from a recycling bin and dreamed about dressing up in the pretty things?

She'd thought she'd gotten that herself with her consignment store dress, but that was nothing compared to being
styled by the fabulous Mario.

Time passed in a whirl of chiffons and satins. Soon,
it was past seven. They'd spent almost four hours in that
dressing room. Chadwick had drunk most of a bottle
of champagne. At some point, a fruit-and-cheese tray
had been brought in. Mario wouldn't let Serena touch a
bite while she was wearing anything, so she wound up
standing in the dressing room in her underthings, eating apple slices.

She was tired and hungry. Chadwick's eyes had begun
to glaze over, and even Mario's boundless energy was
seeming to flag.

"Can we be done?" Serena asked, drooping like a
wilted flower in a pale green dress.

"Yes," Chadwick said. "We'll take the blue, the purple, the blue-and-white and...was there another one that
you liked, Serena?"

She goggled at him. Had he just listed *three* dresses?
"How many times do you expect me to change at this
thing?"

"I want you to have all options available."

"One is plenty. The blue one with the single strap."

Mario looked at Chadwick, who repeated, "All three,
please. With all necessary accessories. Have them sent
to Serena's house."

"Of course, Mr. Beaumont." He gathered up the gowns
in question and hurried from the room.

Still wearing the droopy green dress, Serena kicked
out of her towering shoes and stalked over to Chadwick.
She put her hands on her hips and gave him her very best
glare. "*One.* One I shouldn't let you buy me in the first
place. I do *not* need three."

He had the nerve to look down at her and smile his ruthless smile, the one that let everyone in the room know that negotiations were finished. Suddenly, she was aware that they were alone and she wasn't wearing her normal suit. "Most women would jump at the chance to have someone buy them nice things, Serena."

"Well," she snapped, unable to resist stamping her foot in protest, "I'm not most women."

"I know." Then—almost as if he were moving in slow motion, he stood and began taking long strides toward her, his gaze fastened on her lips.

She should do…something. Step back. Cross her arms and look away. Flee to the dressing room and lock the door until Mario came back.

Yes, those were all truly things she *should* do.

But she *wanted* him to kiss her.

He slipped one arm around her waist, and his free hand caught her under the chin again. "You're not like any woman I've ever known, Serena. I could tell the very first time I saw you."

"You don't actually remember that, do you?" Her voice had dropped down to a sultry whisper.

His grin deepened. "You were working for Sue Colman in HR. She sent you up to my office with a comparison of new health-care plans." As he spoke, he pulled her in tighter, until she could feel the hard planes of his chest through the thin fabric of the gown. "I asked you what you thought. You told me that Sue recommended the cheaper plan, but the other one was better. It would make the employees happier—would make them want to stay with the brewery. I made you nervous—you blushed—but—"

"You picked the plan I wanted." The plan she'd needed. She'd just been hired full-time. She'd never had health

benefits before and she wanted the one with a lower copay and better prescription coverage. She couldn't believe he remembered—but he did.

Her arms went around his chest, her hands flat on his back. She wasn't pushing him away. She couldn't. She wanted this. She had since that day. When she'd knocked on the door, he'd looked up at her with those hazel eyes. Instead of making her feel like she was an interruption, he'd focused on her and asked for her opinion—something he did *not* have to do. She was the lowest woman on the totem pole, barely ranking above unpaid intern— but the future CEO had made her feel like the most important worker in the whole company.

He had looked at her then the same way he was looking at her right now...like she was far more than the most important worker in the company. More like she was the most important woman in the world. "You were honest with me. And what's more than that, you were *right*. It's hard to expect loyalty if you don't give people something to be loyal to."

She'd been devoted to him from that moment on. When he'd been named the new CEO a year later, she'd applied to be his assistant the same day. She hadn't been the most qualified person to apply, but he'd taken a chance on her.

She'd been so thankful then. The job had been a gift that allowed her to take care of herself—to not rely on Neil to pay the rent or buy the groceries. Because of Chadwick, she'd been able to do exactly what she'd set out to do—be financially independent.

She was still thankful now.

Still in slo-mo, he leaned down. His lips brushed against hers—not a fierce kiss of possession, but something that was closer to a request for permission.

Serena took a deep breath in satisfaction. Chadwick's scent surrounded her with the warmth of sandalwood on top of his own clean notes. She couldn't help it—she clutched him more tightly, tracing his lips with her tongue.

Chadwick let out a low growl that seemed to rumble right out of his chest. Then the kiss deepened. She opened her mouth for him and his tongue swept in.

Serena's knees gave in to the heat that suddenly flooded her system, but she didn't go anywhere—Chadwick held her up. Her head began to swim again but instead of the stark panic that had paralyzed her earlier, she felt nothing but sheer desire. She'd wanted that kiss since the very first time she'd seen Chadwick Beaumont. Why on God's green earth had she waited almost eight years to invite it?

Something hard and warm pressed against the front of her gown. A similar weight hung heavy between her legs, driving her body into his. This was what she'd been missing for months. Years. This raw passion hadn't just been gone since Neil had left—it'd been gone for much longer.

Chadwick wanted her. And oh, how she *wanted him*. Wanted to forget about bosses and employees and companies and boards of directors and pregnancies and everything that had gone wrong in her world. This—being in Chadwick's arms, his lips crushed against hers—this was right. So very *right*. Nothing else mattered except for this moment of heat in his arms. It burned everything else away.

She wanted to touch him, find out if the rest of him was as strong as his arms were—but before she could do anything of the sort, he broke the kiss and pulled her into an even tighter hug.

His lips moved against her neck, as if he were smiling

against her. She liked how it felt. "You've always been special, Serena," he whispered against her skin. "So let me show you how special you are. I *want* to buy you all three dresses. That way you can surprise me on Saturday. Are you going to refuse me that chance?"

The heat ebbed between them. She'd forgotten about the dresses—and how much they probably cost. For an insane moment, she'd forgotten everything—who she was. Who he was.

She *absolutely* should refuse the dress, the dinner, the way he had looked at her all afternoon like he couldn't wait to strip each and every dress right off her, and the way he was holding her to his broad chest right now. She had no business being here, doing this—no business letting her attraction to Chadwick Beaumont cloud her thinking. She was pregnant and her job was on the line, and at no point in the past, present or future did she require three gowns that probably cost more than her annual salary.

But then that man leaned backward and cupped her cheek in his palm and said, "I haven't had this much fun in...well, I can't remember when. It was good to get out of the office." His smile took a decade of worry off his face.

She was about to tell him that the champagne had gone to his head—although she was painfully aware that she had no such excuse as to why she'd kissed him back—when he added, "I'm glad I got to spend it with you. Thank you, Serena."

And she had nothing. No refusal, no telling him off, no power to insist that Mario only wrap up one dress and none of the jewelry, no defense that she did not need him to buy her anything because she was perfectly able to buy her own dresses.

He'd had fun. With her.

"The dresses are lovely, Chadwick. Thank you."

He leaned down, his five-o'clock shadow and his lips lightly brushing her cheek. "You're welcome." He pulled back and stuck out his arm just like Mario had done to escort her to the dais. "Let me take you to dinner."

"I…" She looked down at the droopy green dress, which was now creased in a few key areas. "I have to get back to work. I have to go back to being an executive assistant now." Funny how that sounded off all of a sudden. She'd been nothing but an executive assistant for over seven years. Why shouldn't putting the outfit back on feel more…natural?

A day of playing dress-up had gone right to her head. She must have forgotten who she was. She was really Serena Chase, frugal employee. She wasn't the kind of woman who had rich men lavish her with exorbitant gifts. She *wasn't* Chadwick's lover.

Oh God, she'd let him kiss her. She'd kissed him back. What had she *done*?

Chadwick's face grew more distant. He, too, seemed to be realizing that they'd crossed a line they couldn't uncross. It made her feel even more miserable. "Ah, yes. I probably have work to do as well."

"Probably." They might have been playing hooky for a few hours that afternoon, but the world had kept on turning. The fallout from the board meeting no doubt had investors, analysts and journalists burning up the bandwidth, all clamoring for a statement from Chadwick Beaumont.

But more than that, she needed to be away from him. This proximity wasn't helping her cause. She needed to clear her head and stop having fantasies about her boss. Fantasies that now had a very real feel to them—the feeling of his lips against hers, his body pressed to hers.

Fantasies that would probably play out in her dreams that night.

She couldn't accept dinner on top of the dresses. She had to draw the line somewhere.

But she'd already crossed that line.

How much farther would she go?

Six

Chadwick did not sleep well.

He told himself that it had everything to do with the disastrous board meeting and nothing to do with Serena Chase, but what the hell was the point in lying? It had *everything* to do with Serena.

He shouldn't have kissed her. Rationally, he knew that. He'd fired other executives for crossing that very same line—one strike and they were out. For way too long, Beaumont Brewery had been a business where men took all kinds of advantage of the women who worked for them. That was one of the first things he'd changed after his father died. He'd had Serena write a strict sexual harassment policy to prevent exactly this situation.

He'd always taken the higher road. Fairness, loyalty, equality.

He was not Hardwick Beaumont. He would not seduce his secretary. Or his executive assistant, for that matter.

Except that he'd already started. He'd told her he was taking her to the gala. He'd taken her shopping and bought tens of thousands of dollars worth of gowns, jewels and handbags for her.

He'd kissed her. He'd wanted to do so much more than just kiss her, too. He'd wanted to leave that gown in a puddle on the floor and sit back on the loveseat, Serena's body riding his. He wanted to feel the full weight of her breasts in his hands, her body taking his in.

He'd wanted to do something as base and crass as take her in a dressing room, for God's sake. And that was exactly what Hardwick would have done.

So he'd stopped. Thankfully, she'd stopped, too.

She hadn't wanted the dresses. She'd fought him tooth and nail about that.

But the kiss?

She'd kissed him back. Tracing his mouth with her tongue, pressing those amazing breasts against him— holding him just as tightly as he had been holding her.

He found himself in his office by five-thirty the next morning, running a seven-minute mile on his treadmill. He had the international market report up on the screen in front of him, but he wasn't paying a damn bit of attention to it.

Instead, he was wondering what the hell he was going to do about Serena.

She was pregnant. And when she'd come out in those gowns, she'd *glowed*. She'd always been beautiful—a bright, positive smile for any occasion with nary a manipulating demand in sight—but yesterday she'd taken his breath away over and over again.

He was totally, completely, one hundred percent confounded by Serena Chase. The women in Chadwick's world did not refuse expensive clothing and jewelry. They

spent their days planning how to get more clothes, better jewels and a skinnier body. They whimpered and pleaded and seduced until they got what they wanted.

That's what his mother had always done. Chadwick doubted whether Eliza and Hardwick had ever really loved each other. She'd wanted his money, and he'd wanted her family prestige. Whenever Eliza had caught Hardwick *in flagrante delicto*—which was often—she'd threaten and cry until Hardwick plunked down a chunk of change on a new diamond. Then, when one diamond wasn't enough, he started buying them in bulk.

Helen had been like that, too. Oh, she didn't threaten, but she did pout until she got what she wanted—cars, clothes, plastic surgery. It had been so much easier to just give in to her demands than deal with the manipulation. In the last year before she filed for divorce, she'd only slept with him when he'd bought her something. Not that he'd enjoyed it much, even then.

Somehow, he'd convinced himself he was fine with that. He didn't need to feel passion because passion left a man wide open for the pain of betrayal. Because there was always another betrayal around the next corner.

But Serena? She didn't cry, didn't whine and didn't pout. She never treated him like he was a pawn to be moved until she got what she wanted, never treated him like he was an obstacle she had to negotiate around.

She didn't even want to let him buy her a dress that made her feel beautiful.

He punched the treadmill up another mile per hour, running until his lungs burned.

He could not be lusting after his assistant and that was final.

This was just the result of Helen moving out of their bedroom over twenty-two months before, that was all.

And they hadn't had sex for a couple of months before that. Yes, that was it. Two years without a woman in his arms—without a woman looking at him with a smile, without a woman who was glad to see him.

Two years was a hell of a long time.

That's all this was. Sexual frustration manifesting itself in the direction of his assistant. He hadn't wanted to break his marriage vows to Helen, even in the middle of their never-ending divorce. Part of that was a wise business decision—if Helen found out that he'd had an affair, even after their separation, she wouldn't sign off on the divorce until he had nothing left but his name.

But part of that was refusing to be like his father.

Except his father totally would have lavished gifts on his secretary and then kissed her.

Hell.

Finally his legs gave out, but instead of the normal clarity a hard run brought him, he just felt more muddled than ever. Despite the punishing exercise, he was no closer to knowing what he was supposed to do when Serena came in for their morning meeting.

Oh, he knew what he wanted to do. He wanted to lay her out on his desk and lavish her curves with all the attention he had. He wanted her to straddle him. He wanted to bring her to a shuddering, screaming climax, and he wanted to hold her afterwards and fall asleep in her arms.

He didn't just want to have sex.

He wanted to have Serena.

Double damn.

He threw himself into his shower without bothering to touch the hot water knob. The cold did little to shock him back to his senses, but at least it knocked his erection down to a somewhat manageable level.

This was beyond lust. He had a need to take care of

her—to *not* fail her. That was why he'd bought her nice things, right? Sure. He was just rewarding her loyalty.

She'd said that her ex hadn't responded to her email. There—that was something he could do. He could get that jerk to step up to the plate and at least acknowledge that he'd left Serena in a difficult situation. Yeah, he liked that idea—making Neil Moore toe the line was a perfectly acceptable way of looking out for his best employee, and it didn't involve kissing her. He doubted that Serena would hold Neil responsible for his legal obligations—but Chadwick had no problem putting that man's feet to the fire.

He shut the water off and grabbed his towel. He was pretty sure he had Neil's information in his phone. But where had he left it?

He rummaged in his pants pocket for a few minutes before he remembered he'd set it down on his desk when he came in.

He opened the door and walked into his office—and found himself face-to-face with Serena.

"Chadwick!" she gasped. "What are you—"

"Serena!" It was then that he remembered the only thing he had on was a towel. He hadn't even managed to dry off.

Her mouth was frozen in a totally kissable "oh," her eyes wide as her gaze traveled down his wet chest.

Desire pumped through him, hard. All he'd have to do would be to drop the towel and show her exactly what she did to him. Hell, at the rate he was going, he wouldn't even have to drop the towel. She wasn't blind and his body wasn't being subtle right now.

"I'm…I'm sorry," she sputtered. "I didn't realize…."

"Just checking my phone." *Just thinking about you.*

He glanced at his clock. She was at least an hour ahead of schedule. "You're early."

"I wanted...I mean, about last night..." She seemed to be trying to get herself back under control, but her gaze kept drifting down. "About the kiss..." A furious blush made her look innocent and naughty at the same time.

He took a step forward, all of his best intentions blown to hell by the look on her face. The same look she'd had the night before when he'd kissed her. She wanted him.

God, that made him feel good.

"What about the kiss?"

Finally, she dropped her gaze from his body to the floor. "It shouldn't have happened. I shouldn't have kissed you. That was unprofessional and I apologize." She rushed through the words in one breath, sounding like she'd spent at least half the night rehearsing that little speech. "It won't happen again."

Wait—what? Was she taking all the blame for that? No. It's not like she'd shoved him against the wall and groped him. He was the one who'd pulled her into his arms. He was the one who'd lifted her chin. "Correct me if I'm wrong, but I thought I was the one who kissed *you*."

"Yes, well, it was still unprofessional, and it shouldn't have happened while I was on the job."

For a second, Chadwick knew he'd screwed up. She was serious. He'd be lucky if she didn't file suit against him.

But then she lifted her head, her bottom lip tucked under her teeth as she peeked at his bare torso. There was no uncertainty in her eyes—just the same desire that was pumping through his veins.

Then he realized what she'd said—while she was on the job.

Would she be "on the job" on Saturday night? Or off the clock?

"Of course," he agreed. Because, even though she was looking at him like that and he was wearing nothing more than a towel, he was not his father. He could be a reasonable, rational man. Not one solely driven by his baser needs. He could rein in his desires.

Sort of.

"What time shall I pick you up for dinner on Saturday?"

Her lower lip still held captive by her teeth—God, what would it feel like if she bit his lip like that?—he thought he saw her smile. Just a little bit. "The gala starts at nine. We should arrive by nine-twenty. We don't want to be unfashionably late."

He'd take her to the Palace Arms. It would be the perfect accompaniment to the gala—a setting befitting Serena in a gown. "Ms. Chase," he said, trying to use his normal business voice. It was harder to do in a towel than he would have expected. "Please make dinner reservations for two at the Palace Arms for seven. I'll pick you up at six-thirty."

Her eyes went wide again—like they had the day before when he'd informed her he was sending her to Neiman's to get a dress. Like they had when he'd impulsively ordered all three dresses. Why was she so afraid of him spending his money as he saw fit? "But that's…"

"That's what I want," he replied.

And then, because he couldn't help himself, he let the towel slip. Just a little—not enough to flash her—but more than enough to make her notice.

And respond. No, she didn't like it when he flashed his wealth around—but his body? His body appeared to be a different matter entirely. Her mouth dropped open into

that "oh" again and then—God help him—her tongue flicked out and traced over her lips. He had to bite down to keep the groan from escaping.

"I'll…I'll go make those reservations, Mr. Beaumont," she said breathlessly.

He couldn't have kept the grin off his face if he tried. "Please do."

Oh, yeah, he was going to take her out to dinner and she was going to wear one of those gowns and he would…

He would enjoy her company, he reminded himself. He did not expect anything other than that. This was not a quid pro quo situation where he bought her things and expected her to fall into bed out of obligation. Sex was not the same as a thank-you note.

Then she held up a small envelope. "A thank-you note. For the dresses."

He almost burst out laughing, but he didn't. He was too busy watching Serena. She took two steps toward the desk and laid the envelope on the top. She was close enough that, if he reached out, he could pull her back into his arms again, right where she'd been the night before.

Except he'd have to let go of the towel.

When had restraint gotten this hard? When had he suddenly had trouble controlling his urges? Hell, when was the last time he'd had an urge he had to control?

Years, really. Long, dry years in a loveless marriage while he ran a company. But Serena woke up something inside of him—and now that it was awake, Chadwick felt it making him wild and impulsive.

The tension in the room was so thick it was practically visible.

"Thank you, Ms. Chase." He was trying to hide behind last names, like he'd done for years, but it wasn't working. All his mouth could taste was her kiss.

"You have Larry coming in for his morning meeting." She didn't step back, but he saw the side-eye she was giving him. "Shall I reschedule him or do you think you can be dressed by then?"

This time, he didn't bother to hold back his chuckle. "I suppose I can be dressed by then. Send him in when he gets here."

She gave a curt nod with her head and, with one more glance at his bare chest, turned to leave.

He couldn't help himself. "Serena?"

She paused at the door, but she didn't look back. "Yes?"

"I..." He snapped off the part about how he wanted her. Even if it was the truth. "I'm looking forward to Saturday."

She glanced back over her shoulder and gave him the same kind of smile she'd had when she'd been twirling in the gowns for him—warm, nervous and excited all at once. "Me, too."

Then she left him alone in his office. Which was absolutely the correct thing to have done.

Saturday sure seemed like a hell of a long time off.

He hoped he could make it.

Serena made sure to knock for the rest of the week.

Not that she didn't want to see Chadwick's bare chest, the light hairs that covered his body glistening with water, his hair damp and tousled....

And certainly not because she'd been fantasizing about Chadwick walking in on her in the shower, leaning her back against the tiled wall, kissing her like he'd kissed her in the store, those kisses going lower and lower until she was blind with pleasure, then her returning the favor....

Right. She knocked extra hard on his door because it was the polite thing to do.

Thursday was busy. The fallout from the board meeting had to be dealt with, and the last-minute plans for the gala could not be ignored. Once Chadwick got his clothes on, she hardly had more than two minutes alone with him before the next meeting, the next phone call.

Friday was the same. They were in the office until almost seven, soothing the jittery nerves of employees worried about their jobs and investors worried about not getting a big enough payout.

She still hadn't heard from Neil. She did manage to get a doctor's appointment scheduled, but it wasn't for another two weeks. If she hadn't heard anything after that, she'd have to call him. That was all.

But she didn't want to think about that. Instead, she thought about Saturday night.

She was not going to fall into bed with Chadwick. Above and beyond the fact that he was still her boss for the foreseeable future, there were too many problems. She *was* pregnant, for starters. She was still getting over the end of a nine-year relationship with Neil—and Chadwick wasn't divorced quite yet. She didn't want whatever was going on with her and Chadwick to smack of a rebound for either of them.

That settled it. If, perhaps in the near future—a future in which Serena was not pregnant, Chadwick was successfully divorced and Serena no longer worked for him because the company had been sold—*then* she could be brazen and call him up to invite him over. *Then* she could seduce him. Maybe in the shower. Definitely near a bed.

But not until then. Really.

So this was just a business-related event. Sure, an extra fancy one, but nothing else had changed.

Except for that kiss. That towel.
Those fantasies.
She was in *so* much trouble.

Seven

Her hair fixed into a sleek twist, Serena stood in her bedroom in her bathrobe and stared at the gowns like they were menacing her. All three were hung on her closet door.

With the price tags still on them.

Somehow, she'd managed to avoid looking at the tags in the store. The fabulous Mario had probably been working overtime to keep them hidden from her.

She had tens of thousands of dollars worth of gowns. Hanging in her house. Not counting the "necessary accessories."

The one she wanted to wear—the one-shoulder, cornflower blue dress that paired well with the long, dangly earrings? That one, on sale, cost as much as a used car. *On sale*! And the earrings? Sapphires. Of course.

I can't do this, she decided. This was not her world and she did *not* belong. Why Chadwick insisted on dressing her up and parading her around was beyond her.

She'd return the dresses and go back to being frugal Serena Chase, loyal assistant. That was the only rational thing to do.

Then her phone buzzed. For a horrifying second, she was afraid it was Neil, afraid that he'd come to his senses and wanted to talk. Wanted to see her again. Wanted frugal, loyal Serena back.

Just because she was trying not to fall head over heels for Chadwick didn't mean she wanted Neil.

She picked up her phone—it was a text from Chadwick.

On my way. Can't wait to see you.

Her heart began to race. Would he wear a suit like he usually did? Would he look stiff and formal or...would he be relaxed? Would he look at her with that gleam in his eye—the one that made her think of things like towels and showers and hot, forbidden kisses?

She should return these things. *All* of them.

She slipped the blue dress off the hanger, letting the fabric slide between her fingers. On the other hand... what would one night hurt? Hadn't she always dreamed about living it up? Wasn't that why she'd always gone to the galas before? It was a glimpse into a world that she longed to be a part of—a world where no one went hungry or wore cast-off clothing or moved in the middle of the night because they couldn't make rent?

Wasn't Chadwick giving her exactly what she wanted? Why shouldn't she enjoy it? Just for the night?

Fine, she decided, slipping into the dress. One night. One single night where she wasn't Serena Chase, hardworking employee always running away from poverty. For one glorious evening, she would be Serena Chase, queen amongst women. She would be escorted by a man

who wouldn't be able to take his eyes off her—a man who made her feel beautiful.

If she ever saw the fabulous Mario again, she was going to hug that man.

She dressed carefully. She felt like she was going too slowly, but she wasn't about to rush and accidentally pop a seam on such an expensive dress. She decided to go with a bolder eye, so she spent more time putting on eyeliner and mascara than she had in the last month.

She'd barely gotten her understated lipstick into the tiny purse that Mario had put with this dress—even though it was a golden yellow—when she heard the knock on the door. "One moment!" she yelled, as she grabbed the yellow heels that had arrived with everything else.

Then she took a moment to breathe. She looked good. She felt good. She was going to enjoy tonight or else. Tomorrow she could go back to being pregnant and frugal and all those other things.

Not tonight. Tonight was hers. Hers and Chadwick's.

She opened the door and felt her jaw drop.

He'd chosen a tux. And a dozen red roses.

"Oh," she managed to get out. The tux was exquisitely cut—probably custom-made.

He looked over the top of the roses. "I was hoping you'd pick that one. I brought these for you." He held the flowers out to her and she saw he had a matching rose boutonnière in his lapel.

She took the roses as he leaned forward. "You look amazing," he whispered in her ear.

Then he kissed her cheek. One hand slid behind her back, gripping her just above her hip. "Simply amazing," he repeated, and she felt the heat from his body warm hers from the inside out.

They didn't have to go anywhere. She could pull him

inside and they could spend the night wrapped around each other. It would be perfectly fine because they weren't at work. As long as they weren't in the office, they could do whatever they wanted.

And he was what she wanted to do.

No. No! She could not let him seduce her. She could not let herself *be* seduced. At least, not that easily. This was a business-related event. They were still on the clock.

Then he kissed her again, just below the dangly earring, and she knew she was in trouble. She had to do something. Anything.

"I'm pregnant," she blurted out. Immediately her face flushed hot. And not the good kind of hot, either. But that was exactly what she'd needed to do to slam on the brakes. Pregnant women were simply not amazing. Her body was crazy and her hormones were crazier and that had to be the *only* reason she was lusting after her boss this much.

Thank heavens, Chadwick pulled back. But he didn't pull away, damn him. He leaned his forehead against hers and said, "In all these years, Serena, I've never seen you more radiant. You've always been so pretty, but now... pregnant or not, you are the most beautiful woman in the world."

She wanted to tell him he was full of it—not only was she not the most beautiful woman in the world, but she didn't crack the top one hundred in Denver. She was plain and curvy and wore suits. Nothing beautiful about that.

But he slipped his hand over her hip and down her belly, his hand rubbing small circles just above the top of her panties. "This," he said, his voice low and serious and intent as his fingers spread out to cover her stomach, "just makes you better. I can't control myself around you anymore and I don't think I want to." As he said it, his

hand circled lower. The tips of his fingers crossed over the demarcated line of her panties and dipped down.

The warmth from his touch focused heat in her belly—and lower. A weight—heavy and demanding and pulsing—pounded between her thighs. She didn't want him to stop. She wanted him to keep going until he was pressing against the part of her that was heaviest. To feel his touch explore her body. To make her *his*.

If she didn't know him, she'd say he was feeding her a line of bull a mile long. But Chadwick didn't BS people. He didn't tell them what they wanted to hear. He told them the truth.

He told *her* the truth.

Which only left one question.

Now that she knew the truth, what would she do with it?

The absolute last place Chadwick wanted to be was at this restaurant. The only possible exception to that statement was the gala later. He didn't want to be at either one. He wanted to go back to Serena's place—hell, this restaurant was in a hotel, he could have a room in less than twenty minutes—and get her out of that dress. He wanted to lay her down and show her *exactly* how little he could control himself around her.

Instead, he was sitting across from Serena in one of the best restaurants in all of Denver. Since they'd left her apartment, Serena had been…quiet. He'd expected her to push back against dinner like she'd pushed back against the gown that looked so good on her, but she hadn't. Which was not a bad thing—she'd been gracious and perfectly well-mannered, as he knew she would be—but he didn't know what to talk about. Discussing work was both boring and stressful. Even though this was supposed

to be a business dinner, he didn't want to talk about losing the company.

Given how she'd reacted to him touching her stomach—soft and gently rounded beneath the flowing dress—he didn't think making small talk about her pregnancy was exactly the way to go, either. That wasn't making her feel beautiful. At least, he didn't think so. He was pretty sure if they talked about her pregnancy, they'd wind up talking about Neil, and he didn't want to think about that jerk. Not tonight.

Chadwick's divorce was out, too. Chadwick knew talking about exes and soon-to-be-exes at dinner simply wasn't done.

And there was the part where he'd basically professed how he felt about her. Kind of hard to do the chitchat thing after that. Because doing the chitchat thing seemed like it would minimize what he'd said.

He didn't want to do that.

But he didn't know what else to talk about. For one of the few times in his life, he wished his brother Phillip was there. Well, he *didn't*—Phillip would hit on Serena mercilessly, not because he had feelings for her but because she was female. He didn't want Phillip anywhere near Serena.

Still, Phillip was good at filling the silence. He had an endless supply of interesting stories about interesting celebrities he'd met at parties and clubs. If anyone could find *something* to talk about, it'd be his brother.

But that wasn't Chadwick's life. He didn't jet around making headlines. He worked. He went to the office, ran, showered, worked, worked some more and then went home. Even on the weekends, he usually logged in. Running a corporation took most of his time—he probably worked a hundred hours a week.

But that's what it took to run a major corporation. For so long, he'd done what was expected of him—what his father had expected of him. The only thing that mattered was the company.

Chadwick looked at Serena. She was sitting across from him, her hands in her lap, her eyes wide as she looked around the room. This level of luxury was normal for him—but it was fun seeing things through her eyes.

It was fun *being* with her. She made him want to think about something other than work—and given the situation, he was grateful for that alone. But what he felt went way beyond simple gratitude.

For the first time in his adult life—maybe longer—he was looking at someone who meant more to him than the brewery did.

That realization scared the hell out of him. Because, really—who *was* he if he wasn't Chadwick Beaumont, the fourth-generation Beaumont to run the brewery? That was who he'd been raised to be. Just like his father had wanted, Chadwick had always put the brewery first.

But now...things were changing. He didn't know how much longer he'd have the brewery. Even if they fended off this takeover, there might be another. The company's position had been weakened.

Funny, though—he felt stronger after this week with Serena.

Still, he had to say *something*. He hadn't asked her to dinner just to stare at her. "Are you doing all right?"

"Fine," she answered, breathlessly. She did look fine. Her eyes were bright and she had a small, slightly stunned smile on her face. "This place is just so...fancy! I'm afraid I'm going to use the wrong fork."

He felt himself relax a bit. Even though she looked like a million dollars, she was still the same Serena.

His.

No. He pushed that thought away as soon as it cropped up. She was not his—she was only his assistant. That was the extent of his claim to her. "Your parents never dressed you up and took you out to eat at a place like this just for fun?"

"Ah, no." A furious blush raced up her cheeks.

"Really? Not even for a special event?"

That happened a lot. He'd be eating some place nice—some place like this—and a family with kids who had no business being in a five-star restaurant would come in, the boys yanking on the necks of their ties and tipping over the drinks, the girls being extra fussy over the food. He'd sort of assumed that all middle-class people did something like that once or twice.

She looked up at him, defiance flashing in her eyes. The same defiance that had her refusing dresses. He liked it on her—liked that she didn't always bow and scrape to him just because he was Chadwick Beaumont.

"Did your parents ever put you in rags and take you to a food pantry just for fun?"

"What?"

"Because that's where we went 'out to eat.' The food pantry." As quickly as it had come, the defiance faded, leaving her looking embarrassed. She studied her silverware setting. "Sorry. I don't usually tell people that. Forget I said anything."

He stared at her, his mouth open. Had she really just said...*the food pantry?* She'd mentioned that her family had gone through a few financial troubles but—

"You picked the food bank for this year's charity."

"Yes." She continued to inspect the flatware, everything about her closed off.

This wasn't the smooth, flowing conversation he'd wanted. But this felt more important. "Tell me about it."

"Not much to tell." Her chin got even lower. "Poverty is not a bowl full of cherries."

"What happened to your parents?" Not that his parents had particularly loved him—or even liked him—but he'd never wanted for anything. He couldn't imagine how parents could let that happen to their child.

"Nothing. It's just that…Joe and Shelia Chase did everything to a fault. They still do. They're loyal to a fault, forgiving to a fault—generous to a fault. If you need twenty bucks, they'll give you the last twenty they have in the bank and then not have enough to buy dinner or get the bus home. My dad's a janitor."

At this, a flush of embarrassment crept over her. But it didn't stop her. "He'll give you the shirt off his back—not that you'd want it, but he would. He's the guy who always stops when he sees someone on the side of the road with a flat tire, and helps the person change it. But he gets taken by every stupid swindle, every scam. Mom's not much better. She's been a waitress for decades. Never tried to get a better job because she was so loyal to the diner owners. They hired her when she was fifteen. Whenever Dad got fired, we lived on her tips. Which turns out to not be enough for a family of three."

There was so much hurt in her voice that suddenly he was furious with her parents, no matter how kind or loyal they were. "They had jobs—but you still had to go to the food pantry?"

"Don't get me wrong. They love me. They love each other…but they acted as if money were this unknown force that they had no power over, like the rain. Sometimes, it would rain. And sometimes—most of the time—it wouldn't. Money flows into and out of our lives

independent of anything we do. That's what they thought. Still think."

He'd never questioned having money, just because there had always been so much of it. Who had to worry about their next meal? Not the Beaumonts, that was for damn sure. But he still worked hard for his fortune.

Serena went on, "They had love, Mom always said. So who needed cars that ran or health insurance or a place to live not crawling with bugs? Not them." Then she looked up at him, her dark brown eyes blazing. "But I do. I want more than that."

He sat there, fully aware his mouth had dropped open in shock, but completely unable to get it shut. Finally, he got out, "I had no idea."

She held his gaze. He could see her wavering. "No one does. I don't talk about it. I wanted you to look at me for what I am, not what I was. I don't want *anyone* to look at me and see a welfare case."

He couldn't blame her for that. If she'd walked into the job interview acting as if he owed her the position because she'd been on food stamps, he wouldn't have hired her. But she hadn't. She'd never played the sympathy card, not once.

"Did Neil know?" Not that he wanted to bring Neil into this.

"Yes. I moved in with him partly because he offered to cover the rent until I could pay my share. I don't think… I don't think he ever really forgot what I'd been. But he was stable. So I stayed." Suddenly, she seemed tired. "I appreciate the dresses and the dinner, Chadwick—I really do. But there were years where my folks didn't clear half of what you paid. To just *buy* dresses for that much…"

Like a bolt out of the blue, he understood Serena in a way he wasn't sure he'd ever understood another per-

son. She was kind and she was loyal—not to a fault, not at the sacrifice of her own well-being—but those were traits that he'd always admired in her. "Why did you pick the brewery?"

She didn't look away from him this time. Instead, she leaned forward, a new zeal in her eyes. "I had internship offers at a couple of other places, but I looked at the employee turnover, the benefits—how happy the workers were. I couldn't bear the thought of changing jobs every other year. What if I never got another one? What if I couldn't take care of myself? The brewery had all these workers that had been there for thirty, forty years—entire careers. It's been in your family for so long…it just seemed like a stable place. That's all I wanted."

And now that was in danger. He wasn't happy about possibly failing to keep the company in family hands, but he had a personal fortune to fall back on. He'd been worried about the workers, of course—but Serena brought it home for him in a new way.

Then she looked up at him through her dark lashes. "At least, that's all I *thought* I wanted."

Desire hit him low and hard, a precision sledgehammer that drove a spike of need up into his gut. Because, unlike Helen and unlike his mother, he knew that Serena wasn't talking about the gowns or the jewels or the fancy dinner.

She was talking about *him*.

He couldn't picture the glamorous, refined woman sitting across from him wearing rags and standing in line at a food pantry. And he didn't have to. That was one of the great things about being wealthy. "I promised you I wouldn't fail you, Serena. I keep my promises." Even if he lost the company—if he failed his father—

he wouldn't leave Serena in a position in which welfare was her only choice.

She leaned back, dropping her gaze again. Like she'd just realized she'd gone too far and was trying to back-track. "I know. But I'm not your responsibility. I'm just an employee."

"The hell you are." The words were out a little faster than he wanted them to be, but what was the point of pretending anymore? He hadn't lied earlier. Something about her had moved him beyond his normal restraint. She was so much *more* than an employee.

Her cheeks took on that pale pink blush that only made her more beautiful. Her mouth opened and she looked like she was about to argue with him when the waiter came up. When the man left with their orders—filet mignon for him, lobster for her—Chadwick looked at her. "Tell me about you."

She eyed him with open suspicion.

He held up his hands in surrender. "I swear it won't have any bearing on how I treat you. I'll still want to buy you pretty things and take you to dinner and have you on my arm at a gala." *Because that's where you belong,* his mind finished for him.

On his arm, in his bed—in his life.

She didn't answer at first, so he leaned forward and dropped his voice. "Do you trust me when I say I'll never use it against you?"

She tucked her lower lip up under her teeth. It shouldn't look so sexy, but on her it did. Everything did.

"Prove it."

Oh, yeah, she was challenging him. But it didn't feel like a battle of wills.

He didn't hesitate. "My dad beat me. Once, with a belt." He kept his voice low, so no one could hear, but it

didn't matter. The words ripped themselves out of a place deep inside of his chest.

Her eyes went wide with shock and she covered her open mouth with her hand. It hurt to look at her, so he closed his eyes.

But that was a mistake. He could see his father standing over him, that nice Italian leather belt in his hand, buckle out—screaming about how Chadwick had gotten a C on a math test. He heard the belt whistle through the air, felt the buckle cut into his back. Felt the blood start to run down his side as the belt swung again—all because Chadwick had messed up how to subtract fractions. Future CEOs knew how to do math, Hardwick had reminded him again and again.

That's all Chadwick had ever been—future CEO of Beaumont Brewery. He'd been eleven. It was the only time Hardwick Beaumont had ever left a mark on him, but it was a hell of a mark. He still had the scar.

It was all such a long time ago. Like it had been part of a different life. He thought he'd buried that memory with his father, but it was still there, and it still had the capacity to cause him pain. He'd spent his entire life trying to do what his father wanted, trying to avoid another beating, but what had that gotten him? A failed marriage and a company that was about to be sold out from under him.

Hardwick couldn't hurt him now.

He opened his eyes and looked at Serena. Her face was pale and there was a certain measure of horror in her eyes, but she wasn't looking at him like he feared she would—like she'd forgotten about the man he was now and only saw a bleeding little boy.

Just like he saw a woman he trusted completely, and not a little girl who ate at food pantries.

He kept going. "When I didn't measure up to expec-

tations. As far as I know, he never hit any of his other kids. Just me. He broke my toys, sent my friends away and locked me in my room, all because I had to be the perfect Beaumont to run his company."

"How…how could he do that?"

"I was never his son. Just his employee." The words tasted bitter, but they were the unvarnished truth. "And, like you said, I don't tell people about it. Not even Helen. Because I don't want people to look at me with pity."

But he'd told her. Because he knew she wouldn't hold it against him. Helen would have. Every time they fought, she would have thrown that back in his face because she thought she could use his past to control him.

Serena wouldn't manipulate him like that. And he wouldn't do that to her.

"So," he said, leaning back in his chair, "tell me about it."

She nodded. Her face was still pale, but she understood what he was saying. She understood him. "Which part?"

"All of it."

So she did.

Eight

Serena clung to Chadwick's arm as they swept up the red-carpeted stairs, past the paparazzi and into the Denver Art Museum. Part of her clinginess was because of the heels. Chadwick took huge, masterful strides that she was struggling to keep up with.

But another part of it was how unsettled she was feeling. She'd told him about her childhood. About the one time she and her mom had lived in a women-only shelter for three days because her dad didn't want them to have to sleep on the streets in the winter—but her mom had missed him so much that she'd bundled Serena up and they'd gone looking for him. She'd told him about Missy Gurgin in fourth grade making fun of Serena for wearing her old clothes, about the midnight moves to stay ahead of the due rent, about eating dinner that her mom had scavenged from leftovers at the diner.

Things she'd never told anyone. Not even Neil knew about all of that.

In turn, he'd told her about the way his father had controlled his entire life, about punishments that went way beyond cruel. He'd talked in a dispassionate tone, like they were discussing the weather and not the abuse of a child too young to defend himself, but she could hear the pain beneath the surface. He could act like it was all water under the bridge, but she knew better. All the money in the world hadn't protected Chadwick.

She put her hand over her stomach. No one would ever treat her child like that. And she would do everything in her power to keep her baby from ever being cold and hungry—or wondering where her next meal was coming from.

They walked into the Art Museum. Serena tried to find the calm in her mind. God knew she needed it. She pushed aside the horror of what Chadwick had told her, the embarrassment of sharing her story with him.

This was more familiar territory. She'd come to the Art Museum for this gala for the previous seven years. She knew where the galleries were, where the food was. She'd helped arrange that. She knew how to hold her champagne glass—oh, wait. No champagne for her tonight.

Okay, no need to panic. She was still perfectly at ease. She was only wearing a wildly expensive dress, four-inch heels and a fortune in jewels. Not to mention she was pregnant, on a date with her boss and....

Yeah, champagne would be *great* right about now.

Chadwick leaned over and whispered, "Are you breathing?" in her ear.

She did as instructed, the grin on her face making it easier. "Yes."

He squeezed her hand against his arm, which she found exceptionally reassuring. "Good. Keep it that way."

It was almost ten o'clock. Once they'd started sharing stories at dinner, it had been hard to stop. Serena was both mortified that she'd told any of that to Chadwick and, somehow, relieved. She'd buried those secrets deep, but they hadn't been dead. They'd lived on, terrorizing her like a monster under the bed.

At some point during dinner, she'd relaxed. The meal had been fabulous—the food was a little out there, but good. She'd been able to just enjoy being with Chadwick.

Now they were arriving at the gala slightly later than was fashionable. People were noticing as Chadwick swept her into the main hall. She could see heads tilting as people craned their necks for a better view, could hear the whispers starting.

Oh, this was not a good idea.

She'd loved her black dress because it looked good—but it had also blended, something Mario had forbidden. Now that she was here and standing out in the crowd in a bold blue, she wished she'd gone with basic black. People were *staring*.

A woman wearing a fire engine red gown that matched her fire engine red hair separated from the crowd just as Serena and Chadwick hit the middle of the room. She fought the urge to excuse herself and bolt for the ladies room. Queens amongst women did not hide in the bathroom, and that was *that*.

"There you are," the woman said, leaning to kiss Chadwick on the cheek. "I thought maybe you weren't coming, and Matthew and I would have to deal with Phillip all by ourselves."

Serena exhaled in relief. She should have recognized Frances Beaumont, Chadwick's half sister. She was well liked at the Beaumont Brewery, a fact that had a great deal to do with Donut Friday. Once a month, she person-

ally delivered a donut to every single employee. Apparently, she'd been doing it since she was a little girl. As a result, Serena had heard more than a few of the workers refer to her as "our Frannie."

Frances was the kind of woman people described as "droll" without really knowing what that meant. But her razor-sharp wit was balanced with a good nature and an easy laugh.

Unlike everyone else at the brewery, though, Chadwick didn't seem to relax around his half sister. He stood ramrod straight, as if he were hoping to pass inspection. "We were held up. How's Byron?"

Frances waved her hand dismissively as Serena wondered, *Byron?*

"Still licking his wounds in Europe. I believe he's in Spain." Frances sighed, as if this revelation pained her, but she said nothing else.

Chadwick nodded, apparently agreeing to drop the topic of Byron. "Frannie, you remember Serena Chase, my assistant?"

Frances looked her up and down. "Of course I remember Serena, Chadwick." She leaned over and carefully pulled Serena into a light hug. "Fabulous dress. Where did you get it?"

"Neiman's." Breathing in, breathing out.

Frances gave her a warm smile. "Mario, am I right?"

"You have a good eye."

"Of course, darling." She drawled out this last word until it was almost three whole syllables. "It's a job requirement when you're an antiquities dealer."

"Your dress is stunning." Serena couldn't help but wonder how much it cost. Was she looking at several thousand dollars of red velvet and rubies? The one good

thing was that, standing next to Frances Beaumont in that dress, no one was noticing Serena Chase.

Chadwick cleared his throat. She glanced up to find him smiling down at her. Well, no one but him would notice her, anyway.

He turned his attention back to his sister. "You said Phillip is already drunk?"

Frances batted away this question with manicured nails that perfectly matched the color of her dress. "Oh, not yet. But I'm sure before the evening is through he'll have charmed the spirits right out of three or four bottles of the good stuff." She leaned forward, dropping her voice to a conspiratorial whisper. "He's just that charming, you know."

Chadwick rolled his eyes. "I know."

Serena giggled, feeling relieved. Frances wasn't treating her like a bastard at a family picnic. Maybe she could do this.

Then Frances got serious, her smile dropping away. "Chadwick, have you thought more about putting up some money for my auction site?"

Chadwick made a huffing noise of disapproval, which caused a shadow to fall over Frances's face. Serena heard herself ask, "What auction site?"

"Oh!" Frances turned the full power of her smile on Serena. "As an antiquities dealer, I work with a lot of people in this room who'd prefer not to pay the full commission to Christie's auction house in New York, but who would never stoop to the level of eBay."

Ouch. Serena had bought more than a few things off the online auction site.

"So," Frances went on, unaware of the impact of her words on Serena, "I'm funding a new venture called Beaumont Antiquities that blends the cachet of a tradi-

tional art auction house with the power of social media. I have some partners who are handling the more technical aspects of building our platform, while I'm bringing the family name and my *extensive* connections to the deal." She turned back to Chadwick. "It's going to be a success. This is your chance to get in on the ground floor. And we could use the Chadwick Beaumont Seal of Approval. It'd go a long way to help secure additional funding. Think of it. A Beaumont business that has nothing to do with beer!"

"I like beer," Chadwick said. His tone was probably supposed to be flat, but it actually came out sounding slightly wounded, as if Frances had just told him his life's work was worthless.

"Oh, you know what I mean."

"You always do this, Frannie—investing in the 'next big idea' without doing your homework. An exclusive art auction site? In this market? It's not a good idea. If I were you, I'd get out now before you lose everything. Again."

Frances stiffened. "I haven't lost *everything*, thank you very much."

Chadwick gave her a look that was surprisingly paternal. "And yet, I've had to bail you out how many times?" Frances glared at him. Serena braced for another cutting remark, but then Chadwick said, "I'm sorry. Maybe this one will be a success. I wish you the best of luck."

"Of course you do. You're a good brother." Instantly, her droll humor was back, but Serena could see a shadow of disappointment in her eyes. "We're Beaumonts. You're the only one of us who behaves—well, you and maybe Matthew." She waved her hand in his general direction. "All respectable, while the rest of us are desperately trying to be dissolute wastrels." Her gaze cut between Chadwick and Serena. "Speaking of, there's Phillip now."

Before Serena could turn, she felt a touch slide down her bare arm. Then Phillip Beaumont walked around her, his fingers never leaving her skin. He was quite the golden boy. Only an inch shorter than his brother, he wore a tux without a bow tie. It made him look disheveled and carefree—which, according to all reports, he was. Where Chadwick was more of a sandy blond, Phillip's coloring was brighter, as if he'd been born for people to look at him.

Phillip took her hand in his and bent low over it. "*Mademoiselle,*" he said as he held the back of her hand against his lips.

An uncontrollable shiver raced through her body. She did not particularly like Phillip—he caused Chadwick no end of grief—but Frances was one-hundred-percent right. He was exceedingly charming.

He looked up at Serena, his lips curled into the kind of grin that pronounced him fully aware of the effect he was having on her. "*Where* did you come from, enchantress? And, perhaps more importantly, why are you on *his* arm?"

Enchantress? That was a new one. And also a testament to Mario's superpowers. Phillip stopped by the office on a semi-regular basis to have meetings with Chadwick and Matthew about his position as head of special promotions for the brewery. She'd talked to him face-to-face dozens, if not hundreds, of times.

Chadwick made a sound that was somewhere between clearing his throat and growling. "Phillip, you remember Serena Chase, my executive assistant."

If Phillip was embarrassed that he hadn't recognized her, he gave no sign of it. He didn't even break eye contact with her. Instead, he favored her with the kind of smile that probably made the average woman melt into

his bed. As it was, she was feeling a little dazzled by his
sheer animal magnetism.

"How could I forget Ms. Chase? You are," he went on,
leaning into her, "*unforgettable*."

Desperate, she looked at Frances, who gave a small
shrug.

"That's *enough*." No mistaking it this time—that was
nothing but a growl from Chadwick.

If Chadwick had growled at anyone else like that, he
would have sent them diving for cover. But not Phillip.
Good heavens, he didn't even look ruffled. He did give
her a sly little wink before he touched her hand to his lips
again. Chadwick tensed next to her and she wondered if
a brawl was about to break out.

But then he released his grip on her hand and turned
his full attention to his brother. Serena heaved a sigh of
relief. No wonder Phillip had such a reputation as a ladies' man.

"So, news," he said in a tone that was only slightly
less sultry than the one he'd been using on her. "I bought
a horse!"

"Another one?" Frances and Chadwick said at the
same time. Clearly, this was something that happened
often.

"You've got to be kidding me." Chadwick looked...
murderous. There really was no other way to describe
it. He looked like he was going to throttle his brother in
the middle of the Art Museum. "I don't suppose this one
was only a few thousand?"

"Chad—hear me out." At this use of his shortened
name, Chadwick flinched. Serena had never heard anyone call him that but Phillip. "This is an Akhal-Teke
horse."

"*Gesundheit*," Frances murmured.

"A *what*?" Chadwick was now clutching her fingers against his arm in an almost desperate way. "How much?"

"This breed is extremely rare," Phillip went on. "Only about five thousand in the world. From Turkmenistan!"

Serena felt like she was at a tennis match, her head was turning back and forth between the two brothers so quickly. "Isn't that in Asia, next to Afghanistan?"

Phillip shot her another white-hot look and matching smile. "Beautiful *and* smart? Chadwick, you lucky dog."

"I swear to God," Chadwick growled.

"People are staring," Frances added in a light, sing-song tone. Then, looking at Serena for assistance, she laughed as if this were a great joke.

Serena laughed as well. She'd heard Chadwick and Phillip argue before, but that was usually behind Chadwick's closed office door. Never in front of her. Or in front of anyone else, for that matter.

For once, Phillip seemed to register the threat. He took an easy step back and held out his hands in surrender. "Like I was saying—this Akhal-Teke. They're most likely the breed that sired the Arabians. Very rare. Only about five hundred in this country, and most of those come from Russian stock. Kandar's Golden Sun isn't a Russian Akhal-Teke."

"*Gesundheit*," Frances murmured again. She looked at Serena with a touch of desperation, so they both laughed again.

"He's from Turkmenistan. An incredible horse. One to truly found a stable on."

Chadwick pinched the bridge of his nose. "How much?"

"Only seven." Phillip stuck out his chest, as if he were proud of this number.

Chadwick cracked open one eye. "Thousand, or hundred thousand?"

Serena tried not to gape. Seven thousand for a horse wasn't too much, she guessed. But seven *hundred* thousand? That was a lot of money.

Phillip didn't say anything. He took a step back, though, and his smile seemed more...forced.

Chadwick took a step forward. "Seven *what*?"

"You know, one Akhal-Teke went for fifty million—and that was in 1986 dollars. The most expensive horse ever. Kandar's Golden Sun—"

That was as far as he got. Chadwick cut him off with a shout. "You spent seven *million* on a horse while I'm working my ass off to keep the company from being sold to the wolves?"

Everything about the party stopped—the music, the conversations, the movement of waiters carrying trays of champagne.

Someone hurried toward them. It was Matthew Beaumont. "Gentlemen," he hissed under his breath. "We are having a *charity* event here."

Serena put her hand on Chadwick's arm and gave it a gentle tug. "A very good joke, Phillip," she said in a slightly too-loud voice.

Frances caught Serena's eye and nodded in approval. "Chadwick, I'd like to introduce you to the director of the food bank, Miriam Young." She didn't know where, exactly, the director of the food bank was. But she was sure Ms. Young wanted to talk with Chadwick. Or, at least, had wanted to talk to him before he'd started yelling menacingly at his relatives.

"Phillip, did I introduce you to my friend Candy?" Frances added, taking her brother by the arm and pulling him in the opposite direction. "She's *dying* to meet you."

The two brothers held their poses for a moment longer, Chadwick glaring at Phillip, the look on Phillip's face almost daring Chadwick to hit him in full view of the assembled upper crust of Denver society.

Then the men parted. Matthew walked on the other side of Chadwick, ostensibly to lead the way to the director. Serena got the feeling it was more to keep Chadwick from spinning and tackling his brother.

"Serena," Matthew said simply. "Nicely done. *Thus far*," he added in a heavy tone, "the evening has been a success. Now if we can just get through it without a brawl breaking out—"

"I'm fine," Chadwick snapped, sounding anything but. "I'm just *fine*."

"Not fine," Matthew muttered, guiding them into a side gallery. "Why don't I get you a drink? Wait here," he said, parking Chadwick in front of a Remington statue. "Do *not* move." He looked at Serena. "Okay?"

She nodded. "I've got him."

She hoped.

Nine

Chadwick had never really believed the old cliché about being so mad one saw red. Turns out, he'd just never been mad enough, because right now, the world was drenched in red-hot anger.

"How could he?" he heard himself mutter. "How could he just buy a horse for that much money without even thinking about the consequences?"

"Because," a soft, feminine voice said next to him, "he's not you."

The voice calmed him down, and some of the color bled back into the world. He realized Serena was standing next to him. They were in a nearly empty side gallery, in front of one of the Remington sculptures that made the backbreaking work of herding cattle look glorious.

She was right. Hardwick had never expected anything from Phillip. Never even noticed him, unless he did something outrageous.

Like buy a horse no one had ever heard of for seven
million damn dollars.

"Remind me again why I work myself to death so that
he can blow the family fortune on horses and women?
So Frances can sink money into another venture that's
bound to fail before it gets off the ground? Is that all I'm
good for? A never-ending supply of cash?"

Delicate fingers laced through his, holding him tightly.
"Maybe," Serena said, her voice gentle, "you don't have
to work yourself to death at all."

He turned to her. She was staring at the statue as if it
were the most interesting thing in the world.

Phillip had done whatever the hell he wanted since he
was a kid. It hadn't mattered what his grades were, who
his friends were, how many sports cars he had wrecked.
Hardwick just hadn't cared. He'd been too focused on
Chadwick.

"I…" He swallowed. "I don't know how else to run
this company." The admission was even harder than what
he'd shared over dinner. "This is what I was raised to do."

She tilted her head to one side, really studying the
bronze. "Your father died while working, didn't he?"

"Yes." Hardwick had keeled over at a board meeting,
dead from the heart attack long before the ambulance
had gotten there. Which was better, Chadwick had always figured, than him dying in the arms of a mistress.

She tilted her head in the other direction, not looking
at him but still holding his hand. "I rather like you alive."

"Do you?"

"Yes," she answered slowly, like she really had to
think about it. But then her thumb moved against the
palm of his hand. "I do."

Any remaining anger faded out of his vision as the
room—the woman in it—came into sharp focus.

"You told me a few days ago," she went on, her voice quiet in the gallery, "that you wanted to do something for yourself. Not for the family, not for the company. Then you spent God only knows how much on everything I'm wearing." He saw the corner of her mouth curve up into a sly smile. "Except for a few zeros, this isn't so different, is it?"

"I don't need to spend money to be happy like he does."

"Then why am I wearing a fortune's worth of finery?"

"Because." He hadn't done it because it made him happy. He'd done it to see her look like this, to see that genuine smile she always wore when she was dressed to the nines. To know he could still *make* a woman smile.

He'd done it to make her happy. *That* was what made him happy.

She shot him a sidelong glance that didn't convey annoyance so much as knowing—like that was exactly what she'd expected him to say. "You are an impossibly stubborn man when you want to be, Chadwick Beaumont."

"It has been noted."

"What do you want?"

Her.

He'd wanted her for years. But because he was not Hardwick Beaumont, he'd never once pursued her.

Except now he was. He was walking a fine line between acceptable actions and immoral, unethical behavior.

What he really wanted, more than anything, was to step over that line entirely.

She looked up at him through her thick lashes, waiting for an answer. When he didn't give her one, she sighed. "The Beaumonts are an intelligent lot, you know. They'll learn how to survive. You don't have to protect them.

Don't work for them. They won't ever appreciate it because they didn't earn it themselves. Work for you." She
reached up and touched his cheek. "Do what makes *you*
happy. Do what *you* want."

She did realize what she was telling him, didn't she?
She had to—her fingers wrapped around his, her palm
pressed against his cheek, her dark brown eyes looking
into his with a kind of peace that he couldn't remember
ever feeling.

What he wanted was to leave this event behind, drive
her home, and make love to her all night long. She *had*
to know that was all he wanted—however not-divorced
he was, pregnant she was, or employed she was by him.

Was she giving him permission? He would not trap his
assistant into any sexual relationship. That wasn't him.

God, he wanted her permission. *Needed* it. Always
had.

"Serena—"

"Here we are." Matthew strode into the gallery leading
Miriam Young, the director of the Rocky Mountain Food
Bank, and a waiter with a tray of champagne glasses. He
gave Serena a look that was impossible to miss. "How
is everything?"

She withdrew her hand from his cheek. "Fine," she
said, with one of those beautiful smiles.

Matthew made the introductions and Serena politely
declined the champagne. Chadwick only half paid attention. Her words echoed around his head like a loose
bowling ball in the trunk of a car.

Don't work for them. Work for you.

Do what makes you happy.

She was right. It was high time he did what he
wanted—above and beyond one afternoon.

It was time to seduce his assistant.

* * *

Standing in four-inch heels for two hours turned out to be more difficult than Serena had anticipated. She resorted to shifting from foot to foot as she and Chadwick made small talk with the likes of old-money billionaires, new-money billionaires, governors, senators and foundation heads. Most of the men were in tuxes like Chadwick's, and most of the women were in gowns. So she blended in well enough.

Chadwick had recovered from the incident with Phillip nicely. She'd like to think that had something to do with their conversation in the gallery. With the way she'd told him to do what he wanted and the way he'd looked at her like the only thing he wanted to do was *her*.

She knew there was a list of reasons not to want him back. But she was tired of those reasons, tired of thinking she couldn't, she *shouldn't*.

So she didn't. She focused on how painful those beautiful, beautiful shoes were. It kept her in the here and now.

Shoes aside, the evening had been delightful. Chadwick had introduced her as his assistant, true, but all the while he'd let one of his hands rest lightly on her lower back. She'd gotten a few odd looks, but no one had said anything. That probably had more to do with Chadwick's reputation than anything else, but she wasn't about to question it. Even without champagne, she'd been able to fall into small talk without too much panic.

She'd had a much nicer time than when she used to come with Neil. Then, she'd stood on the edge of the crowd, judiciously sipping her champagne and watching the crowd instead of interacting with it. Neil had always talked to people—always looking for another sponsor for his golf game—but she'd never felt like she was a part of the party.

Chadwick had made her a part of it this time. She wasn't sure she'd ever truly feel like she fit in with the high roller crowd, but she hadn't felt like an interloper. That counted for a great deal.

The evening was winding down. The crowd was trailing out. She hadn't seen Phillip leave, but he was nowhere to be seen. Frances had bailed almost an hour before. Matthew was the only other Beaumont still there, and he was deep in discussion with the caterers.

Chadwick shook hands with the head of the Centura Hospital System and turned to her. "Your feet hurt."

She didn't want to seem ungrateful for the shoes, but she wasn't sure her toes would ever be the same. "Maybe just a little."

He gave her a smile that packed plenty of heat. But it wasn't indiscriminately flirtatious, like his brother's. All night long, that goodness had been directed at only one woman.

Her.

He slid a hand around her waist and began guiding her toward the door. "I'll drive you home."

She grinned at this statement. "Don't worry. I didn't snag a ride with anyone else."

"Good."

The valet brought up Chadwick's Porsche, but he insisted on holding the door for her. Then he was in the car and they were driving at a higher-than-average speed, zipping down the highway like he had someplace to be.

Or like he couldn't wait to get her home.

The ride was quick, but silent. What was going to happen next? More importantly, what did she want to happen next? And—most importantly of all—what would she *let* happen?

Because she wanted this perfect evening to end per-

fectly. She wanted to have one night with him, to touch the body she'd only gotten a glimpse of, to feel beautiful and desirable in his arms. She didn't want to think about pregnancies or exes or jobs. It was Saturday night and she was dressed to the nines. On Monday, maybe they could go back to normal. She'd put on her suit and follow the rules and try not to think about the way Chadwick's touch made her feel things she'd convinced herself she didn't need.

Soon enough, he'd pulled up outside her apartment. His Porsche stuck out like a sore thumb in the parking lot full of minivans and late-model sedans. She started to open her door, but he put a hand on her arm. "Let me."

Then he hopped out, opened her door and held his hand out for her. She let him help her out of the deep seats of his car.

Then they stood there.

His strong hand held tight to hers as he pulled her against his body. She looked up into his eyes, feeling lightheaded without a drop of champagne. All night long, he'd only had eyes for her—but they'd been surrounded by people.

Now they were alone in the dark.

He reached up and traced the tips of his fingers over her cheek. Serena's eyelids fluttered shut at his touch.

"I'll walk you to your door," he said, his voice thick with strain. He stroked her skin—a small movement, similar to the way he'd touched her on Monday.

But this was different. Everything was different now.

This was the moment. This was her decision. She didn't want sex with Chadwick to be one of those things that "just happened," like her pregnancy. She was in control of her own life. She made the choices.

She could thank him for the lovely evening and tell

him she'd see him bright and early Monday morning. She could even make a little joke about seeing him in a towel again. Then she could walk into her apartment, close the door and...

Maybe never have another moment—another chance—to be with Chadwick.

She made her choice. She would not regret it.

She opened her eyes. Chadwick's face was inches from hers, but he wasn't pressing her to anything. He was waiting for her.

She wouldn't make him wait any longer. "Would you like to come in?"

He tensed against her. "Only if I can stay."

She kissed him then. She leaned up in the painful, beautiful shoes and pressed her lips to his. There was no "kissing him back," no "waiting for him to make the first move."

This was going to happen because she wanted it to. She'd wanted it for years and she was darn tired of waiting. That was reason enough.

"I'd like that."

The next thing she knew, Chadwick had physically swept her off her feet and was carrying her up to her door. When she gave him a quizzical look, he grinned sheepishly and said, "I know your feet hurt."

"They do."

She draped her arms around his neck and held on as he took the stairs, carrying her as if she were one of the skinny women from the party instead of someone whose size-ten body was getting bigger every day. But then, she'd seen all his muscles a few days before. If anyone could carry her, it was him. His chest was warm and hard against her body.

Things began to tighten. Her nipples tensed under-

neath the gown, and that heavy weight between her legs seemed to be pulling her down into his body. Oh, yes. She wanted him. But the thing that was different from all her time with Neil was how intense it felt to want Chadwick.

Obviously, it'd only been a few months since the last time she'd had sex with Neil. Just about three months. That was how far along she was. But she hadn't felt the physical weight of desire for much, much longer than that. She couldn't remember the last time just thinking about sex with Neil had turned her on this much. Maybe it was her crazy hormones—or maybe Chadwick did this to her. Maybe he'd always done this to her and she'd forced herself to ignore the attraction because falling for her boss just wasn't convenient.

He set her down at the door so she could get her key out of the tiny purse. But he didn't let her go. He put his hands on her hips and pulled her back into his front. They didn't talk, but the huge bulge that pressed against her backside said *lots* of things, loud and clear.

She got the door open and they walked inside. She kicked off the pretty shoes, which made Chadwick loom an extra four inches over her. He hadn't let go of her. His hands were still on her hips. He was *grabbing* her in a way that was quickly going from gentle to possessive. The way he filled his palms with her hips didn't make her feel fat. It made her feel like he couldn't get enough of her—he couldn't help himself.

Yes. That was what she needed—to be wanted so much that he couldn't control himself.

He leaned down, his mouth against her ear. "I've been waiting for you for years." The strain of the wait made his voice shake. He pulled her hips back again, the ridge in his pants unmistakable. "*Years*, Serena."

"Me, too." Her voice came out breathy, barely above a

whisper. She reached behind her back and slid her hand up the bulge. "Is that for me?"

"Yes," he hissed, his breath hot against her skin. One hand released a hip and found her breast instead. Even through the strapless bra, he found her pointed nipple and began to tease it. "You deserve slow and sensual, but I need you too much right now."

As if to prove his point, he set his teeth against her neck and bit her skin. Not too hard, but the feeling of being consumed by desire—by him—crashed through her. Her knees began to shake.

"Slow later," she agreed, wiggling her bottom against him.

With a groan, he stepped away from her. She almost toppled over backward, but then his hands were unzipping her dress. The gown slid off her one shoulder and down to the ground with a soft rustle.

She was extra glad she hadn't gone with the Spanx. Bless Mario's heart for putting her in a dress that didn't require them. Instead, a matching lacy thong had arrived with the bra. Which meant Chadwick currently had one heck of a view. She didn't know if she should strut, or pivot so he couldn't see her bottom.

Once the gown was gone, she stepped free of it. Chadwick moaned. "Serena," he got out as he slid his hands over her bare backside. "You are…amazing." His fingers gripped her skin, and he pressed his mouth to the space between her neck and her shoulder.

Strut, she decided. Nothing ruined good sex like being stupidly self-conscious when he already thought she was amazing. She pulled away from him before he could take away her power to stand.

"This way," she said over her shoulder as she, yes, *strutted* toward the bedroom, her hips swaying.

Chadwick made a noise behind her that she took as a compliment, before following her.

She headed toward the bed, but he caught up with her. He grabbed her hips again. "You are better than I thought," he growled as his hands slipped underneath the lace of the thong. He pulled the panties down, his palms against her legs. "I've dreamed of having you like this."

"Like how?"

He nimbly undid her bra, tossing it aside. She was naked. He was not.

He directed her forward, but not toward the bed. Instead, he pushed her in the direction of her dresser.

The one with the big mirror over it.

Serena gasped at the sight they made. Her, nude. Him, still in his tux, towering over her.

"This. Like this." He bent his head until his lips were on her neck again, just below the dangling earrings. "Is this okay?" he murmured against her skin.

"Yes." She couldn't take her eyes off their reflections, the way her pale skin stood out against his dark tux. The way his arms wrapped around her body, his hands cradled her breasts. The way his mouth looked as he kissed her skin.

The driving weight of desire between her legs pounded with need. "Yes," she said again, reaching one arm over her head and tangling her fingers in his hair. "Just like this."

"Good. So good, Serena." Without the bra, she could feel the pads of his fingertips trace over her sensitive nipple, pulling until it went stiff with pleasure.

She moaned, letting her head fall back against his shoulder. "Just like that," she whispered.

Then his other hand traced lower. This time, he didn't pause to stroke her stomach. His fingers parted her neatly

trimmed hair and pressed against her heaviest, hottest place.

"Oh, Chadwick," she gasped as he moved his fingers in small, knowing circles, his other hand stroking her nipple, his mouth finding the sensitive spot under her ear—his bulge rubbing against her.

Her knees gave, but she didn't go far. Her wet center rode heavy on his hand as his other arm caught her under both breasts.

"Put your hands on the dresser," he told her. His voice was shaking as badly as her knees were, which made her smile. He might be pushing her to the brink, but she was pulling him along right behind her. "Don't close your eyes."

"I won't." She leaned forward and braced herself on the dresser. "I want to see what you do to me."

"Yeah," he groaned, a look of pure desire on his face as he met her gaze in the mirror. A finger slipped inside. So much, but not enough. She needed more. "You're so ready for me." Then she felt him lean back and work his own zipper.

"Next time, I get to do that for you."

"Any time you want to strip me down, you just let me know. Hold on, okay?" Then he withdrew his fingers.

She watched as he removed a condom from his jacket pocket. It wasn't like she could get more pregnant than she already was, but she appreciated that he didn't question protecting her.

He rolled the condom on and leaned into her. She quivered as she waited for his touch. He bent forward, placing a kiss between her shoulder blades. Then he was against her. Sliding into her.

Serena sucked in air as he filled her. And filled her. And *filled* her. In the mirror, her eyes locked onto his as

he entered her. She almost couldn't take it. "Oh, Chadwick," she panted as her body took him in. "Oh—oh—
oh!"

The unexpected orgasm shook her so hard that she
almost pulled off him—but he held her. "Yeah," he
groaned. "You feel so beautiful, Serena. So beautiful."

He gripped her hips as he slid almost all the way out
before he thrust in again. "Okay?" he asked.

"Better than okay," she managed to get out, wiggling
against him. The boldness of her action shocked her. Was
she really having sex with Chadwick Beaumont, standing up—in front of a mirror?

Oh, hell yes, she was. And it was the hottest thing
she'd ever done.

"Naughty girl," he said with a grin.

Then he began in earnest. From her angle, she couldn't
see where their bodies met. She could only see his hands
when he cupped her breasts to tweak a nipple or slid his
fingers between her legs to stroke her center. She could
only see the need on his face when he leaned forward to
nip at her neck and shoulder, the raw desire in his eyes
when their gazes met.

She held on to that dresser as if her life depended on
it while Chadwick thrust harder and harder. "I need you
so much," he called out as he grabbed her by the waist
and slammed his hips into hers. "I've always needed
you *so* much."

"Yes—like that," she panted, rising up to meet him
each time. His words pushed her past the first orgasm.
She couldn't remember ever feeling this needed, this sexual. "I'm going to—I'm—" Her next orgasm cut off her
words, and all she could do was moan in pleasure.

But she didn't close her eyes. She saw how she looked

when she came—her mouth open, her eyes glazed with desire. So hot, watching the two of them together.

A roar started low in Chadwick's chest as he pumped once, twice more—then froze, his face twisted in pleasure. Then he sort of fell forward onto her, both of them panting.

"My Serena," he said, sounding spent.

"My Chadwick," she replied, knowing it was the truth. She was his now. And he was hers.

But he wasn't. He couldn't be. He was still married. He was still her boss. One explosive sexual encounter didn't change those realities.

For tonight, he was hers.

Tomorrow, however, was going to be a problem.

Ten

Chadwick laid in Serena's bed, his eyes heavy and his body relaxed.

Serena. How long had he fantasized about bending her over the desk and taking her from behind? Years. But the mirror? Watching her watch him?

Amazing.

She came back in and shut the door behind her. Her hair was down now, hanging in long, loose waves around her shoulders. He couldn't remember ever seeing her hair down. She always wore it up. He could see her nude figure silhouetted by the faint light that trickled through her drapes. Her body did things to him—things he didn't realize he could still feel. It'd been so long….

She paused. "You need anything?"

"You." He held out his hand to her. "Come here."

She slipped into bed and curled up against his chest. "That was…wow."

Grinning, he pulled her in for a kiss. A long kiss. A kiss that involved a little more than just kissing. He could *not* get enough of her. The feeling of her filling his hands, pressed against him—she was so much a woman. He'd brought three condoms, just in case. He had the remaining two within easy reach on her bedside table.

So he broke the kiss.

"Mmmm," she hummed. "Chadwick?"

"Yes?"

She paused, tracing a small circle on his chest. "I'm pregnant."

"A fact we've already established."

"But why doesn't that bother you? I mean, everything's changing and I feel so odd and I'm going to blow up like a whale soon. I just don't think...I don't feel beautiful."

He traced a hand down her back and grabbed a handful of her bountiful backside. "You are amazingly beautiful. I guess you being pregnant just reminds me how much of a woman you are."

She was quiet for a moment. "Then why didn't you ever have kids with Helen?"

He sighed. He didn't want Helen in this room. Not now. But Serena had a right to know. Last week, they might not have discussed their personal lives at the office—but this was a different week entirely. "Did you ever meet her? Of course you did."

"At the galas. She never came by the office."

"No, she never did. She didn't like beer, didn't like my job. She only liked the money I made." Part of that was his fault. If he'd put her before the job, well, things might have been different. But they might not have been. Things might have been exactly the same.

"She was very pretty. Very—"

"Very plastic." She'd been pretty once, but with every

new procedure, she'd changed. "She had a lot of work done. Lipo, enlargements, Botox—she didn't want to have a baby because she didn't want to be pregnant. She didn't want me."

That was the hard truth of the matter. He'd convinced himself that she did—convinced himself that he wanted to spend the rest of his life with her, that it would be different from his father's marriages. That's why he'd struck the alimony clause from the pre-nup. But he'd never been able to escape the simple fact that he was Hardwick's son. All he'd ever been able to do was temper that fact by honoring his marriage vows long after there was nothing left to honor.

"She moved out of our bedroom about two years ago. Then filed for divorce almost fourteen months ago."

"That's a *very* long time." The way she said it—air rushing out of her in shock—made him hold her tighter. "Did you want to have a kid? I mean, I get her reasons, but..."

Had he ever wanted kids? It was no stretch to say he didn't know. Not having kids wasn't so much his choice as it had been the path of least resistance. "You haven't met my mother, have you?"

"No."

He chuckled. "You don't want to know her. She's—well, in retrospect, she's a lot like Helen. But that's all I knew. Screaming fights and weeks of silent treatment. And since I was my father's chosen son, she treated me much the same way she treated Hardwick. I ruined her figure, even though she got a tummy tuck. I was a constant reminder that she'd married a man she detested."

"Is that what Helen did? Scream?"

"No, no—but the silent treatment, yes. It got worse over time. I didn't want to bring a child into that. I didn't

want a kid to grow up with the life I did. I didn't…I didn't want to be my father."

He couldn't help it. He took her hand and guided it around to his side—to where the skin had never healed quite right.

Serena's fingertips traced the raised scar. It wasn't that bad, he told himself. He'd been telling himself that same thing for years. Just an inch of puckered skin.

Helen had seen it, of course, and asked about it. But he hadn't been able to tell her the truth. He'd come up with some lie about a skiing accident.

"Oh, Chadwick," Serena said, in a voice that sounded like she was choking back tears.

He didn't want pity. As far as the world was concerned, he had no reason to be pitied. He was rich, good-looking and soon to be available again. Only Serena saw something else—something much more real than his public image.

He still didn't want her to feel sorry for him. So he kept talking even as she rubbed his scar. "Do you know how many half siblings I have?"

"Um, Frances and Matthew, right?"

"Frances has a twin brother, Byron. And that's just with Jeannie. My father had a third wife and had two more kids with her, Lucy and David. Johnny, Toni and Mark with his fourth wife. We know of at least two other kids, one with a nanny and one with…" He swallowed, feeling uncertain.

"His secretary?"

He winced. "Yes. There are probably more. That was why I fought against *this*," he said, pressing his lips against her forehead, "for so long. I didn't want to be him. So when Helen said she wanted to wait before we

had kids—and wait and wait—I said fine. Because that's different than what Hardwick did."

Serena pulled her hand away from his scar to trace small circles on his chest again. "Those are all really good reasons. Mine were more selfish. I didn't marry Neil because my parents were married and that piece of paper didn't save them or me. I always thought we'd have kids one day, but I wanted to wait until my finances could support us. I put almost every bonus you've ever given me into savings, building up my nest egg. I thought I'd like to take some time off, but the thought of not getting that paycheck every other week scared me so much. So I waited. Until I messed up." She took a ragged breath. "And here I am."

He chewed over what she'd said. "Here with me?"

"Well…yes. Unmarried, pregnant and sleeping with my boss in clear violation of company policy." She sighed. "I've spent my adult life trying to lead a stable life. I stayed with a man I didn't passionately love because it was the safe thing to do. I've stayed in this apartment— the same place I've lived since I moved in with Neil nine years ago—because it's rent-controlled. I drive the same car I bought six years ago because it hasn't broken down. And now? This is not the most secure place in the world. It…it scares me. To be here with you."

Her whole life had been spent running away from a hellish childhood. Was that any different from his? Trying so hard to not let the sins of the father revisit the son.

Yet here he was, sleeping with his secretary. And here she was, putting her entire livelihood at risk to fall into bed with him.

No. This would not be a repeat of the past. He would not let her fall through the cracks just because he wasn't strong enough to resist her. At the very least, he hadn't

gotten her pregnant and abandoned her like his father would have—even if someone else had done just that.

"I want to be here with you, even if it complicates matters. You make me feel things I didn't know I was still capable of feeling. The way you look at me...I was never a son, never really a husband. Just an employee. A bank account. When I'm with you, I feel like...like the man I was always supposed to be, but never got the chance to."

She clutched him even tighter. "You never treated me like I was an afterthought, a welfare kid. You always treated me with respect and made me feel like I could be better than my folks were. That I *was* better."

He tilted her face back. "I will *not* fail you, Serena. This complicates things, but I made you a promise. I *will* keep it."

She blinked, her eyes shining. "I know you will, Chadwick. That means everything to me." She kissed him, a tender brush that was sweeter than any other touch he'd ever felt. "I won't fail you, either."

The next kiss wasn't nearly as tender. "Serena," he groaned as she slipped her legs over his thighs, heat from her center setting his blood on fire. "I need you."

"I need you, too," she whispered, rolling onto her back. "I don't want to look at you in a mirror, Chadwick. I want to see you."

He sat back on his knees and grabbed one of the condoms. Quickly, he rolled it on and lowered himself into her waiting arms. His erection found her center and he thrust in.

She moaned as he propped himself up on one arm and filled his other hand with her breast. "Yes, just like that."

He rolled his thumb over her nipple and was rewarded when it went stiff. Her breast was warm and full and *real*.

Everything about her was real—her body, her emotions, her honesty.

Serena ran her nails down his back as she looked him in the eye, spurring him on. Over and over he plunged into her welcoming body. Over and over, waves of emotion flooded his mind.

Now that he was with her, he felt more authentic than he had in years—maybe ever. The closest he'd ever come to feeling real was the year he'd spent making beer. The brewmasters hadn't treated him with distrust, as so many people in the other departments had. They'd treated him like a regular guy.

Serena worked hard for him, but she'd never done so with the simpering air of a sycophant. Had never treated him like he was a stepping stool to bigger and better things.

This was real, too. The way her body took his in, the way he made her moan—the way he wanted to take her in his arms and never let her go....

Without closing her eyes—without breaking the contact between them—she made a high-pitched noise in the back of her throat as she tightened on his body then collapsed back against her pillow.

He drove hard as his climax roared through his ears so loudly that it blotted out everything but Serena. Her eyes, her face, her body. *Her.*

He wanted her. He always had.

This didn't change anything.

"Serena..." He wanted to tell her he loved her, but then what did that mean? Was he actually in love with her? What he felt for her was far stronger than anything he'd ever felt for another woman, but did that mean it was love?

So he bit his tongue and pulled her into his arms, burying his face into her hair.

"Stay with me," she whispered. "Tonight. In my bed."

"Yes." That was all he needed right now. Her, in his arms.

What if this was love? With Serena tucked against his chest, Chadwick started to drift off to sleep on that warm, happy thought. He and Serena. In love.

But then a horrifying idea popped into his mind, jerking him back from peaceful sleep. What if this wasn't love? What if this was mere infatuation, something that would evaporate under the harsh light of reality—reality that they might have ignored tonight but that would be unavoidable come Monday morning?

He'd slept with his assistant. Before the divorce was final.

It was exactly what his father would have done.

Eleven

The smell of crisp bacon woke him.

Chadwick rolled over to find himself alone in an unfamiliar bed. He found a clock on the side table. Half past six. He hadn't slept that late in years.

He sat up. The first thing he saw was the mirror. The one he'd watched as he made love to his assistant.

Serena.

His blood began to roar in his ears as his mind replayed the previous night. Had he really crossed that line—the one he'd sworn he would never cross?

Waking up naked in her bed, his body already aching for her, seemed to say one hell of a *yes*.

He buried his head in his hands. What had he done?

Then he heard it—the soft sound of a woman humming. It was light and, if he didn't know better, filled with joy.

He got out of bed and put his pants on. Breakfast

first. He'd think better once he had a meal in him. As he walked down the short hallway toward the kitchen, he was surprised at how sore his body was. Apparently, not having sex for a few years and then suddenly having it twice had been harder on him than running a few extra miles would have been.

He looked around Serena's place. It was quite small. There was the bedroom he'd come out of. He made another stop at the bathroom, which stood between the bedroom and another small room that was completely empty. Then he was out into the living room, which had a shabby-looking couch against one wall and a space where a flat-screen television must have been on the other. A table stood between the living room space and the kitchen. The legs and the chairs looked a bit beat up, but the table was covered by a clean, bright blue cloth and held a small, chipped vase filled with the roses he'd brought her.

His wine cellar was bigger than this apartment. The place was clearly assembled from odds and ends, but he liked it. It looked almost exactly how he'd imagined a real home would look, one in which babies might color on the walls and spill juice on the rug. One filled with laughter and joy. A place that was a *home*, not just a piece of real estate.

He found Serena standing in front of the stove, a thin blue cotton robe wrapped around her shoulders, her hair hanging in long waves down her back. Something stirred deep in his chest. Did she have anything on under the robe? She was humming as she flipped the bacon. It smelled *wonderful*.

He had a cook, of course. Even though he didn't eat at home very often, George was in charge of feeding the household staff. If Chadwick gave him enough warn-

ing, George would have something that rivaled the best restaurants in Denver waiting for him. But if Chadwick didn't, he'd eat the same thing that the maids did. Which was the norm.

He leaned against the doorway, watching Serena cook for him. This felt different than knowing that, somewhere in his huge mansion, George was making him dinner. That was George's job.

Serena frying him bacon and, by the looks of it, eggs?

This must be what people meant by "comfort food." Because there was something deeply comforting about her taking care of him. As far as he could remember, no one but a staff cook had ever made him breakfast.

Was this what normal people did? Woke up on a Sunday morning and had breakfast together?

He came up behind her and slid his arms around her waist, reveling in the way her hair smelled—almost like vanilla, but with a hint of breakfast. He kissed her neck. "Good morning."

She startled but then leaned back, the curve of her backside pressing against him. "Hi." She looked up at him.

He kissed her. "Breakfast?"

"I'm normally up before six, but I made it until a little after," she said, sounding sheepish about it.

"That's pretty early." Those were basically the same hours he kept.

"I have this boss," she went on, her tone teasing as she flipped another strip of bacon, "who keeps insane hours. You know how it is."

He chuckled against her ear. "A real bastard, huh?"

She leaned back, doing her best to look him in the eye. "Nope. I think he's amazing."

He kissed her again. This time he let his hands roam away from her waist to other parts. She pulled away and playfully smacked the hand that had been cupping her breast. "You don't want your breakfast burned, do you? The coffee's ready."

She already had a cup sitting in front of the coffeemaker. Like everything else in her place, the coffeemaker looked like it was either nine years old or something she'd bought secondhand.

She hadn't been kidding. By the looks of her apartment, she really had put every bonus in savings.

It was odd. In his world, people spent money like it was always going out of style. No one had to save because there would always be more. Like Phillip, for example. He saw a horse he wanted, and he bought it. It didn't matter how much it was or how many other horses he had. Helen had been the same, except for her it was clothing and plastic surgery. She had a completely new wardrobe every season from top designers.

Hell, he wasn't all that different. He owned more cars than he drove and a bigger house than he'd ever need, and he had three maids. The only difference was that he'd been so busy working that he hadn't had time to start collecting horses like his brother. Or mistresses, like his father. For them, everything had been disposable. Even the horses. Even the people.

Serena wasn't like that. She didn't need a new coffeepot just because the old one was *old*. It still worked. That seemed to be good enough for her.

He filled his mug—emblazoned with the logo of a local bank—and sat at the table, watching her. She moved comfortably around her kitchen. He wasn't entirely sure where the kitchen was in his family mansion. "You make breakfast often?"

She put some bread into a late-model toaster. "I've gotten very good at cooking. It's…"

"Stable?"

"*Reassuring*," she answered with a grin. "I bring home my own bacon *and* fry it up in the pan." She brought plates with bacon and eggs to the table, and then went back for the toast and some strawberry jam. "I clip coupons and shop the sales—that saves a lot of money. Cooking is much cheaper than eating out. I think last night was the first time I'd gone out to dinner in…maybe three months?" Her face darkened. "Yes. Just about three months ago."

He remembered. Three months ago, Neil and she had "mutually" decided to end their relationship.

"Thank you for making me breakfast. I've never had someone cook for me. I mean, not someone who wasn't on staff."

She blushed. "Thank you for dinner. And the dresses. I think it's pretty obvious that I've never had anyone spend that kind of money on me before."

"You handled yourself beautifully. I'm sorry if I made you uncomfortable."

That had been his mistake. It was just that she fit in so well at the office, never once seeming out of place among the high rollers and company heads Chadwick met with. He'd assumed that was part of her world—or at least something close to it.

But it wasn't. Now that he saw her place—small, neatly kept but more "shabby" than "shabby chic"—he realized how off the mark he'd been.

She gave him a smile that was part gentle and part hot. "It was fun. But I think I'll get different shoes for next time."

Next time. The best words he'd heard in a long, long time.

They ate quickly. Mostly because he was hungry and the food was good, but also because Serena shifted in her seat and started rubbing his calf with her toes. "When do you have to leave?"

He wanted to stay at least a little bit longer. But he had things to do, even though it was Sunday—for starters, he had an interview with *Nikkei Business*, a Japanese business magazine, at two. He couldn't imagine talking about the fate of the brewery from the comfort of Serena's cozy place. How could those two worlds ever cross?

The moment the thought crossed his mind, he felt like he'd been punched in the stomach. Really, how *could* their two worlds cross? His company was imploding and his divorce was draining him dry—and that wasn't even counting the fact that Serena was pregnant. And his assistant.

He'd waited so long for Serena. She'd done admirably the night before at dinner and then the gala, but how comfortable would she really be in his world?

They still had this morning. They finished breakfast and then he tried to help her load the dishwasher. Only he kept trying to put the cups on the bottom rack, which made her giggle as she rearranged his poor attempts. "Never loaded a dishwasher before, huh?"

"What gave me away?" He couldn't bring himself to be insulted. She was right.

"Thanks for trying." She closed the dishwasher door and turned to him. "Don't worry. You're better at other things."

She put her arms around his neck and kissed him. Yeah, he didn't have to leave yet.

He stripped the robe from her shoulders, leaving it in a

heap on the floor. No, nothing underneath. Just her wonderful body. With the morning light streaming through
the sheers she had hung over her windows, he could finally, fully see what he'd touched the night before.

Her breasts were large and firm. He bent down and
traced her nipple with his tongue. Serena gasped as the
tip went hard in his mouth, her fingers tangling through
his hair. *Sensitive*. Perfect.

"Bed," she said in a voice that walked the fine line
between fluttery and commanding.

"Yes, ma'am," he replied, standing back to give her a
mock salute before he swept her off her feet.

"Chadwick!" Serena clutched at him, but she giggled
as he carried her back down the short hall.

He laid her down on the bed, pausing only long enough
to get rid of his pants. Then he was filling his hands with
her breasts, her hips—covering her body with his—loving the way she touched him without abandon.

This was what he wanted—not the company, not
Helen, not galas and banquets and brothers and sisters
who took and took and never seemed to give back.

He wanted Serena. He wanted the kind of life where
he helped cook and do the dishes instead of having an
unseen staff invisibly take care of everything. He wanted
the kind of life where he ate breakfast with her and then
went back to bed instead of rushing off for an interview
or a meeting.

He wanted to have a life outside of Beaumont Brewery. He wanted it to be with Serena.

He had no idea how to make that happen.

As he rocked into Serena's body and she clung to him,
all he could think about was the way she made him feel—
how he hadn't felt like this in…well, maybe ever.

This was what he wanted.

There had to be a way.

Finally, after another hour of lying in her arms, he managed to tear himself away from Serena's bed. He put on his tuxedo pants and shirt and headed for the car after a series of long kisses goodbye. How amazing did Serena look, standing in the doorway in her little robe, a coffee cup in her hand as she waved him off? It almost felt like a wife kissing her husband goodbye as he went off to work.

He was over-romanticizing things. For starters, Serena wouldn't be happy as a stay-at-home wife. It would probably leave her feeling too much like she wasn't bringing home that bacon. He knew now how very important that was to her. But they couldn't carry on like this at work. The office gossips would notice something sooner or later—and once she began to show, things would go viral in a heartbeat. He didn't want to subject her to the rumor mill.

There had to be a way. The variables ran through his mind as he drove home. He was about to lose the company. She worked for him. A relationship was against company policy. But if he lost the company...

If he lost the company, he wouldn't be her boss anymore. She might be out of a job, too, but at least they wouldn't be violating any policy.

But then what? What was next? What did he *want* to do? That was what she'd asked him. Told him, in fact. Do what he wanted.

What was that?

Make beer, he realized. That was the best time he'd had at Beaumont Brewery—the year he'd spent making beer with the brewmasters. He *liked* beer. He knew a lot about it and had played a big role in selecting the sea-

sonal drafts for the Percheron Drafts line of craft beers. What if…

What if he sold the brewery, but kept Percheron Drafts for himself, running it as a small private business? Beaumont would be dead, but the family history of brewing would live on in Percheron Drafts. He could be rid of his father's legacy and run this new company the way he wanted to. It wouldn't be Hardwick's. It would be Chadwick's.

He could hire Serena. She knew as much about what he did as anyone. And if they formed a new company, well, they could have a different company policy.

And if they got sixty-five dollars a share for the brewery…maybe he could walk into Helen's lawyer's office and make her that offer she couldn't refuse. Everyone had a price, Matthew had said, and he was right. He quickly did the math.

If he liquidated a few extraneous possessions—cars, the jet, property, *horses*—he could make Helen an offer of $100 million to sign the papers. Even she wouldn't be able to say no to a number like that. And he'd still have enough left over to re-incorporate Percheron Drafts.

As he thought about the horses, he realized this plan would only work if he did it on his own. He would get $50 million because he actually worked for the company. But his siblings would get about $15 to $20 million each. He couldn't keep working for them. Serena had been right about that, too. If he took Percheron Drafts private, he would have to sever all financial ties with his siblings. He couldn't keep footing the bill for extravagant purchases, and what's more, he didn't want to.

The more he thought about it, the more he liked this idea. He'd be done with Beaumont Brewery—free from his father's ideas of how to run a company. Free to do

things the way he wanted, to make the beer he wanted. It would be a smaller company, sure—one that wouldn't be able to pay for the big mansion or the staff or the garage full of cars he rarely drove.

He'd have to downsize his life for a while, but would that really be such a horrible thing? Serena had lived small her entire life and she seemed quite happy—except for the pregnancy thing.

He wanted to give her everything he could—but he knew she wouldn't be comfortable with extravagance. If he gave her a job in a new company, paid her a good wage, made sure she had the kind of benefits she needed...

That was almost the same thing as giving her the world. That was giving her stability.

This could work. He'd call his lawyers when he got home and run the idea past them.

This *had* to work. He had to make this happen. Because it was what he wanted.

After Serena watched Chadwick's sports car drive away, she tried not to think about what the neighbors would say about the late arrival and very late departure of such a vehicle.

But that didn't mean she didn't worry. What had she done? Besides have one of the most romantic nights in memory. A fancy dinner, glamorous gala, exquisite sex? It'd been like something out of a fairy tale, the poor little girl transformed into the belle of the ball.

How long had it been since she'd enjoyed sex that much? Things with Neil had been rote for a while. A long while, honestly. Something that they *tried* to do once a week—something that didn't last very long or feel very good.

But sex with Chadwick? Completely different. Com-

pletely *satisfying*. Even better than she'd dreamed it would be. Chadwick hadn't just done what he wanted and left it at that. He'd taken his time with her, making sure she came first—and often.

What would it be like to be with a man who always brought that level of excitement to their bed? Someone she couldn't keep her hands off—someone who thought she was sexy even though her body was getting bigger?

It would be *wonderful*.

But how was that fantasy—for that's what it was, a fantasy of epic proportions—going to become a reality? She couldn't imagine fitting into Chadwick's world, with expensive clothes and fancy dinners and galas all the time. And, as adorably hot as he'd looked standing in her kitchen in nothing but his tux trousers, she also couldn't imagine Chadwick being happy in her small apartment, clipping coupons and shopping consignment stores for a bargain.

God, how she wanted him. She'd been waiting for her chance for years, really. But she had no idea how she could bridge the gap between their lives.

In a fit of pique, Serena started cleaning. Which was saying something, as she'd already cleaned in anticipation of Chadwick possibly seeing the inside of her apartment—and her bedroom.

But there was laundry to be done, dishes to be washed, beds to be made—more than enough to keep her busy. But not enough to keep her mind off Chadwick.

She changed into her grubby sweat shorts and a stained T-shirt. What the heck was going to happen on Monday? It was going to be hard to keep her hands off him, especially behind the closed door of his office. But doing anything, even touching him, was a violation of

company policy. It went against her morals to violate policies, especially ones she'd helped write.

How was she supposed to be in love with Chadwick while she worked for him?

She couldn't be. Not unless...

Unless she didn't work for him.

No. She couldn't just quit her job. Even if the whole company was about to be sold off, she couldn't walk away from a steady paycheck and benefits. The sale and changeover might take months, after all—months during which she could be covered for prenatal care, could be making plans. Or some miracle could occur and the whole sale could fall through. Then she'd be safe.

So what was she going to do about Chadwick? She didn't want to wait months before she could kiss him again, before she could hold him in her arms. She was tired of pretending she didn't have feelings for him. If things stayed the same...

Well, one thing she knew for certain was that things wouldn't stay the same. She'd slept with him—multiple times—and she was pregnant. Those two things completely changed *everything*.

She was transferring the bedsheets from the washer to the dryer when she heard something at the door. Her first thought was that maybe Chadwick had changed his mind and decided to spend the day with her.

But, as she raced for the door, it swung open. *Chadwick doesn't have a key*, she thought. And she always kept her door locked.

That was as far as she got in her thinking before Neil Moore, semi-pro golf player and ex-everything, walked in.

"Hey, babe."

"Neil?" The sight of him walking in like he'd never

walked out caused such a visceral reaction that she almost threw up. "What are you doing here?"

"Got your email," he said, putting his keys back on his hook beside the door as he closed it. He looked at her in her cleaning clothes. "You look…good. Have you put on weight?"

The boldness of this insult—for that's what it was—shook her back to herself. "For crying out loud, Neil. I sent you an email. Not an invitation to walk in, unannounced."

Another wave of nausea hit her. What if Neil had shown up two hours before—when she was still tangled up with Chadwick? Good lord. She fought the emotion down and tried to sound pissed. Which wasn't that hard, really.

"You don't live here anymore, remember? *You* moved out."

Then he said, "I missed you."

Nothing about his posture or attitude suggested this was the case. He slouched his way over to the couch—*her* couch—and slid down into it, just like he always had. What had she seen in this man, besides the stability he'd offered her?

"Is that so? I've been here for three months, Neil. Three months without a single call or text from you. Doesn't seem like you've missed me very much at all."

"Well, I did," he snapped. "I see that nothing's changed here. Same old couch, same old…" He waved his hand around in a gesture that was probably supposed to encompass the whole apartment but mostly seemed directed at her. "So what did you want to talk to me about?"

She glared at him. Maybe it would have been better if Chadwick *had* still been here. For starters, Neil would have seen that nothing was the same anymore—

she wasn't, anyway. She wasn't the same frugal executive assistant she'd been when he'd left. She was a woman who went shopping in the finest stores and made small talk with the titans of industry and looked damn good doing it. She was a woman who invited her boss into her apartment and then into her bed. She was pregnant and changing and bringing home her own bacon and frying it up in her own pan, thank you very much.

Neil didn't notice her look of death. He was staring at the spot where the TV had been before he'd taken that with him. "You haven't even gotten a new television yet? Geez, Serena. I didn't realize you were going to take me leaving so hard."

"I don't need one. I don't watch TV." A fact she would have thought he'd figured out after nine years of cohabitating—or at least figured out after she told him to take the TV when he moved. "Did you come here just to criticize me? Because I can think of a lot better ways to spend a Sunday morning."

Neil rolled his eyes, but then he sat up straighter. "You know, I've been thinking. We had nine good years together. Why did we let that get away from us?"

She could not believe the words coming out of this man's mouth. "Correct me if I'm wrong, but I believe 'we' let that get away from 'us' when you started sleeping with groupies at the country club."

"That was a mistake." He agreed far more quickly than he had when Serena had found the incriminating text messages. They'd gone out to dinner that night to try and "work things out," but it'd all fallen apart instead. "I've changed, babe. I know what I did was wrong. Let me make it up to you."

This was Neil "making it up to her"—criticizing her appearance and her apartment?

"I'll do better. Be better for you." For a second, he managed to look sincere, but it didn't last. "I heard that the brewery might get sold. You own stock in the company, right? We could get a bigger place—much nicer than this dump—and start over. It could be really good, babe."

Oh, for the love of Pete. That's what this was. He'd gotten wind of the AllBev offer and was looking for a big payout.

"What happened? Your lover go back to her husband?"

The way Neil's face turned a ruddy red answered the question for her, even though he didn't. He just went back to staring at the space where the television used to be.

The more she talked to him, the less she could figure out what she had ever seen in him. The petty little criticisms—it wasn't that those were new, it was just that she'd gotten used to not having her appearance, her housekeeping and her cooking sniped at.

In three months, she'd realized how much she'd settled by staying with Neil. No wonder the passion had long since bled out of their relationship. Hard to be passionate when the man who supposedly loved you was constantly tearing you down.

Chadwick didn't do that to her. Even before this last week had turned everything upside down, he'd always let her know how much he appreciated her hard work. That had just carried over into her bed. Boy, had he appreciated her hard work.

Serena shook her head. This wasn't exactly an either/or situation. Just because she didn't want Neil didn't necessarily mean her only other option was Chadwick. Even if whatever was going on between her and Chadwick was nothing more than a really satisfying rebound—for both of them—well, that didn't mean she wanted to throw her-

self at Neil. She was no longer a scared college girl exist-
ing just above the poverty line. She was a grown woman
fully capable of taking care of herself.

It was a damn good thing to realize.

"I'm pregnant. You're the father." There. She'd gotten
it out. "That's what I needed to talk to you about. And
because *you* were sleeping around, *I* have to get tested."

For a moment, Neil was well and truly shocked. His
mouth flopped open and his eyes bugged out of his head.
"You're…"

"Pregnant. Have been for three months."

"Are you sure I'm the father?"

Her blood began to boil. "Of course you're the father,
you idiot. Just because you were sleeping around doesn't
mean I was. I was faithful to you—to *us*—until the very
end. But that wasn't enough for you. And now you're not
enough for me."

"I…I…" He seemed stuck.

Well, he could just stick. She was the one that was
pregnant. She'd spend the rest of her life raising his—
her—baby. But that didn't mean she had to spend the
rest of her life with him. "I thought you should know."

"I didn't want—I can't—" He wasn't making a lot of
progress. "Can't you just *end* it?"

"Get out." The words flew from her mouth. "Get out
now."

"But—"

"This is my child. I don't need anything from you, and
what's more is I don't *want* anything from you. I won't
sue you for child support. I never want to see you again."
She hadn't said that when he'd left the last time. Maybe
because she hadn't believed the words. But now she did.

Neil's eyes hadn't made a lot of progress back into

his skull. "You don't want money? Damn—how much is Beaumont paying you now?"

Was that all she was—a back-up source of funding? "If you're still here in one minute, I'm calling the police. Goodbye, Neil."

He got up, looking like she'd smacked him. "Leave your key," she called after him. She didn't want any more surprise visits.

He took the key off his key ring and hung it back on the hook.

Then he closed the door on his way out.

And that was that.

She looked around the apartment as if the blinders had suddenly been lifted from her eyes. This wasn't her place. It had never been hers. This had been *their* place —hers and Neil's. She'd wanted to stay here because it was safe.

But Neil would always feel like he was entitled to be there because it had been his apartment before she'd moved in.

She didn't want to raise her baby in a place that was haunted by unfaithfulness and snide put-downs.

She needed a fresh start.

The thought terrified her.

Twelve

"Ms. Chase, if you could join me in my office."

Serena tried not to grin as she gathered up her tablet. He was paging her a full forty minutes earlier than their normal meeting time. What a difference a week made. Seven days before, she'd been shell-shocked after realizing she was pregnant. This week? She was sort of her boss's secret lover.

No, best not to think of it in those terms. Company policy and all that.

She opened the door to Chadwick's office and shut it behind her. That was what she normally did, but today the action had an air of secrecy about it.

Chadwick was sitting behind his desk, looking as normal as she'd ever seen him. Well, maybe not *that* normal. He glanced up and his face broke into one huge grin. God, he was so handsome. It almost hurt to look at him, to know that he was so happy because of her.

He didn't say anything as she walked toward her regular seat. Instead, he got up and met her halfway with the kind of kiss that melted every single part of her body. He pulled her in tight, and his lips explored hers.

"I missed you," he breathed in her ear as he wrapped his arms around her.

She took in his clean scent, her body responding to his touch. How different was this from Neil telling her he missed her the day before? Chadwick wasn't all talk. He followed up everything he said with actions.

"Me, too." Now that she knew exactly what was underneath that suit jacket, she couldn't stop running her hands over the muscles of his back. "I've never wanted Monday to get here so fast."

"Hmmm" was all he replied as he took another kiss from her. "When can I see you again?"

She gave him a look that was supposed to be stern. It must not have come across the way she intended it to, because he cracked a goofy grin. "This doesn't count?"

"You know what I mean."

She did. When could they spend another night wrapped in each other's arms? She wanted to say tonight. Right now. They could leave work and not come back until much, much later.

That wasn't an option.

"What are we going to do? I hate breaking the rules."

"You wrote the rule."

"That makes it even worse."

Instead of looking disgruntled with her, his grin turned positively wicked. "Look, I know this is a problem. But I'm working on a solution."

"Oh?"

"It's in process." She must have given him a look because he squeezed her a little tighter. "Trust me."

She stared into his eyes, wanting nothing more than to go back to Saturday night. Or even Sunday morning.

But reality was impossible to ignore. "If you need any help solving things, you just let me know."

"Done. When's your doctor's appointment?"

She touched the cleanly shaven line of his chin. "Friday next week."

"You want me to come with you?"

Love. The word floated up to the top of her consciousness, unbidden. That's what this was—love. Even if she hadn't said the exact word, she felt it with all of her heart.

Her throat closed up as tears threatened. Oh, God, she was in love with Chadwick Beaumont. It was both the best thing that had ever happened to her and one hell of a big problem.

He ran his finger under her chin again—much like he had the week before—and smiled down at her. "You all right?"

"I am. You wouldn't mind coming with me?"

"I've recently discovered that it's good to get out of the office every so often. I'd love to accompany you."

She had to swallow past the lump in her throat.

"Are you sure you're all right?"

She leaned her head against his shoulder, loving the solid, strong way he felt against her. "I hope you get that solution figured out soon."

"I won't fail you, Serena." He sounded so serious about it that she had no choice but to believe him. To hope that whatever he was planning would work. "Now, I believe I have time tonight to have a business dinner with my assistant, don't I? We can discuss my schedule in a little more…detail."

How could she say no to that? It was a business-pro-

fessional activity, after all. "I believe we can make that happen."

"So," Chadwick said, pulling back and leading her toward the couch. "Tell me about your weekend."

"Funny about that." Sitting on the couch, her head against his shoulder, she related what had happened with Neil.

"You want me to take care of it?"

The way he said it—sounding much like he had when he'd nearly started a fight with his brother at the gala—made her smile. It should have been him being something of a Neanderthal male. As it was, it made her feel…secure.

"No, I think he got the message. He's not getting anything out of me or this company."

She then told Chadwick how she was thinking of moving to a new place and making a clean break with the past.

He got an odd look on his face as she talked. She knew that look—he was thinking.

"Got a solution to this problem yet?"

He cupped her face in his hands and kissed her—not the heated kiss from earlier, but something that was softer, gentler. Then he touched his forehead to hers. "You'll be the first to know."

That lump moved up in her throat again. She knew he'd keep his promise.

But what would it cost him?

"Mr. Beaumont." Serena's voice over the intercom sounded…different. Like she was being strangled.

"Yes?" He looked at Bob Larsen sitting across the desk from him, who froze mid-pitch. It wasn't like Serena to interrupt a meeting without a damn good reason.

There was a tortured pause. "Mrs. Beaumont is here to see you."

Stark panic flooded Chadwick's system. There were only a few women who went by that name and all of the options were less than pleasant. Blindly, he chose the least offensive option. "My mother?"

"Mrs. *Helen* Beaumont is here to see you."

Oh, *hell*.

Chadwick locked eyes with Bob. Sure, he and Bob had worked together for a long time, and yes, Chadwick's never-ending divorce was probably watercooler fodder, but Chadwick had worked hard to keep his personal drama and business life separate.

Until now.

"One moment," he managed to get out before he shut the intercom off. "Bob..."

"Yeah, we can pick this up later." Bob was hastily gathering his things and heading for the door. "Um... good luck?"

"Thanks." Chadwick was going to need a lot more than luck.

What was Helen doing there? She'd never come to the office when they were semi happily married. He hadn't talked to her without lawyers present in over a year. He couldn't imagine she wanted to reconcile. But what else would bring her there?

He knew one thing—he had to play this right. He could not give her something to use against him. He took a second to straighten his tie before he opened his door.

Helen Beaumont was not sitting in the waiting chairs across from Serena's desk. Instead, she was standing at one of the side windows, staring out at the brewery campus. Or maybe at nothing at all.

She was so thin he could almost see through her, like

she was a shadow instead of an actual woman. She wore a high-waisted skirt that clung to her frame, and a silk blouse topped with a fur stole. Diamonds—ones he'd paid for—covered her fingers and ears. She wasn't the same woman he'd married eight years before.

He looked at Serena, who was as white as notebook paper. Serena gave him a panicked little shrug. So she didn't have any idea what Helen was doing there, either.

"Helen." In good faith, he couldn't say it was nice to see her. So he didn't. "Shall we talk in my office?"

She pivoted on her five-inch heels and tried to kill him with a glare. "Chadwick." Her eyes cut to Serena. "I don't concern myself with what servants might hear."

Chadwick tried his best not to show a reaction. "Fine. To what do I owe the honor of a visit?"

"Don't be snide, Chadwick. It doesn't suit you." She looked down her nose at him, which was quite a feat given that she was a good eight inches shorter than he was. "My lawyer said you were going to make a new offer—the kind of offer you've refused to make for the last year."

Damn it. His lawyers were going to find themselves short one influential client for jumping the gun. Floating a trial balloon was different than telling Helen he had an offer. He hadn't even had the time to contact AllBev's negotiating team yet, for crying out loud. There was no offer until the company was sold.

He couldn't take control of his life—get the company he wanted, live the *way* he wanted—until Beaumont Brewery and AllBev reached a legally binding agreement. And what's more, none of this was going to happen overnight or even that week. Even if things moved quickly, negotiations would take months.

Plus, he hadn't told Serena about the plan to sell Beau-

mont but keep Percheron. God, he'd wanted to keep this all quiet until he had everything set—no more ugly surprises like this one.

"There's a difference between 'refused' and 'been unable' to make."

"Is there? Are you trying to get rid of me, Chadwick?" She managed to say it with a pout, as if he were trying to hurt her feelings.

"I've been trying to end our relationship since the month after you filed for divorce. Remember? You refused to go to marriage counseling with me. You made your position clear. You didn't want me anymore. But here we are, closing in on fourteen months later, and you insist on dragging out the proceedings."

She tilted her head to the side as she fluttered her eyelashes. "I'm not dragging anything out. I'm just…trying to get you to notice me."

"*What*? If you want to be noticed, suing a man is a piss-poor way of going about it."

Something about her face changed. For a moment he almost saw the woman who'd stood beside him in a church, making vows about love and honor.

"You *never* noticed me. Our honeymoon was only six days long because you had to get back early for a meeting. I always woke up alone because you left for the office by six every morning and then you wouldn't come back until ten or eleven at night. I guess I could have lived with that if I'd gotten to see you on the weekends, but you worked every Saturday and always had calls and interviews on Sunday. It was like…it was like being married to a ghost."

For the first time in years, Chadwick felt sympathy for Helen. She was right—he'd left her all alone in that

big house with nothing to do but spend money. "But you knew this was my job when you married me."

"I—" Her voice cracked.

Was she on the verge of crying? She'd cried some, back when they would actually fight about...well, about how much he worked and how much money she spent. But it'd always been a play on his sympathies then. Was this a real emotion—or an old-fashioned attempt at manipulation?

"I thought I might be able to make you love me more than you loved this company. But I was wrong. You had no intention of ever loving me. And now I can never have those years back. I lost them to this damn brewery." She brightened, anything honest about her suddenly gone. He was looking at the woman who glared at him from across the lawyers' conference room table. "Here we are. I'm just getting what I deserve."

"We were married for less than ten years, Helen. What is it you think you deserve?"

She gave him a simpering smile and he knew the answer. *Everything.* She was going to take the one thing that had always mattered to him—the company—and she wouldn't stop until it was gone.

Until he had nothing left.

The phone rang on Serena's desk, causing him to jump. She answered it in something that sounded like her normal voice. "I'm sorry, but Mr. Beaumont is in a...meeting. Yes, I can access that information. One moment, please."

"My office," he said under his breath. "*Now.* We don't need to continue this conversation in front of Ms. Chase."

Helen's eyes narrowed until she looked like a viper mid-strike. "Oh? Or is it that you don't want to have *Ms. Chase* in front of me?"

Oh, no. He'd finally done something he wanted—taken Serena out, spent a night in her arms—and he was going to pay for it. Damn it all, why hadn't he kept his hands off her?

Because he wanted Serena. Because she wanted him.

It'd all seemed so simple two days before. But now?

"I beg your pardon," Serena said in an offended tone as she hung up the phone.

Helen's mouth twisted into a smirk. "You should. Sleeping with other people's husbands is never a good career move for a secretary."

"You can't talk to me like that," Serena said, sounding more shocked than angry.

Helen continued to stare at her, fully aware she held the upper hand in this situation. "How could you, Chadwick? Dressing up this dumpy secretary and parading her about as if she was *worth* something? I heard it was a pitiable sight."

Damn it all. He'd forgotten about Therese Hunt, Helen's best friend. Serena's face went a blotchy shade of purplish red, and she actually seemed to sway in her seat, like she might faint.

If Helen wanted his attention, she had it now. He was possessed with a crazy urge to throw himself between Serena and Helen—to protect Serena from Helen's wrath. He didn't do that, but he did take a step toward Helen, trying to draw her attention back to him.

"You will watch your mouth or I will have security escort you out of this building and, if you ever set foot on brewery property again, I'll file a restraining order so fast your head will spin. And if you think I'm not making a big enough offer now, just wait until the cops get involved. You will get nothing."

"After what you put me through, you owe me," she screeched.

Keeping his cool was turning out to be a lot of work. "I already offered you terms that are in line with what I owe you. You're the one who won't let this end. I'd like to move on with my life, Helen. Usually, when someone files for divorce, they're indicating that they, too, would like to move on with their lives—separately."

"You've been *sleeping* with her, haven't you?" Her voice was too shrill to be shouting, but loud enough to carry down the halls. Office doors opened and heads cautiously peeked out. "For how long?"

This whole situation was spiraling out of control. "Helen—"

"How long? It's been years, right? Were you banging her before we got married? *Were you*?"

Once, Helen had seemed sweet and lovely. But it had all been so long ago. The vengeful harpy before him was not the woman he had married.

It took everything he had to keep his voice calm. "I *was* faithful to you, Helen. Even after you moved out of our bedroom. But you're not my wife anymore. I don't owe you an explanation for what I do or who I love."

"The hell I'm not your wife—I haven't signed off!"

Anger roared through his body. "You are *not* my wife. You can't cling to the refuge of that technicality anymore, Helen. I've moved on with my life. For the love of God, move on with yours. My lawyers will be in contact with yours."

"You lying bastard! You stand here and take it like a man!"

"I'm not doing this, Helen. Ms. Chase, if you could join me in my office."

Serena gathered her tablet and all but sprinted through his open office door.

"You can't ignore me. I'll take everything. *Everything!*"

He positioned himself between her and the doorway to his office. "Helen, I apologize that I wasn't the man you needed me to be. I'm sorry you weren't the woman I thought you were. We both made mistakes. But move on. Take my next offer. Start dating. Find the man who *will* notice you. Because it's not me. Goodbye, Helen."

Then, over the hysterical sound of her calling him every name in the book, he shut the door.

Serena hunched in her normal chair, her head near her knees.

Chadwick picked up his phone and dialed the security office. "Len? I have a situation outside my office—I need you to make sure my ex-wife makes it out of the building as quietly as possible without you laying a hand on her. Whatever you do, *don't* provoke her. Thanks."

Then he turned his attention to Serena. Her color was not improving. "Breathe, honey."

Nothing happened. He crouched down in front of her and raised her face until he could see that her eyes were glazed over.

"Breathe," he ordered her. Then, because he couldn't think of anything else to shock her back into herself, he kissed her. Hard.

When he pulled back, her chest heaved as she sucked in air. He leaned her head against his shoulder and rubbed her back. "Good, hon. Do it again."

Serena gulped down air as he held her. What a mess. This was all his fault.

Well, his and his lawyers'. *Former* lawyers.

Outside the office, the raging stopped. Neither he nor

Serena moved until his phone rang some minutes later. Chadwick answered it. "Yes?"

"She's sitting in her car, crying. What do you want me to do?"

"Keep an eye on her. If she gets back out of the car, call the police. Otherwise, just leave her alone."

"Chadwick," Serena whispered so quietly that he almost didn't hear her.

"Yes?"

"What she said…"

"Don't think about what she said. She's just bitter that I took you to the gala." The blow about Serena being a dumpy secretary had been a low one.

"No." Serena pushed herself off his shoulder and looked him in the eye. Her color was better, but her eyes were watery. "About her being alone all the time. Because you work *all the time*."

"I did."

But that wasn't the truth, and they both knew it. He still worked that much.

She touched her fingertips to his cheek. "You *do*. I know you. I know your schedule. You left my apartment on Sunday exactly for the reason she said—because you had an interview."

All of his plans—plans that had seemed so great twenty-four hours before—felt like whispers drifting into the void.

"Things are going to change," he promised her. She didn't look like she believed him. "I'm working on it. I won't work a hundred hours a week. Because Helen was right about something else, too—I didn't love her more than I loved the company. But that's…" His voice choked up. "But that's different now. I'm different now, because of you."

Her lip trembled as two matching tears raced down either cheek. "Don't you see the impossible situation we're in? I can't be with you while I work for you—but if I don't work for you, will I ever see you?"

"Yes," he said. She flinched. It must have come out more harshly than he'd meant it to, but he was feeling desperate. "You will. I'll make it happen."

Her mouth twisted into the saddest smile he'd ever seen. "I've made your life so much harder."

"Helen did—not you. You are making it better. You always have."

She stroked his face, tears still silently dripping down her cheeks. "Everything's changed. If it were just you and me…but it's not anymore. I'm going to have a baby and I have to put that baby first. I can't live with the fear of Helen or even Neil popping up whenever they want to wreak a little havoc."

The bottom of his stomach dropped out. "I'm going to sell the company, but it'll take months. You'll be able to keep your benefits, probably until the baby's born. It doesn't have to change right now, Serena. You can stay with me."

Tears streaming, she shook her head. "I can't. You understand, don't you? I can't be your dumpy secretary and your weekend lover at the same time. I can't live that way, and I won't raise my child torn between two worlds like that. I don't belong in your world, and you—you can't fit in mine. It just won't work."

"It will," he insisted.

"And this company," she went on. "It's what you were raised to do. I can't ask you to give that up."

"Don't do this," he begged. The taste of fear was so strong in the back of his mouth that it almost choked him. "I'll take care of you, I promise."

Helen had left him, of course. But underneath the drama, he'd been relieved she was gone. It meant no more fights, no more pain. He could get on with the business of running his company without having to gauge everything against what Helen would do.

This? This meant no more seeing Serena first thing every morning and last thing every night. No more Serena encouraging him to get out of the office, reminding him that he didn't have to run the world just so his siblings could spend even more money.

The loss of Helen had barely registered on his radar. But the loss of Serena?

It would be devastating.

"I can't function without you." Even as he said it, he knew it was truer than he'd realized. "Don't leave me."

She leaned forward, pressing her wet lips to his cheek. "You can. You will. I have to take care of myself. It's the only way." She stood, letting her fingers trail off his skin. "I hereby resign my position of executive assistant, effective immediately."

Then, after a final tear-stained look that took his heart and left it lying in the middle of his office, she turned and walked out the door.

He watched her go.

So this was a broken heart.

He didn't like it.

Thirteen

The door to Lou's Diner jangled as Serena pulled it open. Things had been so crazy that she hadn't even had time to tell her mom and dad that she was pregnant. Or that she had quit her great job because she was in love with her great boss.

Mom and Dad had an old landline phone number that didn't have voice mail or even an answering machine, if it worked at all. The likelihood of her getting a "this number is out of service" message when Serena called was about fifty percent. Catching her mom at work was pretty much the only guaranteed way to talk to her parents.

She'd put off going there for a few nights. Seeing her parents always made her feel uncomfortable. She'd tried to help them out through the years—got them into that apartment, helped make the payments on her dad's car—and there'd been the disastrous experiment with prepaid cell phones. It always ended with them not being able

to keep up with payments, no matter how much Serena put toward them. She was sure it had something to do with sheer, stubborn pride—they would not rely on their daughter, thank you very much. It drove Serena nuts. Why wouldn't they work a little harder to improve their situation?

Why hadn't they worked harder for her? Sure, if they wanted to be stubborn and barely scrape by, she couldn't stop them. But what about her?

Yes, she loved her parents and yes, they were always glad to see her. But she wanted better than a minimum wage job for the rest of her life, pouring coffee until the day she died because retirement was something for rich people. And what's more, she wanted better for her baby, too.

Still, there was something that felt like a homecoming, walking into Lou's Diner. Shelia Chase had worked here for the better part of thirty years, pulling whatever shift she could get. Lou had died and the diner had changed hands a few times, but her mom had always stuck with it. Serena didn't think she knew how to do anything else.

Either that, or she was afraid to try.

It'd been nine days since Serena had walked out of Chadwick's office. Nine long, anxious days that she'd tried to fill by keeping busy planning her new life.

She'd given her notice to her landlord. In two weeks, she was going to be moving into a new place out in Aurora, a good forty minutes away from the brewery. It wasn't a radically different apartment—two bedrooms, because she was sure she would need the space once the baby started crawling—but it wasn't infused with reminders of Neil. Or of Chadwick, for that matter. The rent was almost double what she was paying now, but if she

bought her baby things used and continued to clip coupons, she had enough to live on for a year, maybe more.

She'd applied for ten jobs—office manager at an insurance firm, administrative assistant at a hospital, that sort of thing. She'd even sent her resume to the food bank. She knew the director had been pleased with her work and that the bank was newly flush with Beaumont cash. They could afford to pay her a modest salary—but health insurance...well, she was covered by a federal insurance extension plan. It wasn't cheap, but it would do. She couldn't go without.

She hadn't had any calls for interviews yet, but it was still early. At least, that's what she kept telling herself. Now was not the time to panic.

Except that, as she slid into a booth that was older than she was, the plastic crackling under her growing weight, the old fear of being reduced to grocery shopping in food pantries gripped her.

Breathe, she heard Chadwick say in her head. Even though she knew he wasn't here, it still felt...comforting.

Flo, another old-timer waitress with a smoker's voice, came by. "'Rena, honey, you look good," she said in a voice so gravelly it was practically a baritone. She poured Serena a cup of coffee. "Shelia's waiting on that big table. She'll be over in a bit."

So just the thought of being back in this place that had barely kept her family above water was enough to make breathing hard. There was still something comforting about the familiar—Flo and her scratchy voice, Mom waiting tables. Serena's world might have been turned completely on its ear in the last few weeks, but some things never changed.

She smiled at Flo. "Thanks. How are the grandkids?"

"Oh, just adorable," Flo said, beaming. "My daugh-

ter got a good job at Super-Mart stocking shelves, so I watch the kids at night after I get off work. They sleep like angels for me."

As Flo went to make her coffee rounds, Serena pushed back a new wave of panic. A good job stocking shelves? Having her mom watch the kids while she worked the night shift?

Yes, a job was better than no job, but this?

She'd thought that she could never be a part of Chadwick's world and he could never be a part of hers—they were just too different. But now, sitting here and watching her mother carry a huge tray of food over to a party of ten, Serena realized how much her world had really and truly changed. Once upon a time, when she was in college, a night job stocking shelves *would* have been a good job. It would have paid the rent and the grocery bills, and that was all she would have needed.

But now?

She needed more. No, she didn't need the five-thousand-dollar dresses that she hadn't been able to bring herself to pack up and return to the store. But now that she'd had a different kind of life for so long—a life that didn't exist in the spaces between paychecks—she knew she couldn't go back to one of menial labor and night shifts.

A picture of Chadwick floated before her eyes. Not the Chadwick she saw every day sitting behind his desk, his eyes glued to his computer, but the Chadwick who had stood across from her in a deserted gallery. He had been trying just as hard as she was to make things work—even if those "things" were radically different for each of them. He had been a man hanging on to his sanity by the tips of his fingers, terrified of what would happen if he let go.

In that moment, Chadwick hadn't just been a hand-

some or thoughtful boss. He'd been a man she understood on a fundamental level.

A man who'd understood her.

But then Helen Beaumont had come in and reminded Serena exactly how far apart her world and Chadwick's really were.

Deep down, Serena had known she couldn't carry on with Chadwick while she worked for him. An affair with her boss—no matter how passionate or torrid—wasn't who she was. But hearing how Chadwick had neglected his wife in favor of his company?

It'd been like a knife in the back. Were she and Chadwick only involved because they'd spent more time together in the past seven years than he'd ever spent with his wife—because, as Chadwick's employee, she was the only woman he spent any time with at all?

What if he was only with her because she was available? Hadn't she stayed with Neil for far too long for the exact same reason—because that was the path of least resistance?

No. She would not be the default anymore. Stability wasn't the safest route. That's what had kept her mother chained to this diner for her entire life—it was a guaranteed job. Why risk a bird in the hand when two in the bush was no sure thing?

If whatever was going on between Chadwick and Serena was more than just an affair of convenience, it would withstand her not being his executive assistant. She was sure of it.

Except for one small thing. He hadn't called. Hadn't even texted.

She hadn't really expected him to, but part of her was still disappointed. Okay, *devastated*. He'd said all those lovely things about how he was going to change, how she

made him a better person—words that she had longed to hear—but actions spoke so much louder. And he hadn't done anything but watch her go.

She might love Chadwick. The odds were actually really good. But she couldn't know for sure while she worked for him. More than anything else, she didn't want to feel like he held all the cards in their relationship. She didn't want to feel like she owed everything to him—that he controlled her financial well-being.

That was why, as painful as it had been, she'd walked away from his promise to take care of her. Even though she wanted nothing more than to know that the man she loved would be there for her and that she'd never have to worry about sliding back into poverty again, she couldn't bank on that.

She was in control of her life, her fate. She had to secure her future by herself.

Serena Chase depended on no one.

Which was a surprisingly lonely way to look at the rest of her life.

Her head swimming, Serena was blinking back tears when her mother came to her table. "Sweetie, look at you! What's wrong?"

Serena smiled as best she could. Her mother was not many things, but she'd always loved her *sweetie*. Serena couldn't hide her emotional state from her mom.

"Hi, Mom. I hadn't talked to you for a while. Thought I'd drop in."

"I'm kinda busy right now. Can you sit tight until the rush clears out? Oh, I know—I'll have Willy make you some fried chicken, mashed potatoes and a chocolate shake—your favorite!"

Mom didn't cook. But she could order comfort food like a boss. "That'd be great," Serena admitted. She was

eating for two now, after all. "Dad coming to get you tonight?"

That was their normal routine. If he still had a car that worked, that was.

Mom patted her on the arm. "Sure is. He got a promotion at work—he's now the head janitor! He'll be by in a few hours if you can wait that long."

"Sure can." Serena settled into the booth, enjoying the rare feeling of her mother spoiling her. She pulled out her phone and checked her email.

There was a message from Miriam Young. "Ms. Chase," it read, "I'm sorry to hear that you're no longer with the Beaumont Brewery. I'd be delighted to set up an interview. The Rocky Mountain Food Bank would be lucky to have someone with your skills on board. Call me at your earliest convenience."

Serena felt her shoulders relax. She would get another job. She'd be able to continue being her own stability.

Mom brought her a plate heaped with potatoes and chicken. "Everything okay, sweetie?"

"I think so, Mom."

Serena ate slowly. There was no rush, after all. Yes, if she could get another job lined up, that would go a long way toward being *okay*.

Yes, she'd be fine. Her and the baby. Just the two of them. Tomorrow, at her first appointment, she might get to hear the heartbeat.

The appointment Chadwick had offered to attend with her.

She knew she'd be fine on her own. She'd hardly missed Neil after a couple of weeks. It'd been a relief not to have to listen to his subtle digs, not to clean up after his messes.

Even though she'd only had Chadwick in her bed for

a night, that night had changed everything. He had been passionate and caring. He'd made her feel things she'd forgotten she needed to feel. In his arms, she felt beautiful and desirable and wanted. Very much wanted. Things she hadn't felt in so long. Things she couldn't live without.

Now that she'd tasted that sort of heat, was she really going to just do without it?

As she ate, she tried to figure out the mess that was her life. If she got a job at the food bank, then she would be able to start a relationship with Chadwick on equal footing. Well, he'd still be one of the richest men in the state and she'd still be middle class. *More* equal footing, then.

Finally, the rush settled down just as Joe Chase came through the door. "Well, look who's here! My baby girl!" he said with obvious pride as he leaned down and kissed her forehead.

Mom got him some coffee and then slid into the booth next to him. "Hey, babe," her dad said, pulling her mom into the kind of kiss that bordered on not-family-friendly.

Serena studied the tabletop. Her parents had never had money, never had true security—but they'd always had each other, for better or worse. In a small way, she was jealous of that. Even more so now that she'd glimpsed it with Chadwick.

"So," Dad said as he cleared his throat. Serena looked back at them. Dad was wearing stained coveralls and Mom looked beat from a day on her feet, but his arm was around her shoulder and she was leaning into him as if everything about the world had finally gone right.

"How's the job?"

Serena swallowed. She'd had the same job, the same apartment, for so long that she didn't know how her parents would deal with this. "Well…"

She told them how she'd decided to change jobs and

apartments. "The company may be sold," she said as both of her parents looked at her with raised eyebrows. "I'm just getting out while I can."

Her mom and dad shared a look. "This doesn't have anything to do with that boss of yours, does it?" Dad asked in a gruff voice as he leaned forward. "He didn't do nothing he shouldn't have, did he?"

"No, Dad, he's fine." She wished she could have sounded a little more convincing when she said it, because her parents shared another look.

"I don't have to work weekends now," her dad said. "I can round up a few buddies and we can get you moved in no time."

"That'd be really great," she admitted. "I'll get some beer and some pizzas—dinner for everyone."

"Nah, I got a couple of bucks in my sock drawer. I'll bring the beer."

"*Dad*..." She knew he meant it. A couple of bucks was probably all he had saved away.

Mom wasn't distracted by this argument. "But sweetie, I don't understand. I thought you liked your job and your apartment. I know it was rough on you when you were young, always moving around. Why the big change now?"

It was hard to look at them and say this out loud, so she didn't. She looked at the table. "I'm three months pregnant."

Her mom gasped loudly while her dad said, "You're *what* now?"

"Who—" was as far as her mom got.

Her dad finished the thought for her. "Your boss? If he did this to you, 'Rena, he should pay. I got half a mind to—"

"No, no. Neil is the father. Chadwick wasn't a part of

this." Or, at least, he hadn't been two weeks ago. "I've already discussed it with Neil. He has no interest in being a father, so I'm going to raise the baby by myself."

They sat there, stunned. "You—you okay doing that?" her dad said.

"We'll help out," her mom added, clearly warming to the idea. "Just think, Joe—a baby. *Flo!*" she hollered across the restaurant. "I'm gonna be a grandma!"

After that, the situation sort of became a big party. Flo came over, followed by Willy the cook and then the busboys. Her dad insisted on buying ice cream for the whole restaurant and toasting Serena.

It almost made Serena feel better. They couldn't give her material things—although her proud dad was hellbent on trying—but her parents had always given her love in abundance.

It was nine that night before she made it back to her cluttered apartment. Boxes were scattered all over the living room.

Serena stood in the middle of it all, trying not to cry. Yes, the talk with her parents had gone well. Her dad would have all of her stuff moved in an afternoon. Her mom was already talking about layettes. Serena wasn't even sure what a layette was, but by God, Shelia Chase was going to get one. The best Serena had been able to do was to get her mom to promise she wouldn't take out another payday loan to pay for it.

Honestly, she wasn't sure she'd ever seen her parents so excited. The change in jobs and apartment hadn't even fazed them.

But the day had left her drained. Unable to deal with the mess of the living room, she went into her bedroom. That was a mistake.

There, hanging on the closet door, were the dresses. Oh, the dresses. She could hardly bear to look at the traces of finery Chadwick had lavished on her without thinking of how he'd bent her over in front of the dresser, how he'd held her all night long. How he'd promised to go with her to the doctor tomorrow. How he'd promised that he wouldn't fail her.

He was going to break his promise.

It was going to break her heart.

Fourteen

Serena got up and shaved her legs in preparation for her doctor's appointment. It seemed like the thing to do. She twisted up her hair and put on a skirt and a blouse. The formality of the outfit was comforting, somehow. It didn't make sense. But then, nothing made a lot of sense anymore.

For example, she needed to leave for the doctor's office by ten-thirty. She was dressed by eight. Which left her several hours to fret.

She was staring into her coffee cup, trying to figure out the mess in her head, when someone knocked on the door.

Neil? Surely he wouldn't have come back. She'd done a pretty thorough job of kicking him out the last time.

Maybe it was her mom, stopping in early to continue celebrating the good news. But, after another round of knocks, she was pretty sure it wasn't her mom.

Serena hurried to the door and peeked through the peephole. There, on her stoop, stood Chadwick Beaumont.

"Serena? I need to talk to you," he called, staring at the peephole.

Damn. He'd seen her shadow. She couldn't pretend she wasn't home without being totally rude.

She was debating whether or not she wanted to be *totally* rude when he added, "I didn't miss your appointment, did I?"

He hadn't forgotten. Sagging with relief, she opened the door a crack.

Chadwick was wearing a button-up shirt and trousers, with no tie or jacket. The informality looked good on him, but that might have had something to do with the grin on his face. If she didn't know better, she'd say he looked…giddy?

"I didn't think you were going to come."

He stared at her in confusion. "I told you I would." Then he looked at what she was wearing. "You already have an interview?"

"Well, yes. I quit my job. I need another one." She cleared her throat, suddenly nervous about this conversation. "I was counting on a letter of recommendation from you."

The grin on Chadwick's face broadened. It was as if all his worry from the last few years had melted away. "I should have guessed that you wouldn't be able to take time off. But you can cancel your interview. I found a job for you."

"You *what*?"

"Can I come in?"

She studied him. He'd found her a job? He'd come for her appointment? What was going on? Other than him

being everything she'd hoped he'd be for the last week and a half. "It's been ten days, you know. Ten days without so much as a text from you. I thought…"

He stepped into the doorway—not pushing her aside, but cupping her face with his hand and stroking her chin with his fingertips. She shuddered into his touch, stunned by how much it affected her. "I was busy."

"Of course. You have a business to run. I know that."

That's why Serena walked out. She needed to see if he would still have feelings for her if she wasn't sitting outside his office door every day.

"Serena," he said, his voice deep with amusement. "Please let me come in. I can explain."

"I understand, Chadwick. I really do." She took a deep breath, willing herself not to cry. "Thank you for remembering the appointment, but maybe it's best if I go by myself."

He notched up an eyebrow as if she'd thrown down the gauntlet. "Ten minutes. That's all I'm asking. If you still think we need some time apart after that, I'll go. But I'm not walking away from you—from what we have."

Then, just because he apparently could, he stroked his fingers against her chin again.

The need to kiss him, to fall back into his arms, was almost overpowering. But that emotion was in a full-out war with her sense of self-preservation.

"What did we have?"

The grin he aimed at her made her knees suddenly shake. He leaned in, his cheek rubbing against hers, and whispered in her ear, "*Everything.*"

Then he slipped a hand around her waist and pulled her into his chest. His lips touched the space underneath her ear, sending heat rushing from her neck down her back and farther south.

God, how she wanted this. Why had she thought she could walk away from him? From the way he made her feel? "Ten minutes," she heard herself murmur as she managed to push him far enough back that she could step to the side and let him in.

So she could stop touching him.

Chadwick walked into her apartment and looked around. "You're already moving?"

"Yes. This was where I lived with Neil. I need a fresh start. All the way around," she added, trying to remember why. Oh, yes. Because she couldn't fall for Chadwick while she worked for him. And work was all he did.

She expected him to say something else, but instead he gave her a look she couldn't quite read. Was he... amused? She didn't remember making a joke.

As he stood in the middle of the living room, she saw for the first time that he was holding a tablet. "I had this plan." He began tapping the screen. "But Helen forced my hand. So instead of doing this over a couple of months, I had to work around the clock for the last ten days."

If this was him convincing her that he'd find a way to see her outside of work, he was doing a surprisingly poor job of it. "Is that so?"

He apparently found what he was looking for because he grinned up at her and handed her the tablet. "It won't be final until the board votes to accept it and the lawyers get done with it, but I sold the company."

"You *what*?" She snatched the tablet out of his hands and looked at the document.

Letter of intent, the header announced underneath the insignia of the brewery's law firm. *AllBev hereby agrees to pay $62 a share for The Beaumont Brewery and all related Beaumont Brewery brands, excluding Percheron Drafts. Chadwick Beaumont reserves the right to*

keep the Percheron Drafts brand name and all related recipes....

The whole thing got bogged down in legalese after that. Serena kept rereading the first few lines. "Wait, what? You're keeping Percheron?"

"I had this crazy idea," he said, taking the tablet back from her and swiping some more. "After someone told me to do what I wanted—for me and no one else—I remembered how much I liked to actually make beer. I thought I might keep Percheron Drafts and go into business for myself, not for the Beaumont name. Here." He handed her back the tablet again.

She looked down at a different lawyer's letter—this one from a divorce attorney. *Pursuant to the case of Beaumont v. Beaumont, Mrs. Helen Beaumont (hereby known as Plaintiff) has agreed to the offer of Mr. Chadwick Beaumont (hereby known as Defendant) for alimony payments in the form of $100 million dollars. Defendant will produce such funds no later than six months after the date of this letter....*

Serena blinked at the tablet. The whole thing was shaking—because she was shaking. "I...I don't understand."

"Well, I sold the brewery and I'm using the money I got for it to make my ex-wife an offer she can't refuse. I'm keeping Percheron Drafts and going into business myself." He took the tablet from her and set it down on a nearby box. "Simple, really."

"*Simple?*"

He had the nerve to nod as if this were all no big deal—just the multi-billion dollar sale of an international company. Just paying his ex-wife $100 million.

"Serena, breathe," he said, stepping up and wrapping his arms around her. "Breathe, babe."

"What did you do?" she asked, unable to stop herself from leaning her head against his warm, broad chest. It was everything she wanted. He was everything she wanted.

"I did something I should have done years ago—I stopped working for Hardwick Beaumont." He leaned her back and pressed his lips against her forehead. She felt herself breathe in response to his tender touch. "I'm free of him, Serena. Well and truly free. I don't have to live my life according to what he wanted, or make choices solely because they're the opposite of what he would have done. I can do whatever I want. And what I want is to make beer during the day and come home to a woman who speaks her mind and pushes me to be a better man and is going to be a great mother. A woman who loves me not because I'm a Beaumont, but in spite of it."

She looked up at him, aware that tears were trickling down her cheeks but completely unable to do anything about it. "This is what you've been doing for the last ten days?"

He grinned and wiped a tear off her face. "If I could have finalized the sale, I would have. It'll still take a few months for all the dust to settle, but Harper should be happy he got his money *and* got even with Hardwick, so I don't think he'll hold up the process much."

"And Helen? The divorce?"

"My lawyers are working to get a court date next week. Week after at the latest." He gave her a look of pure wickedness. "I made it clear that I couldn't wait."

"But...but you said a job? For me?"

His arms tightened around her waist, pulling her into his chest like he wasn't ever going to let her go. "Well, I'm starting this new business, you see. I'm going to need someone working with me who can run the offices, hire

the people—a partner, if you will, to keep things going while I make the beer. Someone who understands how I operate. Someone who's not afraid of hard work. Someone who can pick a good health care plan and organize a party and understand spreadsheets." He rubbed her back as he started rocking from side to side. "I happen to know the perfect woman. She comes very highly recommended. Great letter of reference."

"But I can't be with you while I work for you. It's against company policy!"

At that, he laughed. "First off—new company, new policies. Second off, I'm not hiring you to be my underling. I'm asking you to be my partner in the business." He paused then and cleared his throat. "I'm asking you to marry me."

"You *are*?"

"I am." He dropped to his knees so suddenly that she almost toppled forward. "Serena Chase, would you marry me?"

Her hand fluttered over her stomach. "The baby…"

He leaned forward and kissed the spot right over her belly button. "I want to adopt this baby, just as soon as your old boyfriend severs his parental rights."

"What if he won't?" She was aware the odds of that were small—Neil had shown no interest in being a father. But she wasn't going to just throw herself into Chadwick's arms and believe that love would solve all the problems in the world.

Even if it felt like that were true right now.

Chadwick looked up at her, his scary businessman face on. "Don't worry. I can be *very* persuasive. Be my wife, Serena. Be my family."

Could they do that? Could she work with him, not *for* him? Could they be partners *and* a family?

Could she trust that he'd love her more than he loved his company?

He must have sensed her worry. "You told me to do what makes me happy," he told her as he stood again, folding her back into his arms. "*You* make me happy, Serena."

"But…where will we live? I don't want to live in that big mansion." The Beaumont Estate was crawling with too many ghosts—both dead and living.

He smiled down at her. "Anywhere you want."

"I…I already signed a lease for an apartment in Aurora."

He notched an eyebrow at her. "We can live there if you really want. Or you can break the lease. I'll have enough left from my golden parachute that we won't have to worry about money for a long, long time. And I promise not to drop thousands on gowns or jewels for you anymore. Except for this one."

He reached into his pocket and pulled out a small dark blue box. It was just the right size for a ring.

As he opened it, he said, "Would you marry me, Serena? Would you make me a happy man for the rest of my life and give me the chance to do the same for you? I won't fail you, I promise. You are the most important person in my life and you will always come first."

Serena stared at the ring. The solitaire diamond was large without being ostentatious. It was perfect, really.

"Well," she replied, taking the box from him. "Maybe a gown every now and then…."

Chadwick laughed and swept her into his arms. "Is that a yes?"

He was everything she wanted—passion and love and stability. He wouldn't fail her.

"*Yes.*"

He kissed her then—a long, hard kiss that called to mind a certain evening in front of a mirror. "Good," he said.

It was.

* * * * *

Seven

Ian may have had the best sexual experience of his life last night, but any desire he felt for Cassie was quickly squelched when he'd discovered her with a baby. A baby, for crying out loud.

It wasn't that he didn't like children. Kids were innocent in life, innocent in the actions of adults. How could he not love them? He just didn't see any in his future. And Cassie having a child certainly wasn't a problem in and of itself.

No, the issue had been when he'd seen her holding her child and he'd instantly flashed back to his mother, who would drag him from sitter to sitter while she went out at night.

But he wouldn't blame his past for his present problems. His body seemed to forget how angry he was and continued to betray him. Cassie was still sexy as hell and he'd forever be replaying just how hot their encounter had been.

But now that he knew she had a daughter, messing

around on a whim was definitely out. He wasn't cut out for the long term, and he refused to be the lover floating in and out of a kid's life the way his mother's lovers had floated through his.

Shaking off the unpleasant memories seeing Cassie with her baby had inspired, Ian approached Max Ford. His client had recently married his high school sweetheart and the couple had adopted a little girl. Ian couldn't be happier for the guy, but he wanted no part in the happily-ever-after myth himself.

"Hey," Max greeted him as he headed toward the makeup trailer. "Coming in with me?"

"Yeah."

Ian fell into step behind Max. The actor tugged on the narrow door and gestured for Ian to enter first. After climbing the three metal steps, Ian entered the cool trailer and nodded a greeting to the makeup artist.

Max closed the door behind him and exchanged pleasantries with the young lady. Ian took a seat on the small sofa across from the workstation and waited until the two finished their discussion of the day's events.

"You're working out in the stables and field today?" Ian asked. "I saw the script. Looked like the scene with you and Lily when the first horses were brought onto the estate after the wedding."

Max nodded as the makeup artist swiped over his face with a sponge full of foundation. "Yeah. It's a short scene. This afternoon and evening we'll be shooting some of the wedding scenes at the small church in town."

Ian settled deeper into the sofa, resting an arm across the back of the cushion. "Everything going okay so far?"

"Great," Max told him. "Raine is planning on joining me in a few days. She was excited I was shooting on the East Coast."

Ian knew Max and Raine had been through hell after years apart before finally finding their way back to each other in Max's hometown of Lenox, Massachusetts. Ian couldn't imagine trying to juggle a family while working in this crazy industry, let alone from across the country. Speaking of crazy, Ian never thought Hollywood heart-throb Max Ford would settle down, much less on some goat and chicken farm in New England, but to each his own and all that. Love apparently made you do some strange things.

"You talking to Lily soon?" Max asked.

Max had been one of Ian's first clients. They'd both taken a chance on each other, the risk had paid off and here they were, at the top of their games. They had no secrets and oftentimes their relationship was more like friends than business associates.

"Yeah. Hoping to get a few more minutes with her today."

The makeup artist reached for a brush and started stroking a shadow across Max's lids. Yeah, Ian would much rather stay on this side of the industry…the side where his face stayed makeup-free.

"I'll keep you posted," Ian said, not wanting to get too detailed since there were other ears in the room. "I plan on being on set for the next several weeks, so hopefully something will come from that."

Something positive. There was no way Ian wanted his ex-partner to get his clutches on Lily. Not to mention Ian was selfish and now that Lily was between agents, he wanted her because she was one of the top Hollywood leading ladies.

Added to that, she was the rare celebrity who hadn't been jaded or swayed by the limelight. Lily was the real deal who made a point to keep her nose out of trouble.

Any agent's dream client.

"I've discussed some things with her," Max stated. "She's

interested in hearing your terms and ideas, so hopefully she makes the right decision."

Ian was counting on it. Lily was smart enough to know the industry. After all, she'd just left her agent, who'd been a bit shady with her career. She'd put a stop to that immediately.

Ian could only hope she saw the hands-on way he worked and how invested he was as an agent. Visiting movie sets was his favorite job perk. Getting out of a stuffy office and being on location was always the highlight. Plus he wanted to make sure his clients were comfortable and there were no glitches.

"I'll be around if you need me." Ian came to his feet and moved toward the trailer door, pulling his phone from his pocket to check his emails. "I plan on being at both scenes today."

"Sounds good. I assume you've met all the Barringtons?" Max asked as the makeup artist ran the powder brush over his neck.

Ian swallowed. "Yeah. I've met them."

Met them, slept with one and still felt the stirrings from the continuous play of memories.

"They're one impressive family," Max went on, oblivious to the turmoil within Ian. "Damon is an amazing man with all of his accomplishments, but I swear, Cassie and Tessa are a force to be reckoned with."

Ian bit the inside of his cheek to avoid commenting on one of those "forces." The image of her in that body-hugging dress still made his knees weak, his heart quicken.

"That's why this movie is going to kick ass," Ian said, circling back to work, where his mind needed to stay. "Everyone loves a story like this, and having it on the big screen with two of Hollywood's top stars will only make it pull in that much more at the box office."

"I hope you're right."

Ian was confident this movie would be one of the biggest for both Max and Lily. Hollywood's heartthrob and sweetheart playing a married couple in a true story? It was a guaranteed slam dunk for everybody.

Which reminded him, he needed to check his emails and hopefully line up another client's role.

"I'll see you in a bit," Ian said as he exited the trailer.

He refused to glance toward Cassie's cottage. He wasn't some love-struck teen who'd slept with a woman and now wondered what she was doing every waking minute.

Okay, so he did wonder what she was doing, but love had absolutely nothing to do with it. His hormones were stuck in overdrive and they would just have to stay there because he refused to see her in any type of personal atmosphere again.

Even flings warranted a certain type of honesty, and getting involved, in any manner, with a woman who reminded him of the past he'd outrun was simply not an option.

A flash of movement from the field in the distance caught his eye. He headed toward the white fence stretching over the Barrington estate. As he neared, his gut tightened.

Cassie sat atop a chestnut-colored horse flying through the open field. Her hair danced unrestrained in the wind behind her and the breeze carried her rich laughter straight to him...and his body responded...work and emails instantly forgotten.

Ian stood frozen and admired the beauty. From behind her came Tessa on her own horse, but Ian's gaze was riveted on Cassie. He hadn't heard that deep laugh. She all but screamed sex with that throaty sound, her curves bouncing in the saddle, hair a wild mass of deep crimson curls.

Her carefree attitude would've been such a turn-on, but in the back of his mind he couldn't forget where he came from. From a father who had standards so high nobody could reach them and a mother who spent her time entertaining boyfriends and husbands, leaving a young Ian a distant second in her life.

He never wanted to go back to that emotional place again.

"You've got an audience."

Breathless and smiling, Cassie turned to her sister as Tessa came to a stop beside her. This felt good, to get out and not worry about training or anything else for a few minutes. Just getting back to their roots and racing was something she and her sister didn't do nearly often enough.

"Who's the audience?" Cassie asked, fully expecting to see some of the film crew. The cameramen and lighting people seemed to be all over the estate, moving things around, making the place their own for the sake of the film. The Hollywood scene was definitely a far cry from the usual relaxed atmosphere of Stony Ridge.

A sense of pride welled deep within her at the fact that Hollywood loved her family's story as much as she did. Horses, racing and family... That was what it meant to be a Barrington, and they excelled at it all because they worked hard and loved harder.

"Your agent," Tessa replied, nodding back toward the fence line. "I saw him stop when you raced by. He hasn't moved."

Cassie risked a glance and, sure enough, Ian stood turned in her direction. He was just far enough away that she couldn't make out his facial expression...not that she cared. But damn, why did he have to be a jumbled mess? He'd wanted her with such passion last night, had made her

feel so special and wanted. How dare he pull such emotions out of her when she was still trying to piece the shards of her heart back together after her divorce?

Today when he'd seen Emily, he'd become detached, angry and not at all the same man she'd been with last night. His silence had hurt her, had made the night before instantly ugly.

And after coming home, she'd checked her phone and found a missed call from Derek. Seriously? After months of no contact whatsoever, now he decided to call? Cassie had deleted the message without listening. She didn't care what he had to say, and, after her emotional morning with Ian, she wasn't in the mood.

"He's not my anything." Cassie turned back toward Tessa, turning her back on Ian and willing him to go away.

"He was something to you last night."

Squinting against the sun, Cassie shrugged. "He was my temporary mistake. Nothing more."

Leaning across the gap between the horses, Tessa slid her hand over Cassie's. "I'm not judging at all. I just want you to know people aren't perfect. We all make rash decisions, and beating yourself up won't change what happened."

Cassie knew Tessa would be the last person to judge her, but that didn't stop the embarrassment from settling in her gut.

"I just hate that I gave in to the first man to show me any attention since being divorced," Cassie explained, gripping the reins.

Tessa's warm smile spread across her face. "Honey, Ian is a very attractive man, you're a beautiful woman and you all were locked in an attic all night. Instant attraction is hard to ignore, especially when you have nothing else to focus on."

"Self-control is a beautiful thing," Cassie murmured. "Too bad I didn't have any."

Laughing, Tessa squeezed Cassie's hand before pulling back. "Yeah, well, I didn't have any where Grant was concerned, either, and look how well it worked out for us."

Cassie's eyes darted down to the impressive diamond band surrounding Tessa's ring finger. Grant had gotten a flat band because of Tessa's riding career; he knew she wouldn't want to work with anything too bulky.

And that proved just how beautiful a relationship her sister and Grant had. The man knew Tessa inside and out, loved her and her career. He'd even overcome his own personal demons to be with her.

Cassie couldn't be happier for the two of them, but her situation was different.

"I'm pretty sure my attic rendezvous will not be leading to any proposals," Cassie joked. She had to joke with Tessa, otherwise she'd cry, and she refused to let this experience pull her down and make her feel guilty for having needs. "Besides, I think seeing Emily was like a bucket of cold water in Ian's face. I won't be with anybody who can't accept that I'm a package deal."

"I saw Ian's face when he found out Emily was yours," Tessa said, shoving her hair behind her ear. "He was definitely caught off guard, but the man wasn't unaffected by whatever happened between the two of you or he wouldn't have just stopped to watch you ride by. He may be torn, but he's still interested. You can't blame him for being shocked you're a mother."

Yeah, well, Ian's interest more than likely consisted of getting in her pants again...which she wouldn't allow.

But the memory of last night still played through her mind. His touch had been perfect. His words had seduced

her until she'd forgotten about anything else but the moment they were locked in.

No matter how her body craved to be touched by his talented hands again, Cassie knew she deserved better than the way she'd been treated afterward.

So if Ian wanted her, that was his problem and he'd have to deal with it. She had enough on her plate without worrying about some big-time Hollywood agent who was only looking for only a fling.

She had a racing season to finish and a school for handicapped children to get started.

Her soon-to-be brother-in-law, Grant, had a paralyzed sister who used to ride, and her story had inspired Cassie on so many levels. Even though they hadn't met yet, just her story alone was enough to drive Cassie to want more for the next chapter of life. And what better way to teach her daughter to give back and love and care for others? Instilling love in young children made all the difference. She and Tessa were evidence of that.

Throwing a glance over her shoulder, Cassie had mixed emotions when she saw Ian was nowhere in sight. On one hand, she was glad he'd moved on. On the other, she kind of liked knowing she'd left some sort of impression on him.

No matter how things were now, for a time last night, she'd been in a sexy man's arms and that man had been attentive and giving and had made her feel more self-worth than ever.

Having regrets at this point was kind of in vain.

Besides, no matter what common sense played through her mind, she couldn't deny the physical pull she still felt toward Ian. And she was positive she hadn't seen the last of him.

Eight

After shooting wrapped for the day, Ian headed toward the stables to see if Lily was in there. He hadn't seen her for two days, and Max had mentioned he'd seen her heading that way. Ian hadn't had a chance to speak with her yet. The chaos of filming and so many people around had gotten in the way. Other than the usual small talk, he'd not been able to catch her alone.

Hopefully he could find her and perhaps they could arrange for a time to sit down and talk.

The sun was just at the edge of the horizon, casting a vibrant orange glow across the sky. The air had turned warmer as spring approached summer. Soon they'd be off to the Preakness Stakes, where Tessa would try to win the second race on her way toward the coveted Triple Crown.

The entire crew was riding the high of the shoot as well as getting sucked into the excitement of cheering the Barrington girls on toward victory. He had no doubt Tessa and Cassie were a jumble of anticipation and nerves.

Ian shoved his hands into his pockets as he approached the stables. He wasn't letting his mind wander to Cassie, because if he thought of her, he'd think of her sweet curves, her tempting smile and the fact he still wanted her.

Before he could travel too far down that path of mixed emotions, Ian rounded the corner of the open stable door and froze.

Lily was in the stable all right. But she wasn't alone. The groom, Ian believed his name was Nash, had his back to Lily, and Lily's hand rested on his shoulder, a look of concern marring her beautiful face.

She whispered something Ian couldn't make out and Nash's head dropped at the same time Lily's arms slid around his waist and she rested her forehead on his back. The intimate, private moment shocked Ian and he really had no clue what he'd walked in on.

The old-fashioned lanterns suspended from the ceiling cast a perfect glow on them and Ian quickly stepped out of the stable before he could be spotted...or interrupt whatever was happening.

He had a feeling whatever was going on between the groom and the star of the film was on the down low... especially since an affair had nearly cost Grant Carter his job when he'd been sneaking to see Tessa.

But that had all worked out and the two were headed down the aisle in the near future.

Their secret would be safe with him. For one, he wanted Lily to trust him and sign with his agency. And for another, why stir up trouble? Ian couldn't help but laugh. He and Cassie were pretty far-fetched in terms of the possibility of getting together, but look where they were now after a heated night in the attic.

Heading back toward his on-site trailer, Ian stopped when a scream cut through the evening. It was loud enough

to have him trying to figure out where the sound was coming from.

He heard it again and moved toward the row of cottages settled beyond the main house. The grounds were deserted now since the entire crew had left for the hotel in town. Only a handful of people were staying on the property in trailers like the one Max had requested for him. The scream split through the air once more and Ian quickly found the culprit.

Just behind Cassie's cottage there was a small patio area and suspended from the pergola was a child's swing.

Cassie pushed her daughter, and each time the child went high, she let out a squeal. Ian's heart dropped at the sight. He didn't recall ever having that one-on-one playful time with either of his parents. Perhaps when he'd been a toddler, but he doubted it, considering they weren't affectionate when he'd been old enough to recall.

The sweet little girl with blond curls blowing in the breeze giggled and kicked her feet when Cassie grabbed the back of the plastic seat on the swing and held it back.

"Hold on," Cassie warned. "Here comes the biggest push of all."

When she let go of the swing, Cassie laughed right along with her daughter and Ian found himself rooted to his spot at the edge of her concrete patio.

The man in him watched, admiring Cassie's laid-back style, with her hair in a ponytail and wearing leggings and an oversize T-shirt that slid off one delicate, creamy shoulder. Her feet were bare and her face was void of any makeup, which was how he'd seen her since he'd arrived. Everything about her screamed country girl.

While the man in him watched, the lost little boy in him turned his attention to Emily. He took in all the delight from the sweet girl still clutching the rope holding

up her swing and wondered where her father was. Did the man even know he had a child? Did Cassie have any contact with him?

All the questions forming in his head were absolutely none of his business, yet he couldn't help but want to know more.

Ian's gaze traveled from Emily back to Cassie...and he found her looking right back at him with those impressive blue eyes.

"What are you doing here?" she asked, giving the swing another light push.

Ian tried not to focus on the fact that her shirt had slipped in the front, giving him a glimpse of the swell of her breast.

"I heard screaming." He stepped onto the concrete pad, cursing himself for being drawn in even more. "I wasn't sure who it was."

Cassie's eyes held his for a second before she turned her attention back to the swing. She held on to the ropes, thus bringing Emily's fun to a screeching halt.

The little girl twisted in her seat to look back at Cassie. Cassie went to the front of the swing, unfastened the safety harness and lifted Emily out.

"We were just heading in for dinner," Cassie said, propping Emily up on her hip.

Damn if her tilted, defiant chin didn't make him want to stay longer. Why torture himself? He wanted her physically, nothing more. Yet he found himself being pulled ever so slowly toward her.

"Don't go in just because of me."

Emily stared at him with bright, expressive blue eyes like her mother's. Her hand reached toward him and he couldn't stop himself from reaching back. The moment he

looked into those little baby blues something unidentifiable slid over his heart.

Emily's tiny hand encircled his finger as a smile spread across her baby face. That innocent gesture touched so many places in him: the child who'd craved attention, the teen who'd needed guidance and the adult who still secretly wished he had a parent who gave a damn without being judgmental.

Ian didn't miss the way Cassie tensed at the sight of Emily holding on to his finger, but he wasn't pulling back. How could he deny such an innocent little girl human touch? She was smiling, happy and had no clue the turmoil that surrounded her right now.

"Don't you have a client you should tend to?" Cassie asked, her meaning that he was not welcome all too clear.

"I already talked with Max after the shooting wrapped and we came back here." The crew had taken a few shots of the wedding scene in town. "I didn't see you at the church earlier."

Cassie reached up, smoothing away blond curls from Emily's forehead. "I was there. I stayed in the back with Tessa. We didn't want to get in the way."

"What did you think of the shoot?"

Why was he still here talking to her? Why didn't he just leave? He had calls to return, emails to answer, contracts to look over.

Besides the fact a little cherublike toddler had his finger in a vise grip, he could walk away. Cassie had made it clear she didn't like him, and he certainly wasn't looking for a woman with a child.

Yet here he stood, talking to her and eagerly awaiting her answer.

"It was perfect," she said, a soft smile dancing across her lips. "Lily looked exactly like the pictures I've always

seen of my mother on that day. My father teared up, so I know Lily and Max hit that scene beautifully."

Ian wiggled his finger, making Emily giggle as she tugged on him. He took a step forward, now being drawn in by two intriguing ladies.

"I think the fans will fall in love with this film," he told Cassie as his eyes settled on hers. "And your family."

The pulse at the base of her throat quickened and Ian couldn't help but smile. Good to know she wasn't so unaffected. What they'd shared the other night was nothing short of amazing. No matter what transpired afterward, he couldn't deny that had been the most intense night of his life.

Damn it. Cassie and her innocent daughter were the exact picture of the commitment he could never make.

So how could he be drawn to this woman?

"I just want my father to be happy with the end result," she told him. "I want people to see what a hard worker he is and that everything didn't get handed to him."

Ian couldn't help but admire her for wanting people to see the other side of Damon Barrington. The man was a phenomenon, and Ian had no doubt whatsoever that this film would be a mega blockbuster.

Emily let go of his finger and started patting her mother's cheeks. Instantly Ian missed the innocent touch, but he stepped back and shoved his hands into his pockets.

"Was there something else you wanted?" she asked.

Clearing his throat, Ian shoved pride aside and nodded. "Actually, yeah. I'm sorry for how I handled the other morning."

Cassie's brows rose as she reached up to try to pull Emily's hands from her face. "I never expected you to apologize."

He hadn't expected it, either, but he couldn't deny the

fact he'd been a jerk. If he'd learned anything from growing up, it was to know when to apologize. He'd never seen his parents say they were sorry to each other, and he'd always wondered if such a simple gesture would have made a difference.

"I can admit when I make a mistake," he informed her.

Those bright eyes darted down as she sighed. "This is a first for me."

"What's that?"

Glancing back up, she shook her head. "Nothing. I appreciate you apologizing. Since you're going to be here awhile, I really don't want tension. Between you working and me training, I just can't handle more stress."

Ian noticed the soft lines between her brows, the dark circles beneath her eyes. This single mother was worn-out and he'd added to her worry because she hadn't wanted any awkwardness between them.

"Who helps you with Emily?"

Great, now he was asking questions before he could fully process them. He needed a filter on his mouth and he needed to mind his own business. The last thing he wanted was to worry about Cassie and her daughter. He certainly wasn't applying for the position of caregiver.

"My family." Her chin tilted as she held his gaze, unblinking. "Why?"

Yeah, why indeed? Why was this his concern? They'd slept together one night after days of intense sexual tension and now he was all up in her personal space…a space that hit too close to home and touched his heart way too deeply.

He pushed aside the unwanted emotions. He would be here only a short time. Even if his past hadn't mixed him all up, he still couldn't get too involved with Cassie Barrington.

Besides, she had her hands full and they'd definitely